MINDY HAYES

DAYBREAK

a Faylinn novel

Daybreak (Faylinn Novels, Book 5)
Copyright © 2020 by Mindy Hayes
All rights reserved.

Published by Mindy Hayes
Cover design by Regina Wamba
ReginaWamba.com
Edited by Samantha Eaten-Roberts

ISBN: 979-8560066642

To Zoey Sue,
always believe in fairytales

ONE

LIA

BLINK, blink.

Blink.

A grid of intricately carved crown molding high above stared back at me. Why was I on the floor? My back muscles cried out as I propped myself up on my elbows, rolling my stiff neck. The dawning sun filtered into my chambers around the dark red drapery, casting a hazy glow on the wooden floor. Had I slept here all night?

When I flipped through my last memory of the night before, it struck me like a speeding bullet. I tugged on the loose neckline of my tunic. My skin was creamy and smooth, not a single blemish. Gone. It was gone. Had I imagined it? The pain knocked me to my knees and now the black mark was as if it hadn't been there in the first place.

Light knocking echoed through the room before the heavy door opened and Cameron peeked his head inside. When he didn't find me in bed, his gaze fell to the floor.

His ocean eyes studied me with a head tilt, stepping around the door and closing it. "What are you doing on the floor?"

It was a good question. One I didn't have a good answer for. The lie flew as easy as my wings. "I slipped on my way out of the bathroom."

So, maybe it wasn't the best of lies, but it was a lie nonetheless.

Cameron held out his hand with a laugh. "Aren't faeries supposed to be graceful?"

"Aren't boyfriends supposed to be complimentary?" I latched onto his hand and let him help me to my feet.

"Boyfriend, huh?" His smirk was altogether too cheeky.

"Yeah, it sounded weird as soon as I said it."

"No, I like it. Though it sounds a bit too temporary for my taste." His lips pinched to the side. "Considering I *did* give up my life for you."

My lips pursed with a raised eyebrow. "You gave up a human life you didn't like anyway."

"At the risk of dying." Cameron looped his arm around my waist and drew me against his sinewy body. "I feel like that's important to note."

"Fine." I smiled, pressing my hand to his bare chest at the open collar of his ivory tunic, my fingertips grazing the warm skin. "What would you rather be called?"

His eyes grew inquisitive, slimming to slits. "What is it the fae call each other before they bond? Their match?"

Heat filled my cheeks. Did Cameron want to bond with me already? That seemed a bit fast, even under the circumstances. "Yes, they're a match."

"I like that." Leaning in, his nose kissed the tip of mine. "You're my match."

Fireflies flickered in my belly. Quieting the hitch in my breathing, I teased, "Hold your horses there, partner. We're not bonding yet."

Even if Cameron transformed in part because of me and he loved me now, it didn't mean that would last. There were lots of beautiful faeries in Rymidon, and I wasn't always the easiest to get along with. After living with me for the last few months, one would think he'd have figured that out by now. He might find someone more suited for him in time.

This wasn't the human world where we'd be together for another sixty or so more years before we passed away. If lucky enough, we'd breach the thousands. That was a long time to be bound to the wrong faery. We'd need to be sure. Cameron would need to be sure. Very sure.

"Who said anything about bonding?" His mouth nudged mine with a quick kiss, the curve of a smile pressing against my lips. "I mean, of course, at some point down the line. Next week, maybe? Or the following," he joked.

I smirked, patting his chest. "How about we test the faery waters for a bit before you bind yourself to such declarations. You might change your mind."

In human years, Skye and I were together for almost fifty years before I was sent to watch over Calliope. Had I been a Royal, we'd have bonded long before that, but fifty years to

Cameron probably felt a lot longer than it did to me.

"Are you getting cold feet on me?" he asked.

"Not in the slightest, but I'm accustomed to how our realm works. You've still got time. A lot of time. You're going to look and feel in your twenties for several hundred more years."

"Wait, how old are you?"

"I'm twenty."

"But like, if you had to guess how many human years you've lived. How old would you be?"

I scratched my temple. "I can give you a guesstimate, but you know our realm runs differently. It's hard to match up the years correctly. You'll get used to it though."

"So, give me a guesstimate."

"I don't know. Two hundred years?" I shrugged.

Cameron smirked. "So, my match is a cougar. *Rawr.* I always wondered what it would be like dating an older woman."

I smacked his chest and he chuckled.

Cinching me tighter, Cameron's large hands molded to the small of my back as his lips roamed across my cheek and down my neck. Languid, deliberate kisses. "I woke up alone this morning. Where did you go?"

I swallowed, the touch of his mouth turning my brain to mush. "I needed to go to the bathroom." It wasn't a lie. I did leave last night to use my washroom. I just happened to pass out on my way back and slept on the floor for the remainder of the night. Or so it appeared.

"I have a bathroom in my bedroom, you know."

Kiss.

Kiss.

Kiss.

Down.

Down.

Down.

"I…I didn't want to wake you." My whole body tingled as his skilled lips traveled along my sensitive skin, his tongue making an occasional sweep. The air escaping my lungs quivered.

"Well, I'm definitely awake now," he said against my collarbone.

Oh gosh.

My head rolled back, my eyes falling shut.

Tap, tap, tap.

The softest knock interrupted Cameron's magical mouth and I cursed whoever it was.

Taking a step back, Cameron left his arm curled around my waist as I cleared my throat. "Come in." The two words were breathless gravel.

Jessamine appeared around the door, her black hair braided in a crown around her head. "Oh. I'm sorry to disturb you. I can come back." She started to creep behind the door.

"It's okay." I stepped farther away from Cameron, untangling myself from his hold. "What did you come here for?"

Pausing, she stepped inside the doorway, her yellow-green wings fluttering. "Queen Sarai asked if I would come to help you dress this morning."

I'd always dressed myself, considering I wasn't a Royal, but maybe Sarai thought it was normal or that it would make me feel pampered or more welcome in Rymidon.

Jessamine and I had never been friends, more like acquaintances as I'd come to the castle quite a bit for Skye, but I still wouldn't have been comfortable allowing her to dress me.

"Thank you, but I have it handled."

She nodded. "Trilla will have breakfast served soon if you

would like to dine with the Queen. She's on her way to the dining hall now."

At the mention of food, Cameron's stomach rumbled. "We'll be there," he said, and a chuckle tumbled from my lips.

Jessamine left and he pulled me in again. "I feel like I could never stop eating and still be hungry. Is that normal?"

"Beats me, but my transformations have been different from yours."

"And you." Cameron framed my face with his masculine hands and covered my lips with his. He kissed me with a ravenous need, like *I* was his next meal. "You make me insatiable."

What woman wouldn't want to hear a thing like that? But was it me? Or was it his newly heightened senses and abilities? He was now living life on full blast, no longer diminished by ordinary human attributes. Everything had more flavor, more color, more sensation. Just more. No human words could touch the magic of the fae realm.

Cameron's stomach growled again and I laughed. "I think your body needs food."

"But it needs you more." He rolled into me, our hips and lips meeting.

I broke away from his kiss with my hand to his chest, bowing my head to catch my breath, and a smile on my face. "C'mon. We don't want to keep Sarai waiting."

With an exaggerated sigh, he said, "Okay." Tipping my chin up, he kissed my nose. "You're right."

When Cameron let me go, my knees buckled, a dizzying mist muddling my head.

He hurried back to me, helping to steady my wobbly legs. "I make you weak in the knees, huh?"

Rolling my eyes, I covered my unexpected fumble with sarcasm. "Don't let it go to your head, Romeo."

Was that a fluke? Literal weakness from Cameron's kiss? Or was it something more?

TWO

SARAI

I could have strangled Guthron. Wrapped my tiny hands around his lanky neck and squeezed. He wasn't supposed to arrive until this morning. We agreed. What was so urgent that they required a place to stay last night? Was their cavern suddenly inhabitable?

If that was how he held up his end of deals, we were in more trouble than I'd anticipated.

Taking a deep breath, I buried my closed eyes behind my fingers as I waited for Naida to bring my breakfast.

Oh, my fae. How was I going to ease their hearts and minds when I couldn't even ease my own? The enemy was here, and they could not be trusted.

Kayne escorted me to my chambers after the confrontation last night, the faint protests of the heated horde echoing through the corridors. Their shouts of displeasure followed me into my dreams.

I promised to talk with him this morning after a good night's rest and a clear head, but as soon as I entered my chambers, I collapsed on my bed. Before sleep could take me, my tears did. And they kept me up for hours.

What am I going to do?

I made a mistake. I did. I could admit that to myself, but what was the right solution? Slaughter the elves to silence them? Wage a war after a battle that took half our kingdom? Inform the other Royals and send trickling consequences across the realm?

There was no clear-cut answer. Everything led to unavoidable ramifications.

The door to the dining hall creaked open and my head whipped up from my hands. Clearing my throat, I ran my palms down the front of my dress, composing myself.

Cameron slipped in first, followed by Lia.

"Good morning, you two." I smiled. Though it was stiff, it wasn't because of their presence. Granted, that wasn't going to be easy explaining to our kingdom, either.

"I heard this is the place to find food." Cameron grinned.

"You heard correctly. You two came just in time. Trilla should have it ready in a moment."

He plopped down in the seat adjacent to me and Lia sat on his opposite side. "Good. I'm starved."

"I hope you're finding your accommodations satisfactory."

"You have us living like literal Royalty." Cameron laughed. "They're more than satisfactory."

I didn't know what it was like to live any other way. "Good, good."

Cameron lifted the goblet of viga juice and took a sip. His lips smacked, as if to savor the beverage, and he looked into the goblet before taking another sip. "So, how about them elves?"

Buzzerwigging Guthron.

"Are you all right after last night?" Lia asked.

"I'm fine." Physically I was fine, so it wasn't a lie. "I hope the villagers didn't keep you two up."

"Not for very long," she said. "Their concern isn't surprising. What can we do?"

"Nothing." I waved her off. There was nothing. It would eventually die down. It had to. "Just do as we discussed last night. Remain unseen from the rest of the kingdom and you will be safe."

"That we can do. We're just grateful for a place to stay," Cameron said, taking another drink. "What is this stuff? It's delicious."

"Viga juice. You don't have vigas in the human world?"

"Can't say that we do. Super sweet, but really good. Like watermelon and pineapple combined."

"*That's* what they reminded me of," Lia said. "I could never quite put my finger on it."

Trilla and Naida entered with three plates overflowing with food and set them in front of us.

"Before you go, is there more?" Cameron asked them.

Trilla's eyes bulged. Our plates were heaping with food. I'd be surprised if he finished his plate. I surely wasn't going to.

"Yes, if you'd like a second helping, I'll gladly make another plate for you."

"Okay, cool. Thank you. Just checking. I'll start with this

one. It looks so good."

She smiled at the compliment and left with a bow.

"I'm hungry *all the time*," he said as he shoveled in a bite. "I think this new blood has sped up my metabolism or something."

"It's possible, needing the extra nutrients for the energy it takes to transform a human body without fae blood. It might balance out with time."

Cameron had devoured half his plate by the time I'd taken my first bite.

"If, by chance," Lia said, "we do run into someone who isn't in your inner circle who recognizes me, what do you want us to say?"

I took a deep breath. "I really don't know. We could say the Fates allowed you another chance."

"But if they ask how? Who I traded places with?"

"We don't know everyone from every single kingdom, do we? So, why don't you just say someone from Aurorali or Oraelia? Just protect yourselves. For the meantime, if a lie is necessary, a lie is necessary until I can gain control over the situation with the elves."

"Who lost their lives?" Lia asked out of the blue. "By the hand of the elves when they were slaying Rymidonians."

My fork stopped halfway to my mouth. "You don't want to go down that course."

"Sarai, I need to know"

"You don't." I set down my fork with a sigh. "It'll only fill you with guilt and question of whose blood was injected into you. Who died, so you could be fae again? No. No, I'm sorry. I won't let you spiral down that path."

"I've already done that." She leaned forward, her utensil clutched in her hand. "It's the not knowing that's sending me

11

spiraling. At least knowing their names will help me come to terms with it. Help me make anonymous reparations. I can't take back what I did, but I can try to ease the pain of those that lost someone."

I exhaled. "You're never going to let this go, are you?"

Lia shook her head. "I'll find out eventually. This way at least you can give me all the right names the first time around."

"You're not to approach any of the fae left behind."

"Of course."

"Very well. I'll have Kayne draw up a list."

"Thank you," she said softly.

"That goes for you, too." I pointed at Cameron. "No interfering in their lives, no matter your good intentions."

"Yes, ma'am." He swallowed his last bite and pointed to the kitchen door. "Can I just go in there and grab some more or…"

I gawked at his plate. Licked clean. With a light chuckle, I rang the bell and Naida appeared. "Would you mind getting another plate of food for Cameron?"

"Yes, Your Grace." She returned moments later with a second heaping plate and set it in front of him.

"Man, this is the life." He smiled and dug in.

AFTER breakfast, I left Lia and Cameron to meet with Kayne in the study.

"Were the dwellings all finished for the elves when they arrived last night?"

He sat across from me with his arms crossed over his brawny chest. "As far as I'm aware. There may have been some last-minute touch-ups that needed to be done, but I haven't heard otherwise."

"And they were delivered food and provisions this morning? Everything they might need?"

Kayne nodded. "Eitri confirmed with Arleen of the Sowers and Fynbar of the Weavers."

I dared ask, "How is the kingdom acclimating today?"

"There were a few from last night who returned this morning, but Brae sent them on their way. It would probably be wise to hold another gathering and discuss the new arrangements. If you don't have a hold on those protesting, it might escalate."

"Yes, I planned on it. Let's do that this afternoon. Is Guthron aware they must remain in their land for the present time? I agreed that our kingdom was now theirs, but we should ease Rymidon into it. If they wander too close to the village, I worry we might wind up with a rather undesirable feud."

Kayne dipped his chin. "Eitri informed him last night, but it might be wise for you to have a face-to-face conversation with Guthron, reiterate the boundaries. He's more likely to listen to you."

"Yes, of course. Let's do that first, and then call all the fae to the gathering hall."

Before Kayne left the tower, he stopped and turned back to me. "There was something strange Arleen said to Eitri about the harvest, though. There seemed to be a shortage."

I tilted my head. "Because we didn't prepare and harvest more for the elves?"

"I'm not sure. They were told to increase their yields, but maybe it just wasn't enough."

"I don't want to overwork them, but we need to make sure there's enough for everyone. Will you speak with Arleen and see where the problem lies? If there aren't enough Sowers to make up the difference, we're going to have to formulate other solutions."

Kayne bowed at the waist and left.

Was this why my father rationed food before? Were we not equipped to handle the size of our kingdom? Or was it simply our increased population with the elves? After losing so many in the Battle of Faylinn, while we had fewer mouths to feed, there were also fewer Sowers. Hopefully, Arleen would have some insight. Otherwise, we might have more serious problems than the elves living here.

THREE

CAMERON

LIVING in a castle was strange. I guess living in the faery world was strange in and of itself. Not having modern technology or conveniences was going to take some getting used to. I kept reaching for my cell phone, which I tossed out as soon as I transformed, but I kept having the instinct to check on my dad. Had he forgotten me already? I wasn't like Callie, able to visit him whenever I wanted. Even if he did remember me, my pointed ears and bigger, brighter eyes would probably give him a heart attack. There was only hope to hold on to that, with time, missing him would get easier.

This morning I showered under a cloud and was surrounded by a wall of steam. That was it. No glass doors, curtains, or faucets. Just a cascade of rain. It was awesome, but so weird.

One thing I wasn't having an issue with was living without the usual mundane responsibilities. There was no more alarm clock for school, no homework or tests and essays. It was a beautiful thing. And because we had to lay low, we couldn't even go work in one of the colonies. It was like a permanent vacation.

If you didn't count the whole hiding away for our protection part.

I linked my fingers between Lia's as we walked out of the dining room. "So, what are we going to do today?"

"What do you want to do?"

"Well, I've never toured a castle before. You know this one pretty well, don't you?"

"You could say that." Lia's cryptic answer was hard to decipher. Was she ashamed of her familiarity or dreading the memories that might resurrect?

"It's hard for you to be here, isn't it?"

She shrugged, but it was all I needed. It was too noncommittal to be indifferent.

"It's just *different*. While most of the Keepers and staff are the same, they *aren't* the same. They're not working on autopilot or seemingly shackled to their duties. It's a definite change in the vibe. I've had two Sowers smile at me. *Me*." A small laugh passed her lips. "It just doesn't make any sense. When Adair was king, there was a certain layer of tension that lived in the walls. You never felt like you could talk freely or louder than a whisper. Everyone walked on eggshells, not daring to draw his attention. Sarai somehow brings a blanket of peace and comfort, even while disaster hovers a few miles away."

I was mostly thinking in terms of Skye, but only because I hadn't thought about the other aspects. Rymidon must have felt like a completely different kingdom to everyone.

"It's not hard being here where Skye lived?"

Lia gave an evasive nod. "There's that aspect, too, but I've stopped mourning him. I mean, I'll always mourn what once was, but I don't want to change a thing about the present." She squeezed my hand but didn't look at me. It was probably the most I was going to get out of her, and I accepted it.

Winding through the wide corridors, we wound up in front of a towering, dark wooden door. Lia turned the ornate handle and entered. There were no windows, only lanterns to light the room, which was packed, wall-to-wall and floor-to-ceiling, with weapons. Spears, swords, bows and arrows, and more.

"Holy cow. This room is rad."

"I thought it might pique your interest."

"Is that a freaking mace?"

Lia chuckled with a nod. "Adair loved his weaponry, as did his sons. If you can dream it, it's probably here."

"Should I learn how to use one of these things?" My fingers traced along the sleek curve of a sickle. "Not this one specifically, but like, any of these."

"It wouldn't hurt. You've only been a part of our realm for a short time and you already could've benefited from some training more than once."

Benefited was an understatement. My only near-death experiences had been in Faylinn. "What? You don't think my Boy Scout and kickboxing talents are lifesaving skills?"

Lia laughed. "Not in this realm."

"Dang." I smirked. "So, what's your specialty?"

"I'm decent with a bow, but my favorite is the sapierce." Lia pulled two short skinny swords off their hooks. At the tips of the swords were mini spikey balls, like miniature maces. "Rymidon originated."

I tapped the tips, careful not to stab myself. "What are these made out of?"

"Glass, or our version anyway. It doesn't shatter the way human glass does."

"Daaang. I bet that hurts going in."

Lia smirked. "And coming out."

I refrained from letting a dirty joke slip. "What do you think should be my specialty?"

"That you'll have to figure out on your own, but I can give you suggestions to start with, see what piques your interest."

Lia had never been so sexy. I swept my arm around the room. "Carry on, my fair maiden."

With a quiet laugh, she rolled her eyes and stepped up to the back wall. "Most faeries have some experience with a bow and arrow. Archery is really useful for hunting game and fowl, too, which as Sowers we'll end up doing as well."

"Noted. What about this bad boy?" I lifted a hefty ax off the wall, testing the weight of it in my hands.

"I don't really take you for a battle ax man. Not that you couldn't handle it, it would just slow you down. If you like that, maybe learn your way around a halberd." She pointed above the mace to a pole with a smaller axeblade and a hook on the backside.

I skimmed the outline of the blade with my fingertip. "Yeah, that's pretty cool."

"It'll be smart to learn hand-to-hand combat, just in case, but you know what? I think I know the perfect weapon for you."

She moved further down the wall and pulled off a Y-shaped wooden piece with a leather strap.

I blinked once. "A slingshot."

"Hold on there, Mr. Skeptical. You're in the faery realm now. This isn't just any slingshot. You're not using marbles or rubber balls here." Lia held out a metallic sphere about the size of a golf ball and dropped it in my palm.

"What is this?"

"It's a kotrop. As soon as you shoot it from the sling, the force turns it into a spearhead."

My eyes widened. "Whoa. That's cool."

"Here. Watch." Lia took a stance in the middle of the den, facing a circular target at the front and released the slingshot. The kotrop struck the bullseye.

Hot, so hot.

I followed her to the front and sure enough, a small spearhead pierced the wood, the tail end a miniaturized sphere. When Lia pulled it off the board by the sphere, the pointed end sunk back inside, and it returned to the full-size, ready to aim again.

"Yes," I said. "Yes, that's the one."

Lia smiled. "I thought so. And it's easy for you to carry around with you. We're going to want to have weapons on us at all times for now."

"Well, then I guess I better get to training."

I'D landed my last kotrop on the rim just outside the center of the target when the door to the weaponry den opened.

Eitri stepped in. "Kayne said I was to bring this to you." He

19

held out a rolled-up piece of paper to Lia.

She hesitated before taking it. "Thanks."

He nodded and left us, closing the door behind him.

When she unrolled the paper, tears streamed down Lia's face. I stepped behind her to get a better look at what she was reading. My heart constricted at the list of fae who died.

I kept my voice quiet. "Do you know someone on there?"

It took her a moment to respond. "I knew them all." Her jaw quivered and she clamped it shut to stop it.

I peered over her shoulder, wrapping my arm around her waist, reading the names one-by-one.

Sindri Broin

Eldon Cuinn

Senan Paor

Isobel Arnot

Twenty names in all.

"They are no longer nameless, faceless fae," she said, her words raspy and anguished. "They were fathers and mothers, husbands and wives. I grew up with some of their children, some of them, or their siblings."

Lia ran the back of her hand under her nose. "Isobel, she taught me how to heal my first wound." Her fingertip brushed across the woman's name. "I'd fallen outside her cottage and scraped my knee. She found me limping away and knelt down beside me. My parents had always done it for me, coddling me, but Isobel put my hand over the cut and talked me through it, showing me what I could do for myself."

Abruptly, Lia rolled the paper back up. "I just don't understand. I know Sarai didn't know any of them well, but she knew the truth. She knew what the elves had done and still chose to give them a place in Rymidon, gift them our land."

"You know Sarai doesn't have a violent bone in her body. Her heart is too gentle to seek anything but a truce."

Lia nodded. "Yeah, and I know I wasn't in there when she made the deal. I don't know why she did it or what that cavern turned into once I fled. I can't judge, but it's hard not to.

"Sarai has been thrown trial after trial, you'd think she'd harden her skin, toughen that heart after what she's been through. I wouldn't have been able to look Guthron in the eye and call for peace. I'd have shoved my sapierce through his heart and moved onto the next." Lia's teary eyes met mine. "They made their choice. Rymidonians deserved justice."

"I think they'll get it," I said. "It's just going to happen differently than you want. And take a little more patience. But Sarai is doing the best she can with the knowledge she has."

Lia swiped the tears from her face. "And I just let Guthron use their blood on me without question, assumed he was being truthful. *Hoped* he was being truthful. It didn't feel right, but I pushed aside my doubts for my own selfish gain. And then I let you do it, too."

"Lia—"

"Does Isobel's blood run through my veins? Or Senan's? I'll never know who died so I could be fae again. And now, I'm…" Her words got caught in her throat.

"Stop." I gripped the sides of her face. "We're not doing this. Sarai was right. You can't go down that road. It only leads to shame and bitterness."

"I just…" She jerked away from me. The rejection stung, but I tried not to take it to heart. "I need air. Can we get out of here for a bit?"

I nodded. "Whatever you need."

FOUR

LIA

AFTER speeding through the forest, I stopped at the edge of a glen, my heart pummeling my rib cage. I slid down a lichen-coated trunk and took a breath, hiding my sudden weariness from Cameron. He took the bough of the tree across from me and kept silent.

Birds sang and leaves whispered. Acres of lush rolling ridges surrounded the small valley. The sight was meant to remind me of my choice, why I risked everything to return to this form, but all it did was drive the dagger in.

This awe-inspiring scenery was my life again because I stole my transformation back. And now I was being punished. My abilities stripped, my strength and stamina weakened, so I'd always be reminded of the abhorrent choice I made. That was it, wasn't it? It wasn't just my body unable to handle the transformation or some kind of infection. This was my consequence for disturbing the balance.

Maybe it'd eventually kill me.

And maybe I deserved it.

I spared Cameron a glance, and though the most breathtaking landscape was painted before us, he was looking at me.

"I'm fine. Really."

"I know." He said it to appease me. His eyes told a different story.

"Do you think it'll get easier?" My gaze drifted back to the luscious green. "Do you think we'll ever be forgiven if the realm finds out?"

"I can try to come up with some sort of answer to ease your guilt, but I really don't know. I wish I did."

I appreciated his answer. Cameron's normal response was to comfort me, but he'd always been in tune with me. Somehow, he knew what I needed to hear, not what I wanted to hear.

"For what it's worth, I still love you."

Finding him staring at me with such an earnest and open expression, his tender words settled the turmoil in my heart. I chuckled. "And I still have no idea why."

He leaped across the connecting branches and sat in front of me, his legs dangling over one side. "Because even though you put off a stone-cold vibe, I know you have a soft heart. And I kind of dig the whole will-she-murder-me-in-my-sleep thing. Keeps things exciting."

I laughed and shoved his shoulder, which was more of a nudge. He smiled back and clasped my hand, holding it between us.

We stayed on the bough, both talking and reflecting until the sun began to descend before heading back to the castle. When we drew closer, where more fae roamed the land, we slowed our pace to keep a more watchful eye out as to not be seen. Near the border of the main village, a group of fae gathered together mingling with drinks around a bonfire. We were far enough away and high enough in the trees they wouldn't notice us, but I noticed something. Or rather, someone.

The sight of a slim woman with short flaming hair stopped me in my tracks. I slipped behind the wide trunk of the tree I was in, peeking around enough for my eyes to see, but hiding the rest of me. Her head tipped back with a laugh as she clapped the shoulder of another woman. And then, a man with light brown hair joined the gathering. He curled his arm around her waist and she stepped into him without looking to see who he was. It was instinct; she knew his touch without sight. Wrinkles creased the corners of their eyes, white and gray sprinkling their hair. They were older, older than I remembered them, but it *was* them.

Cameron only made it a few feet before he realized I wasn't beside him and he backtracked. "What is it?" he whispered, moving behind me to remain unseen.

"My parents."

They were with a few fae I recognized, but there were a couple unfamiliar faces, too. Emphasizing life continued around them, even when their daughters were gone.

Did they miss us? What would they do if they saw me? If I walked up to them with a "Hi, Mom and Dad" what would they say?

Cameron's hand gripped my shoulder, but he said nothing. What could he say? Even if I wanted, I couldn't show myself to them. Even if they'd want to see me, they never could.

They didn't deserve to.

I tore myself away from staring and bolted back to the castle.

If my parents knew what I did, they'd tell me I brought it upon myself after siding with Skye and Adair.

And maybe I had.

FIVE

SARAI

IT'S been confirmed by Arleen that there's almost a sort of cap on the Sowers' abilities to create a larger yield. They've tried, but they can't accommodate the elves as we've promised," Kayne said, sitting across the desk from me. "And they don't want to."

I leaned back in my chair. "Do you think she's not telling the whole truth? That they might be withholding crops to keep from distributing to the elves?"

"I'm not sure. While they aren't pleased with dividing the harvest, it didn't appear that way. She seemed a bit distressed. This has never happened to them before. To any fae, really."

I nodded, grasping the neckline of my dress. "That is concerning."

Why would that happen to the Sowers? Did the elves' arrival have something to do with it, some sort of dampening to their enchantments? Was a force in Rymidon resisting their presence?

Kayne bent over his knees, resting his elbows there. "If we're not going to be able to harvest enough to feed the elves as well, we need to begin more trade agreements."

"Yes. Set up meetings with Mirrion and Callastonia for now, but we'll need something sooner than they can probably provide. I can talk to Calliope and Marcus. Or, you know what…" After Marcus and I last spoke, I departed. I meant to meet with Queen Aisling and King Ronan, but left almost immediately, the trade agreement forgotten. "Oraelia, first. I'll go now. If the King and Queen are unavailable, I'm sure that Marcus can help. Then I'll go to Calliope."

TWO Keepers I recalled seeing with Marcus—Joran and Radford, I believed—received me and my Keepers at the Waking Oak as we entered Oraelia. They stood to attention in their full black attire. Fitted tunics, leather cuffs, and talon axes.

With a nod of greeting and a smile, I said, "We'd like to meet with King Ronan and Queen Aisling, if possible."

Before responding, their heads bowed together, whispering in indistinguishable tones. Until Radford said, "Yes, Queen Sarai. You may head on to the castle." He swept his arm to the side, allowing us to pass by.

Huh. We'd always had an escort, but I knew my way.

"Thank you."

Before we passed them, Joran darted off while Radford remained guarding the Oak. We shared another cordial smile, but I kept my guard up. That was strange. Where did Joran dash off to in such a hurry?

We were met by another set of Keepers at the Oraelian castle entrance, and they let us pass without a qualm, two taking the lead, escorting us to the great hall, almost as if they knew we were coming. Maybe Joran had raced ahead, but I thought he'd left in a different direction.

Stopping at the closed set of towering double doors, one Keeper opened the right side, while the other opened the left. Passing through, Kayne and Brae followed close behind me, closer than they normally did, as if they sensed something was off, too.

In the two thrones at the end of the great hall sat King Ronan and Queen Aisling, their regal poise set in the posture of their shoulders. I'd never seen such a united front, aside from Kai and Calliope. But even with them, Kai always gave Calliope the lead, beside or behind her. She was the Queen and he her husband. Respected, but not in charge. He trusted her decisions without interference.

For the most part.

My parents had never been either way. Looking back, it seemed my father was the Royal at the top and my mom was a woman he needed in order to be King. Not a partner or silent support, but a marionette who did as she was told.

A brooding Prince Alston stood beside his parents, but there was no sign of Marcus. A mixture of relief and disappointment swirled inside me. Where was he?

After announcing me, the two Keepers excused themselves,

closing the doors with a couple of thuds.

"Queen Sarai, how lovely to see you again." Queen Aisling smiled, gracious and approachable. It eased my nerves from the strange behavior of their Keepers.

"Queen Aisling. King Ronan. Prince Alston." I nodded to each.

King Ronan offered an amiable smile, while Prince Alston didn't so much as blink at me. Marcus must have taken after his brother's silent nature. Though not unkind, Alston observed me like he wanted to understand me. Anything was better than distrust and disdain, I supposed.

"Last time, you left before we were able to speak about the trade agreement. I hope everything was all right." There was a certain glint in Queen Aisling's eyes, one that almost knew the truth. Marcus was the reason I hadn't finished our last visit, but how much did she know? Was it a simple mother's intuition or had Marcus divulged more since we last spoke?

"Life in Rymidon has been quite hectic as of late, so please forgive my swift departure last I was here."

Alston eyed me as if he could see past my version of the truth. Did he know what Marcus did? Marcus said they were close, but I wasn't sure how close.

"Of course, my dear. What is it we can help you with today?" It was obvious Queen Aisling did most of the talking around here, surrounded by these reserved men.

"I wanted to form a trade agreement between our kingdoms. Pucuma and fayote from your harvest in exchange for whatever it is you seek. Puriat hides? Atem glass? Weaponry? Our collection of sapierces and katars is extensive."

"Indeed." Queen Aisling looked to King Ronan.

"The sapierce has always been a favorite of mine," he said.

"No one crafts them quite like Rymidon."

"Thank you." I nodded with a pleased smile. At least my father hadn't tarnished everything in Rymidon.

Silence fell upon the bright hall as King Ronan considered my offer. I struggled to keep my hands still at my sides with the urge to fidget as I waited, his gold eyes assessing me. "All right. How much of our harvest do you seek?"

"Five barrels of each for the next three moon cycles in exchange for three hundred sapierces."

"Done."

The groan of the thick double doors opening had me turning, and Marcus stepped through.

With the sight of him, my heart stumbled, tripping over itself as if wanting to run to him, though I kept it at bay.

"Marcus, my dear boy." Queen Aisling beamed. "We hadn't expected you today. Weren't you hunting branaagh with Cormac?"

Our eyes met, but there was no surprise, as if he knew he'd find me here. *Joran.*

"The hunt was cut short. We'll go out again tomorrow." Marcus was talking to her but staring at me.

How was it that one look could fill me with equal parts resentment and longing?

"Well, are you going to greet our guest or gawk?" his mother chastised.

Marcus cleared his throat and bowed. "Sarai."

I smiled, mostly to be polite in front of his family, but also because I couldn't stop myself. "Marcus." His name got trapped in my throat. I cleared it.

It was strange. Though there was a dose of hostility in my heart, one look from him filled me with an unexpected touch of peace. *We were so close to a happily ever after, Marcus.*

And you ruined it.

But I still couldn't help wanting to be near him. Marcus might have crushed our budding love, but he somehow gave me a sense of strength and resilience when our eyes were locked. It was the same look he gave me before the truth was revealed. I was invincible with him and his unwavering esteem.

"Should we give you two some privacy?" My eyes darted back to the thrones and Alston eyed us with a haughty smirk.

"Thanks, brother, but that choice is up to Sarai." Marcus waited.

"I—" I shifted my attention from him to his parents and back. There was no reason to be alone with Marcus, but the strings attaching my heart to him were pulled taught, begging me to ease up, bridge the space between us.

"I think we've rendered the woman speechless." Alston kept the corner of his mouth curled up, cheeky. Maybe he wasn't silent so much as he was patient and waited for the perfect moment to unleash his boldness, to take his opponent by surprise.

"Oh, you boys. That's enough. You've made the poor girl uncomfortable. You don't have to spend time with my son, Queen Sarai, if you do not wish. The trade agreement is final. We're pleased to be doing business with Rymidon once again."

"Thank you." I bowed my head in respect. "But if I could have a moment with Prince Marcus, that would be appreciated."

My request pulled a bright smile from her. "Of course." She stood and shooed Alston. "Come on. Let's go." King Ronan followed behind, nodding his head in farewell.

"Kayne, Brae," I asked. "Would you mind waiting in the corridor?"

They bowed and left.

Alone.

It'd been only a few days since we last saw one another, but after spending nearly every day together, the time apart was odd. I'd found myself searching for his advice on several occasions, but hadn't wanted to seek him out. We needed the time apart, for me to have a clear head, for me to refocus on what was important. But now, with him standing before me, I couldn't help thinking how I could continue going another day without him.

Marcus took one step toward me. "How are you?"

I faced him fully, heaving a heavy sigh. "I've been better."

His mouth opened, a plea on his tongue before he closed it and began again, "I'm sorry to hear that."

"The trade agreement I just made with your parents was to provide food for my kingdom. Since the elves arrived, we've been lacking enough to go around."

Brows pinched, his eyes swelled with worry. "Anything you need, Oraelia will help. I won't explain the details to my parents, but if I ask, they'll do what they can."

"Thank you. They were helpful enough today; I think we'll be fine for a bit."

He nodded and his throat bobbed as he swallowed. No one had eyes like Marcus. Though I loved the color, the same shade of green as after it rained, it was what he did with them. Their intensity and depth. When he looked at me, they devoured me whole, swathed me in his unceasing affection. There was no hiding it. He didn't bother to try.

"It hurts my heart when you look at me that way."

He took another step, his eyes now frowning, but not shielding his adoration. "In what way?"

Like you love me. "Like I mean something to you."

"But you do." Another step. "Why is that a bad thing?"

"Because even though your eyes say one thing, your actions said another."

Marcus stopped.

"As much as I want to be near you, it hurts even more looking at you. Your betrayal still cuts so deep."

Through his eyes, I watched his heart shatter. The jagged pieces tumbled to his feet, but he said nothing.

"But even as much as it hurts, it heals. So, in an endless loop I remain. Healing and hurting over and over. And when we're apart all I do is hurt, until I see you again and heal. And hurt again."

Marcus closed the distance between us. "I'll never hurt you again. I'll make a vow to only heal. If you can learn to see past my deplorable lapse of judgment, I'll never betray you. Ever."

The closer he was, the tighter the string became between us. It didn't loosen, but tugged until I was in his arms and my hands were holding his face. And my lips were molding to his and his arms were clutching me, wrapping my whole self in his embrace. There was no unrest or realm, there was only us, healing.

And then my mind came back to me. It reversed to the day Marcus walked into my study and told me of his lies, of his deception. And I broke away, hurting.

"No." I gasped and tore myself from his arms, racing to the double doors.

He let me go.

SIX

LIA

THE woodlands of Rymidon were silent and serene. Only the flicker of the leaves and the wind lapping at my ears filled the forest. Air glided over my fiery wings, whipping my hair across my back as Cameron and I raced through the trees, swiftly leaping from branch to branch. I had a slight lead on him, but he was hot on my wings, faster than he'd been in previous days.

With every passing day, he'd only gained more speed and strength, his senses and abilities intensifying. I was grateful, of course. It meant the change was settling well with him. He'd been a faery for a couple of weeks, and each day I worried something would go wrong, but there were times when I looked at Cameron and couldn't remember him as a human. Being fae made so much more sense. It made him more confident in his skin, happier. Carefree.

Even though we've had to keep a low profile, this last cycle of the moon has been the most freeing of my existence. There was no oppressive king, no fight for my life.

The elves were settling into Rymidon, albeit with rocky challenges I was still unsure how Sarai was going to smooth over, but at least another war was averted.

While Skye managed to slip into the back of my mind, especially as I resided in the place we grew up and fell in love, life without him was a liberation. No more forbidden meetings or making decisions to please him. No struggling to bring back the man I once knew. The Skye that was still in my heart was not the one who died. I'd lost the one in my heart long before his death.

Every night, I snuck out of the castle and repaired fences or weeded gardens while the remaining families of those slain slept. On some houses, I left bouquets of flowers or hung wreaths on their doors, small tokens of apology. It wasn't much, but it was all I could give for now.

When I chanced a glance over my shoulder at Cameron, I couldn't stop my heart from jolting, an erratic beat that emerged every time I looked at him. He beamed, grinning from ear to ear as he closely followed my trail, his vibrant eyes gleaming with the challenge of beating me. My chest filled with a lightness whenever he was near that I'd never known in my life. It was a wonder I survived this long without him.

"Are you growing soft on me, Ginge?"

"Ginge?"

"Yeah, because you're a ginger."

My eyeroll could've been seen from miles away. "Please shut up."

Cameron's laughter flew through the trees. "Better pick up the pace, or I might not let you win today."

I laughed. "Let me?" Shouting over my shoulder, I pressed on, pushing myself harder. My lungs fought back, constricting. I would not let Cameron *let me* win. Not in a million moon cycles.

Dashing through leaves and dodging around trunks, my lungs burned, a feeling I was once familiar with as a fragile human. And even then, it'd only been after running a mile during gym class. I ignored it, the way I'd been doing since we moved into the castle, pushing the sensation aside and digging within for my fae speed.

The more I pushed, the harder it became. Black dots formed in my vision, speckling the lush foliage in my view.

Don't pass out. Please don't pass out. Not again.

I tried blinking them away. My limbs quivered, reaching their limit. After hours and hours of constant action and energy, maybe. Not a few miles of frolicking in the trees.

After seeing my parents, we'd stayed confined mostly to the castle. I pretended like I didn't see them, and Cameron didn't bring them up. This race in the forest, as if nothing was wrong, was what we needed. A break from reality.

When I passed the finish line, I clung to a branch, trying not to fall. It was as if my lungs were resisting oxygen. My sight blurred, the black spots flashing in and out. In an instant, Cameron landed next to me and wrapped his arm around my waist, encircling me against his chest.

"You losing your touch, Ginge?" Cameron teased in my ear, his chin grazing the crook of my neck. "One more second and I would've whizzed on past you."

The leather bodice of my top left one shoulder and my stomach bare. Cameron took advantage, his fingers teasing the skin at my sides.

I forced a smile. Honestly, I didn't hate the nickname as much as I thought I would. I'd been called worse things.

His once ordinary blue eyes shimmered like bright sapphires as he peered at me before ducking his head down for a kiss. Sucking in a breath, I met his eager mouth. His lips moved, exhilarated, on mine, his new-found energy taking over. Already breathless, his kiss didn't help my predicament. My knees weakened with this exhausted body. Sensing me drooping, Cameron cupped the back of my head, holding me to his mouth and cinching his arm around my waist.

I pulled back, placing my hand over his bare, muscled chest and dropped my forehead against it. "I need to catch my breath."

He chuckled. "Since when do faeries get tired from a little racing? Or was it my expert kissing skills?" I practically heard the waggle of his eyebrows. "You've been doing that a lot lately."

"Well, maybe it's since I haven't been a faery for a while," I shot back, trying not to show my concern or make a big deal out of it. This wasn't an issue when I changed before. I could soar through the trees for miles and miles without being winded. It was as if no time had passed between transformations, but this time was different.

I didn't want to worry anyone, most of all Cameron, but I wasn't what I used to be. I'd accepted it. Cameron was thriving, and I was struggling to keep up. It wasn't as if my body was rejecting the transformation. I wasn't sick; I just wasn't the same.

That black speck on my chest I thought I'd imagined reappeared the other day and hadn't disappeared, but it hadn't grown either. My fainting spells weren't going away. It'd been three times now. Yesterday was the third after the mark reappeared.

What did it mean? How was it that I was more concerned about my transformation than Cameron's wellbeing? He was originally human, after all.

I didn't want to dwell on it or burden anyone else. I'd caused enough trouble over the years. Sarai was dealing with more than she bargained for, transitioning the elves to our kingdom and how poorly Rymidon was handling it. The weight on her shoulders was crushing. Cameron was in another realm of happiness; I didn't want to dampen his excitement with my worry. If there was anyone I could go to it was Calliope, but she was skeptical enough about our transformations. I wasn't in the mood for a lecture.

Stealing the blood of those Rymidonians so I could change was equivalent to a sin for our kind. It didn't matter that I wasn't aware of how the blood had been ascertained, that I thought it was donated, not murdered for. I was a traitor—in more ways than one. I'd only just begun to atone for what I did for Adair, and now I was only fae again because of unnatural methods.

There had to be a reason why those that transformed with fae blood all those centuries ago were the only ones. Did Evan know more than he let on? We'd been so concerned about Cameron, but me? It hadn't crossed any of our minds that I might've been the one to suffer.

How could I draw more attention to myself by questioning my transformation? I should be grateful I was alive.

This. This had to remain my secret.

For now.

"You okay?" he asked when I didn't lift my head from his chest. His index finger tilted my chin up.

I smirked. "Think you got one up on me because you almost beat me?"

"For the record, I could've beat you. And I'll prove it to you." He lifted a cocky grin. "Race you back?"

Not yet. No possible way. "What's the rush?" I leisurely toed the tree limb, walking backward, out of his arms. "There's a lake just over the hillside. Let's go for a swim."

"My fiery faery, hair all soaking wet? Don't have to ask me twice."

I shoved his shoulder with a laugh before darting down from the branch and flipping onto the dirt floor. My legs wobbled, but I recovered quickly enough.

Cameron landed beside me and I led the way on foot. "There aren't any, like, evil mermaids in the lake, are there?"

"Scared of a little sprite, Cam?"

"That depends on what that is."

"They won't bother us," I teased. "Don't worry."

"What the heck is a sprite, Lia?"

I laughed. "It's just a little water faery. They're mostly harmless."

"Mostly?"

"Just don't threaten them and you should be fine." I waved off his concern.

"You know, I'm thinking I might be coming down with something." Cameron forced a few coughs. "It's probably not the best idea to get in cold water and make it worse. No one likes being sick."

"Not such a tough guy, now are we? Live a little, why don't you?" We reached the top of the mountain overlooking the bluish-white surface of Lake Luna, spanning the entire valley.

"Whoa. I've never seen anything like that. It's like an opal gemstone."

"Beautiful, isn't it?"

"Are all lakes like this in Rymidon?"

I shook my head. "This is the only one. It's my favorite."

"I can see why." Cameron took my hand and tugged me down the other side of the mountain, leaping from boulder to boulder. "C'mon." Obviously, thoughts of the sprites forgotten.

At the water's edge, Cameron jerked to a stop. "I can't see the bottom."

The iridescent water obscured everything below the surface. "Chickening out again?"

"No." He scratched the back of his neck. "I just wasn't sure if I was going to be able to touch the bottom. Do I wade in to test the water, or would I get a nice surprise and sink?"

"You wuss." I laughed, teasing his shoulder with a shove. "It's fairly deep." All the better for the sprites to have their solitude. I kept that tidbit to myself. I'd razzed him enough. "You definitely wouldn't be able to touch the bottom without a strong lung capacity to hold your breath there and back."

"I don't need to be that adventurous today." In only his fitted pants, cropped below the knees, Cameron dove headfirst. When his head popped back up, I clapped.

"Bravo. I'm impressed. Didn't even hesitate."

"Couldn't let you have that hanging over my head forever." Cameron raised a hand above the water, rubbing his fingertips together. "Weird. It's thicker than normal water, like heavy cream. Is this even water? It's super silky."

I chuckled. "Yes, it is. Take a drink."

"Seriously?"

I nodded. "It won't kill you. Try it."

Cameron eyed me with mock suspicion as he lowered his

mouth to the surface and gathered a mouthful. His eyes perked up as he licked his lips. "That's crazy. It tastes like water, but almost sweeter? Huh. This bizarre faery world." He beamed at me. "All right, Ginge. Show me what you got."

Not willing to be outdone by him, I took a running start. Leaping into the air, my body twisted, flipped, and swan-dived into the pearly lake. As soon as I hit the water, I knew I'd overdone it. The momentum and speed sent me deeper than I anticipated. With my already impaired lungs, I sputtered for air, scrambling for the surface. My arms and legs drug through the water, slowing me down. A raging fire burned the inside of my lungs and panic drowned me. I wasn't going to make it to the top. My lungs were going to give out. *No.* This wasn't how it all came to an end. Not after everything.

Closer and closer, the sun rippled. Almost there. My limbs slowed, my lungs giving out.

At the last second, I broke free, flailing and gasping for oxygen. In seconds, Cameron was there, taking hold of my waist and bringing me to the shore. I crawled onto the grass, my fingers clawing at the dirt. I coughed up water before flopping onto my stomach, unable to hold myself up any longer.

"Lia, Lia." Cameron flipped me onto my back and brushed the wet strands from my face. "Breathe, Lia. Just breathe."

I tried. It wasn't easy. To my own ears, it was raspy.

"Are you okay?" he asked. "You with me?"

As I struggled to catch my breath, I nodded.

"What happened?"

"Nothing." I attempted to gain my voice, but it was gravel. "I'm fine. Just landed wrong."

"Landed wrong? That was near perfect acrobatics with an Olympic-worthy dive." Cameron tucked my hair behind one ear, tracing the point. "You did not land wrong. Don't lie to me."

I dug for a better lie. "I just went further to the bottom of the lake than I meant to, didn't have enough air to get me back." It wasn't untrue.

"I might be new to this whole faery business, but even I know that's not normal. You should've had plenty of air."

I was naive in thinking I could've kept this to myself for much longer. Though more than the last five years of my life were one giant deception, I should've been able to lie better. But I didn't want to lie to Cameron. Keep it away from him, sure, but there was no possible way I could look him in the eye and betray his trust. No, I left that life behind me.

When I didn't answer immediately, Cameron asked, "What aren't you telling me, Lia?"

Taking my first deep breath, I said, "Since changing back, I haven't been quite the same." I rose to my elbows. "It's not a big deal. It makes sense, really. There's probably a reason faeries can't transform back to our natural form more than twice. I defied nature. I'd be surprised if there weren't any differences."

While I wasn't about to lie to him, I didn't have it in me to worry him, either.

"Does it hurt? Are you in pain?"

I shook my head. "Just don't have the stamina I once did, but I'm fine. Really, Cam. I just have to push myself a little harder to beat you, is all." I laughed, shrugging off my inner doubt.

"I'm such a jerk. Here I am challenging you to competitions left and right to feed my need for speed, while you suffer in silence. You should've told me."

"No, I shouldn't have because it's not a big deal. I've still got more endurance than a human. I can handle it. Maybe it's like exercise. The more I push myself, the easier it'll become. Don't you dare go soft on me."

It wasn't true. In fact, as the days wore on, the less strength and stamina I had. Cameron could go soft on me and I'd probably still be unable to keep up for much longer.

Worry hung in his eyes, but at my adamance, he covered it. "Never. I didn't choose this life to dwindle my new-found awesomeness." He lifted a crooked smile.

"Cam?"

"Hmm?"

"Will you keep this between us? I don't want to draw more attention to us or worry Calliope, or Sarai especially. She's dealing with enough."

"If you say it's not a big deal, it's not a big deal. Secret's safe with me." He winked and sealed it with a kiss.

SEVEN

CAMERON

WHEN I broke the kiss, I helped Lia to her feet. "How about we take a nice stroll back?"

"It'll take us hours on foot," she said, groaning.

I raised an eyebrow. "Do you have somewhere more important you need to be rather than on a stroll with your one true love?"

With an exaggerated sigh, Lia trekked back up the mountainside, toward Rymidon.

"Don't act like spending time with me is such a chore," I teased.

"It's not, but I don't want you to baby me because you think I can't handle my abilities. I just overdid it a little today. I can handle traveling back normally."

"Well, what if I want a human moment? To mosey hand-in-hand with my best girl."

"I'd ask if you smell something nasty with your lips against my butt."

My nose crinkled. "Gross, Lia. I don't wanna think about you farting."

"Hey, everyone's poop stinks."

I nudged her shoulder with mine. "I'd like to believe faery farts smell like flowers."

"You're in for a rude awakening."

I laughed. "All right. Change the subject."

"Did you hear the keepers talking about us when we left this morning?" Not exactly the change I had in mind. "I think we need to be more inconspicuous," she said. "Maybe create a place for us further outside of the kingdom, so we stop attracting attention."

"Live together?"

"Isn't that basically what we're doing now? We can still have our space, separate rooms. I just don't think hiding out in the castle is the best option. Fae talk and it's only a matter of time before questions start circulating. How it's possible I'm back, who you are. Rymidon might not be small, but when hot new blood shows up, it doesn't go unnoticed."

"Are you calling me hot?"

"Oh, shut up. You know you're hot."

"Maybe." I shrugged. "But I didn't know *you* thought I was hot." I laced my fingers between hers.

"Confessing my love for you on my deathbed wasn't

enough for you?"

"Of course not." I gave her a lopsided grin. "You were on your deathbed; desperate times. Nothing you say can be trusted. And besides, love doesn't equate to attraction. Guys need compliments, too."

Lia rolled her eyes, and I stole a quick kiss. I couldn't stop kissing her. Faery blood heightened all my senses. It was a shock to my system at first, a flood of sensations I didn't have words to describe. As the days wore on, my body learned to acclimate. My senses didn't lessen, they merely became normal, second nature.

Running was more like flying at thirty thousand feet, my legs weightless. Food tasted richer, more flavorful, my tastebuds overloaded daily. Sounds that were background noise or inaudible before infiltrated my ears to sometimes overwhelming volumes. I could detect the flapping wings of a bird yards away. And kissing... Kissing Lia was like entering the gates of heaven, over and over. There was no getting enough.

"You never told me I was hot before, either," I said against her lips.

"Before?" She pulled back.

"In case you forgot, we did date once upon a time."

"Can we even call that dating?" Lia's eyebrow quirked. "We were fourteen, and it lasted like a month before I got tired of you."

"You going to get tired of me again? Is that what you're hinting at?"

"I don't know. I guess it depends on how much longer you insist on *letting* me win." Lia bolted through the trees.

Dang it, Lia. If she wound up blacking out from pushing herself too hard at the end of this, I'd never forgive myself. But I couldn't hold her back. I knew Lia well enough to know she wouldn't do as she was told. She'd push back ten times harder.

As to not appear like I was going easy on her, I kept up my speed, but I didn't put pressure on my new abilities to step it up a notch. I stayed by her side, falling back only a fraction before pressing on, so she didn't catch onto my attempt to placate her.

We arrived at the base of the castle, Lia winning. Because I let her, of course. She stopped, arms pumping the air in victory while she laughed. I smiled, lifting her off the ground and turning us in circles. Her head fell to my shoulder as she breathed heavily into my neck, the only sign of exhaustion she showed.

If I knew anything about Lia, it was that she refused to show weakness. If she didn't have the same stamina she once did, she was struggling with a lot more than that. I wished she'd open up to me so I knew what we were dealing with.

What if the more she pushed herself, the quicker she lost her abilities, one negating the other? Would it store up the less she used her fae abilities? Or was she slowly losing them day by day? Was it possible the donor blood was killing her? I promised to keep this between us, but what if that hurt her in the long run?

Laughter sprang from the trees to the west, and I grabbed Lia's hand, sheltering us behind a stone wall of the castle.

"Where did she go?"

"Tosia, you're crazy. That wasn't her."

"I know what I saw and I saw Magnolia. She was with some blonde guy I didn't recognize. They passed right above us."

Lia and I shared a wide-eyed stare, clamping our mouths shut. How had we not noticed them? Too caught up in our competition and her recent confession. She squeezed my hand tighter.

"You know that's not possible. Isn't she human now?"

"She didn't look human," Tosia said, her voice higher than

the other. "Same flaming wings and everything. That red hair and those wings are unmistakable."

"Cait has wings similar to Magnolia's. It was probably her."

"Then who was the guy?"

"Someone from another kingdom, probably. C'mon, I'm starving. It's odd, but it couldn't have been her. Magnolia transitioned too many times to come back."

There was a sigh. "Maybe you're right."

"And even if it was her, she'd be crazy to return home. Didn't her parents disown her, too?"

"Well, when you make a deal with Mabuz, you kind of become one. She deserved it." Their voices trailed off as they walked away.

Once they were gone, Lia and I scaled the back of the west tower, our entrance into the castle. We climbed in through an open window into Lia's bedroom.

"We've been getting careless." Lia walked to her armoire and pulled out different clothes to change out of her wet ones. "I guess we'll be sticking to the castle again from now on."

"What's a Mabuz?"

She slipped behind a wooden partition with ornate carvings along the top. "It's like the devil. Our version of it anyway, since we don't believe in Hell."

She'd never show it if their words affected her, but I had to say it. "Don't listen to them, Lia."

"Everything they said was true, but whatever." One article of clothing flew over the top of the partition. And then another, landing with a sloppy splat. "I never liked Tosia anyway. She was a huge gossip and most of it she made up herself to stir up drama. Could never believe anything she said."

"Well, hopefully, that works in our favor if she tells

someone else."

Lia stepped out in flowing beige pants and a black crop top that was made of some sort of tight-knit lace. Every time I saw Lia, I half-expected to see her in jeans and a T-shirt. Just a regular woman, but every time I was taken aback. Our daily attire was another reminder we weren't human anymore.

Sweeping her hair from her face, she asked, "What?"

"Nothing. You're just beautiful."

Like she didn't know how to handle the compliment, she laughed. "Okay. I think I'm going to take a nap before dinner."

At any other time, I wouldn't have thought twice about her midday nap. We didn't have much to do while we hid out, but after her confession, everything was different. I'd question every comment and move. Exactly what she didn't want from me.

"Yeah. All right. I'll leave you to it. I'm gonna go stir up whatever trouble I can get myself into."

"I know you're joking, but seriously, don't be stupid. Especially after those nosey fae. Keep a low profile until Sarai figures out how to handle us with the rest of the kingdom. It's a miracle that was our first close call. It's bound to happen soon."

"Yes, ma'am." I saluted Lia and then bent to kiss her. My hand gripped her hip over the edge of the drawstring pants. Her exposed abdomen begged my thumb to circle her satiny skin. The faintest of breaths hitched as she deepened the kiss. I brought my other hand to the nape of her neck, my fingers tangling in her damp hair. Damn, this mouth. I needed more. One step away from throwing her on the bed, Lia stopped me.

"Okay, okay." She pushed against my chest, taking a shaky breath. "You make trouble. I'm going to sleep."

Calming my rapid heartbeat, the corner of my mouth crooked. "Sure thing, Ginge." With one last kiss at the side of her plump lips, I slipped out of her room.

Rymidon's castle was different from Faylinn. Calliope had that way about her; anywhere she was felt like home. While Faylinn's castle was welcoming, almost cozy—as cozy as a stone castle could be—Rymidon's was like no one lived in it. I suppose Adair wasn't much for homey decor or hospitality. *Shocker.* And it wasn't as if Sarai had time to liven up the place. She'd been hit with one conflict after another. Her focus wasn't on the outward appearance, but her fae. Where it should've been, though living in these walls couldn't help her mindset.

After living here for a couple of weeks, I'd become familiar with the layout. The kitchen was my home away from home. Trilla, the cook—or Sower or whatever—and I had become friends. I wasn't sure why, but my appetite had been ferocious those first few days, as though my new abilities ate up every calorie in minutes.

Speaking of food, a pre-dinner snack was in order. I headed down the west stairwell to the main level, passing the gathering hall on my way. I wasn't one for eavesdropping, but Sarai's uncharacteristically firm voice caught my attention. Her words were muffled until I drew closer.

"They can't stay here, Your Highness," a deep voice said.

"What am I supposed to do, Kayne? I agreed to this. It's binding. It's done."

"And what about punishment? After killing our fae, they'll get none? We'll just bend to their every whim day after day?"

"No punishment?" Her voice echoed with its volume. "They lost almost half of the elves in that cavern. You were there. They suffered, maybe not as much as you'd have liked, but they did."

"No, it was not nearly enough. I don't trust them."

"For the last time, it's *not* about trust." Ooo, Sarai was *pissed*. "We don't have to trust them, but that doesn't mean we treat them like scradderons."

Scardderons? Was that their version of garbage? Or a pariah, maybe?

"But that's exactly what they are!"

Whoa. Kayne was being ballsy. Calliope would've put him in his place long before that.

Sarai paused before she calmly said, "Nevertheless, if we treat them as such, there is no room for accord or peace."

Sarai's intimidating Keepers, Eitri and Galdinon, stood guard outside the cracked doors to the gathering hall. When they noticed my approach and obvious interest, Galdinon shut the doors with a look of reproach.

My bad. It wasn't everyday Sarai wasn't a gentle peacemaker. Sue me for being curious. I gave them an innocent smile and continued on.

ᴇ‌IGHT

SARAI

IF I may be so blunt, we can't keep this up for much longer, Your Highness," Kayne lowered his voice with the shutting of the doors. We might be passionate about the issue at hand, but we must also be mindful of our surroundings. Who knew who was roaming the castle? "Even with Oraelia's help, our crops are still dwindling. We can't expect every kingdom to sustain us. And their eyes. There is no end. The dark depths are infinite, staring through my soul. I don't know how to help them when I can't even look them in the eyes."

"What is it that Calliope has said? Keep your friends close, but your enemies closer." I circled the marble floors of the gathering hall. "I understand why you believe I wasn't thinking clearly when I offered Guthron a place in our kingdom, but I assure you, it was either this or start a whole new war. We're still recovering from the Battle of Faylinn. I won't put our fae through another."

"I understand, but—"

"This may seem reckless to you, Kayne, but at least if they are on our land, we'll be able to keep a better watch over them. The elves are notorious for moving from one place to the next. At least here we know where they are at all times. They cannot leave, not without my approval."

"Are we sure all of the fae blood was confiscated? How do we know Guthron hasn't hidden a stash for himself?"

"We don't know, but for now, we have to trust that we can find harmony. We have more pressing issues at the moment."

"Precisely, Your Grace. The Rymidonians are not comfortable with the elves on our land. If the point after losing the Battle of Faylinn was to rebuild this kingdom and create unity, welcoming a known enemy into our homeland was careless. And keeping their involvement in the assassinations confidential will surely cause discord when it comes to light."

"And what would you have me do, Kayne? You said you trusted me. Should I start a war? Slaughter a tribe of elves?" My voice ricocheted off the stone walls. "Cause panic when our fae realize our blood can be used against us? This doesn't affect only us. It affects every other kingdom if word were to spread, or if the scroll were to fall into the hands of another enemy. How am I supposed to release this kind of information without causing pandemonium? Please, please, enlighten me, so that I might better rule my kingdom."

Kayne's jaw clenched, his nostrils flaring as he calmed his breathing. "I do trust you, but now that they're here, it's different. You have to see that. We can either start a war with the elves or risk a rebellion within Rymidon when they learn their queen has been withholding vital information. Take your pick, Your Highness."

We stood our grounds, no compromise in sight, holding our stare.

"I did what I thought was best in a dire situation. Right now, what I need from you is to help me bridge the gap between our kingdom and the elves. We'll move onto the next challenge when this is settled."

Kayne grit his teeth. "They murdered our fae."

I wasn't tall enough to meet him eye-to-eye, but that didn't stop me from moving toe-to-toe with Kayne and leveling my stare as I tilted my head back. "I have not forgotten. You and I may not agree, but I am *still* your queen."

Kayne's shoulders dropped with a heavy exhale and his eyes lowered to the floor. "Yes, Your Grace."

With a creak, the door to the gathering hall opened and Eitri entered. "Prince Marcus of Oraelia is here to see you."

Marcus? After our last encounter, I hadn't intended to see him for quite a while. Space was what we needed. *What is he doing here?*

"Send him in."

Eitri stepped aside and Marcus's imposing figure loomed in the doorway before he entered. My Keepers were not small men, but they were dwarfed in size by Marcus. I snatched a neutral mask, hiding the small intake of breath at the sight of him. It hadn't been long since I'd seen him, half a moon cycle or so, but his hair, once cropped close to the scalp when we first met, was long enough to comb my fingers through.

"Kayne, if you will excuse us."

"Yes, Your Grace."

I waited until the door shut before I spoke. "Prince Marcus."

"Must we return to formalities, Sarai?" Marcus made his way across the hall, one eyebrow cocked until we were close enough to touch.

"I think it's best for now." Because I couldn't think properly with him so close, I took one step back.

He nodded, resigned. "Fair enough."

"To what, do I owe the pleasure of your visit?"

A sigh escaped him. "I came to see how you and your kingdom were fairing with Guthron and the elves."

And there. There was the reason we needed to keep formalities. He was the reason I was forced into the decision of providing the elves with land. He was the reason twenty of our fae lost their lives. The reason I had to inform twenty families their loved ones were not returning.

"We're managing."

With one look in his forest green eyes, it was clear he didn't believe me. "Is there any way I or Oraelia can be of more assistance? More resources? Food? Weaponry? I'm sure we could spare a few Keepers, if you need more guarding the elves."

We needed more food, but I didn't want to be more indebted to Marcus, to draw more attention to our kingdom. "Oraelia has been more than generous with our trade agreement, thank you. And I have Faylinn, as well. Calliope is a very supportive sister."

"Yes, I know. I'm grateful you have her."

Every day my feelings toward Marcus flipped. I forgave

him, but it was still so difficult to trust him, to open my heart once again. One moment I was ready to march toward the Waking Oak and rush into his arms, the next I cursed his name for the choices he made, for the position he forced me into.

Maybe I hadn't fully forgiven him after all.

"My parents are concerned for you. All by yourself. They wish they could do more."

I didn't like thinking about being the last of my family, an orphan. It made me feel weak and lost, like a lesser Royal. There was no room in my life for those kinds of emotions.

"Do they know?" The biting tone of my question gave way to my meaning. Do they know the part he played in this mess?

"I haven't told them yet," he said, his eyes downcast.

Coming clean would put him one step closer to my good graces, but if he couldn't own his mistakes, it was only going to further distance us.

Marcus could've sent anyone to check on us or sent a message. "Why did you really come? Why not send Radford or Joran? You have plenty of other Keepers who could've asked about offering aid."

His gaze lifted. "I just needed to see you. After you left Oraelia last, I haven't been able to get you off my mind. You rushed off so quickly, but I wanted to respect your wishes, to give you time and space."

I stiffened. "It shouldn't have happened. It was a moment of weakness."

"Did you ever think maybe you sought me out for strength?"

"Yes. Strength for my heart, not to confuse it."

"Your heart didn't seem very confused at the time."

I turned away, gathering my senses. "The kiss was a

mistake, Marcus. I knew it the moment it happened. It gave you false hope that I was ready for you when I am not. I don't know when I will be. If ever."

"Have I not suffered enough?" His voice drew closer, his footsteps light on the stone floor. "Even being away from you for a day is agony. I understand I hurt you. I know my choices were disgraceful and reprehensible, but how long will you punish me? How long must I live without you?"

I spun back to him. "I have been surrounded by deceitful men my whole life, Marcus. A father who should have empowered me, but instead, lied and hid me, underestimated me. A brother I should have been able to look up to and seek out for guidance and support, instead betrayed not only his kingdom and family but the entire faery race by handing over the scroll to Guthron. The *one* brother I could trust died in a war he didn't ask for, nor approve of.

"And then I was thrust into a role that was never supposed to be mine, only to have the man I was falling in love with plunge into the vengeful footsteps of those very men and make me a fool. I might have been pretty sheltered growing up, but that does not mean I don't know my worth."

If not for my mother, even at such a young age, I might never have known my worth.

Marcus took his crown of bone from atop his head, looking ready to hurl it across the hall, but instead he let it dangle from his fingertips at his side. With aggravation, his other hand gripped the roots of his hair.

"I know your worth. I *do*. I regret my decisions every day, Sarai. I assure you. Whatever punishment you wish upon me, I've punished myself more." Marcus's eyes rose to the ceiling before he dragged a hand down his face and looked at me. "Can we—" His voice cracked. "Can we at least, please, be friends once again? It doesn't have to be more." *Yet.* It wasn't said but implied. "It doesn't even make sense. We spent less than a moon cycle together, but I only needed a day to know you were something precious and rare. I just...I miss you, Sarai. I miss you so much."

I couldn't deny I missed him, too. I missed his counsel, his direction. I missed how his presence calmed me in a way nothing else could these days. Without Sakari, I felt a constant hole, a never-ending loneliness. While I didn't need a romantic complication, I did need an ally, one who wasn't also trying to run a kingdom. Calliope would always be my ally, but it wasn't quite enough. She had her own obstacles to attend to.

"As long as we can keep it that way," I said. "Friends. Don't expect more from me."

"I won't." He took an eager step. "I just want to help you. What can I do?"

My shoulders relaxed at his question. "Kayne wants me to hold a council with the Royals and inform them of the elves' evildoings, but you and I both know that would cause another war. Not to mention, the information we know about the blood was only meant for True Royal eyes. Calliope has to be the one to make that decision."

"True, but they do have a right to know, don't you think? It's no longer a forgotten secret or irrelevant history. It's a current threat."

"If I held a council with the Royals, it would mean you'd have to come clean with your part."

He kept his features steady, resolute. "And I'd accept whatever punishment they deemed necessary. I have no intention of hiding from my mistakes. It's all up to you on how you want to handle the elves. From now on, I'll make no moves about this without your permission."

I was still mad at him, but I didn't want Marcus to be punished unjustly. He righted his wrongs, at least he tried to. What would the Royal council do if they knew what Marcus did? What was the punishment for committing crimes on another kingdom?

"But, Sarai," he pulled me from my thoughts, "how do we know we can trust the other Royals?"

"Why wouldn't we?"

"The elves twisted with my head. Your father and Skye were corrupt. Who's to say there aren't other Royals who are treacherous? Simply because they haven't outed their darker sides yet? Most of us aren't as pure as you."

"Is that where we are now? Forever unable to trust anyone? Unable to trust *Royals* because of a few miscreants? After everything, I don't see how Rymidon can keep this quiet. I might have it contained for the meantime, but I am not so naïve to believe it's over. This will eventually come out. I'll have to tell my fae and from there, the rest will know."

Marcus nodded, gravely. "I'm with you, Sarai. I am. I understand why you'd feel uncomfortable keeping this quiet after what Adair did, and if you decide to go to them, I'll stand beside you, but we don't know who can be trusted with that kind of knowledge. This is about protection, not deviance."

He was right. Everything was complicated. Calliope and I needed to meet and talk this out a little more.

"I'll speak with Calliope and see if she has any ideas. Find out how she would like to handle the knowledge we've been privy to. Then we'll go from there."

"Whatever you desire."

NINE

LIA

WHEN I woke up, my room was dark, the sun seeming to have set hours ago. A presence in the corner had my senses on high alert. My hand reached for the drawer of the side table next to my bed where I kept a dagger.

The tall figure stepped forward and moonlight shone across his smooth jawline. My hand whipped to my chest. "Cameron, you nearly gave me a heart attack."

He chuckled. "Not my intention. You seemed tense. I thought my voice would've startled you more."

"More than creepily moving away from the shadows? What

were you even doing in the corner?"

"Just staying safe in the confines of your room."

"Why didn't you wake me up?"

The bed jostled with his weight as he sat, his fingers brushing a few strands from my eyes. "How could I possibly disturb such a sleeping beauty?"

"Don't deflect with compliments." I sat all the way up, the covers falling away. "Now that you know about my changes, it comes across as patronizing."

"It has nothing to do with your *changes*. You were so tired and looked so peaceful, I didn't want to bother you. But now that you're awake, you hungry?"

"Starving."

"Trilla made you a plate and has it saved for you in the kitchen." Cameron held his hand out to pull me from bed. Once up, he circled my waist, drawing me into him. His nose brushed mine, slowly, side-to-side, before he stole a kiss. It was uncharacteristically gentle, sweet. He stole another, feather-light. It equally made me swoon and raise my suspicion, but I was too hungry to fight with him.

"About that dinner."

He smiled against my mouth. "You know, you were very good at disguising your little accent for all those years, but now that we're here in Rymidon, especially when you get sassy, an Irish lilt comes through."

I shook my head, cocking it to the side. "Dinner?"

"I dig it. It's hot." Cameron chuckled when I stared at him, ready for food, and grabbed my hand. "Okay. Let's go."

WE sat at the corner of a long, wooden island in the center of the massive kitchen, perched on tall tree stumps.

"I think we should visit Calliope," Cameron said. "I'm not sure staying in Rymidon is the best option anymore."

"Why?" I paused my bite of shemun inches from my mouth. "What happened?"

"You know what happened. Between the mob and those girls seeing you. Who else might have and we just haven't heard them talking about it?"

He had valid points, but we agreed to this. We knew the risks. Our options were limited. Cameron was safer here. His safety was more important than mine.

"Have you thought about what you'd do if you don't just see your parents from afar, but actually bump into them?"

I tensed. It wasn't that I hadn't thought about it, it was that I didn't want to. I wasn't sure what I'd do if I saw them again. They'd made their decision about me a long time ago. Did I still love them? Of course, they were my parents, but it didn't mean I wanted to reconnect. I wouldn't grovel for a place in the family or beg for forgiveness. I was their daughter. Their love should've been unconditional. And if bargaining with Adair wasn't enough to sever ties between us, using the blood of innocent Rymidonian fae to return would.

"I won't run into them."

"It's a possibility, Lia."

"Then I'll stay confined to the castle forever. There are worse prisons."

Cameron sighed, but nodded as he rested his elbows on the counter. "I overheard Sarai arguing with Kayne earlier. Tensions are high. Our presence will only cause more contention in the kingdom if or when what we did gets out. For our safety, as well as easing Sarai's burden, I think we should talk to Calliope and get some advice from her, reassess. See if we can't find somewhere safer to lay low until this dies down."

"Faylinn won't be much better." It was why we chose Rymidon. No one knew Cameron here. He was well known as Calliope's human best friend in Faylinn. How would they react if he was no longer human? Or that I— the betrayer of the realm— –had returned and was now a Faylinn resident. He knew all of this, so I didn't push the issue, but the concerns piled on.

"It'll be better than a kingdom on the verge of a revolutionary war," he said.

I snorted. *Who knows?* Maybe Calliope would surprise us. "Okay. We can go tomorrow. We'll need to be prepared. We can't use anyone here to give advance notice to Calliope. There's no telling who might see us traveling through the Waking Oak."

"We've managed to go mostly unnoticed here so far. I think we'll be all right in Faylinn. How well do you know their kingdom?"

"Not nearly as well as I know Rymidon, which is why we'll have to be on high alert, undetectable."

"Cool. Like a James Bond mission."

"If I were any other faery, that reference would go right over my head."

TEN

SARAI

KAYNE re-entered the gathering hall after Marcus left.

"Oh good. I was just coming to find you. I need to go to Faylinn and discuss the current situation with Calliope."

He nodded. "I came to tell you the Royal council contacted us again. We can't postpone the Royal gathering any longer, My Queen," Kayne said. "The Royals are getting anxious. And I'm getting very tired of dealing with Mirrion's adviser. He's so pompous. He wanted me to remind you there are only two moon cycles left for you to bond."

A nauseating pang struck my stomach. Only two. How had

the time slipped by so quickly? I didn't want to invite every kingdom to Rymidon in the midst of this sort of crisis. What must they think of us opening our land to the elves? That sort of rumor surely spread by now. And how was I supposed to match with another Royal when the one Royal I wanted I couldn't choose? Not yet, anyway.

Maybe not ever.

"I know. I've already spoken with Unterrial and she's fully prepared to get started, so send out the invitations and we'll do it on the first day of the waxing crescent."

"Oh, good. That's soon. And what about the elves?"

"We'll save Faylinn for tomorrow and I'll speak with Guthron this evening. We can let them hold their own celebration, but they won't be allowed near ours. Especially with Mirrion coming. I don't know what discord resides there, but we don't need any more unrest. We've met our allotment."

Kayne nodded before heading to the doorway of the gathering hall. "I'll send word now, and then we can visit the elves."

THE Craftsmen built Guthron's home on the west side of Orchid Mountain, overlooking the dwellings of the rest of his elves. It was strange to have so many residents on the ground and none in the trees. It required so much more land, land I shouldn't have given up. We offered to build stairs or ladders into trees, but Guthron was adamant they didn't want to live as fae. Like it was somehow an insult.

"Queen Sarai. How lovely to be graced with your presence."

His words sent a shiver down my spine and I turned, facing him at the base of Orchid Mountain. "Guthron." I nodded. "I trust you've settled in well by now."

"Yes. Although, a king such as I deserves more than a humble dwelling, do you not agree?" He pointed to his cottage above. It wasn't small by any stretch; it could fit a family of four or five comfortably and he lived alone. "How are my subjects supposed to respect a king who lives the same as they do and shares a common area?"

"You want my Craftsmen to replace what they built with a castle?"

"Precisely."

"That wasn't a part of the agreement."

"Was it not?" His head tilted. "I believe your exact words were, 'Rymidonian Craftsmen will help you build dwellings and whatever you might need.' I need a dwelling fit for a king."

"I believe I also said, 'anything within reason.' You already have fifty acres of Rymidonian land, homes for every elf, as much food as you require, and protection from every other fae kingdom. I'm not asking my Craftsmen to build you a castle. Your home is larger than theirs as it is. And you're all by yourself."

"Just as you are alone."

My eyes narrowed. "I didn't choose my castle, but it also houses a good portion of my staff and their families. Over fifty fae dwell inside."

"You don't think I need staff to cater to me?"

I was perfectly capable of taking care of myself, but I didn't come here to argue with him. "This isn't up for debate, Guthron."

He stroked his long, wrinkled chin. "Of course, I could

always let the rest of our realm know the capabilities of your blood. That kind of knowledge would be worth a large sum."

Kayne moved closer when I stepped up to Guthron, tipping my head back to meet his dark eyes. My wing tips sharpened. "If you do, I'll strip you of this land and everything that comes with it. *And* launch a war you cannot win. Don't test me, Guthron. My mercy will be short-lived. I might have been raised to be docile and agreeable, but the blood of my father still runs through my veins. I'm capable of doing what's necessary to protect my kingdom and my kind."

He arched a brow. "My, my, my, Queen Sarai. Maybe you have what it takes to rule a faery kingdom after all. You are mastering ruthless leader like the rest."

"If by ruthless you mean protective, then yes. I am. You and I are at a bit of an impasse, wouldn't you say? You'd like to destroy the fae race, while I'd destroy the elf race if you tried. And I'd like to evict you from Rymidon, but you'll proclaim delicate *sacred* knowledge about our blood to any creature who will listen. So, around and around we go without either of us getting what we want. You'd like a castle, and I'd like peace. It seems, Guthron, neither of us will ever be satisfied."

Guthron's mouth pinched in restrained fury. "Is there a reason you came here other than to reject my request?"

Why had I even come? I couldn't remember now.

"The Royal gala," Kayne whispered in my ear.

Right. "I'm hosting a gathering for the Royals on the first day of the waxing crescent. You'll need to remain here. No venturing into the forests or into our village. Mirrion will be in attendance, as well as every other kingdom. I'd like to keep a harmonious evening, and as you're aware, your presence would not be welcomed by all."

"Another celebration we are not invited to, how surprising." He snarled.

"You're not fae, Guthron, or a Royal, so I'm not sure what you expect. I'm happy to have Unterrial put together your own festivities that night if you'd like. A sort of welcoming celebration."

Guthron's lips pursed as he stared off. "That would be acceptable."

We left the elf village and Kayne muttered, "I really hate that guy."

It was a popular opinion.

ELEVEN

CAMERON

LIA and I sped through the forest on our way to the Waking Oak the next morning, our guard up and solid. She led us on a serpentine path, one that was less traveled to avoid possible run-ins, taking us twice as long to get there. We weren't about to make the same mistake as yesterday and forget our surroundings and who could be around.

I wasn't sure how much longer it'd take to get to the Oak, but Lia wasn't slowing down. I wondered if she was feeling that fatigue but hiding it. I almost slowed down just so she wouldn't feel like I was pushing her to go faster. It wasn't a race. And then, I nearly collided with Lia as she came to an abrupt stop. Skidding across the dirt, I slid to her side. I shot vigilant looks around the woodlands in case she saw or heard someone close by, but I didn't hear or see a single soul.

"What is it?" I asked in a whisper.

She pointed to a large patch of brown, shriveled bushes and moss. "Dead vegetation."

"Okaaaay. Is it going to bite you?"

"We don't have dead vegetation, Cam. Nothing dies in our realm. Our magic always keeps it alive. Even in the winter, it's not really dead, just hibernating. But for it to be the middle of spring, when new life should be thriving, it doesn't make any sense."

"So, what does it mean?"

Lia lifted her gaze to mine, slow dread forming in her hazel eyes. "I don't know." Her unease was enough to tighten knots in my stomach.

"Is it just this patch or do you think it's spreading?"

She peered around. "I don't see it anywhere else, so it might just be here, or it could be in other parts of the kingdom we haven't seen."

"Should we tell someone?"

"I'm going to try and heal it first." Lia crouched down and set her palm on the ground at the border of the dry plants. Eyes closed in concentration, she stayed silent for a couple minutes. I waited with bated breath, but nothing happened. Not even a puny sprout of green.

"I don't feel anything." Her eyes opened. "Not even a weak beat of life. There's nothing to heal because it's too far gone."

"Can you grow more over the top of it?"

Replacing her hand, she closed her eyes once more, but

after several moments, there was still nothing.

Lia shook her head. "It's not working."

"Do you think it's like a poison or infection of the earth?"

She stood with her hands on her hips. "Maybe. I don't know. I've never heard of anything like that. Even when Adair poisoned the Oak, it didn't dry up the lands, it was a toxin that spread to the fae, making them sick."

"So, what do we do?"

"We have to turn back. We need to tell Sarai now."

ONCE we slipped in an entrance at the back of the castle, I picked up my pace to keep up with Lia as she darted through the wide halls, searching for Sarai or one of her personal Keepers. When we rounded a corner, we spotted Galdinon and Eitri marching down the corridor on their patrol.

"Where's Sarai?"

Galdinon blinked, caught off guard by Lia's abrasive tone. Eitri wasn't as surprised by her, sighing with a roll of his bright eyes.

"C'mon, Galdinon. I don't have all day. It's important."

His eyes narrowed, but he answered, "She's in the gathering hall with Brae and Kayne, but I wouldn't interrupt them. They're discussing private kingdom business."

Lia didn't bother to listen once she found out where Sarai was, nor did she wait for me as she sped down the corridor. For someone who was losing her stamina yesterday, she wasn't messing around.

Not waiting to be announced, she burst through the double doors. Sarai's head whipped up, while Kayne and Brae drew their glassy swords.

When our faces were recognized, the three relaxed, but Sarai's face grew wary. "Lia? Cameron? Is everything all right?"

"I'm sorry to have so rudely interrupted, but we might have a problem."

Sarai widened her eyes waiting for Lia to continue

"On our way to Faylinn this morning, about a mile from the Waking Oak, we stumbled upon a sizable expanse of dead landscape. I tried to heal it, but it wouldn't even let me cultivate new growth."

The faces of all three Rymidonians fell as they met each other's stare.

So, this was bad. This was very, very bad.

"Show me. Now."

LIA brought them back to the same spot without the serpentine, remembering exactly where it was. I'd have been traveling in circles for hours, but she knew these lands like the back of her hand.

Sarai knelt on the ground at the edge of the dry foliage and did just as Lia did, placing both palms on the earth and closing her eyes.

Kayne and Brae stood beside us, looking on. Not a word was spoken, hardly a breath taken. Several minutes passed. Nothing. Nothing happened. If not even a Royal could heal it, that couldn't be good. Maybe Calliope could? With her True Royal powers or something.

"Not a single pulse." Sarai's voice was low as she sat back on her heels. "Have you seen this anywhere else?"

We shook our heads and Sarai's gaze turned to Kayne.

"With the limited harvest," he murmured, and Sarai nodded.

"What's happening with the harvest?" Lia asked.

Sarai sighed and rose to her feet. "Since the elves arrived, we've had a shortage. Nothing that would mean we'd starve, but we can't grow as much as we need. Arleen said they've tried to harvest more, but it's like there's a limit on their powers and it's growing worse."

"Do you think it has to do with the elves?" I asked.

"It wouldn't make sense if it did," Kayne said. "They've lived in all different lands and I've never heard of this happening."

"Us," Lia said. "Is it us?"

Us? Why would it be us?

Sarai's teeth sunk into her lower lip, eyes slanting at the corners in conflict. "I don't know."

I gripped Lia's hand. *Us.* Our unnatural transformation. The balance thing Calliope mentioned before I transformed. We could be causing the land to die.

"Maybe we can ask Callie to try," I suggested. "Maybe her powers are stronger. She fixed the Oak after it was poisoned, didn't she?"

Sarai nodded, but she didn't appear hopeful. "It's worth a shot. Brae, will you go to Faylinn and ask for the presence of Calliope in Rymidon at once? Tell her it's urgent and bring her straight here."

"Yes, Your Highness." He bowed and whizzed away.

If this was caused by us, what were we going to do? Would we have to change back into humans? Could we even do that? Even if *I* could, I didn't think Lia could.

There were so many questions swirling in my head, but I kept them inside for the time being. One step at a time. Maybe this wasn't as big a deal as they were making it out to be, and Calliope would have it green and thriving in no time.

TWELVE

SARAI

WHAT'S going on?" At the sound of Calliope's voice, we turned. "Are you two in danger?" She strode forward, Kai at her side and Declan bringing up the rear.

"It's not us, well, it could be us, but it's more than that." Cameron scratched the back of his neck, unease in his stance.

She offered a questioning look around our circle.

"It's the land." I drew her attention to the foliage drained of life.

"I've tried to heal it," Lia said as Calliope stepped up to it. "Sarai's tried to heal it. Nothing. There's no sign of life beneath the earth."

Kai looked just as troubled as the rest of us, but Calliope didn't quite understand the severity of dead land.

"Huh. Well, let me take a crack at it." She popped her knuckles and wandered to the center of the decayed woodlands. Sweeping aside her sage green dress, she knelt and pressed her palms to the soil.

"When did you find this?" Kai asked in a hushed whisper.

"Lia and Cameron found it this morning, not long ago. I sent Brae to retrieve you as soon as I couldn't heal it myself."

"Did they search for any other similar parts of your kingdom?"

"Not yet, but I will send out a unit if Calliope can't heal it."

The look in Kai's indigo eyes wasn't promising. Even as powerful as his wife was, he didn't believe this was something even a True Royal could restore.

In a quiet voice, I said, "We're also experiencing a shortage with our harvest. We thought it might've been with the arrival of the elves, but my head Sower said it's more than that. We made an agreement with Oraelia, who has been providing extra food, but it's not enough. My Sowers can't grow more, no matter how hard they try."

Kai's worried stare whirled to me, just as stunned as I was.

"Has anything like that ever happened to Faylinn?"

His head shook. "Not that I'm aware of."

Time passed with no change to the vegetation before Calliope stood. "It's strange. For me, it's not just that there's no life, it's almost as if it's pushing back. Like there's a force blocking my power and shoving it away. *You shall not pass!*"

Cameron chuckled, but covered it with a cough.

"What could it be?" I asked.

"You're asking the half-breed?" Calliope smirked.

"Could it be us?" Lia asked. "We know there needs to be a balance in nature. Your dad never told you what would happen if there wasn't?"

She shook her head.

Lia paled. "So, this could be it. We could be killing the realm?"

"I feel like if it were that severe my father would've told me."

"Did you ask him?"

"Well, no. It wasn't the point of our discussion at the time, but even Evan didn't know what would happen. Maybe my father didn't either. He just knew the laws of the transformation. Balance or you don't transform. I always assumed it was because it wouldn't work, or that you'd die."

"We transformed without the balance and lived, so..." Cameron searched the circle for answers.

"As did several other elves, who are still alive and living on our land," I said. "It could very well be them." It was a stupid thing to say, if it was the elves, it was Cameron and Lia, too. They all used the same blood.

"But the elves started transforming like four moon cycles ago," Calliope said. "Would it take that long for the balance to be disturbed?"

I said, "It might've affected more and we just haven't seen it yet, a slow trickle of effects. This might've started out small enough for no one to notice until now."

Calliope's shoulders lifted. "But it's just one patch, right? Maybe it won't spread. It could be nothing."

"Or it could be deadly," Kai said. "We need to have a unit of Keepers sweep every acre of Faylinn, Calliope. We need to go now."

She stepped from the brown foliage. "Is it really that serious?"

"More than you know." He held out his hand for her to take, his eyes begging her to speed up.

A frown broke out across her face. "Well, I guess we're going. I'm sorry. I wish I could've been more help."

"No. Thank you." I squeezed her hand as she passed me. "I'm grateful you came as quickly as you did. If there is anything awry in Faylinn, will you inform us?"

"You'll be the first to know," she said. There wasn't time for much else before Kai dragged Calliope away.

"Kayne." I turned to him.

"I'm already on it. Brae will organize four units. One each for the east, north, west, and south lands."

When I peered around, Brae had already left. "Good, good. Let's head back to the castle."

"What can we do?" Lia asked. Guilt crippled her features: her eyes dipping, her mouth downturned, her shoulders sagging. Desperation seeped through her pores.

If, in fact, this had to do with the balance in nature, she couldn't have known it'd come to this. And Calliope and I both gave Cameron permission to transform. We were all at fault. It didn't matter who was to blame, what mattered was how to fix it.

"Let's wait to hear from my units first and then we'll go from there. If this is the only dead land, maybe we won't have to do anything." Even as I tried to placate them, and myself, none of us believed it.

Cameron and Lia nodded, but they were anything but reassured.

"I'll see you back at the castle." And then Kayne and I took off.

THIRTEEN

CAMERON

LIA dragged her fingers through her hair, peering around the forest. "So, what do we do now?"

"I think we should still go to Faylinn." I skimmed my hand up her arm, pulling it away from her hair, and took her hand in mine with a squeeze. "We're not safe in Rymidon and now with this whole dead faery land, Sarai doesn't need us hanging around making everything worse. Especially if we're the cause of it."

She gnawed on the corner of her lips. "Faylinn won't be much better, especially if their land is affected, too."

"But maybe Callie has some alternate solutions. We at least

have to try. We risked a lot by changing; I don't want our time to run out because we weren't more careful."

Lia hesitated, but then nodded.

THE Waking Oak was nestled between two peaks soaring above Rymidon. Its thick, gnarly limbs stretched from one lush mountainside to the other.

"This thing really is massive, isn't it?"

"I suppose it has to be to power seven kingdoms and all the other lands."

"It's strange that it's the same in all the lands. Have you visited all seven kingdoms?"

Lia shook her head. "Not all. A couple—Callastonia and Oraelia, I had a few friends there—but Skye and I remained confined to Rymidon for the most part. He wasn't comfortable with me leaving. Coming to your world was actually my first time leaving the fae realm."

Skye. Man, I hated that guy. I hated everything about him, except for his taste in women, of course. That was exceptional.

Two Faylinn Keepers greeted us on the other side of the Waking Oak and we froze. They were such a contrast to Rymidon's formal attire of laced up tunics with leather vests and hooded cloaks. Leather cuffs covered Rymidonian Keeper forearms while their boots hit a few inches below the knee.

Faylinn Keepers wore cropped pants. That was it. Just pants. I'd never seen them in anything else. Vines wound up their left arms, a bow and arrows strapped to their bare backs. Their hands readied over sheathed daggers at their waists.

We're in trouble.

When we were in full view, they relaxed as recognition settled in their eyes. The Oak's trunk creaked behind us as it twisted closed.

"Cameron. Lia. We were not expecting you." The one I knew as Dugal, who Calliope stationed in the forest by my apartment, stepped forward.

"We were hoping to speak with Calliope," Lia said, without a hint of uncertainty, like we belonged here just as much as them. "Is that possible?"

Good. Act natural. Smart woman.

"Yes, of course, but weren't you just with the Queen? She just returned from Rymidon not long ago."

"We were, but we have some other matters to discuss."

"We'll need to take some precautions," Dugal turned to the younger of the two. "Brokk, send word of their arrival and see how the Queen would like to proceed."

Brokk, a short but burly guy, nodded and darted into the trees. It wasn't more than five minutes when Declan returned with him, a face of a comrade. *Phew.*

"Is everything all right?" Concern creased Declan's brow. "Did Sarai discover more already?"

"No, not yet," Lia said. "They're sending out troops now."

I slipped my hand in hers. "We just need to chat with Callie, if that's okay."

With a terse nod, he said, "Follow me."

Declan was a man of few words. I'd only been around him a handful of times, but he never smiled. Always seemed to be all business and no play. Maybe that was common practice for a queen's personal Keeper. If you let your guard down for even a second, she could die.

"Since when has the Waking Oak been guarded?" Lia asked

as we leaped through the trees.

"Because of recent...events, Calliope stationed Keepers at the Waking Oak for added protection, so we will always know who is entering and exiting Faylinn."

I guess Rymidonians weren't the only ones worried about Guthron and his band of vampire-eared brothers.

We arrived at the rear side of the castle with six staggering towers, but instead of scaling the wall like we'd done in Rymidon, Declan swept aside a curtain of leaves, exposing a hidden door.

"This way." He entered first, motioning for us to follow behind as he peeked over our shoulders, ensuring we were unseen.

Interlocking our fingers, I guided Lia over the threshold. The door opened to a long stone corridor lit by lanterns filled with fireflies. There was something more magical about that than the fire used to illuminate lights in Rymidon.

At the end of the hallway, Calliope stepped in front of the mouth. She stood in her royal garb, or rather, as royal as Calliope would allow. A long, flowing light green dress and her crown of glass. Every time I saw her, the more regal she became. Royalty suited her.

"You guys miss me already?" Calliope eyed Lia's hand clasped in mine. "It's like freshman year all over again."

"Ha-ha." I pulled her into a one-armed hug and kissed the top of her head. "We didn't really get to say hi when you came."

"There seemed to be a more pressing issue at the time." A corner of her mouth curved up. "Kai just sent out a few troops to search Faylinn. I hope they don't find anything."

"Me, too."

"Lia." Callie smiled and drew her into an embrace, which

Lia accepted with a tentative hold. It was nice knowing their fallout was healing. They might never be where they once were, but Callie was good at forgiveness.

"So, did you guys come to hang out or is there more with the dying forest?"

"We were actually on our way here when we found the dead patch. We wanted to talk to you about some other things."

Her mouth pressed into a thin pursed line. "Let's talk in the atrium. We'll have more privacy there."

Kai was behind the desk when we entered, bent over reading what looked like one of the sacred scrolls. I guess being married to a True Royal had its perks.

He straightened, eyeing us with aggravation. "I'm not turning you away from Faylinn because you're Calliope's best friends, but your presence here puts her at risk just as much as it does you."

"All right, big guy. You wouldn't turn away anyone who needed help." Calliope rested her hand on his arm with an eye roll. "And they wouldn't be here if it weren't important."

I couldn't take offense at his lack of hospitality. I loved Callie, too. His protectiveness of her only made me respect him more. She was his family, his wife, his everything, and my selfish decision to become fae put her at risk.

"What's with the Keepers at the Oak?" I asked. "Are we okay being here with them knowing?"

"I placed Dugal and Brokk there because next to Declan, they are my most trusted Keepers. In case you did need to travel through, I wanted assurance that you would be protected. They will keep your presence in Faylinn to themselves. I promise." Calliope shifted her eyes between Lia and me. "So, what's going on?"

"Rymidon might not be our safest option anymore," I said. "Ever since Guthron showed up things have been tense, to say the least. Did Sarai tell you about the riot outside of the castle the night Guthron showed up?"

"A riot? Like fighting against the elves or the Keepers?"

I shook my head. "Well, they didn't get violent, but they had their torches like they were about to raid the castle. And it's only getting worse. Members of colonies are refusing to help them, questioning Sarai's judgment. Rymidon knows something is up, but since the truth is a little difficult to come out and say, issues aren't resolving. I heard Sarai arguing with Kayne yesterday. I realize I'm new to all of this, but since living in Rymidon I've never heard Kayne contradict Sarai or raise his voice. Not once. It's always, 'Yes, Your Highness. I'll bend over and take it, Your Grace.'"

"Emotions are running very high," Lia said.

"If the truth comes to light while we're there, especially after this new development of the land dying, I worry what will happen to us." I scratched the back of my neck. "*And* while we were traveling through the forest yesterday, we were spotted by one of Lia's old friends."

"*Friend* is a loose term," Lia muttered.

Calliope's eyes widened. "What did you do?"

"We were able to hide in time, making the girl question her sanity, but it was close. And it got me thinking, is there anywhere else we can hide out? Not in this castle or anywhere that would put you in danger, but somewhere we can create a hideaway. Faylinn is the largest kingdom, isn't it? I hoped maybe there was some land that might be less traveled."

Calliope looked to Kai who nodded once. "Kai has a secret safe house in the depths of Faylinn, near where members of the other kingdoms used to live. We haven't used it since Rymidon invaded. No one else knows about it except for Declan. It's small, but no one should find you. You're welcome to stay there until all of this is sorted out."

"Define small." Lia tilted her head.

"It fits one fae comfortably," Calliope said with a chuckle.

"One. As in only one bedroom?"

"As in no bedrooms, but it comes at no cost to you, so you're welcome." Kai crossed his arms.

"It was a question," Lia said. "Doesn't mean I'm not grateful."

To keep them from strangling each other, I asked, "How dangerous do you think it is for us to show our faces in your kingdom? Like, how recognizable do you really think I'd be?"

"Recognizable enough," Callie said. "I wouldn't say it's dangerous. No one is going to attack you, but it wouldn't be wise. Word travels fast. Before you know it, one Weaver has spoken with another who reached out to a Weaver in Rymidon and bam, we've got another war on our hands. It's a very delicate situation."

I ran my fingertips along my bottom lip. "I really screwed this all up, didn't I?"

"Yeah." Kai leaned against the window seat, crossing his ankles and arms with a dry stare. "You did."

"No," Calliope spoke over him with a glare. "No. Whether or not you two used the fae blood, the elves still assassinated faeries, the scroll was still in the wrong hands. They were still creating a mutant army that could've caused an imbalance in the realm. All of the kingdoms would've found out soon enough." She swept her hand to the side. "It just might happen sooner because of...this."

"Can we head to Kai's place tonight?" I asked.

"When the sun goes down I can have Declan show you the way," Callie said. "Go back to Rymidon, gather your things, and tell Sarai. You can come back and we'll do dinner together before Declan takes you. Maybe by then we'll also have more of an idea what we're dealing with with the dead land."

I nodded.

"I worry about Sarai." Lia tightened her hold on my hand as I turned to walk out, holding me in place. "If Rymidon turns on her when all of this comes out, or if the truth comes before she tells them. Either way, it won't end well for her."

"We'll protect Sarai at all costs," Kai said. "Even if it means protecting her from her own kingdom."

FOURTEEN

SARAI

The Keeper units returned not long ago and were meeting with Kayne in the gathering hall before he came to give me a report. As I turned to the mountain outside my tower window, I searched for peace, but my stomach twisted with tension. Something told me it knew what was found and it wasn't what I wanted to hear.

At the sound of a knock, I called, "Come in."

Galdinon appeared in the archway. "Faylinn has reported back about the search in their kingdom."

With the grim tone and hopeless expression on his face, I

already knew what he was going to say.

As Galdinon was leaving, Kayne entered the study with a knock, carrying a rolled up map. "I'm afraid I don't have good news. Each unit found dying land just like the one by the Waking Oak."

"I had a feeling they would." *But what does it mean?*

He spread the map of Rymidon out on my desk. X's were marked on the four quarters. "Here, here, here, and here." Producing a writing instrument, he marked the one we found this morning by the Waking Oak. "And here."

"How big?"

"Smaller than the one by the Oak, but still large enough to cause concern," Kayne said. "Have we heard anything from Faylinn yet?"

"Dugal came and informed Galdinon while you were with our Keepers and said Faylinn found three sections of dead land. Two the size of what we saw, and the other larger, but they were so far into the forest, no one had stumbled upon them yet."

"With Faylinn being largest of our kingdoms, they might've even missed more." Kayne ran a hand down his face. "What are we going to do?"

"If Calliope can't fix it and it does have to do with Lia, Cameron, and the elves transforming, how can we stop it? Transform the same amount of fae into humans? Have them all transform back? How would fae even transform to the human form without a counterpart. It couldn't be in Lake Haven with the pastelline lily, and something tells me injecting human blood wouldn't have the same effect."

I wasn't expecting answers from Kayne as I thought aloud. He knew about as much as I did when it came to the blood of our fae, but there had to be an answer somewhere.

"Let's go to Oraelia. I want to ask Marcus if they've seen anything similar. And if not, inform them it would be wise to send out their Keepers to search. If it's affecting Faylinn while all those who have transformed are here, this may be even more serious than we comprehend."

DYING."

Kayne left Marcus and me in a sitting room off the main corridor to speak in private. With the delicate issue at hand, I assumed it wasn't wise to include Marcus's parents just yet. As far as I knew, he hadn't mentioned his involvement with the elves, and we couldn't very well tell them about Cameron and Lia.

"Dead," I said. "As in shriveled up and unrevivable. Lia, Calliope, and I all tried to heal it. We couldn't get a single blade of grass, not even a miniscule sprout."

"I haven't heard of anything like that in our forests, but Oraelia is quite vast. It doesn't mean it's not there. I'll have Aife gather a patrol to search the kingdom without raising suspicion. If it's happening in Faylinn, too, it's only a matter of time before it strikes the rest of the kingdoms."

"That's what I'm afraid of." I massaged my temples and took a seat on the settee. "What are we going to do, Marcus?"

"I hate it just as much as you, but we're going to have to tell the truth about the elves." He lowered beside me, resting a hand below my wings. "Especially if this is connected."

"I know. But there's also Cameron and Lia to think about. While not innocent in all of this, all they wanted was to be together. And if the lands are dying because of a balance in nature they interrupted, what does that mean for them? What does that mean for us? What will need to happen in order to reset the balance?"

Marcus blinked, a pensive trace to his eyes, as he folded his hands in his lap. "There is folklore about the Mabuz, Viridessa. Have you heard of her?"

"Maybe. My mom was really the only one who told me stories, so I might've heard when I was young, but I couldn't tell you a thing about her."

He nodded, locking and unlocking his fingers. "The folklore has been passed down for millennia. Tales and outlandish stories to frighten or fascinate children. It's told that in the beginning of time, she forged our realm with her own flesh and blood, conceiving us in her own likeness. She is said to be the one who created the Waking Oak, powering our blood of enchantments.

"It took Viridessa fifty years, and when she was finished, she went to sleep below the realm's surface. She slumbers when there is harmony in her creation, but when it is threatened, she rises and tortures the offenders.

"I once heard Viridessa awoke centuries ago when they disrupted her creation, and the bloodbath could've washed Faylinn away, but their iniquity was rectified, and they never woke her again."

My heart hammered in my chest, fear pumping in my veins. "Do you think it's true?"

"I'm sure it's exaggerated. No one wants to hear dull folklore, but stories originate from somewhere, don't you think?"

"So, you think the transformations could have woken her?"

He shrugged. "I don't know, but it's worth a second

thought. Something to talk to the Royals about."

My palm rubbed across my aching heart. "My kingdom will never forgive me. I'm not ready for them to turn against me, and they will, Marcus. They will."

Marcus's hand returned to my back, rubbing up and down between my wings, the most sensitive spot. "You'll move past it together. You aren't the first Royal to keep something from their kingdom for your fae's benefit, but if this is as serious as I think it is, a war is the least of our problems."

"How will we know if it's even connected?"

"As hard and risky as it will be, we'll need to seek knowledge from the rest of the Royals. They've been around much longer than the rest of us."

I bowed my head. He was right. I knew it, but I didn't want to have to turn to the Royals like we were guilty children, confessing to our parents. It was one thing when I was informing them what the elves had done. It's another to tell them everyone might be in danger because of what we allowed Cameron and Lia to do.

"Can we wait until after the Royal gala? It's in three days and the first time the other kingdoms will be entering Rymidon since the battle. We don't need more unrest than there already is."

"It's up to you. I stand by you and your decision."

I nodded, meeting his eyes. We didn't say more, and for a moment, life froze and the world evaporated around us. Marcus was close, so close, with his sincere, faithful eyes. If we leaned in, just a fraction, our lips would meet. His forest eyes told me that was precisely what he wanted, for me to give in, for me to fall into his arms without a guard once again.

I couldn't. Not now. Not again.

Clearing my throat, I stood. "Will you contact me if your Keepers find any dead lands in Oraelia?"

He said nothing for a moment, only speaking with his eyes. They uttered longing and disappointment, but also patience and understanding. "Of course. We should know by this evening."

"Thank you, Marcus."

Standing to escort me out, he said, "Anything for you, Sarai."

His words healed and hurt.

WHEN I entered the corridor on the way to my tower, Lia and Cameron were walking down the hallway with totes slung over their shoulders.

"Oh, good. You're back," Cameron said.

"Where are you going? Is everything all right?"

Cameron took Lia's pack from her shoulder and hefted it across his. "Kai has a safe place we can hide out for a while, so we figured with the events of today, we'd get out of your hair and avoid putting more stress on you."

"You two really don't have to. We'll get to the bottom of this."

"We really do," Lia said. "We've caused enough strife. Especially if we're responsible for the dead lands, Rymidon doesn't need to know you helped us on top of everything else."

I appreciated their consideration, but my lonely heart called to beg them to stay. While it hadn't been long, it'd been a pleasant change to have them here. The walls of the castle would lose a little more life.

But instead of convincing them to stay, I nodded. "Okay. It

probably is a wise decision. Until we know more about the dead lands and have a hold on the elves, Kai's hideaway is a good option. I'm glad you have a safe place."

"We don't want you to think we're ungrateful." Lia took a hasty step toward me. "We are. We're so grateful you welcomed us into Rymidon after what we did."

"No, of course." I shook my head. "Your decision had my blessing. You two know that. But I understand. You're doing what you think is best for you and for me. I appreciate your concern and desire to help, but know you're always welcome here. No matter what."

She smiled. "Thank you, Sarai. And while we're going to a more secure place, we're still available to help with anything. Whatever we can do, whatever consequences we have to face, we're prepared. We're not hiding for that, just everyone else."

"Yeah," Cameron said. "If we screwed everything up, we'll take the punishment without objection."

Their bravery was admirable, but worry hung in their eyes. We had no idea what the consequences could amount to.

I really hoped it didn't come to that, doling out punishments or requiring them to transform back into humans. Maybe we'd find an easier answer. Maybe the answer was staring us right in the face, we just needed someone to open our eyes.

FIFTEEN

CAMERON

AS I roamed the atrium, Kai and Calliope traced locations of the dead lands on a map of Faylinn while we waited for dinner to be ready. One more had been found before we returned. That meant Faylinn had four dead patches. And it had only been one day. How long would it take before the kingdom was overrun?

There were new portraits on the wall by the sacred scrolls I hadn't noticed before, so to keep my mind occupied I mosied over. When one face stuck out to me, I approached. He was younger, but his green eyes and features were familiar enough.

"Cal, is that your dad?"

She came up beside me and nodded. Her fingers brushed the side of the ornately carved, creamy frame. "Prince Finnian himself."

He was so young. Fifteen, maybe. He stood beside another boy who looked around twelve. Behind them, their parents, I assumed—Calliope's grandparents.

"Is that his brother?"

She nodded. "Galvyn. King Galvyn, the last life Favner stole to take the throne."

"Oh, man." I shook my head. "The faery world really had a bout of bad dudes over the last few decades, huh." I pointed along the wall at six other paintings. "Who are the fae in the rest of these paintings?"

"Royal families of the other kingdoms. Favner had a bunch of these buried in storage above the dungeon. I wanted to have this one of my father and our family hung up, but I thought it'd be cool to have the other Royal families displayed, too. Just a reminder that we're one. I'm sure if I mapped it out, I'd see how we were related, but obviously I haven't had much time for that." She chuckled.

Passing from one portrait to the next, I paused in front of Rymidon. Though Calliope probably didn't enjoy looking at Adair and Skye every day, Sakari and Sarai were in the portrait, as well as their mother. She was striking, identical to Sarai with inky hair. Sakari must have been around twelve dressed in black as I'd only seen him; a young Sarai in front of him, his protective arm wrapped around her shoulder. I didn't know the guy well, but seeing Sarai with this family who no longer lived tore my heart apart for her. We were all a little bit like orphans in one way or another, but none of us quite like Sarai.

Moving on, I passed a family in puffy getups like they were

straight out of the 1500s, then a family covered in oversized leaves and flowers, very drafty. And another decked out in bone crowns and talon piercings. I recognized a younger Marcus, still just as unreadable as he was now with a stern brow and endless eyes, next to a guy that could've been his twin, just a couple years older.

Passing from one to the next, I stopped on the last one. A slender woman with fiery red hair and antlers the size of a five-point buck crowning her head stared back at me. The silvery blue flecks of her eyes seized my heart.

"Who is that?"

"That's Queen Elena of Elfland." Calliope's voice was almost reverent.

Huh. "She looks really familiar."

"Maybe you saw her at the Battle of Faylinn. Her kingdom was there in the end. They put an end to the war and helped with recovery."

I pointed a thumb at my chest. "Hiding in a burrow with Kai, remember?"

"Oh, right." Her mouth pinched to the side. "Well, I don't know then."

"There was a lot going on when we made it back to the castle," Kai said, still focusing on the map, "but they could've been there."

Something in the eyes of the faery queen nagged at my brain, a weird sense of deja vu. I guess there was a chance I saw her when Kai and I returned after the battle, but I felt like I would've remembered seeing her. She was pretty unforgettable.

Calliope nudged my shoulder. "Maybe it's the red hair. You have been spending quite a bit of time with a certain redhead lately."

I laughed and peeked over at Lia sitting in the window seat overlooking the meadow in front of the castle, paying us no attention. "Yeah, maybe."

"What are you looking at?" I asked, slipping my hand underneath Lia's hair, cupping the back of her slim neck.

"A few of the villagers are putting on a play." Her full lips lifted in a half-smile.

I followed her gaze to a painted light blue and yellow caravan with a platform attached. A crowd of fae were gathered around as the four on stage performed what looked like a scene straight out of Shakespeare. Dressed a bit like the portrait of the family in pillowy sleeves and MC Hammer-style pants, they walked along the platform like they were reciting sonnets.

"Do they get any money for that?" I asked. "Or is it just for fun?"

"We don't have money," Calliope said. *Oh, right.* "So, it's just for entertainment."

"Do they do it a lot? Perform out in the open just because?"

"The village plays? Oh, yeah." Calliope walked up behind us. "At least once a week. More so since the battle. It's become a source of levity. Sometimes I have the time to go down and watch, but you know how crazy Royal life gets. I wish I could hear them from here, but the sound gets drowned out by everything else."

A throat cleared. We turned to find Declan standing in the open doorway of the atrium. "Dinner is served."

WITH four patches of dead lands," Lia said, "what else could it possibly be, if not linked to us?"

Callie swallowed her bite. "It could be some sort of disease in the earth. Right, Kai? You mentioned that."

Kai wiped his mouth with a cloth napkin. "I mentioned that as a weak possibility, but this is unlike any disease we've ever encountered. Everything we've dealt with before has always been fixable, and rare."

Lia set down her fork, after hardly eating anything on her plate. "I'd transform back in a heartbeat if I knew how, if it would fix the balance."

"We'll figure something out," Callie said, trying to reassure. "There are knowledgeable fae in our world. We just need to find them. This could have nothing to do with you guys. Let's just try to be optimistic for now."

"Sarai mentioned there's been a shortage in their harvest." Kai took a sip of water from his goblet. "We need to touch base with my mother and find out if we're experiencing anything like that."

"I'll do that first thing in the morning. I wanted to visit Lorelle and Violet, anyway. Though, Allura would probably have more to say, give me all the Sower details and more."

Kai chuckled with an affectionate eyeroll.

"What else could it affect?" I asked. "Are there other things we should be looking out for? Especially with Lia and I taking residence so far away from the main village, are there things we should take note of for you?"

Like Lia's lack of stamina. But if that was connected to the balance, then why hadn't I been experiencing any problems? I still felt better than ever. Granted, my only comparison was my human body. What if I was weakened and didn't even know it? Anything was heightened over the human form.

"We need to be diligent in paying attention to anything amiss, not just the land but in every colony," Kai said. "Craftsmen and Weavers unable to finish projects as quickly as before. Keepers losing their endurance and heightened awareness of surroundings, slower reactions. It could be an imbalance in nature, but that could mean anything. The land itself or us."

My gaze shifted to Lia, but she avoided eye-contact, as I assumed she would. She knew she should say something and was keeping it to herself. But what if diagnosing her meant diagnosing the problem with the dead lands? What if what healed her could heal it?

Even with my fixed stare boring into the side of Lia's head, she made no attempt to look at me. I wanted to out her, but I wouldn't betray her trust. She asked me to keep this between us and I'd keep that promise.

At least, until it became life or death. Then all bets were off. *Sorry, Ginge.*

SIXTEEN

LIA

Once the sun set and darkness cloaked the forest, Declan helped us find Kai's safe house. He didn't stick around, eager to get back and guard his queen, but it wasn't as if we needed a tour. The shack was farther away than I thought it'd be, which was good. Less of a chance we'd be spotted.

"Callie wasn't kidding." Cameron squeezed my hand in his.

We stared up at the small hut in the tree. It was constructed of vines and twigs, like a child pieced it together, not a Craftsmen. How long ago did Kai build this? And for what purpose?

"One walk-in closet, coming right up." He chuckled.

"It's probably why they didn't offer it sooner. We were in the lap of luxury in Rymidon. Bedrooms four times the size of this place. Personal chefs serving meals to us all day. This is putting it quite mildly—roughing it. I'm assuming there isn't a bathroom in there, either. Maybe a chamber pot."

"I assume you're correct, but if that's the case, I hope you don't mind if we don't use it and take advantage of the great outdoors instead."

I laughed. "Deal."

We leaped into the tree, landing on a small stoop in front of a flimsy bark door. It creaked open and a small cot lay in one corner, while a couple tree stumps sat next to a make-shift table and a sink. Above the wooden basin were a couple cabinets and one small window cut out above the bed, no glass covering.

"Cozy." Cameron lowered himself onto the bed, getting a hint of a bounce, if that. It wasn't much of a mattress. More like blankets on an elevated slab of wood. "At least it's bigger than a closet."

"Not much, but it's safe."

"It'll be an adventure." He smiled. "Good thing you're shackled to a boy scout. Camping is kind of my jam."

It was better than sleeping in the trees outside Cameron's house like I'd done before, or even the homeless shelter. We didn't have to share the space with anyone but each other.

"Speaking of bathrooms, I actually do need to go," he said. "There's not an actual chamber pot, is there?"

I laughed. "I don't think so."

"Good. I don't want to share a room with Kai's old bodily functions; I wouldn't care how many times he's cleaned that thing." Cameron stood, clapping his hands against his thighs.

"I'll be back."

When the door fell shut, I pulled out one of the stumps and sat down. Okay. Okay, we'd make this work. We could hunt and fish on our own, and sneak into the farmlands at night for a few fruits and vegetables. There wasn't a stove or oven, but we could make a fire. While the bed wasn't big, there were enough blankets to keep us warm. This was doable. We'd be fine.

Maybe.

STIFF and sore, I awoke to the sun rising and blinding me through the window above the bed. No curtains. We'd definitely have to rectify that, especially if it rained. Pin up a blanket or board it up with wood.

I tugged up the quilt to shield my eyes. My shoulder and hip ached as I twisted to my back, away from the light.

Cameron kept his arm around my middle, forming his solid body to the side of mine. While my body throbbed, staying warm was not my problem last night with the mortal furnace next to me.

"Was that the most uncomfortable night of sleep you've ever had or was that just me?" Cameron rasped with his morning voice into my ear.

I groaned out a chuckle. "The mattresses in the Rymidonian castle spoiled us."

"Yeah, I don't know how Kai sleeps on this thing." He rolled away from me, shifting onto his back. "Though, he probably didn't use it for sleep. Maybe this was his bachelor pad for the ladies."

"Gross." I laughed and whacked Cameron in the chest. "I

don't want to think of Kai like that or what he did on this thing that we have to sleep on. And if this was a hook-up spot, I pity every girl he brought here."

"It was probably Callie."

I almost shoved him off the bed.

He chuckled. "C'mon. I can't lay on this thing for much longer. Can we go find something, like a berry patch or, I dunno, anything to get us some breakfast."

"Calliope sent some bread and pruilas with us. They're in my bag."

"Oh, right. Score!" Cameron hopped up and rummaged through my tote, pulling out a couple of croissants. "Bless that woman. I knew I liked her for a reason."

I held out my hand for him to toss me one and sat up. Breaking off a piece, I took in Cameron sitting on the stump, munching on the croissant. Hadn't it only been yesterday I was wallowing on his couch while he griped at me to get a job? If someone had told me this was where we'd be only months later, I'd have choked and then laughed in their face.

He pushed his shaggy bedhead off his forehead. "So, what's on the agenda today all by ourselves in the wild?"

"Let's put your slingshot to use. Get you better acquainted with it while we do a little hunting for lunch. You did pretty well in the weaponry den when we trained. And if we're lucky, maybe we'll catch something for dinner, too."

"I'm game." He shoved the rest of the bread in his mouth, swallowing it down. "Teach me your ways, huntress."

AFTER a few target practices on a tree trunk, Cameron had a

good handle on his aim. We trekked a couple miles from Kai's shack over steep knolls and through a labyrinth of ferns and thorns before we found a thicket, perfect for hunting smaller animals.

"Let's hang out here for a bit," I said, hushed. "See if we can catch something living in the underbrush."

Just then, there was rustling in the dense shrubbery. Cameron and I crouched down, searching for the source. He kept the slingshot, raised and ready to aim. A lone bush shivered.

"There." I pointed at the peak of wiry fur between the ferns and Cameron released the kotrop. The rustling stopped.

"I have no idea what I was aiming at, but hopefully I got it." We waited, just in case we'd only scared it. "Also, in case I didn't already say this today, this thing is so cool." He beamed like a child on Christmas morning.

"I knew you'd love it."

When there wasn't another sign of life, we trekked through the thick shrubs, avoiding thorns. When we hit the spot I had Cameron aim, I bent down and picked up our kill. "A radik. Nice."

"That giant rat is what we've been eating for dinner in Rymidon?" His nose wrinkled at the bridge. "Thank goodness that tail was chopped off. I don't have a queasy stomach, but even that would turn my insides."

"Oh, come on, ya wimp. Can't handle a little carcass?" I laughed, dangling the dead radik by its tail in his face and he reared back. "We can rig up some fishing poles tonight and fish for some shemun and zendan tomorrow, if that would be easier for you."

"Hey, I can take it. I've just never seen the animal I was eating before it became nothing but freezer meat."

"And you call yourself a boy scout." I chuckled. "Time to get used to that, love."

His mouth quirked at my slip of term of endearment. I wasn't normally one to fling out affection; that was Cameron's department. He said nothing as he kissed the corner of my mouth.

"Bag it and let's move further north. Just be on the lookout. I don't know what kinds of predators live in Faylinn."

"Predators." He tucked his slingshot into the holster on his hip and hoisted the bag with the dead radik onto his shoulder. "Lovely."

"You live in the wilderness now, Cam. With all the bonuses of being a magical being come downsides. But our senses are sharper than the other creatures, so we'll be fine." At least Cameron's were sharper. If I were back to my normal self, I would've been able to hone in on my heightened senses and detect the lack of heartbeat on that radik. Of course, I'd never tell Cam that.

After traveling for a couple miles above ground, a twig snap sprang up from the forest floor. I darted down from the branch I'd landed on, tugging Cameron with me.

Finding a large, vine-covered boulder, Cameron and I hopped over some roots, sneaking behind it. I peeked my head around to get a good look at what we stumbled across. Fae or beast?

A lean, black-furred creature stepped from behind the bramble, bowing down to nibble at the moss carpeting the soil.

"What's that?" Cameron whispered.

"Chocat. It's like a deer, but it has three eyes, mostly harmless." It could feed us for months if we nabbed it.

"Well, that's freaky."

My lips curved in a half-smile. It was fun teaching Cameron all these new things, his human mind amazed and baffled by all things of our realm. I pressed my finger to my lips to keep him from saying more so we didn't scare it off.

I was about to pull an arrow from a quiver Calliope sent with us but stopped. Turning to Cameron, I eyed him and then his slingshot attached to his belt.

He pressed his hand to his chest, as if asking, *me*? I nodded. It'd be good practice, and it was five times the size of a radik. Should be easier to kill.

With careful, quiet movements, Cameron slipped the slingshot from his hip and a kotrop from a leather pouch. Lifting his arms as I instructed, he aimed at the chocat.

"His head," I whispered. "To kill him quicker."

Cameron nodded with one eye closed and let the kotrop fly. It whizzed right passed the chocat's head, startling it before it bolted.

"Dang." His head hung. "So close."

"It's all right. We'll have other chances. Let's go cook up this radik."

We'd only taken a few steps when the absence of green caught my eye. I turned to the right. "Cameron." I pointed and his eyes slid across the dense woodland floor.

"Dead lands." He sighed. "Is this one of the ones they already found? Or is this a new one?"

"I don't know. I never looked at the map. We should've asked where their patches were because if this is new since yesterday, how many more new ones are there?"

"I'm sure Kai will have Keepers making rounds daily, looking for any new ones."

"Yeah. He definitely will." I took hold of Cameron's hand

and we began our journey back to the shack. "If nothing else, we can keep an eye on that one and see if it spreads any farther. Let's come back tomorrow."

SEVENTEEN

SARAI

THE harvest shortage is worse today than it was yesterday. Oraelia's barrels for this moon cycle are already gone."

Gone? They should've lasted us at least one more week.

Kayne's forearms rested on his knees as he settled into the chair opposite my desk. "Our food supply is dwindling more and more every day. The Sowers are now refusing to share our crops with the elves altogether. Not out of spite, but preservation."

"Well, we can't let the elves starve, either. I promised Guthron to provide for them. If I can't uphold that part of our arrangement, the elves won't uphold theirs and then no one is safe."

"The elves transforming is most likely the reason why we can't grow more yields. And if we can't even tell our fae why the elves are here, we can't force the Sowers to feed them, unless you want to use your Supremacy."

"No." My answer was quick, firm.

Kayne nodded. "I didn't think so. Then what do you suggest, Your Highness?"

Sighing, I leaned back in the chair behind my desk. "The Royal gala is tomorrow night. After that, I'll hold a council with the Royals and tell them everything. Since Oraelia has dead lands, too, the rest are bound to have them as well. Together, we'll come up with a solution."

"I really hope you're right."

Knock, knock, knock.

Brae appeared in the arched doorway. "Prince Marcus here to see you, Your Grace."

"Send him in." I turned my attention back to Kayne. He was already standing up. "We'll finish this discussion later."

Kayne nodded and passed Marcus on his way out with a bow. I stood.

When the door shut behind him, there was a stretch of silence before I said, "Hi."

"Hi." His deep, elegant voice soaked those two letters.

"Aife sent word last night that two sections of dead lands were found."

"That's actually why I'm here." He lowered into the chair opposite me, resting his ankle across his knee. His large frame dwarfed the chair. "Another was discovered this morning by her unit. It's larger than the other two combined, spanning an acre at the edge of Oraelia."

"It grew that large overnight?"

Marcus nodded.

Whatever this was was aggressive and spreading faster than we could've anticipated. "It's accelerating. Our units found two more this morning; one more in the east and another in the north. If the dead lands increase at this rate, Rymidon will be dried up by the end of the next moon cycle. And that's only if it doesn't rapidly worsen."

"We'll contain it before then." Marcus said it with such confidence, I wanted to believe him, but my gut told me otherwise. "Have you called for the Royal council to meet?"

"Not yet. I'm going to the morning after the gala. Keep them from questioning me while here. I just want one night before this all blows up."

He nodded. Maybe Marcus disagreed with me, but he was letting me handle the situation, and for that, I appreciated him. Being stripped of control for so many years, it was a relief to have someone who trusted my judgment or at least someone who was willing to let me make my own mistakes and learn from them.

"How about your crops?" I asked. "Are your Sowers experiencing any problems with harvesting?"

"Not that I've been made aware, but my parents might know. I didn't ask them about this, having Aife keep her unit's patrols confidential until after the Royal gala."

"Thank you."

"What will you say to them?"

I interpreted the words he wasn't asking. *What will you tell the council about me?* "Everything, I guess." But the moment I said the words, they felt wrong. How had I been so angry with him? So betrayed, and yet, I felt guilty for revealing his part in it?

"Leaving things out would only hurt us further. They need all the knowledge to properly guide us, if they can, that is."

"I should tell them myself," he said. "Come forward, so they understand my remorse and my willingness to accept the consequences. Or at least, tell my parents first, so they aren't ambushed."

"If that's what you feel is right. Would you like to come with me?"

He nodded.

"I'll let you know as soon as the council is set."

"Thank you. I need to get back, but I wanted to ask about the Royal gala." Marcus paused, his jaw clenching as he chewed on his bottom lip. "Are you still treating it as it is intended? To choose a match?"

If he'd asked if I wanted to treat it as it was intended I'd have told him no, but that didn't matter in this scenario. What I wanted wasn't an option. Wants didn't always match up with duty.

"That is the hope."

Marcus said no more, but with the intensity of his tormented eyes and the movement of his soundless mouth, it was obvious he wanted to. Not that any of his words would change the predicament we were in. My heart twisted, tortured by the inability to freely choose. My head fought, reminding it there was more to think about than our complicated love.

Clamping his lips shut, Marcus nodded before he excused himself and left me alone.

With his brusque retreat, somehow, I felt more alone than ever.

KAYNE and I were in the middle of discussing the elves and the harvest when Eitri entered announcing Veren and Moira Byrne. *Lia's parents.*

Since I became queen, we hadn't had much interaction, if any. It was my assumption that they were avoiding me, knowing they disowned Lia when she made the agreement with my father. I probably wasn't their ideal choice for the throne.

Before I could greet them, Moira stepped forward. "Is it true?"

"I'm sorry. Is what true?" There were so many things she could've been referring to.

"Our daughter. Magnolia. Is she here?"

I stiffened but tried hiding my discomfort. "What makes you believe that she is?"

Veren moved to stand beside his wife, placing his hands on her dainty shoulders. "There have been rumors that she was seen in the forest only days ago."

"Interesting." I cleared my throat. "As far as I know she is not in Rymidon. I didn't think she could return." At least that wasn't a lie. While I had a responsibility to my fae, I wasn't about to share something Lia didn't want shared. She didn't tell her parents about the transformation for a reason. If she hadn't trusted them with the information, I wasn't going to either.

Her shoulders deflated, Veren drawing her closer to his side. Tears welled up in her eyes, spilling over as she blinked. "Wishful thinking on our part, I suppose."

From what little Lia shared with me before she left for the human world, they'd never gotten along, but these weren't the faces of two parents who didn't love their daughter, who didn't mourn her absence.

"I'm sorry I don't have the answer you're looking for. I

wish I did."

They nodded, wiping at their cheeks, and bowed at the waist before leaving the gathering hall, Veren stroking Moira's cinnamon hair as she leaned into him.

"Will you tell Lia?" Kayne asked when the door shut behind them.

"I'm not sure that she'll want to hear about it, but yes. When I see Lia again."

What a confusing position to put her in. Were they genuine in their grief? Or seeking information? If Lia did reconcile with them, could they be trusted?

EIGHTEEN

LIA

Cameron and I spent the day in the solitude of the forest. Kai's location truly was ideal. We hadn't heard anyone for miles. Come to think of it, we hadn't heard much of anything. Animals included.

Careful to keep our presence unknown, we'd kept our senses on high alert, but no one came out this far. It made perfect sense for Kai to keep Calliope safe here when Rymidon invaded. Had they never returned to the castle, it would've taken several of Adair's troops to find her.

We stumbled upon a lake not far from the shack and spent

most of the day swimming and fishing, basking in the false calm and security.

"Do you think they've figured out what the dead lands are yet?" Cameron asked as he cast the line.

"If they had, I think they'd have to come tell us. It's only been a day, so I doubt it. We should check on that spot we found yesterday, though. See if it's gotten bigger."

He nodded. "What are we going to do if we're the cause? How can something like that be fixed?"

"Well, balance, right? So, we might have to transform back, though I have no idea how. We can't do it the normal way."

"So, what if we can't? What if there isn't a way to be human without transforming with another human? That'll only cause more of an imbalance."

"I don't know, Cam. I really don't."

Silence fell over us as we sat on the lichen-covered boulders at the edge of the lake, sending out a line, over and over.

After hours of fishing for dinner and only catching one zendan, but not a single shemun—I tried not to think of what only being able to catch one meant—we returned to the section of dead land.

"Wait. Is this the same one as yesterday?" Cameron asked.

I nodded, noting the dried vegetation curling like claws around the surrounding tree trunks, strangling them of life. "It's spreading."

The dead patch that was the size of a cluster of viga plants yesterday, was now the size of Lake Luna. We'd have to return to the castle and tell Calliope. Just in case they missed this one. That kind of deterioration was too rapid.

"I'm going to make a round of the perimeter and see if there are more." Cameron handed off the string with the fish to me. "You can head back to the shack, and I'll meet you there."

"Cameron, I'm fine. I can handle a little jaunt around the forest. We've hardly done anything today but swim and sit by that lake. I'm not tired."

"I know," he slipped his arms around my waist, "but just give this hunky, doting match some peace of mind." His mouth pressed to the underside of my jaw, right where he knew it would make me shiver and cave.

"Fine." My answer was breathless. I shoved against his chest. "I'll make us some dinner before we go to the castle."

"You know the way to my heart." Cameron darted off with a wink.

On the short trek to the shack, I got a little winded, but I shook it off. It was nothing. I was fine.

With a tap of the bark door of the treehouse behind me, I moved to the cabinets to gather a pan for roasting. We'd have to find another lake to fish in tomorrow. Cameron ate more in one meal than I did in an entire day and one fish was not going to sustain us both.

My chest spasmed and I clutched my top, pulling it away. The black ring around the injection site pulsed, spreading farther than it had before, following the veins and then retracting. Spread, retract, spread, retract, like a heartbeat web. I placed my palm over it, concentrating like I'd done so many times before.

Heal. Heal. *Please* heal.

It never did and it wasn't now.

It contracted again, squeezing my heart, and I doubled over. *Soggy sludge.* I tried to breathe through the pain, clutching the wobbly table. It would subside. It would go away.

Another spasm and I dropped to the floor, crying out in pain. Within seconds there was nothing but blackness.

NINETEEN

CAMERON

When my feet touched down on the small landing of the hut, I had the strange urge to wipe off my feet on a mat before I went into the shack made of vines and bark. I chuckled and put my hand on the handle. "I didn't see any other—"

Lia wasn't standing making dinner but laying in a lump, curled on her side just inside the door.

"Lia." I slid to my knees across the floor and brushed her cheek, combing my fingers through her hair. "Lia. Hey, wake up. Wake up."

She remained motionless. *This can't be happening.* I should've gone to Sarai or Calliope as soon as she told me something was off. I should've told Calliope and Kai at dinner last night. I had the perfect opportunity, but to protect Lia's trust in me, I kept my mouth shut. *Idiot!* This wasn't okay, no matter what she said. She wasn't fine.

Pressing my ear to her chest, her heartbeat was there but slow.

"Lia." I tapped her cheek. "C'mon, Lia. Open your eyes. Open your eyes for me. *Please.*"

Her head swiveled back and forth, and I heaved a sigh as her hazel eyes fluttered open.

Finally. "It's about time. You okay?"

She took a deep breath. "Yeah, I think so."

"What happened?"

With a groan, Lia propped herself on her elbows and glanced around, like she couldn't figure out where we were. "I guess I passed out."

"You guess you passed out? You've been out of it for like five minutes. Or what felt like five minutes, maybe an eternity. How long after you got back did it happen?"

She rubbed at her forehead. "Well, I grabbed the pan from the cabinet and was heading for the door to make a fire and that's the last thing I remember."

"*Freak.* Lia, that had to be like twenty minutes ago. We've been doing a lot of nonstop travel over the last couple days. Has it been too much for you?"

"Maybe. I don't know." I didn't like the tone of her voice, so vague, secretive. She knew, and she wasn't telling me. "But I'm fine. I'm good. Just needed a little rest, I guess."

I helped her move to the stump and crouched in front of her, clutching her knees. "Don't mince words or downplay your issues. Be honest with me. Tell me now. What is going on with you?"

Lia met my stare, running her teeth along her bottom lip, before her eyes gave in. She curled her fingers around the neckline of her blouse and tugged it down. I almost stopped her, getting the wrong impression. Now was not the time to distract me with seduction, but then I saw a small black splotch over her heart, the size of the head of a nail.

Reaching out, my fingertips brushed across it. It was flat almost like a large freckle. "What is that?"

"I don't know, but it's where the elves injected the blood."

My head whipped up. "And when did it appear?"

Lia swallowed. "The night we moved into the Rymidonian castle, but then it went away, so I thought maybe I imagined it. Until it reappeared and hasn't gone away since."

I jolted to my feet. "What the hell, Lia? And you kept it from me this long?"

"I hoped it would go away, that I just needed more time to heal…"

"But you keep getting weaker and losing more stamina." I gripped her head between my hands, my voice breaking. "Why didn't you tell me?"

"I didn't want to worry you."

"Worry me! *Devastate* me. I don't care. We can't keep secrets like this. I didn't transform to be with you just to lose you."

Lia nodded, tears brimming her eyes.

"Does it hurt?"

She shrugged, but it was answer enough. That was Lia-speak for it crippled her, clearly enough to make her pass out.

"We're telling Callie. C'mon." I held out my hand. "We're going right now."

"I don't want to bother them with this, Cam. We'll just tell them about the dead land we found. That's more important."

"No. No, it's not. The dead lands can wait. You held out telling me for too long; we're not waiting any longer to tell her. Maybe she's found something in the scroll since she first got it back. Or maybe Evan has some insight. Even if there's nothing, she needs to know. *I* need to know what this thing means."

Lia finally agreed, but she didn't have the energy to travel. So, I swept her up in my arms and flew through the trees with her face nestled in my neck.

LIA sat on the couch in the atrium and cleared her throat. "Every day, I lose more stamina, strength, speed. Any enchantment weakens me, healing takes more energy and it takes more time. I don't know why. Maybe my blood is reacting to the donor's blood. Or maybe this is my punishment. Whatever it is, I'm not the same. I'm…I'm not okay."

Calliope paced the room. "How many times have you fainted?"

Lia ran a hand through her hair, a nonchalant gesture sure to cover up the truth she was about to spill. "Three, maybe four times."

I jumped up from the window seat. "Lia! Seriously?"

"I know. I know," she said. "I should've told you the first time it happened, but you'd just changed for me. Given up everything to be with me. How was I supposed to tell you I might not make it?"

"You're going to make it," I said. There was no other answer. It was us. Together. Forever. She wasn't leaving me.

"Even if you didn't tell Cameron, why didn't you say something earlier to Sarai, or to me?" Calliope asked. "All this time I could've been searching for answers, ways to help you. And with the dead lands, Lia, this is serious."

She shrugged one shoulder. "Sarai has a lot on her plate, and so do you. I thought with time, maybe it would heal on its own. Or that it was just a side effect I'd get used to."

"But it's only getting worse," I interjected.

"So, what does it mean?" Calliope looked to Evan who she'd woken up and brought to the atrium when I told her what had happened.

He sat at the edge of the chaise and rubbed a hand along his wrinkled jaw. "It could mean a number of things. Maybe it's an infection, something that can be treated with bellon root or the purus blossom, which is more powerful. Except...you already used the purus to save the other kingdoms from Adair's poison. It'll be nearly another hundred moon cycles until it blooms again, too late to help you."

"So, the bell root one," I said. "What about that?"

"Maybe. We can give it a try, but if it's not an infection..." Evan's eyes grew weary. "It most likely means your body is rejecting the blood, and I'm not aware of a cure for that. I don't know of anyone who has survived a flawed transformation."

"Do you think it has to do with the dead lands?" Calliope asked.

He shrugged. "It's a possibility."

"Then why aren't I having any issues?"

Evan looked at me. "You're not experiencing any problems? Nothing similar?"

"I've never felt better."

"Hmm..." He sat back, easing into the cushions with a

121

tired, loosened breath. "It most likely has to do with the fact that Magnolia already used her transformations." His attention shifted to her. "Your body can't handle the stress of going back and forth this often. It's been through a lot in a short amount of time."

"There has to be something, some kind of solution or treatment." I stood up. "Don't you guys have doctors or healers or whatever?"

"We don't need them since we can heal ourselves and each other," Calliope said with regret.

"So, there's no one."

"I'm sorry," Evan said, head bowing with regret. "You were both aware there'd be risks. We talked about it. There's nothing I can do for you."

"I'll research." Callie moved to the wall full of scrolls and pulled a few down, not accepting Evan's answer. "Don't lose hope. I've gone through most of these, but maybe I've missed something in one, or I interpreted something wrong. It'll be okay. We'll find the solution."

But what if she didn't or what if she found the answer too late?

TWENTY

LIA

Calliope let us stay in an extra bedroom down the hall from her and Kai for the night so we didn't have to travel back to Kai's shack. Not risking getting caught, we waited in the bedroom until Brokk came to retrieve us the next morning and brought us to the atrium where Calliope and Kai were waiting.

There were two plates of pastries, fruit, and oats on a table next to the couch.

"Here. Sit. Eat," she said.

Cameron didn't hesitate. He swiped the plates, handing me one before digging into the other.

"So, bellon root is fairly common. One of my Sowers should be able to find it in the forest easily. I've already sent out the request for it to be found. Evan said to boil it and then mash it into a paste before spreading it over the wound. It's not instantaneous, but he said if it works, it'd make a difference within a short time."

"Well, we don't have anything to boil it with at Kai's safe house. I mean, we could make a fire, but…"

"I can have Tania do it for us." Calliope nodded to Declan and he bowed out of the atrium. "While we're waiting for that, I've been up all night scouring the scrolls, especially the one about our blood."

Kai stood beside her, rubbing her shoulders and occasionally brushing her curls from her face. She had dark bags under her eyes like she wasn't exaggerating. She really had been up all night.

"I wish it was more of an experimentation log because after Evan admitted we've turned humans before, I seriously doubt they stopped there. They'd have wanted to know what else our blood was capable of. Obviously, that's one of the ways they figured out fae could only transform twice. Had they really not tried to force a transformation again? In the thousands of years that we've existed? Something tells me they did, but there's nothing in the scrolls about it."

"So, how do we find out?" Cameron covered his full mouth.

"I want to talk to other Royals about it. Someone has to know more about our history. So, we're going to need to disclose what we know on the scroll. I'll meet with Sarai and then we'll call for a Royal council. It was inevitable anyway with the dead lands."

"They'll probably figure out the elves' involvement," I said. "Sarai will have to tell them what Skye did. How this all came to be. Are you going to tell them about Cameron?"

"Not yet. With how healthy he is, we'll take this one priority at a time. I'll have to tell them about you, though."

"I figured."

"I wonder if the elves are experiencing any adverse effects," she said.

Kai scoffed. "I honestly doubt Guthron would tell us if they did. Too prideful to own his mistakes."

We all nodded.

"When will you talk to Sarai?" Cameron asked.

"She's holding a Royal gathering this evening, so I'll speak with her afterward. By then we should know if the bellon root worked or not." Calliope rounded the desk, leaning her backside against it. "I'll have you two stay here in the castle so we can keep an eye on Lia. Maybe just hide out in the atrium for now. No one enters but Kai and me, and my personal Keepers. And then we can go from there."

Cameron saluted with a nod, stuffing the last bite of his breakfast in his mouth. I'd hardly touched mine.

Once Declan returned with the bellon root, Cameron helped me lay down on the chaise and gestured for me to move aside my top. I untied the neckline and opened the collar, giving him access to the black mark.

Calliope gasped. When I peered down, I understood why. The mark had almost tripled in size, like a grape.

"Damn it," Cameron said. "It's a lot bigger." Appling a small glob, he rubbed it in, and then sat at my feet at the edge of the lounger.

"How long should we wait?" he asked Calliope.

"I don't know. Evan only said a short time. I'm hoping it means minutes, but it could be hours for all we know."

Great. Whatever. It's not as if we had anything better to do. The worst part was going to be Cameron who wasn't a very patient man.

Calliope took Kai's hand. "We have some other Royal business we need to attend to before the gala."

"We're good," Cameron said. "We'll just chill here. You go about your Queenly duties and get ready for the Royal party."

Calliope hesitated. It was clear she didn't feel comfortable leaving us, whether it was because of fear that we'd be discovered here or my condition, I wasn't sure.

With a nod, she said, "I'll be back." And left us alone.

MY head fell back against the chaise in defeat. "It's not working."

"Maybe it just needs a little more time. Or some fresh bell root."

I smirked. "Bellon root."

"Whatever." Cameron scooped another portion from the bowl, replacing the other salve. "A year ago, who would've thought I'd be at your feet, begging a treatment to heal your fae blood."

I chuckled. "I don't think anyone would've guessed that."

He met my eyes with a sad smile.

We waited.

And waited.

And waited some more.

But the short time Evan promised turned into a full

morning, afternoon, and evening with no changes. Since Declan and Brokk left with Kai and Calliope, Dugal brought us meals. Cameron was going stir crazy. He paced and chewed on his thumbnail as he stared at the mark, willing it to shrink. Then paced some more. I tried napping, but Cameron constantly checking the bellon root made it difficult to do it undisturbed.

As we ate dinner, he paid more attention to the paste on my chest than his plate. He'd only eaten a quarter of it by the time I was done with mine. The black mark never faded or shrunk.

"Let's try one more time." Cameron kneeled beside me and wiped away the mashed up bellon root before reaching for the last of it, but I grabbed hold of his wrist.

"Cameron, it's not working."

"But it might. Maybe each round pulls out toxins or whatever. A fresh layer each time might be helping."

I waited for him to look me in the eye. "It's not working, Cam. I feel no difference. It's not going to make me better. It's just not."

Sighing, he shook his head. "Fine. *Fine.*" He dragged his hand behind his neck. "Then we wait for Callie to visit with the council and we'll get more answers. You'll get better. Something will work. It will."

I didn't want to destroy his hope. It was all we had. So, all I said was, "Okay." My fingers skimmed his stubbled cheek. It had been a couple of days since he'd shaved. The scruffy look worked for him, roughing his boyishly handsome face. He bent his head down to meet my waiting lips.

"You trying to distract me with a kiss?" he asked against my mouth.

"Does that bother you?"

His fingers combed through my hair, a slow sweep across

my forehead. "There are worse things."

Our lips grazed and just as with every other time we connected, the frenzy in my veins ignited.

I needed him. I needed him now.

I didn't know how much longer I had—if these were some of our last moments together—so I tugged on Cameron's bicep, pulling him over me. He braced himself with one hand by my head and kissed me. Even though I was at my weakest, there was nothing delicate about his touch. He didn't treat me like I was a fragile doll. He knew better, thank the Fallen Fae.

Too far away. He was still too far away. To make room, I shifted to the side and he joined me on the chaise, cradling my jaw.

On my back, Cameron laid on his side, hovering above. He licked his bottom lip, eyes roaming my face like I was a revelation only meant for him. I was rare and he was lucky enough to find me.

"If this is like last time and you're kissing me because you think you're dying, it's not happening."

"Just shut up." Looping my arms around his neck, using what strength I had, I sealed his mouth to mine. In an instant, he took control. His newly developed hunger taking over.

Cameron had lips with knowledge. They knew how to kiss me, where to kiss me. They knew how much pressure and the perfect tempo, deliberate yet languid. His lips knew when teeth were wanted and when tongue should lead. Such a delicious symphony.

One of his legs slipped over mine, wedging between my thighs. He hooked his hand behind my head, locking in my hair, and released a feral groan into our kiss.

I could lose myself in his kiss without a care of being found.

Eyes closed, mouths captured, bodies entangled. It was the most blissful surrender. Cameron had the ability to flip a switch inside me. One minute I was rolling my eyes, wanting to strangle him, and in the next, I became a puddle of feelings. Adored and worshiped and loved.

He reached behind, yanking his shirt over his head. I welcomed the warm touch of his skin, encouraging the slip of his hand up my shirt. Our touch evolved from slow passion to heated desperation in seconds.

I wasn't sure how it happened. How I could hardly stand Cameron months ago and now couldn't fathom getting only a short time with him. I couldn't leave him. I didn't want to.

I wouldn't give up. I couldn't lose hope.

We were going to live a long, messy, smitten life together.

It was the only thing I'd accept.

TWENTY-ONE

SARAI

UNTERRIAL really outdid herself. I'd never seen the banquet hall this festive. Teal and purple gossamer material sheathed the ceiling, billowing like clouds above us, matching my eyes and wings. Several long tables on both sides of the hall were brimming with flowers and food. Food imported from all the kingdoms to cover where we lacked. The castle had never been filled with so many faeries and so much joy. The diversity of apparel and culture in one place, mingling and smiling in Rymidon, was a beautiful sight.

I'd dreaded this night for so long, but now that it was here, while I hated the reason for it, I was grateful for the accord nevertheless.

As I meandered around the hall, greeting every fae I came upon, a tall, regal woman with long golden hair piled atop her head beneath a crown of crystals approached me. "Queen Sarai."

I nodded as she outstretched her wrist adorned with multiple bracelets and gems. "I'm Isolda, Queen of Callastonia."

"It's wonderful to meet you." I accepted her Root.

Her amaranth eyes roved over my face. "Aren't you beautiful. Just like your mother. I remember when you were just a little girl running through the maze of the castle gardens. My heart shattered when I heard of you and Saoirse's passing, and here you are."

Here I am.

"My son Tomas will be *very* pleased to meet you."

"Oh." I chuckled with an uneasy shift in my stance, my heart aching with the mention of my mother and a time I barely recalled. "Thank you."

"He should be here soon. There was just a matter in Callastonia my husband asked him to handle before coming."

"I hope everything is all right."

She smiled, a warm glint lacing her reddish-rose eyes. "Perfectly fine. Just some routine checks with our Keepers."

"Well, I'm happy Callastonia decided to join us this evening."

"Of course. Saoirse was a dear friend of mine. I anticipated you'd be just as lovely, and I was right." Her gaze flitted around the grand banquet hall. "And Rymidon is just as magnificent as I remember. You've brought such a graceful light to the castle."

The absence of my father in her compliments was obvious. Not that I wanted him to be brought up this evening, but these were all fae who probably knew him better than I did. Had grown up with him and my mother. How strange it must be to see me in their stead. Not Skye or Sakari, but a girl they thought to be dead.

"Thank you, though I can't say I have much to do with that. I have an incredible staff of fae who keep me sane."

"Indeed, what would we do without them?" She smiled, gently touching my forearm. "Well, as soon as Tomas arrives I'll be sure he doesn't wait to seek you out. I have no doubt you'll be sought after all evening."

A light chuckle trickled from my mouth out of politeness. "I look forward to meeting him." Maybe. I wasn't sure. Queen Isolda seemed pleasant enough, but my heart wasn't in this tonight, not for what it needed to be.

She dipped her head in farewell as she walked away.

"Do you need to step away for a minute?" Kayne asked in a low voice. I blinked, noticing a thin sheen of tears across my eyes. He was becoming more and more in tune with my needs.

I sniffled and cleared my throat. "I'm fine. Thank you, though."

"Would you like a little help picking out a husband?"

I spun at the sound of Calliope's voice and shoved her in the shoulder before hugging her. "Oh, my Fallen Fae. That's exactly what this is, isn't it? It sounds so much worse when you say it like that."

Calliope laughed as she pulled away. "Welcome to the club."

"At least other Royals have their parents as a buffer to negotiate and weigh in with all of these strangers," I said. "Or they've spent their lives getting to know one another. I've got one night to spend with them to try and narrow down my choice all by myself. Could I love him?" I pointed around the room at random. "Could I love *him*?"

"The sad thing is, I might not believe in arranged marriages, but I totally get it. I was in your same shoes. *The Bachelor*, fae style." Her head shook as she chuckled. I pretended to know what she meant and released a soft laugh. "I would've killed to have my dad around giving me advice that night. We live in a weird, weird world. Thankfully, I found love in the end." She swiveled her gaze to Kai with a half-smirk and he winked at her.

Bittersweetness drenched me as I tried to keep a smile on my face. Sakari could've made her happy, too, but I was grateful Kai brought her so much joy.

"But you're not alone, Sarai. I've got you," Calliope said. "Though, I'll be honest. Never in a million years did I ever think *I'd* be the one giving the rundown about the other Royals in this scenario."

"Who helped you?"

"Helped might not be the best term. Offered snarky commentary?" She pointed her thumb in Kai's direction.

"In my defense," he said, crossing his arms over his chest, "I was in love with you and had to keep quiet by your side while helping you choose your match. Wasn't exactly an ideal situation."

Calliope slipped her hand into the crook of his elbow, tugging him close to her. She didn't say anything, just tugged him down and kissed him on the cheek. When she turned back to me, she asked, "Hey, when this is over, do you mind if we chat?"

"Of course. Is everything okay?"

"Umm…well we should probably talk about the scroll, among other things."

"I agree. Everything is becoming out of hand. I actually

need to talk to you, too, but let's forget that stuff for the evening." Whirling around to the room, I swept my dress to the side. "What can you tell me about the Royals? I know who Marcus's parents are, and his brother, Alston." I found the three of them speaking with some Auroralites. As if Prince Alston heard his name, his eyes drifted to me. A knowing smirk curled the corner of his mouth and he raised his goblet in my direction. I nodded, polite.

"What's that about?" Calliope asked.

"I think Marcus told him a little about us, but I don't know what." I sighed, shaking my head. "Moving on. I've met King Steafan and Queen Eimear of Mirrion. We discussed a trade agreement recently. And Queen Isolda of Callastonia introduced herself to me not long ago, but I've yet to meet any of their heirs."

"Well, lucky for me this is the fun part. You see the redhead with green eyes dressed in an excessive amount of blue and black clothes, those puffy sleeves and pants?"

I nodded.

"That's Niall from Mirrion. King Steafan did all the talking for him at my Awakening, so I can't tell you much about him except that he's really good at nodding and agreeing with his father."

"So, he's agreeable. Always a good trait." I laughed. "Are there any other Mirrion Royals?"

Kai cleared his throat and spoke up from the other side of Calliope. "He's got an older brother, Boyden, who will be taking King Steafan's place, and a younger brother, Varik, who just reached the age for bonding. As well as a sister, but she's not old enough to bond yet."

He lifted a finger, pointing to the opposite end of the hall that Niall was. "The one with the blonde hair, dressed in green and orange. That's Varik."

He was scrawny and couldn't have been any taller than me. "He cannot possibly be old enough to bond."

"We're startin' 'em young." Calliope chuckled.

Kai covered his mouth, pretending to scratch his nose. "I think Mirrion is desperate to create ties with another kingdom, especially one with another female heir who is first to the throne. No one really wants to align themselves with King Steafan."

"Why is that?"

Kai kept his voice low. "He can be a little *difficult* to get along with. Not much for compromising. He likes things his way and that is that. As you can imagine, with the history of the Great Divide, most of the Royals like things their way, but at least for amity sake, they compromise when necessary. He rarely does."

I nodded. Good to know, good to know. Not that I would be bonding with Steafan, but I didn't necessarily want to align myself with a kingdom like that, either. Not at a time like this.

"What about Aurorali?"

"Kai has always questioned their affinity for leaves as clothes."

I chuckled.

"I'm sorry," he said, "my man parts need more security than that."

My hand slapped over my mouth, covering my shocked amusement at his openness.

Calliope punched him in the arm with a laugh. "Behave." She turned back to me. "But in all honesty, Cormac is good for a laugh. He was fun to dance with at my Awakening. He kept things light and stress-free, which was exactly what I needed that night."

"Prince Cormac. Of Aurorali?"

"Yeah, why?"

"He's good friends with Marcus."

"Ah." She gave a mischievous half-smile. "Speaking of, is he here yet?"

"No." I would've noticed and my quick response told Calliope she knew just that. His parents were here and so was his brother. Where was he?

"Well, I'm sure he'll turn up eventually."

I equally wanted him to and didn't. I'd have a clearer head if he missed the evening. There was too much conflict between my head and heart when he was around. Reason and sensibility pummeled emotion and passion.

"Watch out for Tomas of Callastonia." Calliope tipped her head in the direction of a strikingly attractive blond with the darkest blue eyes I'd ever seen entering the hall. "That one is ballsy. He'll try to snatch your hand in marriage before catching your name," she whispered in my ear.

"So, when his mother said he'd be very pleased to meet me, she wasn't kidding."

"Not in the slightest." Calliope laughed. "Allura, Kai's sister, gave me the rundown on him after I met him. He might be handsome, but he is well aware of it and unashamed to flaunt it. Granted, it has been nearly an entire moon rotation since my Awakening, so he might've matured a little. Hopefully, for his sake."

"I guess I'll find out soon enough." Tomas was met by Queen Isolda as soon as he walked in and just as quickly his eyes found me.

"Definitely doesn't waste time, that one," she murmured in

my ear.

A charmed smile tipped his lips when he saw that I was already looking at him. *Oops.* His strut across the hall was confident, almost arrogant, but I suppose that fit with Calliope's description of him. Adorned in a cream tunic with a pale blue vest that complimented his eyes, he never took his stare off me. Bold. I already knew he'd be bold.

"Queen Sarai." Prince Tomas bowed and held his hand out. Instead of a Root, he clasped my fingers and brought my hand to his mouth, placing a light kiss on my knuckles. "I am Prince Tomas of Callastonia."

I bowed my head. "It's a pleasure to meet you. Your mother and I had a pleasant conversation earlier."

His cheeks turned a brighter shade of red and he laughed, though he didn't seem flustered. The flush of his cheeks appeared natural, rosy-cheeked. "I am sure you did. I hope she didn't say anything too embarrassing."

"On the contrary, she was quite lovely." And I wasn't lying. Though the conversation about my mother was difficult, I was grateful she hadn't been forgotten. Most were too uncomfortable to bring her up in conversation, assuming I wouldn't want to talk about her. On the contrary, she and Sakari were some of my favorite topics.

"She is, she is. Queen Calliope." He bowed his head. "King Kai. It's good to see you again."

"You, too." Calliope smiled, but she was biting back a laugh.

Prince Tomas offered his hand to me. "Would you care to dance?"

To my surprise, I did actually. He wasn't nearly as off-putting as I expected him to be. I nodded. Guiding me to the center of the hall, with a fluid motion, he spun me into his chest and looped his other arm around my waist at a respectable distance.

"I hope Queen Calliope didn't skew your opinion of me too horribly."

I lifted my eyes to him in question, hoping to shield the truth, and he continued with a timid smirk, "I made a bit of a fool of myself at her Awakening."

"How so?"

His light chuckle was endearing. "Well, you see...I'd been rather nervous and had chugged one too many deoches, clouded my judgment a little. Since she was the first female heir, and a True Royal at that, I hadn't known the proper way to handle a proposal for an arranged bonding."

My eyebrow rose, waiting for him to explain.

"I might have been a bit presumptuous and asked her to bond with me as soon as we started dancing." His eyes closed as he shook his head with an embarrassed smile. "The details are a bit hazy, but I think I said this will be a night we'll remember forever before asking her." He chewed on his bottom lip. "I promise not to do that this evening. I'll be on my best behavior."

I laughed. "That is appreciated."

"I'll wait until the second dance, at least," he joked.

Tomas was...dare I say...charming? And his eyes, they were captivating; blue as the midnight sky. And goodness, he was gorgeous. Sharp jawline with full lips, straight nose. He was the kind of gorgeous that made it difficult to turn away, but you didn't want to get caught admiring, either. It was the kind that made you tongue-tied.

"Do you have any siblings, Prince Tomas?"

"An older brother, and a little sister." He lowered his head, speaking in my ear, "Find the man in the room with the loudest laugh, surrounded by half the Royals and you'll find Tadhg, my brother."

My eyes scanned the banquet hall, dipping from one group to the next and sure enough, one crowd was larger than the rest. It was comprised mostly of Callastonians, but a few Mirrionians and Auroralites mixed in there. And in the center was a tall brunette with the biggest smile of bright white teeth. He tipped his head back with booming laughter as if in the middle of a very animated story.

"Find him yet?" There was an amused smile in Tomas's voice.

I chuckled. "I think so. Brown hair? Orange eyes? Really tall."

"That would be him."

Everyone was enamored with him. It was clear on the faces of those around him, eyes lit with mirth. It wasn't false amusement to get closer to the Royal, but genuine delight in his company. He drew them in like a moth to a flame.

"Your people love him."

"The beloved son." He nodded. "Tadhg will be the perfect king for Callastonia when the time comes."

There was an underlying resentful tone to his words, but I decided not to touch on it. Sibling rivalries were complicated. I didn't want to get in the middle.

"And your sister, is she here?" I asked.

Tomas pulled back, spinning me in a circle as he smirked. "Most likely stealing sweets quicker than your Sowers can replenish them."

I chuckled. My kind of girl.

"Our mother keeps her on a fairly strict diet, so when

there's any sort of celebration, those tables are the first thing Emlyn raids."

I appreciated the fond timbre of his voice, that of a loving brother. Hopefully, Emlyn had in Tomas what I'd had in Sakari.

When the song ended, he escorted me back to Calliope and Kai. She watched me with wide inquisitive eyes as we approached, clamping her lips together.

"Thank you for the dance, Queen Sarai. I hope we can see more of each other. Maybe save another dance for me later." Tomas gave a low bow, winking when he stood, before he walked off.

"Well," Calliope said. "He certainly seemed more charming than when I first met him. You hardly stopped smiling on that dance floor."

"He was a pleasant surprise, I'll say that."

"Good, good." Calliope's gaze fell across the room. "And the man of the hour has arrived at last."

I looked to the entrance as Marcus stopped and surveyed the hall. My heart leaped, my pulse pumping. Without saying a word, he had the presence to command a room, self-assured and smoldering. And he had my full attention. The dark green coat over his black tunic brought out the dark green irises of his eyes. I waited for him to meet my stare, to offer a private hello, but he turned left into the hall before he saw me, moving in the opposite direction.

Why did you have to break my heart, Marcus?

TWENTY-TWO

SARAI

ALL night Marcus avoided me. He never once bothered to look my way. I would've known. Against my better judgment, I hardly took my eyes off him. Prince Alston and I made eye contact more times, and that was only a couple.

Marcus mingled with Oraelians and Auroralites for the most part. Or rather Prince Cormac and two beautiful girls from Aurorali. They couldn't have been much younger than me. And he didn't seem to mind their company, engrossed in conversation. There was the occasional arm grab or shoulder slap, and he took it in stride, offering pleasant looks. Nothing to discourage them. They were awfully familiar with each other.

"Prince Cormac's sisters."

I turned to Calliope. How did she...

"You've been staring at them for the last five minutes."

I shook my head and averted my eyes to the other end of the banquet hall, annoyed with myself. He shouldn't be where my focus was tonight, but this was *my* Royal gala. Why hadn't he come to say hello?

"It's okay to be jealous, to miss him."

"I'm not—"

"Oh, please. Spare me the lies, Sarai. You care about Marcus whether you want to admit it or not, and it's perfectly normal to be jealous of him with other women. But you made your choice, didn't you? That's why we're all here tonight. So, you can choose someone else."

Before I could respond, Prince Cormac must have noticed our attention on their group because he was dancing his way over to us, his leafed loincloth flapping as he went. Hopefully, there was something more secure to cover him up beneath that.

The curls on his head bounced with each leap and prance, drawing the attention of everyone he passed. His carefree nature emanated, evoking smiles and laughter from each fae. He seemed a difficult man to dislike.

A grin stretched across my face and Calliope giggled at my side. "He is a *trip*."

"Queen Sarai." Prince Cormac bowed at the waist, fanning his arms out to the side as he smiled. "May I have this dance?"

How could I possibly say no? I took his outstretched hand and followed him. Not once did he stop moving as we made our way to the center. He danced the whole way, but he didn't pull me close. Cormac held me at arm's length, swinging us around and side-to-side.

"You're even more beautiful than Marcus described."

He talked about me to Cormac?

"Don't look so surprised." He smirked. "When the Princess of Rymidon rose from the dead and caught the attention of Marcus the Impenetrable, I had to know every detail."

Marcus the Impenetrable. That seemed a good title for the man I'd first met in Faylinn, what felt like a lifetime ago.

How much did Cormac know? He ignored the question in my eyes and spun me in circles, heel-kicking as he went. Light on his feet, this one was. And then, for the first time, he pulled me close, placing his hand on the small of my back, holding us chest-to-chest as he twirled us around the room.

Close to my ear, Cormac said, "Uh-oh. Someone wants to unleash the big jealousy monster."

I followed his stare to Marcus in the corner with Cormac's sisters. He wasn't even looking at us, his sole focus on the two girls. They smiled and giggled and shoved Marcus in the shoulder while he offered his subtle smiles. He didn't look all that jealous to me. They'd even been able to draw out his smile.

"What makes you say that?"

"I know my best friend, but I also have no interest in making an enemy out of Marcus." He laughed, putting distance between us once more, another arm's length. "I'm just here as a formality. Royal gathering and all."

"You mean you're not going to vie for a match with me?" I teased.

"Definitely not." He smiled. "You belong to Marcus's heart. That's not something I care to toy with."

My lungs tangled with my heart, stealing my air and pausing its beats. How was it possible to crave his affection and harbor so much anger toward him at the same time?

"Well, Marcus…isn't my match. He did things that hurt me deeply." Understatement if ever there were one. "And I don't know that I'll be able to trust him again."

"I know what he did."

But did he really?

"If you knew Nerida, you'd understand." Cormac's light expression dimmed. "You wouldn't have been able to sit idle either. A friend wasn't the only thing lost that day, but a wife, a daughter, sister, and mother."

My eyes widened.

"You think he'd hide something like that from his best friend?" Cormac pulled me close once more, lowering his mouth to my ear. "Should he have sought the help of the elves? Probably not. But Marcus doesn't always think with his head, he thinks with his heart. And his heart was wrecked, guilt-driven. It's difficult to think clearly with broken pieces."

His words cut deep and stroked the grief I struggled to bury. My bleeding heart and broken pieces invited the enemy into our kingdom.

When I didn't say anything in return, Cormac asked, "They're living here now, aren't they? The elves. How is that fairing for you?"

He pulled back, meeting my eyes which must have spilled the guilt and stress I'd carried because his eyes softened. "He loves you, you know?"

I sucked in a breath.

"Even after he broke things off with Nerida, and after he lost her, I've never seen Marcus this tormented. He'd do anything for you, Sarai. You just have to say the words."

The song ended and Cormac bowed before leaving me

paralyzed in the middle of the dance floor. Marcus…loved me?

"Queen Sarai?" Blinking, I turned and was met by Prince Niall of Mirrion. He introduced himself with a subtle bow. "Might you spare a dance for me?"

As if an automatic response, I placed my hand in his and danced to another song, the stringed instrument's melody filling the room. Calliope was right about Prince Niall. He'd asked me to dance but hardly said a word the entire time, only nodding and offering one-word answers to my limited questions. It suited me just fine. After my dance with Cormac, I couldn't think much beyond his admissions about Marcus.

"You all right?" Calliope asked when I met back with her and Kai near one of the long tables of food. She dished shemun onto a plate, peeking over her shoulder at me.

I nodded, but didn't say anything else.

"You should eat. You haven't yet, have you?"

I shook my head and she passed me a plate to fill. It wasn't common practice for a queen to serve herself, but I followed Calliope's lead. If my stomach wasn't turning on itself, I'd have piled my plate high with more than I'd be able to eat. It must've all been so delicious, but I only snagged a few things, things I knew would be easy on my stomach.

The three of us lined up against the wall, eating and observing the rest of the Royals. I should've mingled with the others since I wasn't even halfway through meeting the rest of them, but I needed some time to breathe. This night was more draining than I anticipated.

"Elfland is still missing," Calliope noted. "Elena might not have come to any of the festivities in Faylinn, but at least her fae did. What is she so worried about? Adair is gone. Rymidon isn't a threat anymore."

"She's kept up those wards for so many decades," Kai said. "It might not be easy to trust, to take them down without taking other precautions first."

"Does she have children?" I asked.

"She has a daughter and a son. Maybe more that we aren't aware of since she and her family remain concealed in Elfland."

"Won't they eventually have to bond with other Royals?" Calliope passed her empty plate off with a 'thank you' when one of my Sowers offered to take it. "What does Elena expect to happen if her children never familiarize themselves with the other kingdoms, with the other Royals? They'll wind up just like Sarai and me, awkwardly choosing a spouse at a party like it's a game of eeny, meeny, miny, moe."

"In context, I have an idea of what that game is, but your guess is as good as mine. And it's a valid question considering they might be old enough to bond soon, if they haven't reached the age already," Kai said. "You can always reach out to Elena again, you know."

"I might. She saved us. And then disappeared all over again. I want to understand why."

Queen Elena's way of surviving was enticing. If I could've disappeared and cut myself off from the other kingdoms, I might've done it, too.

"Incoming," Calliope said under her breath.

I looked up as Prince Tomas was a few feet away. He smiled when our eyes met. "Might I be able to sneak another dance with you before the evening ends?"

"Sure." I smiled and passed off my half-eaten plate to Kayne.

Instead of clasping his hand around mine, Tomas linked our fingers together and it set a whole new mood between us.

My fingers had never locked with another man before. Though Marcus and I had kissed, had hugged, we'd never held hands. It was intimate in a whole different way, and somewhat possessive, but oddly enough I didn't mind it.

Tomas pulled me closer than he had the first time, a more familiar hold, as he whispered in my ear. "Though it's our second dance, I promise to keep my proposal to myself."

I chuckled, squeezing his hand in mine. "Thanks."

"How has your evening been?"

"Oh, it's been delightful," I forced a polite tone.

"You don't have to lie. We're all aware of how uncomfortable a night like this can be." He laughed. "As a queen, at least you're the lucky one, able to choose who you'd like, while the rest of us have to hope we'll impress you enough to be chosen." The humor in his deep blue oceans lightened his words, a refreshing, self-deprecating humor.

"It's true. It's all incredibly awkward, isn't it?" I smiled.

Tomas's head tipped to the side as he raised a hand in the air. "The life of a Royal. Isn't it grand?"

I nodded with a small smirk, but said no more, letting the music fill the silence. I'd never resented being a Royal before. It'd been ingrained in me that it was a privilege and honor. And it was, but it was also a lot of responsibility scrutinized by so many. One wrong move and the entire kingdom could turn on you. And I suppose that was where Supremacy held a place. It took away control and free-will, but it kept the peace. In a sense, I could see the appeal, how a Royal could use Supremacy to keep fae agreeable even when mistakes were made.

With one turn on the dance floor, I caught Marcus's eye. A shiver ran down my spine. It was the first time we'd made eye-contact, something I'd been longing for all night, but this was a look I'd never seen before. A look I wasn't prepared for. Jaw clenched, eyes orbs of fury. What had I done to deserve such anger? He severed our stare and left, slipping out a side door of the hall.

Was he leaving for the night? Without a goodbye, or even a hello?

"Is everything all right?"

"Hmm?"

"You went very stiff and your smile disappeared completely."

"Oh." What could I say to cover the truth? "Just tired, I guess." I feigned a smile. I wasn't a very good liar.

Tomas looked around, but said no more.

When the song ended, he asked, "May I see you outside of this gathering? Perhaps dinner? In Rymidon or Callastonia, whichever you are more comfortable with."

There wasn't a fire lit inside or a spark, but a flutter whispered in my stomach and that had to be enough. For now. I owed it to myself to explore my options.

"That would be lovely. I've never been to Callastonia."

His smile stretched wide. "Wonderful, then I'd be honored to give you a tour. I'll speak with our staff and have Durin, our adviser, set it up with..."

"Oh, he can speak with Kayne. He's my...confidant." Though, at this point, he might as well have been my adviser. I wasn't going to turn to anyone else.

"Very well. I look forward to seeing you again." Prince Tomas lifted my knuckles to his lips and pressed a gentle kiss. "Enjoy the rest of your night."

Maybe the touch of his lips should've done more to the fireflies in my stomach, but they didn't. I was left with nothing but a faint flicker.

"Thank you." I bowed my head and he strutted away.

"You should stay away from him." Warm breath brushed the shell of my ear.

I whipped around, coming face-to-face with Marcus. Or rather, face-to-chest. I lifted my gaze.

He was here. He hadn't left. "Excuse me?"

"Stay away from Tomas, Sarai." There was no teasing, only demand in his tone and eyes.

I reared back. "I'm sorry, but you don't get a say in this matter. I'll spend time with whomever I choose."

Marcus grabbed my hand and for some reason, I didn't resist him. He pulled me along the wall, sneaking out a door at the back of the banquet hall. After searching the corridor and learning we were alone, he pinned me to the wall. "I mean it, Sarai," he whispered. "He's not a good guy. Take it from a Royal who knows every Royal offspring here better than anyone, Tomas is to be avoided."

"Why?" I kept my voice just as quiet. "Because he actually stands a chance to be with me?"

Marcus's expression wilted. "Please don't say that."

"You can't get territorial with me, Marcus. We're friends. Nothing more."

"So you've said, but where have your eyes been all night?"

I clamped my mouth shut. Caught. How had he noticed? He barely spared me a glance.

"That's what I thought."

My eyes darted away. "Well, you seemed perfectly content with Prince Cormac's sisters. All the smiles and giggles and arm touching. Are you sure you don't want one of them?"

I hated the jealousy that oozed from my mouth, but it

couldn't be stopped. As vile an emotion, it festered within me. I hated seeing him with other women. They didn't belong by his side.

Marcus's eyes pinched in confusion. "Why would you...? Brenna and Devona were mocking my irritation of having to watch you with every other Royal here, vying for your hand in bonding. It might come as a surprise to you, but they don't see that side of me very often. They've never seen me...care for someone. Not in the way I care for you."

"Not even Nerida?"

He stiffened, his stare steely. "Nerida was years ago, and in secret, Sarai. They were too young to know any part of that. But let me make this clear, not even Nerida brought out the feelings of longing, protectiveness, and jealousy that you did tonight."

My shoulders sagged, but my heart beat faster. "What do you want me to say?"

"Say you'll trust me, that you're ready to put this all behind us and choose me back. Because I choose you, Sarai. I'd choose you over and over."

I swallowed back tears threatening to break free. "And what happens when my kingdom finds out what we did?" I hissed, breathless. "You teamed up with the elves to have them killed. And *I* welcomed the elves into our kingdom with open arms like they didn't slaughter us. Then I *bond* with you? What a trusting Royal pair we'd make."

His hand smacked the stone wall by my head, frustration saturating his eyes. "It's more complicated than that. We're so much more than our mistakes, and you know it."

"*I* know it. *You* know it. But how will that look to them? They won't see our reasons, our good intentions. Rymidon is too raw after my father. Two Royals, one after another, who should have defended and protected them, betrayed them."

"*You* are *not* your father."

"Aren't I though?" My voice quivered, unable to restrain my tears any longer. "He kept secrets. I'm keeping secrets. He forced them to invade Faylinn. I'm forcing them to live with the enemy. Our motives might be different, but we've both hurt them just the same. And now our lands are *dying*."

"Stop this." Marcus cupped my face, brushing the wetness from my cheeks with his rough thumbs. "We'll heal the lands. It's not over with the elves. You don't have to accommodate them forever. We can find a way. *Together*. Rymidon doesn't have to know what happened until after we've rectified our indiscretions. They'll see what your end goal was. Relocating the elves is just a stepping stone. We can make this right and transform Rymidon into a thriving, stable kingdom. Better than it ever was."

I peered around, making sure we were still alone. "And what about Cameron? Lia? The scroll? The capabilities of our blood can't be hidden forever. Even Calliope knows that."

"We'll figure it out, Sarai. When you set up the council with the Royals, they'll have more answers. I just…I want you. I want you forever. I will do whatever it takes to make this right. I'm here for you." He pressed his forehead against mine, his breathing heavy, gruff. "Please."

If I tipped my head up, just a fraction, I'd have met his lips. Just. One. Tip. Of my chin.

"Your Highness."

My head whipped to the side. Kayne averted his eyes, but remained solid, a confident rise of his head. "King Steafan is looking for you. I believe he wants to finalize the trade agreement."

"Yes, of course." I ducked away from Marcus, offering an apologetic backward glance as I slipped inside the banquet hall. He stood tall, but the slight droop of his shoulders and anguish in his eyes pierced my heart.

MOST of the other kingdoms were gone, so Calliope, Kai, and I moved to my study. After my encounter with Marcus in the corridor, I didn't see him for the rest of the night. He didn't stick around, which was probably for the best.

"I know it's late and you're probably exhausted, but this can't wait any longer," Calliope said.

"Have you made a decision about informing the other Royals about the scroll?"

"Yes. Because of Lia."

"Lia?"

"She's not accepting the transformation very well. Apparently she's been having issues since they moved into the Rymidonian castle."

"And she said nothing?"

Calliope nodded. "She didn't say this, but I think Lia still harbors a lot of guilt for her past mistakes. Asking for help from those she wronged is probably hard for her. I guarantee she didn't want to be a burden."

"Is she all right?"

"Honestly, I don't know." Her shoulders deflated as she exhaled. "It's not looking good. And because of her situation, I think we need to hold an emergency Royal council tomorrow morning. It's possible they already know a lot. I can't imagine that only my family is aware of our blood's properties. As Evan said, Cameron isn't the first human to transform. There's more history that we aren't aware of. And we've been keeping this to ourselves out of fear, but what if the other Royals have solutions or insight? What might they know about our history that isn't on the scrolls? They'd want the knowledge on the scroll protected just as much as we do. It puts them and all of their kingdoms at risk."

"Because of the dead lands, I was going to call the council together. We can both go, but what will we tell them about Cameron and Lia?"

"You and I need to prepare for repercussions, but we can either tell the truth or come up with some sort of cover story. For now, I'd like to keep Cameron's transformation out of this. Lia's health is a top priority. We don't need to muddy the waters with Cameron's decision yet. When the time comes, I'll protect them as best I can, but we all made decisions that have consequences."

I nodded. "Marcus is willing to accept any punishment for consorting with the elves, but I don't want the Royals to make those decisions. Would their punishment be fair? Or would he suffer more than he should?"

"I know my opinion wasn't asked for, but I'm going to give it anyway." Kai shifted forward on the couch, sitting on the edge with his forearms resting on his knees. "Prince Marcus has been a tough one for me to read over the years. I used to hate it because the quiet ones tend to be the most dangerous, their thoughts always kept to themselves for a reason. But, to me, he's proven to be a devoted force, willing to protect and avenge those he loves. If he did that for one woman, imagine what he'd do for his kingdom. Did he go about it the wrong way by joining forces with the elves? Yeah, but he went a fairly mild route, in my opinion."

My head tilted to the side, curious.

"If it were Calliope, or even my sister, Allura, who was killed in the Battle of Faylinn, I wouldn't have gone after possible Adair followers, I'd have burned down the entire kingdom."

While his words stung, I understood. A love like theirs was rare and deep. To know that kind of love was powerful.

"So, when it comes down to it," he said, "I say we leave Marcus out of this. He's not the enemy. The elves are. He's paid his price. I know what it's like being kept from the one you love, watching them with another." We shared a meaningful glance. I couldn't begrudge him for loving Calliope as my brother had. "I assure you. Not having you, Sarai, is punishment enough."

TWENTY-THREE

CAMERON

LIA lay sleeping in my arms on the lounger when Callie walked into the atrium. "How is she?"

"The bellon root didn't work." I kept my voice quiet, stroking Lia's hair. Disappointment wafted off me. "I actually think she's worse than before. She hardly moved from this thing all day, and not just because she had that salve on her chest."

Callie's shoulders sagged, matching the dip of her eyes. "I had a feeling that wasn't going to work, but I held out hope."

I nodded. "How was the shindig?"

"About as fun as gouging out my eyes."

I chuckled. "Sarai ready to swallow her pride and give in to Marcus yet?"

"I wish." Callie groaned and motioned for me to follow her out of the atrium.

I didn't want to leave Lia, but I didn't want to wake her either. Like a ninja, I slipped out from beneath her and pulled a blanket over her shoulders.

Once the door was closed behind us, Callie said, "Sarai and I are going to speak with the Royal council tomorrow. She's going to call for an emergency meeting. We're going to tell them everything, except about you." She looked both ways down the corridor. "I don't know how they're going to react, but if it goes south, I'll send word and I want you to take Lia back to the safe house."

"Done."

"I doubt it'll come to that, but it's better to stay prepared."

I raised the three-finger boy scout salute. "Always."

She chuckled. "All right. Go get that poor girl to bed. I've fallen asleep on that chaise and it's not that comfortable. I'll have breakfast sent to your room in the morning. Just hang out there until I get back from the meeting."

"You got it, Your Ladyship."

Callie shoved me with a smirk as she moved onto Kai waiting with his arms and ankles crossed at the doorway of their bedroom. He grabbed her waist, pulling her inside as she laughed.

My smile, watching them, quickly turned to a frown when it hit me. We had no idea how to help Lia. That life, the one Callie had with Kai, was within reach but could be stripped away from me any day, any moment.

When I carried Lia to the bed, she didn't stir. I'd slept

beside her long enough before to know she wasn't a sound sleeper. No matter how graceful my movements were as a faery, between my conversation with Callie and jostling her down the hallway and into bed, she should've at least had an eyelid flutter or change in breathing, but Lia continued sleeping as if in a short coma.

After I got ready for bed, I curled in behind Lia, tugging her against me. The steady shallowness of her breath calmed me and worried me. Would she wake in the morning or slip away in my arms as she dreamed without me knowing? Would I wake up and find her gone?

I couldn't help myself. I pressed a kiss into her neck, and then another, and another.

Lia took a deep breath, rousing. "Did Calliope get back?" she murmured, rolling into my chest. The sound of her sleepy voice settled my uneasiness. Burying her face, Lia pressed a kiss to my warm skin and I sighed.

"Yeah, her and Sarai are going to take care of you."

She mumbled into my chest, "You can't make promises like that."

"Well, they're going to try." I stroked her hair. "Tomorrow morning they're going to meet with the other Royals. We'll get to the bottom of this."

Lia released a drowsy sigh before nodding and falling back asleep.

Please wake up in the morning.

TWENTY-FOUR

SARAI

I should have told Marcus about when I was meeting with the Royals, but after Kai, my decision to leave him out of it solidified. I wasn't going to let him crucify himself. Or allow the Royals to make him into something he wasn't. A villain.

"Hey, what's wrong?" Calliope rested her hand on my arm.

I blinked, rolling my shoulders back. "Nothing. I'm okay."

"Are you sure?"

One shoulder shrugged. "I guess I'm just nervous about the council. We're about to go in there and drop a lot of information and plead for help. What if they aren't willing? Or they don't have answers?"

"They might not, but we have to do this nonetheless. You don't have to go in there with me, you know? I have all I need to tell them everything. I can be a spokesperson for you or whatever."

"No, no. I want to be in there. My presence is important. Rymidon deserves that from me at least."

"Then let's go. I'm right here beside you."

Mirrion Keepers, in their boldly colored tunics and billowy pants, opened the doors to the great room where the rest of the Royals were waiting.

Each Royal sat in plush chairs in a semicircle, the sight quite intimidating. One Royal from every kingdom. King Steafan of Mirrion—of course, Queen Isolda of Callastonia, Queen Aisling of Oraelia, King Noll of Aurorali, and King Cian of Elfland.

I was surprised to see Elfland in attendance, but it wasn't Queen Elena, which was less than surprising. I'd have loved to meet her, though she might not have felt the same with me being the daughter of Adair.

King Steafan beckoned us further into the great room with a flippant wave of the hand and approving nod, as if we were deemed worthy to approach.

Though Calliope was the True Royal and should've been the one leading the councils, King Steafan was granted control when Calliope became queen because of her lack of knowledge in the fae world and our practices. Hopefully, she'd get to reclaim her place in time because Kai was not wrong; King Steafan was less than desirable.

He wasn't evil—I didn't think—just an arrogant pig. It wasn't any wonder his adviser was so pompous, as Kayne had said. It seemed the other Royals only allowed it to happen because it was easier than arguing with him; let the man feel like he was in charge. The rest knew the truth, and in the end, he didn't have any real pull over any of the Royals.

I'd only been a part of one Royal council before, the one I called together for Calliope to bond with Kai. As tense as that meeting was, I expected nothing less for this one.

"We've called for this emergency council because we have a few critical and time-sensitive matters to discuss," Calliope said as we stood in front of them. She paused, letting me take the lead.

I squared my shoulders. "As you're all aware, about two moon cycles ago, twenty Rymidonian faeries were found on the outskirts of our forests days apart with their throats slashed and drained of blood. It took longer than I'd have liked to discover the culprit, but we now know the elves were responsible."

"Slimy scat faces." King Steafan's voice rose above the others appalled reactions.

I turned to Calliope because it was her place, not mine, to divulge the existence of the Royal scrolls.

"After the Great Divide, my family created scrolls."

"The True Royal scrolls," King Cian said, reverent.

Calliope tilted her head. "Yes. Are you all aware of them?"

The other Royals shook their heads, trepidation flickering in their eyes as they looked to King Cian and back to Calliope. Why did he know, but the others didn't?

"Well, at some point my family started to transcribe our laws, our history, our fae abilities, and so on. Everything so nothing was lost over time. After Rymidon was attacked, I offered my help to Sarai to search for reasons why faery blood would be drained. Upon researching, we found that the scroll which includes the attributes and capabilities of our blood was missing."

"My brother, Skye, gave it to the elves before my fa-
father..." I cleared my throat, the term turning to ash in my
mouth. "Before Adair launched the Battle of Faylinn."

Calliope covered for my choked emotions and proceeded.
"They'd been using our blood to experiment on themselves and
faeries who'd transformed to humans but wanted to return to
their fae form."

"They know our blood can be used to transform other
beings," Queen Aisling said, gasping. Because of course the other
Royals knew. We were babies compared to the thousands of
years they'd been around.

There was a collective gasp as the other Royals caught on to
what the elves were up to.

"They were creating an army of sorts to attack one
kingdom after the next, wanting to become the superior race.
After a short fight, we were able to retrieve the scroll from the
elves and recover the blood they stole."

"But you've invited them into Rymidon, have given them
land, Queen Sarai. Why would you do that?" Queen Isolda asked.

"I'm not my father. I don't want to be responsible for the
death of an entire race of elves, so I negotiated a different
solution."

"So, they suffered no consequences." King Steafan crossed
his arms, eyeing me with judgmental astonishment. "They still
hold the knowledge and can try again. How many other innocent
faeries will be sacrificed in the name of your mercy?"

"We came to an agreement," I said. "They know they don't
stand a chance against us if they try again. Guthron wouldn't
dare."

"Why come to us then, after you've already made your

decision to create peace with the elves?" King Noll asked, stroking his beard.

"Because there is no peace," I said. "We're stuck in a cycle of threats. I didn't want to start a war, so I offered our land, a place where they felt equal and dignified, so they didn't feel the need to use our blood for our powers and abilities. They'll expose the knowledge of our blood if I don't comply with Guthron's demands. And if they do, I'll be forced to retaliate."

"Naive, naive girl." King Steafan tutted. "Obliterate them. Our realm would be better without the elves."

"That would make us no better than the elves," Queen Aisling said before turning her attention back to us. "I assume you brought this matter to us because you'd like a solution that doesn't involve war."

"Yes, that, but there's actually a more pressing reason why we're here," I said. "Our harvest has been dwindling daily since the elves arrived. Oraelia and Faylinn have helped in supplementing what we're lacking, but it's not enough. And a few days ago, a couple of my fae stumbled across a patch of dead land." The horror on their faces mirrored mine inside. "And since then, five more sections have been found. They're spreading wider each day, killing the woodlands."

Calliope said, "After Sarai sought my help to try and heal it, which didn't work, my Keepers discovered several patches in Faylinn, as well. One spanning a quarter of a mile wide."

I almost mentioned Oraelia, but clamped my mouth shut to keep Marcus's involvement quiet.

"Lia, a former Rymidonian—"

"We're familiar with Magnolia's arrangement with Adair," King Steafan said, clipped.

"Right, well, she's made amends," Calliope said. "She gave

up her fae form so that my husband, Kai, could transform back to faery after my father died. But the elves approached her, enticed her. She wasn't aware of how the blood was retrieved at the time. All she knew was that she could have her life back. So, she switched, and now her body isn't accepting the transformation."

"They upset the balance," Queen Isolda said, her face paling.

"Viridessa." King Cian's eyes grew grave, releasing a low gasp.

"Oh, c'mon, Cian. You can't possibly believe in that billbosh." King Steafan scoffed, rolling his eyes.

"Who's Viridessa?" Calliope asked.

King Cian leaned forward. "She's a great and powerful being."

"She's a tale used to frighten children and keep them from taking transformations lightly." King Steafan folded his arms, not even entertaining the idea that King Cian might be telling the truth.

"I assure you, she is more than a tale." While King Cian responded, it was more to confirm to us than defend himself to Steafan, barely offering him a glance.

Calliope shifted her eyes from me to King Cian. "Wha-what's the tale?"

"She created our realm and sleeps when there is peace, but when the balance is disturbed, she awakens in one of us and carries out her punishment."

"Who?" I couldn't help but ask. "Who does she awaken in?"

"We don't know."

"It's just folklore, Cian," Queen Isolda said. "It's a story that's been told for so long it's skewing your outlook on reality."

"I assure you. It is more than folklore."

"What's the punishment?" Calliope asked.

King Cian's eyes grew weary. "She decides the severity from circumstance to circumstance."

Sarai stepped forward. "So, killing our lands could be it?"

His eyes slanted at the corners, grim. "It's only the beginning."

A shiver coursed through my wings.

"Lighten up, Cian." King Noll swatted the air. "There's a perfectly good explanation for the dead lands. It's not some ancient being that has come to terrorize us."

"And you're a fool not to considerate it."

We didn't come here to listen to them bicker, so I asked, "Have any of you been made aware of dead lands in your kingdoms?"

They looked to another as if they had the answers. One by one they shook their heads. Even Queen Aisling. Marcus still hadn't said anything.

"Even if Viridessa isn't the cause," I said, which I wasn't so sure, "it might be wise to dispatch a few units of Keepers to sweep your kingdoms. Just to be sure. If this is something that has affected every kingdom, I fear the balance has been upset and we don't know how to fix it."

"I know how to fix it. Be rid of the elves and Lia." King Steafan folded his arms, not a hint of remorse in his aged eyes.

"We've already established we're not killing the elves, Steafan." Queen Isolda groaned, shaking her head. "We'll all have units circle our kingdoms to check for dead lands. It would be the wisest decision."

Fortunately, the rest nodded in agreement.

King Steafan sighed, but said, "We'll report back here tomorrow."

Calliope's wings perked up, worried at the meeting adjourning. "Is there anything we can do for Lia in the meantime? She really does need help."

King Steafan snorted, crossing his arms over his round belly. "And you want our help for her reckless decision?"

It took Calliope a moment to compose a polite response. The urge to snap at him was swirling in her eyes. "I understand your hesitation. Her choice was not rational or wise, but she is a dear friend of mine. We just want to know if there is anyone who might have more insight, who might know of a situation similar to hers." Pleading soaked her voice. "Or if there are remedies or treatments in your kingdoms that might cure her, heal her, extend her time. *Anything.*"

The room silenced. Time passed with nothing but their stares.

"A human transformation hasn't been done in centuries. There's a reason for that, Queen Calliope," Queen Aisling said, pity in her vibrant iris eyes. "The outcome isn't promising."

"So, there's nothing we can do?"

There wasn't a single response. There were no glances at each other or contemplation. We were met with silence. Whether out of defiance or lack of answers, they weren't going to help.

"Let's focus on something we can do, shall we?" King Steafan pursed his pudgy lips. "The elves need to be dealt with. They know too much."

"We're not going to slaughter the elves, Steafan." Queen Isolda groaned, fed up with his opinions.

"Then what do you suggest, Isolda? Sit in a circle, holding hands until there's understanding and harmony?" His sarcasm was met with a glare, but she ignored him.

"Do you want to continue giving the elves refuge in Rymidon?" she asked me. "Does your kingdom know what they did to their fellow fae?"

I loosened a breath. "No," answering both questions.

Queen Isolda nodded with a knowing, solemn smile, the way a mother would a child. It sunk into the pit of my stomach. I was an orphan with no direction, and they knew I was barely holding my own. I must seem out of my depth. And they weren't wrong. I liked to think of myself as capable as any other Royal, but I was lost, pretending that I could do this all alone.

"Why don't the elves have their own land?" Calliope asked.

"They did." King Steafan drummed his fingers along the armrest of his throne with narrowed, unimpressed eyes. "They were given land just as the trolls and pixies were. Just as every other creature in our realm. But they didn't care for it. Over time, they destroyed it. Then, when they could no longer live off their land, they wanted more and came to me, demanding I share Mirrion. It wasn't my fault they weren't grateful for what the Waking Oak granted them, so I turned Guthron away."

"Did he go to Adair, too?" Calliope asked.

King Steafan nodded. "And he turned him away as well. The elves only have themselves to blame for their lack of respect and appreciation for the forest."

"So, since then, they've been moving from kingdom to kingdom, squatting on land that doesn't belong to them," Calliope concluded.

"Guthron told me they had to keep moving on when their dwellings were no longer habitable for their protection," I said.

"Of course he did," King Steafan spat. "No longer habitable because they are careless wastes of space who don't deserve your mercy and aren't welcome to claim land that doesn't belong to them. They mooch and mooch until they have to move onto the next."

"Steafan," Queen Aisling chided.

His head whipped to her. "You know it's true, Aisling. You'd have turned them away, too."

She didn't contradict him.

"Back to the issue at hand," King Cian said. "You're seeing this as only two options with the elves, Queen Sarai. Give the elves what they want to keep the peace. Or come clean with your kingdom and start a war. The Oak has created entire kingdoms. It's possible to banish the elves. Send them back to the land they destroyed. Force them to rebuild it. Then place wards around it so they cannot leave."

"It's still reachable?" Calliope asked.

"Through the Oak, yes. Engalawood. They might not have lived there for centuries, but it's there. It might even have regrown in their absence."

"What if it's not habitable enough for them to survive?" I asked. There were still children to think about. Not all the elves were fully innocent, but they weren't deserving of starvation. "If Guthron had that option, wouldn't he have tried? They don't have the abilities we do to regrow crops or build dwellings."

"And neither do we if our lands are dying," King Noll said. "Humans have been self-sufficient for millennia. The elves could too, if they were willing to try."

King Cian ignored him. "If you want to offer more mercy, Queen Calliope can create another branch as a sort of prison with a new land. They can do what they please with it and hopefully will learn to tend to it, cultivate it. Learn the art of craftsmanship and build their own dwellings if they know they can't turn to anyone else. Wards could be set up to keep them there. The elves still get their own land, while we remain safe."

"I can create a branch on the Waking Oak?" Calliope asked.

"How do you think the other branches were created? Out of thin air?"

Her brow pinched. "I was told the branches appeared as if the Oak knew it was time, like it was meant to be."

"And it was, but it was King Oscar, a True Royal, who facilitated the growth. It is meant to remain a secret, so not every determined, ignorant fae would think they could branch off and run a kingdom."

"King Oscar? My grandfather?"

King Cian nodded.

"So, I can create a branch?"

"You restored the Waking Oak after Adair poisoned it, didn't you?"

"Well, yes, but that was healing, something I know how to do, something we do all the time. Creating a whole new branch, a whole new land is different."

"You're a True Royal, Calliope," he said, calm confidence in his piercing eyes. "Don't diminish your abilities. Only you can do what you do."

"It's a fair alternative," King Steafan said. "One I don't think they deserve, but it was your fae they slaughtered, Queen Sarai. We'll allow you to dole out the punishment. The branch doesn't have to be as large as our kingdoms. The elves don't deserve to be rewarded with their own kingdom. It's a place of banishment, a prison of sorts."

Calliope looked at me. "Is that something you're comfortable with?"

"It avoids war and gives my kingdom protection once

again. If you think you're capable of creating a branch, then let's do it."

"I can sure try." She smiled, a nervous tilt to the corners. "Maybe it'll reverse the dead lands."

We could only hope, but that seemed too easy a solution.

"There's nothing we can do about Lia?" she tried again.

The Royals regarded her with remorse, every mouth clamping shut.

"There is no easy cure, my dear," Queen Isolda said. "I'm afraid we can't help you. She made a choice that she'll need to deal with, unfortunately. I'm very sorry."

My heart sank. How were we supposed to tell Lia? Cameron? He'd be devastated.

"Well, if that is all the order of business we have today, let us adjourn and meet back at the same time tomorrow." King Steafan stood, followed by one after another as they left us distressed and speechless in the great room.

Calliope remained a statue, staring at nothing. I rested my hand on her arm.

"How am I supposed to tell Cameron?" she whispered. Her hand clutched mine, seeking strength with tears in her eyes.

"I'll tell him with you."

"Queen Calliope, Queen Sarai." We swiveled our heads and were met by the most vibrant shade of orange eyes. Cian. He was the last one except for the two of us left in the great room. "I don't believe we've been properly introduced. I am Cian of Elfland."

"Of course." I took his wrist in a Root. "King Cian, it's wonderful to officially meet you. Thank you for your advice in the council. Your sympathy was appreciated."

He offered an amicable smile before glancing around the

empty hall. "Come and meet with Elena in Elfland," he said, hushed. "I think she may have some insight that could be useful."

"Yes. Absolutely," I said. "Anything would be helpful. Thank you, King Cian. When?"

"Tomorrow, after sun up. I'll let Elena know you'll be coming."

"But the wards..." Calliope said, finding her voice.

"We'll have a Keeper there that will be aware of your arrival. You'll have entry immediately."

"Thank you. Thank you so much."

He nodded with another smile and left us. Our eyes met with hopeful curiosity.

TWENTY-FIVE

LIA

CAMERON bounced on his toes in the corner, looking out the window of my bedroom. It didn't face the direction Calliope would return from the Waking Oak, but he remained anyway as if she'd miraculously appear.

I'd gotten up and showered, but I didn't have strength for much else. Even if we could leave the bedroom, I probably wouldn't have.

Cameron ate his breakfast and most of mine when I couldn't finish it. My first few bites turned my stomach, so I couldn't eat the rest. I laid back down and watched him.

"There are lots of other remedies in other kingdoms, right? Faylinn can't be the only one with options."

"Maybe." I used as much optimism in my voice as I possessed, which wasn't much.

He peered over his shoulder. "Don't worry, Lia. I've got a good feeling about this. It's going to be okay."

I offered him a smile but said nothing more.

A gentle knock echoed in the room and Cameron darted to the door to open it. Calliope passed through, her buttery wings fluttering behind her. I sat up, scooting against the headboard.

"How are you feeling today?"

"I'm hanging in there." What I didn't say was I felt worse than before, that I was so weak I almost fainted in the shower.

"We don't have any answers, but Sarai and I are going to Elfland tomorrow."

My forehead furrowed as I sat up straighter. "What?"

"Yeah, it surprised me, too." Calliope plopped down on the chair in the corner of the room, closest to the bed. "King Cian waited until the other Royals left and said they might have some insight."

"So, what does that mean?" I asked.

"We're hoping they have answers about what will help you, but he kept his invitation vague. It could very well be about the dead lands."

Cameron took a hasty step. "But it *could* mean they can help Lia."

"It could, but we won't know anything for certain until tomorrow morning. We were both so taken by surprise we didn't ask any questions."

Blooming hope sprouted in my chest, fighting the despair. "Did King Cian know it was me they might be helping? If that's what this is about."

She nodded. "Your name was mentioned in the meeting, but no helpful solutions were given."

Would Elena be willing to help when she found out it was me that needed aid?

"I've got some dead lands to deal with and a meeting with Lorelle to speak of our harvest. It seems to be dwindling as well. So, I need to go, but just take it easy for today. Okay?"

That wouldn't be a problem. I mean, for me it wouldn't. Cameron on the other hand was going to wear a hole in the wood floors.

"Stay in here, for me," she said, getting up. "Please. When my meeting is over, I'll have Declan come get you guys so you can hang out in the atrium for the rest of the day. I'll have Tania bring lunch there."

When Calliope left, Cameron came and sat on the edge of the bed. He gripped my hand, limp at my side. "See? I told you I had a good feeling about this. They're going to help you and everything will work itself out."

The skeptic in me shunned his words, but I nodded and pulled his head closer to kiss me. Every last kiss was important.

TWENTY-SIX

SARAI

WHEN I returned to Rymidon after the Royal council, Kayne and I stood in the gathering hall discussing a new patch of dead land found by one of Eitri's units on the outskirts. Six. We now had six areas of lifeless landscape. None of them had breached our villages, but they were inching closer. Too close.

The door burst open, and in stormed Marcus with a forest fire lit in his eyes. Before he said anything, I murmured to Kayne. "Will you give us a moment?"

Without a word, Kayne bowed his head and passed through the open door and shut it behind him.

"Something interesting happened today." Accusation rolled off Marcus's words. "My mother returned from a Royal council meeting, a meeting I thought you were going to tell me about."

"I decided not to."

He cocked his head. "Which I find very interesting since we had an agreement. My mother came home talking about your decision with the elves, knew every detail. But what I found most interesting is that she didn't say a thing about me. She informed me of the circumstances as if I were oblivious." Marcus's throat bobbed as he swallowed and his voice quieted. "You didn't tell them about me? Why?"

I shrugged on an exhale. "Kai and I talked about it late last night after the gala. I didn't want to see you get hurt. And I couldn't handle the thought of your mother's face when she found out."

"Kai? Why?" He straightened and stepped closer to me. "I'd have accepted whatever I deserved, you know that. I was supposed to tell the truth, to own my crime."

I pressed my lips together, my eyes softening. "I know, but it doesn't mean you should've had to."

There was one blink and then another. Marcus didn't know what to make of my change of heart. And neither did I. While I forgave him, trusted him, I still wasn't quite ready to let him into my heart. What I said at the Royal gala was true. How could we be together after what we'd done to Rymidon? How could they ever trust in him if he became their king and they uncovered the truth about his part in the slaying of our fae—even if he did believe they were Adair followers? And in turn, they would never trust me for choosing him. No matter how much I might want to.

"So, what's going to happen now?" he asked, taking a step

closer. Then another.

"Calliope is supposed to be able to create another branch on the Oak, one we can ward off and keep the elves imprisoned in for as long as we decide. We're hoping dealing with the elves will make a difference with the dead lands."

He halted. "And if it doesn't?"

"King Cian mentioned Viridessa, too. Seemed to think she was more than a wild tale, but the rest of the Royals brushed him off."

Marcus nodded like he half-expected as much. It was a fable we'd been told as children, after all. "If Viridessa is who came to mind for him, too. She's someone to learn more about, Sarai. Whether or not there is more to the folklore than we know."

"I agree." I nodded. "After the Royal council this morning, King Cian invited Calliope and me to speak with Queen Elena in Elfland tomorrow. If the new branch doesn't help, I think they might be able to."

His brow skyrocketed. "She's letting you pass through the Elfland wards?"

"That's what he said. Though, I guess another aspect we need to consider is, have they gone mad? Has paranoia taken their minds? There is a reason for their wards, after all. For them to believe in Viridessa, but not a single other Royal to even consider it?"

Marcus's eyes grew leery. "No one knows what's going on beyond those wards. Maybe I don't want you going on your own."

"I won't be on my own. Kayne and I'm sure Declan will accompany us."

"I know that should make me feel better, but it doesn't."

"I'll send word as soon as we return," I said. "Cian also mentioned a part of the tale you didn't mention and I don't recall hearing. That Viridessa enters one of us when she wakes to dispense the punishment she sees fit."

Marcus's features hardened, tense and fearful. "So, with the dead lands, she could already be here. In one of the fae in our kingdoms sucking the life from the land."

My breathing turned shallow, accelerated, my heart hammering in my chest as his revelation flipped a switch in my mind. I nodded.

"How would we know?"

"I don't know, but maybe tomorrow Cian and Elena will be more forthcoming without the Royal council mocking his beliefs."

Marcus nodded. "And you'll tell me as soon as you return?"

"Straight away." I smiled to combat his concern, though I couldn't say I wasn't feeling a bit leery myself.

THE moment we stepped through the Waking Oak into Elfland, Calliope and I were met by an infinite rippling wall of white and a single Keeper. He was burly, giant in stature, and adorned in fur boots with a fur wrap atop his shoulders as if it were winter, but it felt no different than spring.

"Queen Calliope, Queen Sarai." He bowed at the waist. "I am Nikolas, personal Keeper to Queen Elena. King Cian said to expect you this morning." Nikolas's gaze shifted behind us. "I'm afraid your Keepers will not be permitted through with you though."

"That's not going to happen," Declan said, stepping beside

Calliope.

"I have to agree." Kayne stepped forward on my right. "Where my queen goes, I go, too."

"And it's very gallant of you, but I'm afraid I don't answer to either of you or your queens. I answer to the King and Queen of Elfland, and I'm only authorized to admit Queen Calliope and Queen Sarai. If that's not possible, then no one enters."

Marcus's fears of me going alone past the wards sparked mine. What if his suspicions had merit?

"That's absurd. What kind of Keeper to the queen would I be if—"

"Declan, just wait here." Calliope held up her hand. "We'll be fine. Won't we?" She eyed the Elflandish Keeper. Being one of the most powerful of fae, she didn't have as much to fear.

"Yes, Your Majesty." He nodded. "Elfland is the safest place you could be in our realm."

My gut was telling me to trust him, but my gut had been wrong in the past.

"See?" Her eyebrow cocked as she peered to her left at Declan.

He crossed his bare muscular arms over his chest, displeased with the arrangement. "If she doesn't make it back, your head is mine."

"Declan, you are not harming a single hair on this man's head. King Cian was kind enough to invite us here. We're guests and they are not the enemy. You know where we are, if we don't return, then you send for us. Maybe we'll like it so much we'll want to stay." She smirked at me.

"Yes, I'll be sure to tell Kai you're moving to Elfland," he quipped.

"Oh, please don't do that without me. I want to see the

look on his face when you do." Calliope laughed.

I couldn't stop my chuckle as we approached Nikolas.

In all honesty, they were there to protect us, but Calliope and I were more powerful individually than both Kayne and Declan combined. The question was, were we more powerful than the other Royals we were headed to see?

"I can guide you through, but you'll need to take my arms." He offered his elbows.

"What a gentleman." Calliope took one side, while I rested my hand on top of his forearm, keeping just enough distance. I wasn't sure why. He wouldn't dare harm me, but my wariness was raised.

A fleet of Keepers met us as we passed through the wards, the kind of numbers I'd only use for the enemy. We weren't the enemy. They didn't think we were, did they? Was this the number of Keepers they always kept at their wards? Or special just for us? If they didn't trust us, why invite us in the first place?

The Keepers were spaced out in five long rows, dressed in the same attire as Nikolas, as a sort of faery blockade. Others grouped in huts of the high-reaching trees, like lookouts, a vivid rainbow of eyes all on us.

We let go of Nikolas and he stepped forward. The fence of fae parted, allowing us passage as he took the lead.

Elfland was unlike Rymidon or Faylinn, flat, not a mountain or grassy knoll in sight, but it was covered with silver-green moss and trees. Beautiful white-barked trees. In the distance, far beyond the dense line of the forest, light gray towers and spires of the Elflandish castle peaked above.

"Well, that was intimidating," Calliope whispered in my ear.

I nodded with a soft chuckle and shot a glance over my shoulder. The Keepers were back in place, all facing the wards, which from this side were transparent. Declan and Kayne waiting near the Waking Oak were visible to all of Elfland. *Clever, Queen Elena. Very clever.*

We walked straight into the tree line and I wished I'd worn a better dress, or even pants. It wasn't just a forest but an obstruction of trees. With the trunks so close together and the ground nothing but moss-covered rocks and a blanket of lush vegetation, my dress was too full to get through. I lifted the hem and gathered it at my side.

Elfland was not a kingdom that could be infiltrated easily. The real question was, was Queen Elena shrewd or paranoid?

A trickling brook weaved through the trees, following our path to the castle, but not a single sound of life, of fae. No houses or pavilions for bartering. Only woodlands and the whisper of nature.

Once we reached the castle, that was all there was. No village or dwellings but a grand fortress. Miles wide and mountain-high stone walls paralleled with the forest we'd left. The crests of the pristine castle were no longer visible this close up.

Calliope and I shared a questioning look. Why were wards necessary when walls like this existed? A basket large enough for a group of fae to stand, descended the wall, landing before us. Nikolas swung open a woven door helping me in and then Calliope.

"Thank you."

He nodded and tugged on a wooden lever that hoisted us up the wall in seconds. When we reached the top, Nikolas stepped off and offered his hand as Calliope and I hopped off onto the broad pathway. Hundreds of Elflandish Keepers spread out along the top of the wall in both directions strapped with bows and arrows. Maybe Calliope and I could learn a thing or two about security measures from Queen Elena. Apparently, one could never be too careful.

The land below came into view and I moved to the other side, overlooking the scene of Elfland. Acres of cottages spanned the whimsical landscape surrounding the most magnificent castle. It was majestic without being ostentatious. The luster of grandeur was difficult to pry my eyes from, like opening my eyes to our world for the first time.

"Queen Sarai."

I swiveled my head to Nikolas, Calliope at his side, waiting to cross the bridge to the castle.

"My apologies." I hurried to them. "I was admiring Elfland. What a beautiful place."

He offered his first smile and it transformed his face into a gentle giant. "I'm very proud to call it my homeland."

Would my fae ever be proud to call Rymidon their homeland? Or would our offenses chase us for eternity?

When I met them at the entry to the bridge, I nearly stopped my progression. At the end of the lengthy platform stood King Cian, standing tall. Beside him stood a woman with long red hair whirling around her face. She wore grand antlers like a crown. Queen Elena.

I was sure I'd have toppled under the weight of the headpiece, but they perched atop her head like an extension of her. With every step, I grew more stunned into silence by her striking beauty and serene confidence.

Her deep red lips formed a gracious smile on her snowy white skin. "My fellow queens. Welcome to Elfand."

Calliope and I offered gentle nods.

"Thank you for having us," Calliope said. "Your kingdom

is…" She lost words.

"It's enchanting," I supplied. "Really and truly."

"Thank you. We take great pride in it." Her hand swept to the side. "Please, come inside. I'll have Misha brew us some pruila tea."

"You had me at pruila." Calliope smiled.

We were escorted to a quaint room lined with shelves of books and bolstered chairs circling a low-set table. It was a charmingly cozy setting, one that eased my nerves.

"I'm going to excuse myself and allow you ladies to talk." King Cian kissed Queen Elena's cheek. "Welcome to Elfland." He bowed his head with a cordial smile and let himself out.

Queen Elena gestured for us to take a seat. Calliope and I sat side by side while Elena took a chair across from us. A gentleman with his hands behind his back next to her seat bent down. Queen Elena spoke quietly in his ear before he left us.

We sat in silence for a few moments that grew strained. Was she waiting for us? For the tea before we began? King Cian said they might have insight, but that could mean anything. Was this about Lia? The blood? The dead lands? I wasn't sure Calliope or I cared, so much as we were intrigued by King Cian inviting us to a kingdom concealed from the rest of our world, and would do anything if this meant saving lives.

Queen Elena stiffly tilted her head. "Pardon me if I'm a little out of practice. I haven't had guests in quite some time."

"No, it's okay," Calliope said. "I guess it's a matter of where to start."

"King Cian invited us, but I'm not sure we know why we're here," I said. "Do you know how we can save Lia? Or the dead lands?"

"Sarai—" Queen Elena stopped herself. "May I call you,

Sarai?"

"Please, yes. That's fine."

"This goes back a bit farther than a simple answer. Are you all right with me speaking of your father?"

The hairs on my arms stood. "He has something to do with this?"

"A bit. Yes."

How? I took a deep breath. "Then, by all means. I'm aware of the kind of man he was, so say what you need to say."

The Sower I believed was Misha returned with the pruila tea, passing us one wooden saucer at a time with delicate little cups. We nodded our thanks and he left us to speak in private.

"Do you two know the story of why Cian and I branched off?"

Calliope shifted, crossing her legs. "Umm...well, there's rumors that you and Adair were meant to bond, but you fell in love with Cian, who wasn't in your colony. So, you created Elfland to be together." She hid behind her teacup when she said, "Some say there was a bit of a lover's quarrel."

Elena laughed with a hint of somber undertones. "Lover's quarrel indeed," she said under her breath. "Are there any stories of why we've created wards around Elfland?"

"Everyone says it's because of Adair," Calliope said. "Is it not?"

"To a certain extent, yes." Elena set her saucer on the squatty table before easing into the back of her wingback chair, her neck elongated, graceful. "I've heard a great deal about the character of women you are, so I trust that certain things I'm about to disclose will be kept quiet, only shared with those it affects."

Calliope and I eagerly nodded. "Of course. You can trust

183

us," I said. They invited us to their kingdom when no one else was allowed; why would we jeopardize that?

Elena took a deep breath. "My sisters and I have always had a stronger ability to heal. I've brought fae back from the brink of death, some whose hearts have stopped beating, though not those that have been dead for long. I'm not sure how or why. Our father had the same ability, as did his mother, and hers before her. But we'd always been cautioned to keep our healing powers to ourselves, only to use them in dire situations, as to not be exploited."

Calliope and I scooted to the edge of our seat.

Elena tipped her head forward. "So, in short, yes. It's possible I might be able to help Lia. Though my ability does not extend to the dead lands."

Hope. There it was again. Though small, it was the first I'd truly experienced it in a long while.

"What does this have to do with Adair?" Calliope asked. "Did he know about your ability?"

She nodded. "Adair and I *were* supposed to bond. I cared about him deeply, may have loved him in a way, but when Cian and I grew to know one another, it became clear, I could never love another the way I love him.

"When Adair found out, he was furious, as you could assume. Since it wasn't allowed for us to bond outside of our colonies, Adair didn't worry about me not being his, but he didn't like the thought of me bonding with him and loving another man. He threatened to kill Cian. And he almost succeeded."

Anger and horror took hold, my heart straining under their grip.

Elena clasped her hands in her lap, her light gray-blue eyes pinched with a painful memory. "Cian and I were supposed to meet earlier that day, but he never came to our spot. When I couldn't find Adair either, I grew frightened. In my gut, I knew something was wrong, so I scoured the forests of Faylinn. Miles and miles and what felt like an eternity until I found them.

"Cian lay bleeding at Adair's feet. There was so much blood, lacerations all over his body. Adair wasn't free of wounds either. Cian had put up a good fight, but when I knelt beside him and pressed my hand to his heart, there was no beat."

Her hands tightened into fists as she blinked back tears. "Adair was there, but I couldn't live without Cian, even if it meant we couldn't be together. I couldn't let him die… So, against my father's advice, I healed Cian. It didn't take but a few of my heartbeats when he gasped for air. But of course, Adair had seen. He knew what I could do, and he was never going to let me go after that. I was a source of power he didn't possess, a source that could be passed down to his children. Adair told me if I tried to leave him, my family's secret would no longer be safe. He wanted to live forever and having me and children, grandchildren who could make that happen was motivation enough."

"So, you went to the Waking Oak?" Calliope asked.

"I went to King Oscar, your grandfather," she looked at Calliope, "and pleaded for his understanding. I loved Cian. I couldn't bond with a man who'd killed him, *tried* to kill him. And what if he tried again?"

Elena sighed. "Your grandfather was a compassionate king, but laws were laws. They couldn't be abandoned simply because one wanted it so, but I knew I wasn't, couldn't possibly be—out of the tens of thousands of fae—the only one. So, I sought more like-minded fae, observed those fighting and shielding feelings or meeting in secret. By the time I was nearing my bond with Adair, only days away, I'd found a thousand fae. *One thousand fae*," she punctuated the words.

"When I approached King Oscar, he still believed bonding within colonies and breeding stronger fae was more important for the future of our kind, so he wasn't willing to budge on the law, but he was willing to let us leave. Of course, that couldn't be publicized, then everyone would try to branch off or try to break laws. So, the two of us went to the Waking Oak together and the branch for Elfland formed, like the land was waiting for me to claim it.

"As you know over a short time, after seeing Cian and me, five more kingdoms broke off. Adair, followed by Eadric of Callastonia, Steafan of Mirrion, Aisling of Oraelia, and Farrah of Aurorali. But it was strange, King Oscar didn't create all the branches. The Waking Oak formed the others. After Farrah, anyone else who'd tried to couldn't. It stopped being possible." Elena shifted her faith-filled stare between us. "There was a plan for our world, someone just needed to be brave enough to rise up."

I'd never heard the story of the Great Divide this way. But why would I have? My father's version was the version he wanted us to hear. One of greed and selfishness, of betrayal and lies. Not hope and change.

"So, why the wards around Elfland?" Calliope asked. "If Adair created his own kingdom, bonded with Saoirse, he couldn't have you anyway."

Elena nodded. "He tried to come for me, several times before he branched off and bound with Saoirse. My Keepers stopped him, but every time he came, he had more and more fae with him, more followers—more that eventually branched off with him. For the protection of myself and my fae, I had to set up the wards."

"And you weren't worried about him sharing your family's secret?"

"I was, but there were more important things to prioritize, like ruling a brand new kingdom." She smiled. "Representing and standing by those who were brave enough to come forward and follow me was more vital than my safety, than my secret."

"But my father is gone now. And I don't think he ever shared your secret. Rymidon isn't a threat, why do you keep them?"

Elena's mouth curved up with a soft sigh. "There is much you two have to learn, my young queens. There is more to fear than a rotten king or war. I have fae who've sought my protection for many, many different reasons. Behind my wards, they are safe from all who try to harm them. If that means we have to ostracize ourselves from the rest of our world, it's a sacrifice we're willing to make."

"So, Elfland isn't just a kingdom, but a safe haven," Calliope said.

"Precisely."

I smiled. "That's a very noble cause, Elena."

"It's what is right." She returned to her tea, confirming our admiration and praise wasn't why she did it.

"What about the dead lands?" I asked. "Are they affecting Elfland, too?"

Elena's eyes swelled with distress. "There were a few areas found at our border. Even my wards are not strong enough to stop the spread of that kind of malicious power."

If Elena could block the lethal poison my father used to harm the other kingdoms, but she couldn't stop this? Was there any stopping it?

Elena shook her head. "Viridessa is going to make those that disrupted the balance of our realm suffer greatly. Until then, nothing can stop the spread of the dead lands."

"So, she's real," Calliope said. "She's not a tale to frighten children?"

"I wish she were only a tale. My ancestors of yore know firsthand the cruelty of her wrath. When my grandfather, six generations ago, transformed to fae without a counterpart, Viridessa butchered his human family and made him watch, before she retreated and returned Faylinn to its full glory."

Calliope and I gasped, processing the horrific scene she painted. As ruthless as Favner or my father had been, they'd never been that wicked. What were we up against?

"He wasn't allowed to try to reset the balance?" Calliope asked. "She just killed his family?"

Elena nodded. "There is no resetting the balance on your own. Viridessa's consequences *are* the reset. If you mess with her creation, she chooses what she considers a comparable punishment."

I tilted my head. "If this is all true, why was the council so skeptical of King Cian's belief in Viridessa? Why weren't they more concerned?"

With a sigh, Elena said, "Faylinn was a much different kingdom one hundred thousand years ago. Hundreds of thousands of faeries resided there. It was much easier to shield the kingdom from the truth, to give a false sense of security. There were too many of us. And the king at the time, King Gabor, kept the knowledge of the dead lands to a select few, so when Viridessa came to serve her retribution, the others were not aware. I only know the reality of the tale because it has remained in my family, the truth passed down one generation to the next."

"Who does she possess?" Calliope asked. "I mean...who does she wake up in?"

"It will be a fae who can sense life and death. Who knows who's born and who dies. She'll know when transformations take place and when they aren't balanced."

"Do you know anyone like that?"

Elena nodded. "There is a family, where the gift is passed down from generation to generation. He or she might not know if Viridessa has taken over. Their body no longer is their own. Brigantia of the Weavers was the host at the time of my grandfather's repercussions, but she had many children, and they had many children. I don't know who possesses the gift now."

"So, it could be a man or a woman?" I asked. "In any kingdom?"

"Unfortunately, yes. The family resided in Faylinn, but after I left for Elfland, I'm not sure if they chose to stay or move on to a different kingdom."

Anyone. They could be anyone. Or anywhere. My heart sank. When would she reveal herself? Would our kingdoms be overrun with dead lands before then? Would we starve to death?

"And what about Lia?" Calliope asked, dread lacing her voice. "She'll be the one to suffer the consequences?"

"If the flawed transformation doesn't kill her first."

Air snatched from my lungs. Calliope and I shared a look. Not only Lia but Cameron would suffer. How were we supposed to save them from this?

"Will you be able to heal her?"

"I've only healed a human who transformed to fae once before, my niece, so I can't promise my powers will work, but I will try."

My heart leaped with relief, though minimal. It was hope enough.

"When? When can we bring her?" Calliope almost shot out of her seat.

"If she's quite ill, bring her at once. I will see what I can do, but if her illness is connected to Viridessa, there will be nothing I can do."

TWENTY-SEVEN

CAMERON

THEY'VE been gone a while," I said, walking up to Kai in the atrium. "Do you think something happened to them in Elfland?"

"Elena wouldn't save Faylinn, just to hurt their queen," he said, but looked just as anxious as I felt as he stood at the window overlooking the entrance to the castle, waiting for Callie's return.

"Yeah, you're right," I said to assure him, just as much to assure me.

We knew next to nothing about this queen and her kingdom except that she shut everyone else out. For all we know, she could've captured Calliope and Sarai behind her wards and refused to give them up, torturing them for information. What kind of information? I didn't know. My mind was spiraling.

"They're back." Kai bolted from the sky-lit room.

"Well," I turned back to Lia laying on the chaise. "Mr. Play It Cool wasn't so confident after all."

She hadn't moved much since we got here. She'd walk a few steps here and there, but then sit down and play it off as simply that, wanting to sit down. Not because she didn't have the strength to stand any longer. The transformation wasn't killing her as quickly as it tried to kill Kai, but it was accelerating, stealing her essence before my eyes.

Lia chuckled, but it lacked her unusual sardonic amusement.

Calliope and Sarai entered the atrium with Kai, Declan, and Kayne, but their faces held little confidence.

"What happened?" I took a step toward them.

Kai closed the door.

"Sit down by Lia." Calliope pulled up a chair to the chaise, Sarai following.

"I don't like the sound of that." I sat at Lia's feet as she adjusted, sitting up straighter.

"There's a lot." Calliope took a deep breath. "Elena was very informative, and while she was helpful, it wasn't all promising."

"Don't try to shield us," Lia said, firm and tough, as I expected. "What did she say?"

Callie and Sarai took turns sharing the creation of Elfland and Elena's healing ability, which encouraged my hope, but then they finished with the story of Viridessa, annihilating it.

"But can we believe everything she said?" I asked.

"Marcus came to me with the Viridessa theory first," Sarai said. "I think it holds merit. It explains everything. The balance has been disturbed and we're already experiencing the effects of that."

"But we have no idea how to fight against something like this. Lia and I are just supposed to wait for this witch to show up and hurt us? Or hurt people we love?" I shot up, dragging my hands through my hair. "There has to be another way."

"And we're going to keep searching for that other way," Calliope said. "None of us want to see either of you at her mercy, but if Viridessa is the creator of our world—the Waking Oak— who knows what kind of capabilities she holds. Not even with every faery's power combined could we defeat her. If she's the only one who can replenish the dead lands or keep them from spreading, what are we supposed to do?"

"So, that's it." My palms slapped my thighs. "Either we comply with her twisted consequences or she kills the realm?"

Calliope and Sarai both opened their mouths to speak, but nothing came out. They looked to one another and then down at their laps.

With a sigh, Calliope looked up. "Cameron, you know I love you." She turned to Lia who hadn't said a word. "And you know I love you. But you both knew there could be trouble if you messed with the balance in nature. Without knowing what that meant, you were willing to risk the consequences. And it's my fault I let you do it." Her jaw set. "Well, Viridessa is the consequence."

"What about the elves?" I asked.

"I'm sure there will be repercussions for them, too. The good news is, we have an answer. It might not be one we like, but we're not in the dark anymore. There is an end in sight."

"But we have no idea when the end will come. We can't figure out who has this ability to recognize life and death?"

"Not yet. But just because Elena didn't know, doesn't mean no one does. Maybe Evan knows or someone else. We might not be able to defeat her, but we can prepare for her."

"And Elena doesn't think what's happening to me has something to do with the balance?" Lia spoke up, her voice quiet.

"She isn't sure, but she's willing to try," Callie said. "That's what we're going to focus on. Getting you better first."

"Why? Why is Elena willing to help me? Does she know who I am?"

"I believe so."

"And she's still willing to help?"

"What does it matter? She's going to heal you." I walked back to Lia and held out my hand. "Can we go now?"

"Cam, they wouldn't even let Declan through. I don't think they'll let you."

"Well, they'll have to." I grabbed Lia's hand and helped her to her feet. "I'm not letting Lia go in without me. What if something happens? What if she can't be healed. Or what if instead of healing, it hinders her more? I'm not letting her out of my sight."

Lia's knees gave out and she fell into my chest. I caught her and swooped down, lifting her into my arms. "She can't even hold herself up. I'm coming."

"Okay." Callie sighed. "Let's see what we can do."

AFTER passing through the Oak, we were stopped by a wall of

white water and a Keeper dressed for the arctic. How was he not sweating his balls off?

"Queen Calliope." He bowed his head.

"Oh good, Nikolas. I was worried I was going to have to beg another Keeper."

He tilted his head.

"This is Cameron." Callie gestured to me carrying Lia. "He's Lia's...match. And he doesn't want to leave her side. Do you think you can grant him entry into Elfland with me? I promise to keep him in line."

Nikolas pinched his mouth to the side, contemplating. "Queen Elena gave word that you were allowed one other companion aside from Lia since Queen Sarai wasn't returning. I assumed it would be King Kai or your Keeper, but..." He gnawed on his lips. "Okay."

She clasped her hands together. "Thank you, thank you, thank you."

"Well." Nikolas looked between the three of us. "Are you well enough to stand?" he asked Lia. "The three of you will need to hold onto me as we pass through."

Lia rolled her eyes, but when I set her down, her legs wobbled. With one arm on the Elflandish Keeper's shoulder, I cinched my arms around Lia's waist and held her to my chest as we walked through.

An army of Keepers met us on the other side of the wards and I gaped. "They've got some tight security," I mumbled.

"This isn't even half of it."

I lifted a brow and Callie nodded for me to follow the Keeper through the thick grove of trees.

"You'll wanna put Lia on your back," she said. "Lia won't make it on foot. And it's a tight squeeze through the forest, so be careful with her. Knowing you, you'll knock her head on a trunk."

"I resent that."

"She's not wrong," Lia muttered.

"Quiet, you."

After crossing the woodlands and rising in a gigantic basket up a colossal stone wall, we arrived at the top, met by even more Keepers. The measures of protection for this place were like freaking Fort Knox. Holy cow. Maybe Lia and I should've lived here.

Carrying Lia on my back to the opening of a solid wood-slatted bridge that led to the castle, Nikolas led the way.

Lia tapped my shoulder. "Let me stand. I don't want to ride piggyback like an invalid when I meet Queen Elena."

Against my wishes, I set her on her feet, but Lia swayed. Looping my arm around her waist, I held Lia upright, her weight leaning on me.

"Don't be stubborn and let me carry you. You'll lose what energy you have left."

"I think I can handle walking across a bridge." Within two steps her knees buckled and she fell to her knees.

"Suck it up, Ginge. I'm carrying you." Bending down, I swept her legs up in one arm, cradling her back with the other. Her unsteady head rolled against my chest.

"Once I'm better, I'm gonna kick your butt."

"Please do, but be gentle," I murmured. "I don't have as much junk in the trunk as you do."

She snorted and swatted my chest.

As we grew closer to the castle, the woman from the painting strode out of two tall double doors, the entry opening as if automatic. Nice little grand entrance. Her antler headdress was gigantic, the portrait not exaggerating in the slightest. And her eyes were such a piercing silver, I couldn't look away. She was even more captivating in person.

Wait. Could I still say 'in person'? Or was the saying 'in faery'? Tomato. Tomahto.

Calliope stood at my side. "Queen Elena, this is Lia. And her match, Cameron."

She didn't say anything for a moment, her head tilting as she studied me. "Cameron?" It was the way she said my name. Not questioning who I was, more asking for clarification, like my name was familiar. Putting a face to a name.

"Yeah, why?"

"I…" Her eyes drank me in, swallowing the length of my body and face, before her hand clasped over her mouth. Strange woman. "It's not important right now. Lia, you don't look very well. Let's try and make you feel better." She looked at me. "Bring her inside."

I didn't hesitate, and Calliope followed close behind. The double doors closed with an echoing thud.

"I can't make you any promises, but I will try my best to help," Queen Elena said over her shoulder as she led us to a room off the foyer.

A plush cream chaise draped in fox fur—at least it looked like the fur of a fox, soft orange and cream and brown, but it was much larger. Two to three times the size of a regular fox. She gestured for me to lay Lia there as she dragged a chair from a table in the corner beside the lounger.

"Why are you helping me?" Lia asked, her voice barely above a whisper.

"You're worthy of saving, are you not?"

"Yes," Callie and I said in unison.

197

"But she'll tell you otherwise," I muttered.

"And why is that?"

"Because I helped Adair infiltrate Faylinn," Lia rasped. "I brought the war upon us."

"Ignore her," I said. *Good idea, Lia. Provoke the woman who divided Faylinn by creating a kingdom just to escape the man you helped.*

"Well, the fact that that makes you feel unworthy leads me to believe you didn't support his cause."

"She didn't," Calliope said, and Lia's eyes glistened as she shook her head.

"My dear, Adair would've invaded Faylinn with or without you. If not you, then another. That's who he was, a destroyer of good things for his own selfish gain. His claws hooked in deep before you realized they were even there."

Lia nodded, a tear escaping her hazel eye. I brushed it away with my thumb and kneeled down on the other side of her. She gripped my hand, or gripped it as tightly as her strength would allow, which wasn't more than a gentle squeeze.

"Okay," Elena said, leaning forward. "You were injected in the heart, yes?"

Lia nodded and I helped pull aside her gray blouse. The black mark flared farther than before, snaking up her collarbone like someone dumped a bottle of ink on her chest.

A hum of disappointment left Elena's lips. "It's worse than I assumed. Even after I try to heal it, it might take some time to recover. Don't expect to leap all the way home. And you might notice some changes in your abilities. Just know it's normal and not to worry."

"I'd settle for walking at this point," Lia teased.

Elena nodded with a gentle smile, then placed her palm over Lia's heart. She took a deep breath and closed her eyes.

Only a second passed when she pulled back with a hiss, like the mark burned her. That wasn't supposed to happen when you tried to heal someone, was it? I'd only seen it done once before by Calliope, and she hadn't shunned away from any pain.

"Are you okay?" Calliope asked, stepping closer.

"I'm okay. Just a little sting. I wasn't prepared for that." Elena replaced her hand on Lia's chest and winced, but held her touch.

My head whipped back and forth from Lia to Elena. I wanted Lia better, but I hated the thought of the one saving her bearing pain. Lia's body jerked, a slight convulsion of her torso, but Elena held steadfast. Closed eyes, creased brow, mouth firm in concentration. And then, the mark shrank, little by little, but my eyes were drawn to Elena's hand quivering over Lia's heart. Black crept up her fingertips, inching along each finger.

Calliope sprang forward. "Elena!"

"No, it's all right." She warded Callie off. "Let me do this." The black continued across her hand and up her arm, her eyes pinched in pain.

Seconds ticked by that dragged like hours before Elena pulled back, chest heaving with labored breaths. When my eyes focused on Lia's chest the blackness was gone, her skin returned to creamy and untouched.

Raising my gaze to Elena, she held her hand now drenched in black like she'd submerged her arm in a bucket of paint.

"Elena, your arm." Calliope took hold of it, rotating it side to side. "Will it go away?"

"I'm not sure." The skin between her eyebrows puckered. "Nothing like this has ever happened to me before."

I hovered over Lia, combing my fingers through her hair. "How do you feel?"

"Okay, I think." She smiled.

"She'll need to rest for a bit."

"Are *you* okay?" I asked Elena.

She waved me off. "I will be."

"But your arm. Why didn't you stop?"

She ignored my question. "I'll have one of my sisters look at it. I should be fine." And gave a reassuring smile.

With my worst fear lessening as Lia's skin lost the ashy tone and warmed to its natural pink color, I asked the question gnawing at my mind. "Do you know who I am?"

Elena's eyes pierced mine. "I do, but my concern is how you became a faery."

"Maybe I should take the lead on that question," Callie said. "Wait, how do *you* know who he is?"

Elena's gaze traced my face, a hint of a smile on her lips. "I was never supposed to get the chance to meet you, but...this life is unpredictable. Such beautiful unpredictability. I'm your great aunt."

Great aunt. Wait. "What? How is that possible?"

"Oh, sweet child," she said. "There is so much you don't know about your lineage. Where do I even begin?"

"Wait, wait, wait. Hold the phone." Calliope spread her arms out, fingers splayed wide. "Cameron has fae blood in his genes?"

Elena clutched her chest with her good hand as she looked from Calliope to me. "I shouldn't be the one to tell you this."

"If not you, then who?"

Her eyes softened, a sheen of tears glistening. "Your mother."

"My mother? My—" I swept my gaze to Callie, eyes wide. What the hell?

"Follow me, dear boy. I think there's someone who would like to see you." Elena placed her hand between my shoulder blades. My mind was reeling, repeating the bomb she detonated seconds ago.

My mother?

Like a distant resonating echo, I heard Callie tell Lia to rest and that we would return for her, but my pulse was pounding so loudly in my ears, it hardly registered.

We left the castle grounds and turned down a couple different gravel roads, traversing deeper into the village. My heart thundered in my chest, a stampede of elephants crushing my lungs. Elena couldn't really be taking me to my mom. It wasn't possible and didn't make a lick of sense. She had the wrong Cameron. She didn't even know my last name. There wasn't fae blood in my genes. I would've known, like Callie. Wouldn't I?

Calliope took my hand and squeezed. I looked at her, too scared to hope, too dazed to think clearly. We rounded a bend, and a small stone cottage with a sloped roof was nestled in a cluster of birch trees. A short white fence bordered the front with a brimming garden and a woman kneeling beside a flower box. Her back was to us, golden hair twisted into a bun at the base of her neck.

As if she felt our presence, the woman slowly turned her head over her shoulder, shielding her eyes from the sun. The memory of my mother was fuzzy, but as my eyes roamed her features, it was clear why Elena had looked so familiar in that painting on Calliope's atrium wall. They shared the same eyes. The same bright gray eyes.

When our gazes locked, my heart stopped. Everything stopped. There was no time or heartbeats. No oxygen or gravity.

"Cameron?" Her breathless gasp carried in the wind.

"Mom?" My voice matched hers.

She bolted up and leaped through the garden, over the fence. In seconds, I was enveloped in her arms, in arms that hadn't held me since the last day she hugged me and sent me off to school nine years ago.

One of her hands stroked the back of my head as her body shook. "My boy. My dear, sweet, sweet boy," she sobbed.

"How is this…" I swallowed, gathering my scattered thoughts.

She pulled back and gripped my face in her hands, head tilted back as I was about a foot taller than her now. Tears leaked down her flushed cheeks as she took in my face. "You're so grown up. That happened so quickly. Too quickly."

Time ran differently in the fae world, so what had our time apart felt like to her? The near ten years it was for me, did it feel like weeks? Months? Years? Without me, without Dad.

"What are you doing here?" she asked.

"What am *I* doing here?" I ran a hand through my hair, disbelief fogging my brain. Reality was now the fairy tale. "What are *you* doing here?"

"I…"

"Senja," Elena rested her hand on my mom's shoulder. "Let's take this inside."

"Okay. Yes. Come inside." She opened a gate in her fence, inviting us through.

I glanced over my shoulder at Calliope. Her eyes widened as she mouthed, "What is going on?"

I shrugged with a humorless laugh, shaking my head. Hell if I knew. I followed my *mom* and Elena into the tiny cottage.

"Can I get you anything to eat? Drink?"

I shook my head, numb, while Calliope politely declined.

We sat next to each other on a periwinkle loveseat under a circular window. There wasn't much to the cottage. A kitchen with a table and a couple chairs, a small bed in the far corner behind an accordion partition, and the couch Calliope and I sat on. My mom lived here? Did she live alone? Did someone share her bed?

I wasn't sure why it was harder to believe my mom was fae and living in Elfland than it was to find out about the existence of faeries through Calliope.

None of this made sense.

My mom dragged the two chairs from the kitchen into the sitting room, offering one to Elena. "Forgive my manners. You are?" She extended her wrist to Callie.

"I'm Calliope, Cameron's best friend."

"Queen Calliope of Faylinn," Elena said.

My mom's forehead creased as she looked between me and Callie. "Finnian's daughter. You two…"

"Let's start with you first." I bent forward, resting my forearms on my knees.

"Right. Well." She took a seat in the wooden chair across from Calliope and me. "Where to begin."

"How about with how you're a faery."

"I could ask you the same thing." Her lips pursed in such a familiar reprimanding facial expression. "But, no, I think we need to go further back than that."

Sharing a look with Elena, my mom began, "Six generations ago, your grandfather, Arthur, was a human who was kidnapped and injected with fae blood."

"The first human transformed to faery?" Calliope gasped and looked to Elena. "The one who had to face Viridessa."

Elena nodded, solemn.

"After his family was slaughtered, he found love with a woman named Dorene. Our family lived for centuries in Faylinn until the Great Divide when Elena created Elfland.

"Lilja, my mother, couldn't follow Elena into Elfland because she needed to remain in Faylinn with her husband, Leon. He refused to leave Faylinn, and since bonds are forever, she couldn't leave him. He'd never been a pleasant man, but when your grandmother had vocalized her desire to leave with her sister, he grew increasingly possessive and violent toward her. For many years she endured, but it became too much. She tried to escape to Elfland, but..."

Elena filled in, "At the time, my wards were fresh. I was new to creating them and it took time to understand how they worked. Initially, wards are permanent. There is no going in or out to preserve their strength and make them last. I didn't know Lilja needed me. If I had, I never would've set up the wards in the first place. Or I would've taken her with me. Leon be damned."

"So, what did she do?" Calliope asked.

"The only other thing she could think of. She transformed into a human," my mom said. "She was aware of our heritage, it hadn't been a secret—just kept in the family—and had faith the transformation would succeed. And it did. She met your actual grandfather and had me.

"But Leon didn't stop looking for her. It took him many, many years, but he found her when you were about eight years old and killed her."

She'd told me my grandma died of a heart attack.

"Being the planner your grandma was—in case he ever came looking for her—she wrote a letter to me explaining everything and said if I ever found myself in danger to seek out

Finnian Holbrook and find my way to Elfland."

"You knew my father?" Calliope gasped.

"Only briefly. My mother was actually the reason your family wound up in Walhalla. Before Finnian transformed into a human, he'd found out why Lilja disappeared and sought her out, wanted to make sure we remained safe. 'Once a Royal always a Royal,' he'd said."

Calliope's gaze hit the side of my face, but I was taking in every last drop of information. I needed more before I could say anything in return.

"After she passed," my mom continued, "I found the letter among her belongings when your grandpa asked me to go through them. Of course, I thought she'd been losing her mind, talk of a faery realm and transforming into a human, but when Leon showed up at our house, his appearance was more than convincing."

"He found you, too?" Calliope asked. "You saw him?"

"Several times, actually. The first time I was in the backyard, in our vegetable garden when he appeared. He was surprised I could see him and so was I. I didn't understand what this strange bare-chested man was doing in my backyard. At first, I thought I was seeing things, but then he spoke. Leon was a twisted individual. He wanted to take me back to Faylinn as his bride." She shrugged with a sad smile. "I looked a lot like my mother."

"How did you get away from him?" Calliope scooted to the edge of the cushion.

"Thankfully, I was close enough that I raced into the house and locked him out. He was cocky enough that he didn't think I'd need convincing, so he was surprised I fled. When he tried to enter, the door weakened him, and he retreated to the forest."

"But he came back," Calliope said.

My mom nodded. "He'd hover in the forest behind our house, day after day, his pointed ears visible, dressed in trousers and nothing more, a vine winding up his arm, wanting me to know he was there, wanting me to know I couldn't escape him."

A Faylinnian Keeper.

"Leon returned several times while Cameron was at school, waiting to catch me outside again, with the aversion to metal weakening his strength. After that, I knew I needed help, I needed to take a leap of faith."

"But how did you get to Elfland?" Calliope asked. "You were a human, for one. You'd never have made it through the wards without help. And the only way in is through Faylinn, and if I'm calculating the timeline right, Favner was king. He never would've let you leave Faylinn. You'd have been seized by Keepers almost instantly, if not Leon himself."

My mom nodded. "I had a bit of help, yes. That's where your father came in. Finnian said he couldn't come with me, but he gave me a detailed map and said there'd be someone near the entrance that would help me, that I needed to give his name and I'd be taken care of.

"There wasn't anyone there. I followed his instructions down to the boulder shaped like an old man's face, but I couldn't find the Hedge or anyone for miles. I wandered around, thinking maybe I'd taken a wrong turn or misread something when a handsome young Keeper named Declan found me lost in the woods."

"Declan?"

"Do you know him?"

"He's my personal Keeper. He watched over me for years, protecting me from Favner."

"Well, when I explained what my mother had written in her letter and mentioned Finnian's name, he snuck me into Faylinn and through the Waking Oak."

Elena said, "By then I had a Keeper at my wards who informed me who was seeking entrance into Elfland. I was able to help transform her into fae as one of my own had been wanting to transform to human for quite some time and needed a counterpart."

I took a deep breath, falling back against the couch, and ran my hand through my hair. My head hurt. This was a lot to take in.

"What happened to Leon?" Calliope asked.

"I don't know. After I spoke with Finnian, he said he'd make sure nothing happened to my family."

"Do you think he killed him?" she asked.

My mom shook her head. "I really don't know. Once I entered Elfland, I was safe. He never came looking here."

"I had no clue," Calliope uttered and turned her attention to me. "If my father knew who you were, why didn't he ever say anything to me?"

That question was the last on my mind. We moved after my mom left, not out of Walhalla, but out of the home I was born in. I never understood why. Was Finnian the reason? Moving us to protect us? I'd always resented my dad for that, worried my mom would never be able to find us if we didn't live in the same home.

And she'd turned to fae, that was why my father stopped mentioning her and buried himself in work. He stopped remembering her.

Now he'd stop remembering us both.

I had fae blood, that was why I didn't—couldn't forget her.

207

Why I couldn't forget Calliope. Why I remembered everything about Lia and Faylinn. Why the transformation didn't have any adverse effects on me. This form lived deep in my veins.

"Why didn't you bring me with you? Or move us to a different state? Across the country? Around the world? I don't know, how could you leave me?"

Tears poured down her cheeks. "I'm so sorry, Cam. I wanted to come back, after I was settled and knew what my mother had said was true, I wanted to come back for you and your father, but there was the matter of Favner and the wards he'd put in place. There was no way for me to travel back through the Waking Oak without getting caught. I couldn't send word to Declan because all the Keepers were under Favner's Supremacy. I wanted to keep you safe. You and your father's safety were all I could think about. I thought my presence only brought you more danger, that he wouldn't stop coming after me, no matter where we moved."

"And you never came back to check on us? Never wondered if we were okay?"

"Of course I wondered. I worried every day, but I couldn't risk leaving Elfland after that. Favner would've captured me. And what if Leon caught wind of my presence in the fae world? I would've wound up like your grandma."

"And what if he came after us next?"

"That has been my greatest fear every day since."

I wanted to understand. I wanted to forgive her, but I couldn't. I couldn't wrap my head around any of this.

She reached forward. "I never stopped loving you, missing you, wishing I could bring you here."

"But then after, when Callie took over Faylinn, you couldn't come for me then?"

"Adair," Calliope murmured under her breath. "There is the whole Adair bit and the war. We've kind of had a lot going on, Cam."

"That was my fault," Elena said. "I didn't trust Adair. It was more important for my family to remain here and safe than to take any chances, so I kept them behind the wards."

"How are *you* here?" my mom asked. "When did you become fae?"

When I didn't respond right away Calliope answered for me. "It's a long story, really, but the short version is he fell in love with Lia, or you may know her as Magnolia, who'd been injected with the fae blood by the elves. There was blood left over, so...we used it on him as well."

"You could've died," my mom said.

"It wouldn't have been the first time in this world."

Her head whipped back. "What are you talking about?"

"I was there, during the Battle of Faylinn. Adair had me kidnapped to use me against Calliope, so that she'd comply with him to bond with Sakari."

Her body deflated, shoulders curling in, her head hanging as more tears appeared. "This whole time I thought I was protecting you, you were in the thick of it."

"Funny how life works."

"And now Viridessa." My mom's eyes shot to Elena, who nodded. "How can we protect my son from her?"

"We can't."

"We have to." She gripped Elena's hand on the armrest of her chair. "Elena, you can't let my son suffer at her hand. *Please*."

"It's not my choice, Senja. I have no power against her. None of us do. You *know* that. I would love to protect him, and I would in a heartbeat, if it were possible."

"But there has to be something. *Anything!*"

Elena could only stare with remorse. Silence dragged on while we soaked in everything thrown at our feet. My lineage. The helplessness of the situation.

Calliope cleared her throat. "We should probably go check on Lia."

Lia. "Yeah." I abruptly stood.

"Where are you staying?" my mom asked, darting to her feet.

"We have a safe place in Faylinn."

"Is that wise?" she asked. "With all the history with Magnolia."

"What do you know about Lia?" Maybe I should've kept the bite out of my tone, but I was tired of everyone's unfair opinion of her.

"Enough to know the fae world isn't safe for her, or you, if anyone knew you were human before."

"We're managing."

My mom turned in her seat, gripping the armrest of the chair Elena sat in. "Elena, can they not stay here?"

"This is a place of sanctuary. Too many others rely on me. If I could protect everyone from Viridessa, I would. But I can't, and I can't allow Viridessa here, not when I have so many others to protect. It would be unwise to bring them here."

"I think I need some space from this place anyway. Cal, can we go?"

"Yup." She hopped up and we headed for the door.

"When will I see you again?" My mom's voice stopped me with my hand on the handle of her front door.

I paused. "I don't know. I just...I need some time to digest all of this." I glanced over my shoulder.

She hadn't aged a day since I last saw her, her face exactly the same as I remembered. My mom swallowed back emotion and nodded. "Okay."

When the door shut behind us, I tore out of the garden, sprinting to get to Lia.

Calliope met my pace. "You all right there? That was a lot to take in."

"Can we just not talk about this yet?"

"Sure thing. We'll get Lia and head back to Faylinn. I have a prison branch to try and create, anyway."

I snorted. What was this world we chose to live in?

TWENTY-EIGHT

SARAI

WHEN I returned to Rymidon after speaking with Cameron and Lia, I sought solace in my tower, gazing out the window, admiring the lush green mountains. Everything Elena said about Viridessa was disheartening and troublesome. She could be here in Rymidon right now and I wouldn't know. I had to simply sit back and continue to watch my lands die, my fae suffer.

Kayne entered the study with a knock. "Durin, Callisonia's adviser, contacted us to see if you'd be available to have dinner with Tomas this evening."

Tonight? After the day I'd had, my heart and mind were

exhausted, but maybe a dinner with Tomas would be a good distraction. If I stayed here, the conversations of the morning would be on a continual loop.

"Tell him I'll be there."

"Are you sure?" Kayne asked. "You look as though you should lie down for a bit, My Queen."

"And maybe I will, but I can still go." I stepped away from the window. "How was the harvest today?"

"Less than yesterday. Enough to go around with rationing, but it's getting scarce. There might be some bellies that go hungry tonight. I've managed to get the Sowers to agree with dispersing some to the elves, but Guthron was not happy with their portion."

"Was he informed that his transformations might have something to do with the lack of crops?"

"No, Your Grace. Would you like us to inform him of that?"

I shook my head. "I should be the one to speak with him. He'll need to know about Viridessa, as well."

"Would you like to go to him now or...?"

I shook my head. "I actually have another assignment for you. And you alone. Will you see what you can find out about a family with the ability to recognize life and death? They know when fae die and when they are born. Or rather, it would be one person in the family, but the trait has been passed down for generations."

"Are they Rymidonian?"

"They might be, but they could be in any other kingdom. Male or female. You don't need to bother with Faylinn or Oraelia. Just start with our kingdom and we'll go from there."

I'd need to talk to Marcus as well, and hope that the other

Royals would start taking Viridessa seriously.

I did need to lay down though. Some sleep would help me think more clearly. "Will you have Jessamine wake me in time to get ready for the evening?"

Kayne nodded and bowed at the waist before stepping aside so I could leave for my bedchamber.

WHEN we arrived in Callastonia, Prince Tomas had a carriage waiting for us. Two animals I wasn't familiar with were attached to the front. They were large, sleek beasts with brown and cream stripes along their coarse fur. Two black horns curled around their heads like hooks.

"Queen Sarai."

At one side of the carriage, a Callastonian Keeper stood at attention, holding open a door. "Prince Tomas is expecting you."

"Thank you." I took his hand as he helped me into the carriage. Galdinon stepped in behind me, sitting across the small space. Our knees knocked.

Before Kayne followed, the Keeper said, "It's good to see you, Kayne. Under less…tense circumstances."

Guilt flickered in Kayne's eyes before he blinked it away. Tense circumstances?

"Indeed. We'll have to catch up at a more appropriate time. I'd like to…make amends."

The Callastonian nodded with an understanding curve of his mouth, not quite a smile, but amiable nevertheless.

Was this something personal or…

The door closed with the two of us inside. "What was that about?"

"Conor was…is a good friend of mine. We haven't seen each other since the Battle of Faylinn." Kayne looked away, out the window at the rich landscape passing by.

The Battle of Faylinn. It clicked. The same battle my father forced his Keepers to fight—against friends, distant family members. Who had they killed that they once knew? That they'd cared for? Loved?

"I don't think I've ever apologized to you, either of you."

Kayne's gaze slid in my direction. "Apologized for what?"

"For what my father did to you."

His brow furrowed. "Because you have nothing to apologize for. You didn't do anything."

"I know, but he's still my blood. The fallout of his actions are mine to bear. He's not here to make things right, but I am."

Kayne's shoulders fell as he sighed. "My Queen, I have never, nor will I ever hold his actions against you."

"Nor I," Galdinon said.

"We've known you long enough to know his evil never touched you."

I nodded, but their words did nothing to ease the pain my father caused. I'd forever carry the weight of his actions. It was my burden to bear, always there, encouraging me to make the right decisions for my fae, better decisions than he made.

We rode in silence along a smooth road through the trees until the Callastonian castle appeared around a curve. Though not wide, it was tall. Five towers soaring to the skies as the sun set behind, reds and pinks radiating around the light stone.

Pulling right up to the iron gates, they opened and Prince Tomas was standing at the grand castle entrance with a couple of his personal Keepers.

He opened the door, helping me down. "You're here."

215

"Was I not supposed to be?"

"No, of course. It's just…I'm happy you came." Prince Tomas leaned in and kissed my cheek.

Oh, we were there, that level of familiarity. Okay.

"Dinner should be served as soon as we get inside. You made perfect timing."

When we reached the dining hall, the long table was overflowing with lavish floral centerpieces and ornate candelabras from one end to the other, as if for a large dinner party. But our two lone place settings were the only ones, side by side, at the center of the table. A bit extravagant for only the two of us, but if Prince Tomas was trying to make an impression, he made a grandiose one.

"Conor, Lorcan, Gerard," Prince Tomas addressed his Keepers. "You may go."

They slipped out the door without a word or nod. Not that Prince Tomas was looking at them anymore to acknowledge one. His eyes were searching the room, like he was looking for someone else.

Galdinon and Kayne hovered by the door, watching the Callastonian Keepers exit. "Will you be all right, My Queen?" Kayne asked.

I'd been alone with Marcus dozens of times. I could handle one dinner with Prince Tomas.

"Thank you, Kayne. I'll be fine." I smiled. "Reconnect with your friends." They deserved that much.

With a bow, they followed the other Keepers out.

Prince Tomas pulled out a chair for me, gliding it back in once I was seated, and then took the chair beside me. It was closer than I was comfortable with, but I let it slide. We wouldn't have been able to see each other across the table with the enormous flower arrangements down the center anyway.

"Where is the food?" he muttered. "Orla!" His voice rose with an irritated edge.

A moment later, a woman rushed in, her rich moss wings fluttering rapidly. With wide eyes, she curtsied. "Yes, Your Excellency."

"Fiona was supposed to have everything ready. Where are our meals?"

Her hands knotted together. "They'll be out shortly. She's in the middle of adding the final touches, making everything perfect as you requested."

He didn't say more when he gave her a curt nod and she rushed out of the room.

Turning in his seat, Prince Tomas leaned into me with his elbow on the table. "Sometimes the help just can't be controlled." He shrugged with an eyeroll and a smile as if to soften his words, but they were less than charming and certainly not humorous.

I shifted back a fraction, hoping not to offend him, but needing a respectable space between us. "I don't mind. I'm sure it'll be delicious and worth the wait."

"Indeed." Prince Tomas's eyes traveled down my body and back up as he bit down on his bottom lip.

Offering an uncomfortable smile, I swiped the goblet of wine on the table and took a drink. Maybe I should have had Kayne and Galdinon stay.

No, that would have been silly. I was reading into his answer. Surely, he wouldn't forget his decorum with another Royal—and a queen, no less. One he was trying to impress enough to bond with.

Prince Tomas shifted back in his seat, giving me space

again, and I breathed easier. But then his arm stretched along the back of my chair.

"Tell me more about yourself. I'm afraid what I know is solely from word of mouth."

"Well, Prince Tomas," I said, reminding him of his place. "What would you like to know?"

"Oh, we can forget the formalities. Just call me Tomas. Or Tommy. That's what my friends call me."

"Tomas, okay." I lifted a slight smile. I didn't want to give him the wrong impression, but I didn't hate the sound of friends. I had so few.

"Do you have any nicknames?" he asked.

Only one. Raven. And it hadn't been used in years. Not since my mother, who used to call me Raven because of my black hair, but I wasn't ready to share that with him. Not even Calliope or Marcus knew.

"No, not really. Sarai will have to do."

His lips curled into a flirtatious smirk. "That's perfectly fine with me. Sarai is a beautiful name. Beautiful name for a beautiful woman."

"Thank you." I took another sip of my wine, busying my hands. He was only trying to compliment me. There was no reason to feel uneasy. Though, somehow, if the words had come from Marcus, I knew they'd have sounded more genuine, less sleazy.

Where was the food? And what happened to the pleasant vibes Tomas was emitting the other night?

Just then the door swung open and two women flitted in, wings flickering as if they'd been dashing through the kitchen like their lives depended on it. Orla set a plate in front of me and I thanked her, while the other, I was assuming was Fiona, placed

Tomas's plate in front of him. Her cheeks were flushed, her pearly pink eyes strained.

Fiona apologized for taking so long before they curtsied and scurried from the dining hall. Tomas didn't thank her or accept her apology, not that she had any reason to apologize. There was hardly an acknowledgment of their presence at all. How a Royal treated their staff said a lot about them, and I was quickly realizing Tomas wasn't who I thought he was. This was going to be a shorter evening than I anticipated. We clearly were not a good match. The last thing I wanted was to waste more time than necessary when my kingdom needed me more.

Our meal was eaten with intermittent conversation, but mostly I was counting down the time to leave. I had much more pressing affairs to attend to.

"Are you close with your siblings?" More than anything it was a topic to fill the silence, but I also hoped he might change my mind about this evening's impression of him.

"Closer with Emlyn than Tadhg. The perfect son and future heir to Callastonia is a busy man, taking on new roles and catering to my father's every whim doesn't leave much time for brotherly bonding." He rolled his eyes. "I'm sure you dealt with that quite a bit with Skye and Sakari, especially Skye."

Though he wasn't wrong, it was the way in which he said it. As if we need to criticize our siblings in order to find common ground. He'd get no such connection with me.

I squared my shoulders. "Skye looked up to my father, yes. And Sakari was an honorable man. Fought for what he believed was right until the very end. I was blessed to have him as a brother."

Tomas's eyes widened. Surprised I'd spoken up for myself? Or embarrassed he overstepped?

"Yes, of course. I didn't mean anything by it. I'm sorry." Though his apology seemed less than sincere.

"It's all right." I gave a close-lipped smile, setting my fork down, my plate clean. "Well, that meal was lovely. May we call Fiona in here, so I might thank her properly?"

He waved away my request. "That's not necessary. I'll tell her."

Somehow, I doubted that.

"Well, in that case, I think it's time I head back to Rymidon." I stood, stepping around the chair and sliding it back in. "Thank you for the invitation. Callastonia is beautiful."

"Wait." Tomas darted up, grabbing my hand. "Leaving so soon? I haven't even given you a tour yet."

"Maybe another time. I really should go. My kingdom is in a bit of a fragile state at the moment, and I hate to leave them for long." Fragile state barely explained the depth of our troubles. With the elves and the crops, Viridessa, and Cameron and Lia. We were in tatters. And I didn't care to share any of that with Tomas.

My decision solidified. I wouldn't bond with him. Ever.

I tried pulling my hand away, but his grip tightened.

"I think you have a few minutes to spare." Tomas backed me against a wide pillar. My head hit with a *thump*. Fear slithered beneath my skin. "We should get to know each other better, on a more intimate level. A bond between us would be rather favorable. Don't you feel it? We have so much in common."

"I don't think we do, actually." I shrunk away from him, turning my head. "I think you've gotten the wrong impression. I'm really sorry, Tomas, but I don't think we're a good fit. If you'll just—"

"No? You don't think? Because I do." His body weighed

against mine, pinning me against the hard wood as his head leaned into mine. "You're exquisite, Sarai."

The hairs on my arms raised, my body tensing. "What are you doing?"

"Indulging. It's only fair since Marcus already got a taste."

"What? What are you talking about?"

"You don't need to play coy with me. Just let this happen, Sarai. I think you'll be pleasantly surprised. Most women love me, thank me when we're done. You'll see."

My wings sharpened, sensing the change in Tomas. "No. Stop it. This night is over. I'm not going to bond with you. I will *never* bond with you." I wriggled my arms and shoved against his chest, but he didn't budge. "Get off me, Tomas. *Now.* Before I scream."

"Oh, I don't think you will. You see, I seem to have a few little secrets I can unleash, if you do."

My eyes held all the questions.

And he smiled, triumphant, truly arrogant. "The real reason the elves live in Rymidon. How Prince Marcus helped slay your fae. The scroll. Cameron and Lia."

Every muscle tensed. What did he know of...? How did he...?

"Did you think you were careful at the Royal gala? If you didn't want to be heard, slipping a few feet away from the doorway of the banquet hall wasn't the best way to keep your secrets quiet."

Tomas heard? He listened to Marcus and me? Did anyone else hear?

"Aligning yourself with the man who betrayed your kingdom. What a wicked woman." He ran his moist lips across my cheek and back to my ear. "What would your kingdom say?"

I flinched.

"See? We're the same, you and I. Deviant little hearts that we keep hidden. No one else would understand, but I do." His tongue flicked my earlobe. "Don't worry. We'll just keep this naughty secret between you and me."

"No, stop it." I wasn't above begging. Every inch I gained away from him closed as he found a way to meet every part of my body. "Please. *Please* stop."

"I'm not good enough for you? Is that it? The daughter of a tyrant and mass murderer. Can't deem my presence worthy? I'm the best you'll get, sweetheart."

My head whipped forward, my eyes slits of offense. "Excuse me?"

His head leaned into the curve of my neck and he licked a line to my earlobe before he bit it. I cringed. Why was this happening? What had I done to deserve this? With one hand he squeezed my jaw and forced his lips on mine.

I shook my head, trying to disentangle from his grip. "Please. Please, don't."

"It's okay." The dark blue of his eyes deepened to black. "You'll like this. I promise."

Tomas pressed his hand over my mouth, muffling my shrill, "*no,*" as he ripped the neckline of my dress. His mouth bent down and tears fell as his tongue met my skin. I screamed, but the sound was stifled, a fractured whisper.

This wasn't happening. Where was Kayne? Galdinon? Why weren't they coming for me?

I struggled beneath his hold, but the weight of his body against mine was too strong. I couldn't fight him off. Tomas used his other hand to lift the heavy fabric of my dress, shoving his knee between my legs to keep me in place, and unbuttoned his pants.

Shaking my head, I pleaded with my eyes, but his stare was focused on my body, not my face.

"You want me." Tomas rasped, staring at my bare chest. "No need to deny yourself."

The scrape of a door cut through his last word. "Oh, I'm sorry, Your Excellency. I didn't mean to disturb you."

I didn't know if it was Orla or Fiona and I didn't care, but all she could see was Tomas's back. His broad figure covered me just enough that she couldn't see the horror in my eyes, couldn't see his hand over my mouth.

"I was coming to clear the dishes. I didn't think you were still in here."

"*Leave*, Orla," he growled. "This instant."

Feet shuffled and the door snicked shut. *NO*.

Tomas released a heavy, aggravated sigh. "It's just as well." He let down the skirt of my dress as his lips slid up my chest. I trembled with revulsion. "Who knows who else might walk in on our little tryst and ruin all our fun?"

"I won't remain silent forever, Tomas." My voice shook.

I was going to be sick. The contents of my stomach rolled. Everything hurt. My body. My bones. My head, heart, skin. I didn't even know skin could hurt. Tears soaked my face.

Tomas kept his body pressed against me as his wet mouth skimmed the shell of my ear. "Won't you? And who exactly do you think they would believe? The daughter of Adair, the betrayer of our realm?" Tomas laughed, a terse, mocking laugh. "Or the son of Isolda the gracious, the brother of Callastonia's future beloved king?"

I wanted to bite back, to prove him wrong, but I couldn't. My kingdom's transgressions had fallen on me over and over. I was continually judged based on my father's actions.

Tomas grabbed a handful of me. This time I was able to get an arm free and my palm cracked across his cheek.

A villainous grin turned his mouth and he removed his hand from me, snatching my wrist. "Save some of that for next time. It's more pleasurable that way." He leaned back in and bit my neck. "Dream of me."

When Tomas stepped back, leaving me alone in the dining hall, I sunk to the ground, covering my bare chest and cried.

I'M not sure how long it took to collect myself. I was in the middle of fashioning a shawl from part of the tablecloth to cover my torn dress when Kayne entered. He opened his mouth as if to address the room but stopped short.

When he took note of my shredded bodice and tear-stained face, he rushed to my side. "What happened? Did Prince Tomas do this to you?"

"I...I..." I was at a loss for words. I cleared the emotion from my throat to try again, but it was useless.

Thunderous rage boiled in Kayne's eyes. "My Queen, tell me who did this so I can burn his body alive."

"I can't..."

"What do you mean you can't?" When I couldn't meet his stare, Kayne's tone gentled, "Sarai, look at me. It was Tomas, wasn't it? Where is he?"

My eyes betrayed me. I was never much of a liar.

Kayne spun on his heel, charging for the door.

"No!" I shouted in a panic, halting his steps. "No, he knows. Tomas knows about Marcus, the scroll, Cameron, Lia. All of it." My voice cracked, tears streaming from my eyes again. "I just...you can't do anything. Keep this between us, Kayne. Promise me."

His head shook. "I don't think I can do that."

"You must. As your queen, I'm telling you, you must."

"But the Royals, you just held a council divulging everything. We can go to them and they'll deal with Tomas. They'd never allow this. Queen Isolda would be appalled."

"The Royals don't know about Marcus or Cameron, and they never can." Keeping my bodice closed, I said, "Bring me my cloak so I can cover up and we can leave."

If it were possible steam would've pooled from his nostrils and ears. "He won't get away with this."

Maybe, maybe not. "For now, he has to."

TWENTY-NINE

LIA

HOW are you feeling?" Cameron's fingers caressed the outside of my delicate wings wrapped around my torso. A shiver trembled through my limbs at his soft, sensitive touch.

"I've been better, but I'm definitely not where I was before Elena helped me. With time, I think I'll get back to my original self. Or at least whatever self that might be with those possible changes she spoke of."

"I hope so." His lips brushed my cheek, a whisper of a kiss as he cinched his other arm around my waist, curling me into his body. "It's such a relief you're okay."

Okay was a relative term. Was I physically doing better? Yeah, sure. Better than before. But the threat of Viridessa loomed, like an ominous tempest. Death by flawed transformation seemed a lot more humane than the uncertainty of Viridessa's vengeance.

I finally understood how humans felt when they learned that we were real, that the fairytales they'd been told all their lives weren't all false. A chilling fable my parents used to tell me was coming to life and would hunt me and the man I loved down. She'd make us atone.

"How are you doing with…" Did I dare breach the subject? After Calliope told me on the way back from Elfland, not a word had been spoken of Cameron's mother for the rest of the day. "…with finding your mom?"

His fingers stilled. A few faint breaths passed his lips across my neck before he said, "It doesn't seem real. I don't know what to think."

"It's a shocking revelation, for sure."

The stroking of my wings resumed as he said, "I get why she would think leaving would protect my dad and me, but what if she'd brought us with her? We could've all still been a family. And I wouldn't have needed to use that blood because I'd already have been fae." Cameron went quiet. "But then, you and I never would've happened."

And I wouldn't have had Cameron to help me navigate the human world when I returned. I probably wouldn't have stuck around, having moved around wherever I could've survived. Guthron's elves might've never found me. And Viridessa wouldn't be coming after us but only after Guthron.

"Even after all of that, I'm having a very difficult time regretting our choices." His nose followed the path of my jaw where he placed a tender kiss below my ear.

I trembled. "Would your dad have believed your mom? Gone with her on this insane whim that an old faery king was going to help keep her safe from your grandmother's ex-husband who now wanted to bond with your mom, and hide away in a magical faery realm through an invisible wall?"

He snorted.

"I don't mean to make light of it, but you don't think he would have thought your mom was certifiably psychotic and stolen you away to protect you from her?"

A chuckle rumbled through his chest, vibrating my back. "I don't know. Maybe," he said. "I believed Callie."

"Who had wings and pointed ears to prove it."

His amusement continued. "Yeah. That was a bizarre day," he said. "What I don't get is why my mom or I didn't get ears or anything like Callie did."

I interlaced my fingers with Cameron's splayed on my stomach. "Well, Calliope is a True Royal, and even Finnian wasn't sure if her fae features would form. From what I understand, she was the first of our kind. The Waking Oak called her to return to Faylinn to save it. She was special.

"Most faeries that transform to human don't have fae offspring. Or rather, don't have children that grow fae features. They remain human, or the fae blood remains dormant, anyway."

"So, if Viridessa created the Waking Oak and the Waking Oak was calling to Callie, does that mean Viridessa was calling to her?"

The hairs on my arms stood. "I don't know. I guess it could be possible. Maybe Viridessa isn't all bad but reacts in anger when her creation is threatened. Our realm is essentially her child. That's something in everyone's nature. To protect what

228

they love, what we create. I think that's all she's doing. A mother protecting her offspring."

"But to make that man watch as she murdered his family. That feels a bit extreme."

"I never said she was rational. She's an all-powerful being. Do you expect a slap on the wrist?"

"No, but at least the chance to right my wrongs. Punishment should match the crime. And from what I understand, my however-many-greats grandpa didn't make the choice. He was kidnapped as an experimentation. And yet, *he* was still the one to pay the steep price."

"There might have been more who suffered, the ones who kidnapped him. Elena just only knows about your family."

"Yeah, maybe. But it doesn't make it right."

"No, it doesn't."

CAMERON and I joined Kai, Calliope, and Declan at the Waking Oak the next morning. It was time for Calliope to see what she was really made of.

"So," Cameron said, "While we wait for this witch to show, you're going to create another kingdom branch or whatever on the Oak, and Sarai is just going to banish the elves. And we're going to hope it makes a difference. Can you *do* that?"

"Well, I'm going to try." Calliope shrugged. "The Royals seemed to believe I was capable. I suppose there's a first time for everything."

Kai leaned his shoulder against the trunk and crossed his ankles, stuffing his hands in his front pants pockets. "The last time you connected with the Oak, you nearly died."

Calliope rolled her eyes. "I passed out from exhaustion. There's a difference. I'm half-human, cut me some slack."

Kai folded his arms. "Forgive me for being concerned about my wife."

"Kai, in a matter of like twenty-fours I'd turned nectar into rain and drenched all of Faylinn, fought and killed countless Rymidonians, and lost my father. Of course restoring the Waking Oak on top of all that was going to affect me." She placed her hand on his cheek. "I'll be okay. It's just a branch, right?"

His hand covered hers and he nodded once.

"Okay. Let's do this."

Calliope stood at the base of the Waking Oak and pressed her hand against the gnarly wood. The rest of us moved up on the grassy hill of the ravine, silent. Declan and Kai's heads bent together as they whispered low enough that Cameron and I couldn't hear.

We waited for a good ten minutes as she remained, eyes closed tight, fingers gripping the bark. As time passed, tension thickened.

Nothing happened. Not a creak of wood, a rumble of the earth, even a rustle of the leaves.

Calliope stepped away and threw her head back with a frustrated growl.

"Maybe you need to concentrate harder," Cameron joked.

Poor timing. I elbowed him in the side as Kai shot him a glare.

"Your commentary is less than helpful, Cam," Calliope muttered, eyes on the Oak.

"Sorry. I'll zip my lips."

"Wise choice," I said under my breath.

She rolled her shoulders back and tried once more, but just

as the dead lands were unchanged by her touch, so was the Waking Oak.

"I can't do it," she cried, kneeling at the base. Kai sprung up and flew over the roots to get to her.

As Kai consoled her, I whispered, "What's Sarai going to do if this doesn't work?"

"Well, if Viridessa gets here soon, maybe nothing," Cameron said. "She might wipe out all the elves so Sarai doesn't have to."

Comforting. Though not wrong.

The five of us traveled back to the Faylinnian castle together. With Viridessa, Calliope didn't want us returning to Kai's shack, so she had Evette and Adelaide set us up permanently next door to her and Kai's chambers.

"Hey, Dec," Calliope said. "Do you remember several years back, helping a woman lost in the woods? A woman who needed help getting to Elfland."

His head cocked, eyes wide, like he didn't know how Calliope could've known about that. "Yeah. That was around the time we were ordered to look for you and hadn't found you yet. I'd just come back from one of my daily searches. She wasn't anywhere near the Hedge and she was distressed, raving about one of our Keepers trying to kidnap her. Your dad had given her a map, but she was all turned around, but even if she did find it, we hadn't had a Keeper at the Hedge in ages. I wasn't sure how she hoped to get through without another faery, but my gut told me helping her was the right thing." He slowed his pace. "Why are you asking me about her?"

"She's my mom."

Declan reared back, eyes darting to Cameron. "What?"

"Crazy, right?" Calliope said.

Cleared his throat, Cameron said, "She left me and my dad when I was around ten years old. I had no idea what happened to her. One day she was just...gone."

Declan stopped and the rest of us did, too. "Cameron, if I'd known she was your mother, I'd have said something a long time ago. All I'd known was that she was a woman in trouble who knew Finnian and she was lucky enough to stumble across me and not one of the other Keepers."

"It's fine." He waved off Declan. "I'm not really stuck on that detail."

"So, wait, Cameron has fae lineage?"

Callie laughed, disbelief still there. "Yeah. It's like it was meant to be. Maybe now if people find out he had fae blood in him, we'll be able to spin it in our favor."

"I'm not really sure it'll work that way, considering the lands are still dying and crops are getting low," Cameron said. "And the small detail that I still used the blood of unwilling faeries, knowingly, unlike Lia."

"We'll figure out how to make it right, Cam. I promise," she said.

"I knew Leon," Declan said. "He was awful, one of Favner's faithful followers, but you don't have to worry about him anymore. He died in the Battle of Faylinn."

Good. I wished it was me that did it, but I'd already switched sides at that point.

I was still trying to wrap my head around it all. I couldn't imagine how Cameron was dealing. Would Elena even let him go back into Elfland to visit his mom with Viridessa after him? Apparently, she'd made it clear we weren't welcome there to stay, but would Elena really keep Cameron from his mom?

"Good riddance," Calliope said. "Otherwise I'd have

tracked him down and put him in prison. Even if the murder of your grandma wasn't on Faylinn soil, I'd have made an exception."

"There are laws about faeries killing humans," Declan said. "So, you'd be in the clear."

She nodded. "Good to know."

"Are we any closer to finding out who Viridessa could be inhabiting?" I asked.

"I have a meeting with Evan when we return. He couldn't meet with me yesterday evening, but I'm hoping he'll have some insight."

"Can we be there, too?" Cameron asked.

"Yeah, I was going to include you guys anyway."

"Cool." He nodded. "Then what are we waiting for? Time to track down the faery of mortality."

"Did you come up with that one all on your own?" Calliope teased.

"Yeah." Cameron smirked. "Pretty clever, huh?"

We laughed, shaking our heads.

THIRTY

CAMERON

AS we walked down the hallway to Calliope's atrium to meet with Evan, I studied Lia. The way she walked and held herself. I honed into her breathing, making sure she hadn't overdone it this morning. She seemed okay. Better than yesterday, so that was promising.

"Do you feel any different?" I asked. "Any signs of weakness?"

Lia slid an annoyed stare my way. "I made it to the Waking Oak and back on my own. Was that not good enough for you?"

I chuckled and wrapped my arm around her shoulder,

kissing the top of Lia's head. "Well, at least your sass is in full swing."

"I should probably test out my abilities at some point, though. Try to grow something or heal. I could try enticement on you, though it wouldn't require much." She smirked.

"Enticement?"

"Yeah, it's a luring ability all faeries possess, making yourself irresistible."

Calliope turned over her shoulder. "Kai tried it on me and I nearly smacked him."

"I stand by my original defense," he said, arms raised. "At least I didn't take your memories."

"Can you do that?" Cameron's eyes widened.

"Some of us can, but not everyone," he said.

"Have any of you done that?" Cameron asked.

I shook my head. I didn't have the ability, and I was grateful for that. Kai shook his head, too. "I can, but I haven't. And I won't."

"Why would you take someone's memories?"

"Lots of reasons," Kai said. "People want to forget pain and grief. Or the more devious side, who don't want to get caught breaking the law or want their match to forget infidelity."

"That sounds incredibly manipulative and unethical."

"It is. Which is why I've never done it."

When we entered the atrium, Evan was already waiting with his arms clasped behind his back. "What can I do for you, Calliope?"

VIRIDESSA." Evan surveyed us. "Are you sure?"

"Elena was very adamant. Viridessa has woken up and she has the temper of the devil. And Cameron and Lia are probably the target of her fury."

"Mabuz," he gasped. "Of course I've heard the stories, but no one had ever claimed they were true. I've been with your family for three generations and not once was that confirmed."

"Maybe they didn't believe it either," she said.

"If she's so dangerous, why would they keep that a secret?" I asked. "Why make it out to be a tale to scare kids? Wouldn't knowing the truth encourage faeries to be more careful with the realm?"

Evan rubbed his chin. "Yes, but my assumption is that the previous kings didn't want to cause panic. Faylinn was meant to be a place of peace and merriment, freedom to do as you chose until the Great Divide happened. We've been taught since the beginning of our existence that we are the most powerful beings in our realm. If a mightier force could awaken and torture them all with the slightest mistake, the psyche might spiral. Fae could turn on one another. They probably thought it was better to have our fae live in blissful ignorance than initiate mass chaos."

"So, who could Viridessa turn up in?" Calliope asked. "Do you know which family has the ability to recognize life and death? That would know the elves or Lia and Cameron transformed."

He nodded, grim. "I do, and so do you."

"I do?" Calliope reared back. "Who?"

"Oliviana."

Calliope's forehead creased, her eyes squinting. "What? No. She sings with the voice of an angel for the Fallen ceremonies. That woman is peace and harmony and serenity reincarnated."

"She is when the spirit of Viridessa doesn't live within her.

But, Calliope, how do you think Oliviana knows to begin the Fallen ceremonies?"

Calliope's face slackened. "No…"

"What does this mean?" I asked. "She lives in Faylinn? She's here, like right now?"

Evan nodded, but Calliope was still in a sort of comatose state as she processed it.

"So, what can we do? Do we go find her?"

Lia's eyebrows arched. "You want to go out there right now and approach the woman who might be the one to end us like we're going to check on the weather?"

My eyes narrowed. "I want to know if Viridessa really is who they think she is. I want to know if this Oliviana lady is actually possessed or whatever, or if we're chasing an actual fictional creature."

"And what are you going to do? Knock on her door and ask?" Lia shook her head. "You think she's going to just carry on a polite conversation if Viridessa *is* inside her?"

"Well, maybe not you and me specifically, but one of Calliope's Keepers or something. Are you saying we're just supposed to sit on our butts and continue to wait? Like sitting ducks?"

"You two." Calliope stood up. "Enough. You bicker like an old married couple." She pinched the bridge of her nose "No one is going to approach her. I'll send a unit to scout out her home, to keep an inconspicuous eye on her, see if they notice anything out of the ordinary. If she's not acting like herself, then we'll go from there."

"If Viridessa is in Oliviana or whatever, then why hasn't she come after us already?" I asked.

"You're asking questions like we have the answers. We all

know as much as you."

"I just find it odd is all. Why wait?" I laughed. "We're such a bunch of amateurs."

Calliope's hip popped. That was never a good sign. "Do you have a better suggestion?"

I raised my arms, stifling my laughter. "No, I just realized how ridiculous we sound. What if there is no physical proof? I'm just picturing your Keepers hiding in the bushes, spying on her waiting for some strike of lightning. It's like a bunch of humans trying to prove the existence of God."

"Yeah, except instead of being as loving and forgiving as your human God," Lia said, "we've got the female Lucifer who will want us to suffer like we're in her own version of Hell."

THIRTY-ONE

SARAI

CHURNING, rolling, and twisting. My upset stomach jolted me out of bed. I raced to the washroom and emptied its contents. One heave after another.

Tomas's bluish-black eyes. *Heave.*

His saccharine breath. *Heave.*

His earthy myrrh musk. *Heave.*

His forceful hands. *Heave.*

His vile smile. *Heave.*

Tomas tormented my dreams last night; and in one, succeeded in finishing what he started after dinner while I screamed and screamed but no sound came out. Not because his hand covered my mouth, there was simply no voice. He stole that, too.

I heaved again at the memory, but there was nothing left.

"Your Highness?" someone called into my bedchambers.

I was on my knees next to the toilet bowl when Kayne entered. He rushed to my side, kneeling in front of me.

"My Queen, are you all right?"

I tried to brush him off, but another wave of nausea hit me, and I curled over the toilet. Nothing but saliva. A hand settled between my wings and I flinched.

Spitting out the taste in my mouth, I faced him. "Sorry."

As if realization dawned, Kayne sat back on his heels. "You need to inform someone."

I wiped the back of my hand across my mouth. "And tell them what exactly?"

His cornflower eyes fumed. "That Tomas attacked you. That he humiliated you. That he *violated* you."

"He didn't." I bowed my head. "Not in the sacred sense."

Kayne gripped shoulders. "Do not diminish what he did to you, My Queen. I was there. I saw you after he left you in that dining hall." Dress torn. Makeup smeared. Eyes swollen and red. I looked at myself in the mirror when we returned after I'd let my composure break. I saw what Kayne saw. "He should be imprisoned for what he did to you. And don't think for one second I will not out him if it becomes necessary."

I got off the floor and onto my feet. "We have more important things to attend to than my tussle with Tomas. The elves remain a problem. Rymidon is dying. Cameron and Lia are in danger. And Viridessa is at our doorstep."

Kayne's expression was hard as stone. "What I saw was not simply a tussle, Your Grace. It is just as important as the other matters, if not more. He needs to be punished for his horrific actions."

Collecting myself, I straightened my spine. Kayne had seen enough weakness from me today. "For Marcus's sake, for Cameron's sake, this will remain between us."

Kayne huffed a frustrated sigh. Giving in, he nodded. "Speaking of Prince Marcus, he is in the study, waiting for you."

No. I couldn't face him this morning. I couldn't.

But if I sent him away, he'd sense something was wrong. He couldn't know anything was awry, apart from the obvious.

"Send Fern in straight away to help me get ready. Let Prince Marcus know I'll be a little longer. Do not tell him I've only just awoke."

Kayne wasn't pleased, but he bowed and left me to gather myself before Fern arrived.

WHAT was the best way to handle this? With the door to the study closed, I remained on the other side. Should I enter and walk straight to my desk, business as usual? Greet Marcus with a gracious nod and sit on the couch by his side? Would I even be able to meet him in the eye? Be able to pretend I was the same woman he saw two days ago.

After Elfland and Callastonia two days felt like two millennia.

Okay. I could do this.

With a deep exhale, I shook the tension from my neck and opened the door. The turn of Marcus's head was gradual, enough for my heart to pause, waiting for our eyes to meet. And when they did, relief lifted my heart and its beats stumbled. His green eyes were such a welcome sight after the blue haunting my night.

There was a moment when we only looked at one another, a one-sided conversation with our eyes. We were in a strange limbo. The me from a couple of days ago might have been brave enough to greet him with a kiss on the cheek, but today, I could hardly offer him a nod as I rounded my desk to give me space.

"You didn't send word about your meeting with Queen Elena. I was worried about you."

Right. I promised him I would. I was surprised he hadn't shown up without warning yesterday. Maybe if he had I'd never have gone to Callastonia.

"I'm so sorry. The day got away from me. It was quite...eventful." There wasn't a good word for what yesterday was. After I returned from Callastonia, I'd locked myself in my chambers and hadn't left until now.

"Is everything all right?"

"Hmm?"

"You don't seem well." Marcus took one step and another until he was at the back of the chair. "I realize a man should never say that, but I don't mean you don't look beautiful. You do. You just..." *I just am not myself. I know.* "Are you all right?"

I fluffed my hair, as if that would make me look more put-together. "Oh. I'm well enough, but there's much to discuss. Yesterday was quite grueling in Elfland." Come to think of it, I hadn't even gotten the chance to send a message to Calliope and ask if Elena helped Lia. I'd have to have Galdinon touch base.

"You seem to be alive, so at least there's one positive outcome." Marcus moved around the chair and sat. "Was the visit helpful?"

I nodded and shared everything I could with him about Viridessa and Elena's grandfather.

"So, we were right," he said. "Until the consequences are

met, our realm will continue to die."

I nodded.

Marcus exhaled, reclining in the chair. "Our harvest is dwindling, as well. There was another Royal council yesterday morning. Apparently, you and Calliope didn't make it?"

The council. Yes. *Buzzerwig*. We forgot. "With Elfland, it must've slipped both of our minds. Did your mother tell you what was said?"

"Every kingdom discovered dead lands. Some were worse than others, but none as bad as what you've told me about in Rymidon."

I gripped the side of my neck. Everything hurt, the weight of his words adding to the tension.

"I need to speak with Guthron. The elves will most likely have to suffer the same fate. We should find out if they're experiencing anything out of the ordinary."

Marcus stared at me, an unsettled stare. "This won't be able to remain secret much longer, Sarai. And if we have to divulge the origin of the dead lands, Guthron will surely reveal my part. He won't go down without taking me with him."

"Not if Calliope creates the branch in time. We'll banish them back to their uninhabitable land, if we have to. I'm done letting our fae suffer."

A small smile quirked one side of his mouth, a crinkle at the corner of his eyes.

"What?"

"Confidence looks good on you."

Tears glossed over my eyes. Now was not the time. Why was I crying?

Oh, maybe because I felt anything but confident. I blinked, trying to clear them, but it was like the more I blinked, the more tears I produced.

Marcus stepped around the desk in an instant and kneeled at my feet, turning my chair to face him. "Hey." His large hands cradled my jaw. My flinch instinct flared, but I shoved it away. I needed his touch. His kind and tender touch. I needed the reminder; good existed even when evil lived and breathed.

"What did I say?"

My head shook. "Nothing." I blinked and more tears skated down my cheeks. "Nothing."

Why? Why had I gone to Callastonia? Why did Marcus conspire with the elves? Last night never would've happened if I'd never accepted Tomas's invitation. If I'd used the gala as a place to declare Marcus as my match. And now Tomas held the power to destroy Marcus and me. He had the power to hurt Cameron and Lia. And strike fear into every faery in the realm with the knowledge on that scroll.

I put my kingdom first, as I'd always been taught. Selfish desires of the heart had no place in ruling a kingdom. Though, ironically, my father ruled with only selfish desires. And where had that gotten me?

Marcus's thumbs brushed my cheeks. "Tell me what I can do, Sarai. Tell me how to help you. Let me lighten your burdens."

I didn't know. I didn't know how. A ghost of Tomas's talons curled around my throat and choked.

You're exquisite, Sarai.

Aligning yourself with the man who betrayed your kingdom. What a wicked woman.

No one would believe the daughter of Adair.

I recoiled from Marcus. His jaw slacked, like a wounded animal, dropping his hands.

"I'm sorry. I didn't—" He could never know my reaction had nothing to do with him. "We need to go see Guthron." I bolted up and away from Marcus and his crushed eyes.

He spun, still kneeling down, following my movement with confused uncertainty. "Do you...do you want me to go with you?"

I did. I didn't want him to see through my barely fixed facade, but I wanted him by my side, needed his presence and silent support. "Yes, of course. Will you?"

Marcus stood to his full height, his face unreadable as he studied me. *Please don't study too closely*. With one nod, he followed me out of the tower.

GUTHRON was in a circle of his transformed elves when we arrived with my Keepers in tow at the base of Orchid Mountain. Her grand peaks cast shadows over the scattered withering landscape.

I couldn't remember their names, but the harsh eyes of the one who attacked me in the cavern watched me with a hungry stare. Not of desire, but for my blood. The deep set of their eyes would never not send a pit to my stomach.

"Guthron," I called him away.

He strode toward us with a slow, measured gait, flicking the dry leaves off a shriveled tree. They tore from the dead branch and drifted to the forest floor. "Your trees are dying."

"That's why we're here." It took everything to keep the accusation out of my tone, even though this all began with him. I gestured to his dwelling on the side of the mountain. "Inside. We need to have a private discussion."

"I do not take orders from you, little one." His eyes slithered to Marcus at my side. "Did you bring your lackey to intimidate me?"

Marcus's voice wasn't loud, but assertive. "Sarai is perfectly capable of handling you herself if she so chooses."

My eyebrows lifted at Guthron. *Test me, Guthron. I dare you.* "Do you want to know why my kingdom is dying or not? And why this affects you, too?"

Guthron snarled but led the way up the mountainside.

HIS head tossed back as he scoffed. "Viridessa sounds preposterous. We began transforming several moon cycles ago. Why would she act now?"

"I wish I had the answer, but all I know is that your transformed elves started the imbalance in our realm, and soon they will have to answer to the repercussions. Your elves haven't been experiencing any illnesses? No aversions to the transformation?"

His head shook, haughty. "It is as though this was the form they always should have taken."

Why couldn't they be the ones to fall ill, to react poorly to the fae blood? Let them die off as nature intended.

His top lip curled. "And what of your friend? Will she have to face the consequences, or will you shield her from Viridessa's wrath?"

Guthron didn't know about Cameron. I'd nearly forgotten. I'd keep it that way.

"If we could, we would, but we can't. Lia is already preparing herself. No one can run from Viridessa. Even you,

Guthron."

With an easy sigh, he uncrossed his arms over his lanky frame and leaned back in his high-back chair. Some make-shift throne. "I think we will manage just fine. Thank you for your concern."

"You do realize what this means." I leaned forward. "Our harvest will grow smaller and smaller. You will not be able to sustain your tribe much longer until Viridessa gets what she wants. We don't have enough to go around as it is. It's why your portions have not been generous. We have to start making more sacrifices."

Guthron's head tilted, black eyes narrowing. "Are you sure this is not some excuse to keep from holding up your end of the bargain? No protection and now no food? What else will you take from us? The dwellings? The land? As far as I can tell, your end of the agreement is already falling quite short, and you know what that means."

"This is out of my hands. If you harm even a hair on any faery from any kingdom, you will answer to me, Guthron." My voice was like venom. Even to my own ears, I didn't recognize it. "And I promise you, you do not want to answer to me."

Not after all I'd been through.

His cackle echoed through his home. "We shall see."

Marcus took a step, away from the corner he hovered in behind me. "Sarai will not be alone in her retaliation. She will have the backing of every Royal in the realm, Guthron. Don't test your limits."

"Was that a threat, oh mighty Marcus?"

"Only the truth. You may have a few transformed elves, but they will not stand against the rest of the realm. And if Viridessa doesn't finish you off first, the others will."

Guthron rose to his feet and stepped forward, meeting Marcus burly chest to gangly chest. "I will keep that in mind."

I tugged on Marcus's arm. "It's pointless to reason with him." I glared at Guthron. "He'll learn soon enough, and he'll wish he'd listened to us."

Guthron met my stare with smug superiority. "Doubtful."

The fool.

YOUR Highness." Eitiri bowed when we returned to the castle. "The Queen and King of Faylinn are in the gathering hall waiting for you."

I rushed through the corridors, Marcus close behind. Calliope and Kai awaited us, sitting on the platform to my throne, heads bent close together.

At the sound of our entrance, Calliope hopped up. "Oh good. You're back."

"What's happening?" I dashed forward.

"Other than the end of our realm as we know it?" Kai shrugged as he slowly stood. "Not much."

Calliope nudged him in the ribs with a dry laugh. "We just wanted to come and update you in person."

I nodded. "Lia? Is she well? Was Elena able to help her?"

"So far, yes. She's really lucky. I don't think she's at her full fae abilities yet, but she's close."

A deep sigh of relief left me. "Good, good. So, what is going on?"

Calliope flicked her eyes to Marcus next to me. "How much does Marcus know?"

I peered up at him and his eyes questioned me. "Everything

I know, I guess," I said.

Do I? His deep green eyes asked in return, and I dropped my gaze. I couldn't let him catch my lie.

Calliope took in the gathering hall, most likely checking if we were alone, and still her voice lowered. "We know, or rather, have an inclination, of where Viridessa is going to present herself. There's a woman in Faylinn, Oliviana, who sings and draws the kingdom together for a Fallen ceremony."

I nodded. "We have someone like that, Iona."

"As do we," Marcus said. "Marvina. It's tradition."

"Do all kingdoms have someone?" She looked between the two of us.

"I believe so," Marcus answered. "But you'd have to ask the other Royals to be sure that they carried on with the tradition."

"Dang. Here I was thinking we had the jump on someone. We've had Keepers covertly patrolling her around the clock since I spoke with Evan."

"Well, it doesn't mean it's not her," I said. "Maybe Evan knows more. Does she discern life and death?"

Calliope nodded. "It's how she knows to begin the Fallen ceremonies."

Made sense. "I'm not sure that Iona does," I said. "When the elves killed Eldon and Sindri, I was able to keep their deaths quiet until we told their families. Iona didn't sing until we mourned everyone who was killed by the elves."

Marcus stroked the side of his face. "I'd have to ask my parents. I'd always assumed Marvina began singing after being told it was time, but if this is some sort of ability that wasn't meant to be known…" He shrugged.

"That's what I'd assumed about Oliviana." Calliope nodded. "And maybe she does wait to start when she's told. I'm not sure if this is a trait that's been kept secret, like Elena's family, or if it's more well known."

"I didn't know," Kai said. "I don't think most Faylinnians are aware."

"We'll have to find out if any of them are related," Calliope said. "Elena said the family isn't in Elfland, so at least we can cross them off the list. Seven kingdoms down to six faeries. That's a better pool than we were working with before."

"We could ask. What's the worst thing that could happen?" I shrugged. "She'd strike sooner than later? At least then we wouldn't be taken by surprise."

"I guess at this point it's worth a shot. My Keepers haven't noticed anything different about Oliviana. I gathered a unit that know her well, and none of them seem to think she's anything but herself, which might not mean anything at all. Viridessa could be in her head, not in possession of her body."

"The only thing you can do is go to her," I said. "Or bring her to you. You're in a better position inside the castle, without the listening ears of your fae."

She nodded.

"How about the Waking Oak for the elves? Have you made any progress with the branch?"

Calliope shook her head. "I tried first thing this morning, but it didn't work. Then attempted once more before we came to see you, and I'll try again tomorrow, but I'm feeling less than confident in my abilities."

"It doesn't matter. If you can't, you can't. We'll send the elves to their old land."

Calliope's eyes squinted, skeptical. "Are you sure?"

Mercy delivering Sarai was fading. The stakes were rising too high and my kindness had been taken advantage of one too many times.

"I'm done negotiating with Guthron. Viridessa is more of a priority. We just came back from discussing everything with him, to warn him of what's to come, and Guthron accused me of making it all up to force them out of Rymidon."

They both shook their heads and Calliope snorted. "He really is a jackass."

"Let them suffer the consequences when Viridessa appears," Kai said. "They'll get what's coming to them."

"I hate that it needed to come to this."

"You did everything you could, Sarai." Marcus rested his hand on my shoulder. With his unexpected touch, I couldn't suppress my flinch no matter how hard I tried.

"Sorry." I raised my gaze to him. "I'm just jumpy today."

He nodded, but his eyes couldn't cover the hurt as he pulled his hand back. I hated myself for that flinch. He didn't deserve it.

After Calliope and Kai left, Marcus stayed. I was torn between relief and dread. I didn't fear Marcus. Being alone with him wouldn't end in a violation of my body or with my control revoked; but he'd been watching me so closely, I'd done a terrible job hiding the underlying edge of my hysteria.

Inviting him to stay wasn't my smartest move, but I couldn't ask him to leave, either.

"It's past time for lunch and I haven't even had breakfast yet. Are you hungry?"

I wasn't, but my body needed something to function on for the rest of the day. If I was lucky, I'd be able to keep something down.

Marcus nodded, uncharacteristically hesitant. "If you don't mind me joining you."

With a gentle smile, I said, "I never mind a bit of company." At least that wasn't a lie.

"Do you think Guthron will try to continue his crusade for our blood?" I sat down at the head of the table, waiting for Naida to bring our meals.

"It's hard to tell. It would be foolish of him to try. As soon as a Rymidonian went missing or was found dead, you'd know exactly where to turn. But that only means he'd try to be smarter, kidnap fae he thinks would go unnoticed or discard the bodies where you couldn't find them."

I snorted, very ladylike. "I'd hand him right over to the other Royals, King Steafan in particular. Let him decide what to do with them. I promise Guthron would've wished he'd thought better of my mercy."

Marcus took a sip of water from his goblet with a subtle smirk. "King Steafan hates the elves that much?"

"More than the realm hated my father." I laughed, but it held little humor.

The door to the kitchen swung open and Naida entered with two plates of modest-portioned food. "Thank you, Naida."

"Yes, thank you," Marcus said.

She nodded with a sweet smile.

As soon as she set the plate in front of me, my stomach recoiled. It wasn't the thought of eating but the scent that wafted off the zendan. There was some sort of seasoning Trilla must have used. Saffron or cloves. Shots of the meal Fiona made last night flashed on the plate with Tomas's arm draped along the back of my chair, leaning in. The cloves mixed with his earthy musk. My head spun and I swallowed back my dry-heave.

"Sarai?" Marcus placed his hand on the table close to the tips of my fingers gripping my fork.

Oh no.

"I'm feeling a bit ill. Please excuse me." I darted from the dining hall, but only made it around the corner of the empty corridor before I heaved into a planter. Nothing came out. I hadn't eaten since last night. My body attempting to expel nothing was worse than a full stomach, constricting my weakened stomach muscles.

I was Queen of Rymidon. A thoughtless run-in with Prince Tomas shouldn't cripple me. He didn't deserve to strip me of my spirit and strength, especially at a time like this. Sliding down the wall, I buried my face in my hands and wept.

It wasn't long before Kayne found me. "Would you like me to ask Prince Marcus to leave?"

I could only nod, keeping my face down, away from Kayne's eyes that were surely pleading with me to speak the truth.

There was no way I could face Marcus after this. My shield was down, I'd confess everything from last night. And knowing Marcus, he'd bring war to the gates of Callastonia. We couldn't risk that during a time like this.

After several moments, Kayne returned and bent down in front of me. "I told Prince Marcus you came down with something. He said he'd check on you tomorrow."

I raised my head and nodded once.

"What else needs to be done today?" Kayne asked.

So much. Too much. This couldn't be me. I had work to do; fae to question, dead lands to examine, food to find. Rymidon needed me at my strongest. I wouldn't cower in my chambers. Tomas didn't get to do that to me.

Without the help of Kayne, though he tried, I got to my feet. "First, we need to speak with Iona."

THIRTY-TWO

LIA

You're going to bring her here?" Cameron stared at Calliope, unblinking.

"Better than to corner her in the village and have a spectacle," she said. "Containment is key, especially now that the rumor of the dead lands is spreading across the kingdoms. If she becomes dangerous or volatile, I want the least amount of fae near her as possible."

"And what about us?" I asked.

"I want you near, but unseen. I'm still not sure what I'm going to say, but if you're there, then maybe you'll get to see what we're up against."

Cameron rubbed his forehead. "This could be a suicide mission."

"We have to put an end to this soon, Cam. Our kingdoms are on the verge of starvation. Do you have a better idea?"

"No, no. I get your position. And I know this is my fault, Cal. I'm just trying to mentally prepare."

She nodded. "Well, hopefully, this is just a conversation. Something to confirm if Viridessa lives in Oliviana or not. If all we can get is confirmation, we'll be one step closer to understanding what we're up against."

I gripped Cameron's hand and squeezed. "When is she coming?"

"I'm sending Brokk right now."

"It hasn't even been a day since you started her surveillance," he said. "Do you really think it's wise to do it now, tonight?"

"You were just going on about how you wanted us to march up to her door and figure out if she is who we think she is and now you're wussing out?"

"I'm not wussing out. I just don't understand what changed from this morning, bringing her here into what should be a safe place."

For the *love*, they quarreled like siblings. And to think, Calliope had a crush on him for so many years. A chuckle escaped before I could stop it.

"Is something funny?" Cameron raised an eyebrow at me.

I bit my lips together and shrugged. "Just you two. What does it matter how and when she's approached? Oliviana could bring us one step closer. We might as well see what she knows."

"Exactly," Calliope said. "After talking with Sarai, I realized we're running out of time. I'm not going to accuse her of anything, just ask her some questions to see if she'll be any help."

"And what better way than having the upper hand here?" I said, trying to calm Cameron.

With a deep exhale, he nodded, gripping my hand like a lifeline. Cameron was scared and it trampled my heart. I couldn't blame him. There was little we could do to protect ourselves and that was all we wanted to do for each other.

THERE was a closet in the atrium where Calliope kept pillows and blankets for a midday nap. Cameron and I hid inside, facing the doors. They were made of angled slats, enough so we could see out, but no one could see in. Not without close inspection anyway.

"I feel like I'm hiding from my girlfriend's parents after sneaking into her bedroom without them knowing," Cameron whispered.

My lips pursed. "You did that with Isla, didn't you?"

"Only once." He smirked at the salty gleam in my eyes.

I thumped him in the chest.

"Ouch." He chuckled.

Kai sat in the window seat, knee propped up with his back against the wall, displaying a relaxed front, but I noticed the tension of his shoulders and the way he gripped the flute in his hand. This was a conversation best had between Calliope and Oliviana alone, but he'd refused to leave Calliope's side. Even if she was the one more likely to protect him than her, he wouldn't back down.

With the click of the door, a lithe woman with soft-hued

pink wings and hair so blonde it was almost white glided into the atrium after Brokk. Angelic. Calliope had said her voice was like an angel. With such delicate features, I was surprised she wasn't one.

Cameron and I stilled, observing their side profiles.

"Oliviana, thank you for coming to see me." Calliope smiled. Though trying to remain natural, it was tight.

"Of course, Your Grace." She curtsied low, her nose nearly touching the ground, a ballerina type move. "What is it I can do for you?"

Even Oliviana's speaking voice, the words strung together were like an aria.

"I'm hoping you can help me, actually." Calliope slipped her hands behind her back as they fidgeted. "I'd like to know more about your family. How you became the voice of the Fallen ceremony."

"I…" Oliviana's mouth clamped shut, not in defiance but more in thought, like no one had ever asked her that question before. "Well, my mother taught me, as her mother taught her, and so on."

"And how do you know when to sing?"

"It's a feeling, Your Highness." She shrugged. "My heart knew the song before my tongue did. When someone passes on, I can't control the music. It's like I'm the one responsible for bidding them farewell to the other side."

Calliope nodded. "When Favner was king, there were no Fallen ceremonies. What did you do then?" Her fidgeting fingers stalled, waiting for an answer.

"I still sang, but he locked me in the castle so no one could hear."

A loosened breath left Calliope. "It truly is uncontrollable.

Your need to sing. That's a travesty, to keep such a celestial voice from our world."

The brightest pale yellow of Oliviana's eyes flashed her sorrow. "Thank you."

"Umm…" Calliope clenched her hands into fists behind her back, struggling to keep them calm, struggling to remain composed. "Oliviana, do you know anything about Viridessa?"

"Viridessa," her voice was so quiet, I had to strain my ears. "The Mabuz?"

Calliope nodded. "Have you heard about the dead lands in Faylinn?"

Oliviana gasped. "Is it her? Did she return? Has someone forsaken our realm?"

The genuine concern in her voice, on her face, creased the lines on Calliope's forehead. Either Oliviana was a superb liar or Viridessa wasn't inside her.

"That's what I'm trying to find out," Calliope said slowly. "So, you believe in her existence?"

Oliviana curled into herself, almost embarrassed. "I know most don't, but something in my veins has always livened at the mention of her, this internal reaction as if sensing her existence."

"Do you…sense her presence?"

There was a collective holding of breaths as we waited for Oliviana to respond.

"Not her presence so much as feeling she is real, intuition, maybe?"

Calliope nodded. Watching her body language, it was so clear she was trying not to jump out of her skin.

"I've been told you're blessed with the ability to know when someone is born and dies, or when they transform. Is that true?"

Oliviana nodded. "I do detect that, yes."

"So, have you noticed anything off with transformations lately? An imbalance between our realm and the human world."

Her head shook, eyes worried. "No, Your Grace. Should I?"

"Maybe not." Calliope paused as if weighing the truth of her words. "I just hoped if anyone knew, it would be you."

"I wish I could be more helpful, but the last transformation I felt was when our king switched with Magnolia." Her attention flickered to Kai on the window seat and he offered a cordial close-lipped smile.

Calliope nodded. "Right. Okay." She unfurled her fists, her arms relaxing at her sides. "You know, I think that's all. You have been helpful. Thank you, Oliviana."

She curtsied once more. "If there's anything I can do, please come to me, Your Grace. I want to resurrect the lands as much as everyone else."

"I will. Enjoy the rest of your day." Calliope smiled and Brokk escorted Oliviana out.

When the door shut, Cameron and I burst out of the closet.

"Do you believe her?" I asked.

"Wouldn't you?" Calliope said, pointing at the closed door. "She's the closest thing to innocence I've ever seen, almost childlike. She wouldn't hurt a snake if it bit her."

"But she senses Viridessa's existence?" Cameron ran a hand through his hair. "If that's not an admission, I don't know what is."

"She also said she didn't detect your transformations."

"And how is that possible if she detects all life and death and yada yada yada? She could've been lying, or Viridessa could've been shielding her mind or something. I don't know."

Calliope released a deep breath. "It's possible. You're right,

259

but there was still no proof. She could be just as innocent as us."

"We're not innocent," Cameron mumbled.

She groaned. "Oh, you know what I mean."

"If it's not her, then who?" I asked.

"We've still got five other faeries who might be the key." Calliope slipped around the circular table. "I need to ask the other Royals what they know, but before I do that, I need to try with the Waking Oak again before sundown. The longer the elves remain in Rymidon, the quicker Sarai's kingdom will starve having to provide for those leeches."

"Can we come with you?" Cameron asked.

"Yeah, I don't want you guys out of my sight right now."

ANOTHER day, another failure. Calliope was defeated. I was defeated *for* her. After trying again last night for the third time and failing, we returned first thing the next morning. And nothing.

So much pressure rested on her shoulders to make this happen, responsible once again for saving our world from an adversary.

Thanks, Favner. If it weren't for him, she wouldn't be the last True Royal. Our world would have more of a fighting chance.

If only we could help her.

And then, a thought came to me. Maybe... It couldn't be that easy. Surely she's already tried.

"Have you ever tried to grow something?" I asked.

Calliope turned to me, where she was seated on the mammoth roots of the Waking Oak. "What?"

I stood, walking down into the ravine. "You've created

wind and fire. You've burst geysers from the earth and a deluge from the sky, but have you tried to make anything grow?"

"I repaired the Oak; was that not similar?" Calliope's head cocked to the side.

"You healed it, you weren't trying to create something new. You were restoring what once was. You need to think of it differently." I turned to Kai. "You were a Sower once, weren't you?"

"I've grown a thing or two." He nodded.

"So, you know we think of it as cultivating a new life. Maybe, Callie, you need to—" Her expression changed from concentration to curious. "What?"

"Nothing." A reminiscent smile tugged on her lips. "You just haven't called me Callie since…"

Since we both pretended to be nothing but human, an eternity ago.

"Is it okay if I call you Callie?" Our friendship had shifted so drastically when it all came to a head. I never dared to dream we could be what we once were.

She nodded, blinking rapidly, like she was clearing away tears. "Yeah, go on. Explain this to me."

"Right. Okay. So, maybe you need to start by picturing the limb, not as what it's going to be, not a place for the elves, but the actual branch." I grabbed her hand and placed it on the trunk. "Close your eyes. Imagine it as a seed first, sprouting from the trunk, lengthening and flourishing. Sprigs spreading and leaves unfurling. Hold onto the images and play them on repeat."

She exhaled and pinched her eyes shut, wrinkles forming at the edges with her concentration. After a minute, nothing happened.

And then…

Creaks and groans. A fluttering of leaves in the mild breeze. When I looked up, a new branch sprouted from a knotted bough, stretching farther and wider.

"Holy crap, it's working," Cameron's stunned words carried in the wind.

"That's good, Callie. You're doing it. Focus." I kept my voice calm and steady. "Now, move onto the land it'll sustain. What's there? Grass? Trees? Briars and hedges? Flowers and vines? What about hills and valleys? Are there bodies of water? Other animals? This is your world, Callie. Create it."

She shut her eyes tighter and I stepped back along the roots until my back collided with a solid body. I looked over my shoulder and Cameron tugged me into his arms, kissing my forehead. "You're amazing. Look what you helped her do."

"It was just a few flowery words," I whispered back.

"A few flowery words that could help save Rymidon."

When the branch was done it wasn't like the boughs for the kingdoms but a limb forking off of one. Smaller, but no less grand.

"Should we go test it out?" Calliope whirled around with glee in her eyes.

"I don't know," Cameron said. "Are we going to fall into a bottomless pit?"

"Guess you'll have to wait and see." She winked and touched the trunk. It twisted open with a decrepit groan. With excited eyes and a lopsided smirk tossed over her shoulder, Calliope stepped through, followed closely by Kai, a hand molded to her back.

"Well?" I asked, and Cameron shrugged.

"Why not?"

Passing through the darkness, I blinked at the new light.

The land was modest, not vast. There was an end in sight, a sort of mirrored sky-like backdrop a couple of miles around, like a sphere border. We were in a dome. It soared high enough, nothing that might cause claustrophobia, but you could see a curve in the clouds. Not even the highest leaping faery could reach it.

Calliope had grown trees and vegetation, blossom-speckled meadows and green-carpeted knolls. Nothing overly abundant, nothing like our fae kingdoms, but it had a simple beauty.

"It's not much. I didn't want to leave them without food sources or resources for building homes, but it is a sort of prison, so…"

"Cal, you grew a freakin' land." Cameron laughed. "You don't need to be humble about it."

Her grin spread. "I did, didn't I?"

"What are you going to call it?" Kai asked.

"I guess I should name it, huh? Well, Elena has the market cornered on Elfland, so, how about…Arcshire?"

Cameron nodded as he studied the domed-sky, and patted her on the back. "I dig it."

When we crossed back into Faylinn, Calliope nudged her shoulder into mine. "Thanks."

"I didn't do much. You just needed a little encouragement."

"Yeah. And you somehow knew exactly what I needed to hear."

"Well, I wasn't your best friend for all of those years without learning a thing or two."

She smiled, reminiscent. "I can't wait to tell Sarai."

THIRTY-THREE

SARAI

ARCSHIRE was perfect. More than Guthron and his tribe deserved, but it gave me a sense of peace knowing they weren't being sent to a desolate land where they'd soon die without resources. Even if that would be their own fault.

This was the right choice. After everything, I didn't want to lose myself, to lose the light in my heart I'd protected for so long. Sakari wouldn't have wanted that for me, or my mother.

After Calliope and Kai left through the Waking Oak for Faylinn, I turned to Kayne. "I need all our Keepers to head to Orchid Mountain. Surround the elf village, let no one escape.

And have Galdinon summon every Rymidonian to the castle. It's time I fill in some gaps."

SHOUTS rang out around the gathering hall, drowning the conclusion to my confession.

"You think we don't know they are the reason our fae went missing? As soon as they took residence, we haven't had a single soul lost," Eoghan of the Craftsmen hollered. "Of course they're the reason our lands are dying and our harvest is dwindling."

"They murdered our fae, and yet you invited them to join our kingdom. Gave them food and shelter, protection," another yelled, but I could see him. His fist raised above the rest before his deep wine eyes pinned me with their wrath. "You're worse than Adair. He might've forced his Supremacy on us, but he did it to better our kingdom. He did it *for* us."

I wanted to wrap my heart in armor, for their words to ricochet off me, but I deserved to feel their frustration, their feelings of betrayal. I'd kept them from the truth for so long, and we'd suffered. Even if my intentions were pure, they put us all at risk.

"I hear you. I feel your betrayal and your fears. They are the same as my own. I promise you that. War was imminent without the negotiation. My decision to bring the elves to Rymidon was not an easy choice and I did not make it lightly. Precautions were made for your safety. And there is a plan. As your queen, your advocate, I promise there will be consequences to their actions.

"As we speak, our Keepers are surrounding the elves and taking measures to ensure the elves never harm again. Any of us. Queen Calliope has formed a prison in the Waking Oak. They will be warded there, never to leave again."

Confused and skeptical murmurs spread through the mass.

"And what of the dead lands? What of the imbalance they caused? How will that be repaired?" Robyn of the Weavers asked.

I now understood why the Royals kept Viridessa a secret, simple folklore. If this was how they'd reacted to the elves, what were they going to do with the knowledge of Viridessa? The panic would be near impossible to manage.

"The dead lands have affected every kingdom. We are not alone in that. The Royals are working together to swiftly find a solution."

"Kill the elves!"

"Kill the ones that transformed! It's the only way!"

"Make them suffer!"

"Killing them will rectify the balance!"

I raised my voice above the cacophony. "We're considering all options. Please, give us patience. We will fix this. You will not suffer much longer. Until the elves are contained, for your safety, please remain here."

My plea was met with more shouts of disapproval.

The moment I stepped off the platform, Brae and Eitri burst through the side door. Based on the tense looks of their faces, I gestured for them to head back out and I followed.

"Your Grace." As soon as Brae addressed me, I knew I wasn't going to like what he had to say. "They're gone."

"What do you mean they're gone?"

"I mean every dwelling is deserted, not a single sign of the elves."

My heart stopped, my blood draining from my face. "How did we manage to lose thousands of elves? Where was the unit that was supposed to be guarding them?"

"There was a change in guard," he said. "It must've happened then."

I couldn't breathe. "We had them. We had them right where we needed them and you're telling me they vanished?"

"I don't know how it's possible. I'm sorry, Your Grace."

"I don't need you to be sorry, Brae. I need every Keeper on duty. We need a patrol in the village, guarding every home. I want a unit at the Waking Oak ensuring no one comes in or out without my knowledge. Place a unit at their deserted village in case they return. Every available Keeper needs to scour Rymidon. No stone unturned until the elves are either found or it's clear they're no longer here."

"Yes, Your Grace." He bowed and Eitri followed.

I turned to Kayne, hand over my chest. "I stood there and promised our fae justice. Promised them the elves were no longer a problem." I took a deep breath, willing my tears to stay at bay. I couldn't let my emotions get the best of me. That wouldn't help anyone. "What am I supposed to tell them now? They'll overrun the castle. You saw how angry they were. This will be the catalyst to a revolt."

"You don't say anything yet." Kayne remained calm. "Maybe we'll find the elves. They couldn't have gone far. The Waking Oak was guarded. No one would've allowed them to leave. They're here. We just need to find them." Kayne rested a hand on my shoulder. "What would you like to do about our fae in the meantime?"

"Keep those that are in the banquet hall here to ensure their safety. Feed them, keep them calm, do whatever is necessary to ensure we don't have a riot. Once I get a report about the elves, we'll go from there."

He nodded and left me in the corridor alone. It was then I gave myself permission to break.

THEY were gone. Another unit of Keepers found those guarding the Oak unconscious. Alive—thank the Fallen Fae—but unconscious with no recollection of what happened. With Guthron's enhanced elves, they could be anywhere.

Kayne managed to calm our fae when he informed them of the elves' departure from Rymidon—not to Arcshire, mind you. However, he didn't mention they were gone because we lost them. Though I didn't know how long that would last, how many Keepers were aware of the elves disappearing act.

Everything would continue to be kept on a need to know basis. And the Rymidonians definitely didn't need to know we had no clue where the elves were.

I kept an extra unit stationed at the Waking Oak in case they tried to return. It was a relief to have them out of Rymidon, but the knowledge of them still roaming, free to harm any kingdom, distressed me. I'd have to inform the Royals. We all needed to be on guard.

But another nagging question begged an answer. Why did they run? Were they warned? Had they overheard Calliope and I at the Waking Oak?

Where had they gone?

THIRTY-FOUR

CAMERON

LIA and I sat at the dining table with Kai and Calliope, our plates no longer piled with food, but portion-controlled. A half of a radik, a spoon full of vegetables, and a roll. This was a snack for this new form, but my body had to deal with it. Faylinn couldn't starve because of my decision.

"Our animal population is shrinking, which means not only are our crops dwindling but all our food sources."

Lia sat back in her chair, having already finished her plate. Not that it was difficult. "When we went fishing a few days ago, we were at a lake near Kai's shack for hours and only caught one zendan."

Kai paused his bite halfway to his mouth. "That lake is hardly ever fished." He looked to Callie. "It should've been brimming with fish."

"It's not like the sprites don't need food, too," she said. "All they have is the fish and algae and kelp. If that's dying off too…"

"Cameron and I can go without food." Lia took a sip of water, pushing her plate away.

"I'm not going to make you starve." Callie rolled her eyes. "Not yet anyway. At that point, we won't have a choice. The Faylinnians come first, of course—"

"And you." Kai eyed her. "Without you, Faylinn doesn't exist. You need to take care of yourself. I'll go without if the kingdom needs to see we're making sacrifices, but you can't starve yourself. That helps no one."

Callie took his hand. "I'll eat what's necessary, but I'm not going to overdo it. I don't need a lot. I want children to be fed first and fed well. Adults can handle being a little hungry. Our children shouldn't have to."

Kai pulled her in, kissing her cheek.

"You really don't think Oliviana was faking?" I asked.

"Of course she could have been. I don't know her very well, but she was really convincing. You saw."

I nodded, tempted to lick the juices off my plate. "It was a pretty authentic performance if that's all it was. She looked like she fell straight from heaven and I don't mean that as a pick-up line. Her eyes even shined like stars."

"I've always thought that, too," Calliope said. "They're gorgeous."

"So, are you going to talk to the other Royals about it?" Lia asked.

Calliope nodded. "Sarai and I are going in front of the Royal council tomorrow to tell them about the branch and hopefully the good news that the elves are safe inside. Then we'll talk to them about Oliviana. I'm praying they'll be more helpful this time around."

"Don't bank on it," Lia said.

AS I was passing through the hallway on my way to our bedroom, I stopped at the conversation of the Keepers.

"The Rymidonian Keepers were sent to collect the elves, but they were gone."

"Gone?" Dugal halted. "Gone from Rymidon?"

Brokk nodded.

"Have you passed this information onto Queen Calliope?"

"Not yet."

Dugal nodded before striding toward the atrium with Brokk on his heels.

I knocked on our bedroom door before entering.

Lia sat in the corner of the room, carving some sort of bracelet.

"The elves are missing."

"What?"

"Yeah, I just heard Dugal talking about it with Brokk in the hall."

She straightened. "We need to find them, Cam. After everything, the least we can do is get off our butts and search for them. We're useless hiding out in the castle. I'm sick of it."

"I'm up for it, but we'll need to tell Callie so she doesn't send a fleet out looking for us."

Lia got up, setting the wooden bangle on the chair. "Do you think she'll stop us?"

"She wasn't able to stop me from using the blood. I don't see how she can stop us from trying to atone for what we messed up."

We strode hand-in-hand down the hall to the atrium and raised voices flowed through the door.

"I can't believe this. We were so close!" Calliope shouted.

I gave Lia an *oh crap* face before opening the door. Calliope was surrounded by her Keepers and Kai.

"Could they be here?" she asked.

"No, Your Grace," Brokk said. "Even though Lia and Cameron are here, we never stopped guarding the Waking Oak. For this very reason. The elves are too unpredictable. There's been no sign of them."

Calliope was no longer in her crown and gown from earlier today but a thin light blue nightgown and robe with her hair like a lion's mane. "Okay, but still, just to be sure. I want every available Keeper searching Faylinn. They need to search harder than they do for the dead lands every day. For Sarai's sake, we need to help find those elves."

Brokk and Dugal nodded before bowing and leaving.

"I can't believe this." Her palms slapped the sides of her thighs.

"Did anyone else know you made the branch?" Declan asked.

"Aside from Sarai, her Keepers, the Royals, and everyone else in this room, no."

That wasn't a small amount of fae, but most seemed trustworthy enough.

"Would any of the Royals or Sarai's Keepers have given them a heads up?" I asked.

She shook her head. "The only one who has been sympathetic to the elves during this whole mess has been Sarai. No one wants to see them free."

"Why don't Cameron and I help?" Lia stepped up. "We can go search the other kingdoms and lands not inhabited by fae. We could even go to the elves' original stomping ground, too, if I can figure out how to get the Oak to open up a passageway there."

"You think it's a good idea right now?" Calliope's eyebrow cocked. "While we're still searching for Viridessa?"

"We don't even know for sure that she's who we should be worried about," I said. "If she is, what's taking her so long? Is part of the punishment making everyone else starve? Maybe banishing the elves is the key. It could be as simple as that, and if we just find them. We can test the theory."

Calliope sighed. "I want to know every detail. Where you go, who you see, and what else is out there. If the other lands are dying too."

"We'll come and check in every couple of days to update you and keep you from worrying about us, Mom." The corner of my mouth quirked.

"Joke about it all you want, but you know it's dangerous. Everything about it. Showing your faces, entering other kingdoms. Most know who Lia is; you realize that, don't you?"

"Why don't we just search the other lands first?" Lia asked. "Fortenberry and Novalora. Most of the other kingdoms probably have Keepers guarding their Waking Oak entrances. The elves aren't going to risk being caught that way. And it's less ground to cover."

"I feel better about that," Calliope said. "And you know what, you shouldn't run into anyone unless you enter the other kingdoms, but just in case." She bent over her desk, jotting something down on a piece of paper.

"Here."

We are on official confidential Royal business. Please refrain from hindering our task.

Calliope Willow
Queen of Faylinn

I chuckled "Look at you getting all fancy and eloquent in your royalness."

She rolled her eyes. "I have no idea if that will hold up, but it's a last resort. No one can know you're looking for the elves. I'm not sure what each Royal has decided to divulge to their kingdoms. The last thing we need are fingers pointed at Faylinn because we screwed up more. And keep your identity hidden, too, Cam. The Royals still don't know you transformed, and neither do the elves."

"Mums the word." I zipped my lips.

"Just don't be stupid. That's all I ask. Respect the other lands. Lay low. And if you happen to find the elves, do *not* approach them. You go straight to Sarai or straight to me. Whoever is faster."

"Yes, ma'am." I saluted her as we slipped out of the atrium.

"So, sleeping under the stars tonight? Or head out at first light?" I squeezed her hand.

Lia shook her head. "I'm not going to be able to sleep. We

can get a jumpstart on finding them by going now."

"You're not concerned about creatures that might come out at night?" Because it didn't sound too appealing to me, but if that's what Lia wanted.

"We'll be fine. You have your slingshot and kotrops, right?"

I nodded.

"And I've got my sapierces and bow and arrows. We should be good. We'll start with Novalora. The pixies are harmless, and I don't think there are any lethal creatures living there, so we won't have to constantly watch our backs."

This place was sounding better and better. "Novalora, it is."

THIRTY-FIVE

SARAI

ONCE again we stood before the Royal council. All of the same Royals were in attendance as before, which made me curious if they ever switched? Not King Cian and Queen Elena, of course, but did any of the others? Would Marcus come in my stead?

I shook my head. *Where did that thought come from?*

"You both were noticeably missing from our last meeting. For Queens who were so concerned about the dead lands, you didn't seem too concerned with following up on your fellow kingdoms."

"Don't talk to us like we're children, Steafan," Calliope said.

"It's rude. We might not have as much as experience as the rest of you, but we've earned our place here."

King Steafan's eyes bulged. Both Queens Isolda and Aisling hid stifled smiles behind their hands while he gaped at Calliope. It was difficult for me not to smile, too. I couldn't wait for her to lead these councils. She was more powerful than all of them combined. I bet King Steafan felt threatened.

"We weren't here because we were buried in this mess, trying to figure out solutions, not because we don't care." *Let him have it, Calliope.* I bit my lips to crush my smile. "And in case you don't recall, my adviser reached out to yours. And a representative from Oraelia briefed Sarai. We've remained informed."

I was grateful she left Marcus's name out of it. Queen Aisling probably knew, but I didn't want the speculation of what they might think of our communication. The less Marcus's name was mentioned, the better.

She turned to me and I assumed that was my cue. "The reason we asked to meet this morning was because Calliope created the branch on the Waking Oak. And it's perfect for our needs. The issue we've run into is the elves went missing yesterday evening."

"You lost them?" King Steafan thundered.

I squared my shoulders. "I assure you this causes me just as much distress as it does you. And my Keepers have been searching nonstop since their land was discovered vacated. I'd spoken to Guthron the day before, trying to warn him of the consequences of the transformation imbalance—"

"Well, there was your first mistake." King Steafan scoffed.

Queen Isolda sighed, glaring at him. "Your interruptions are less than helpful, Steafan. Let the women speak. Maybe if you had more compassion and respect for others, your kingdom would like you better."

He scowled at her and Calliope choked on a laugh.

"Forgive my cousin." She addressed us. "He doesn't know when to shut up."

While I appreciated Isolda's defense, I couldn't look her in the eye. Though a different color, her eyes reminded me too much of her son. A part of the missed Royal council day I yearned to erase. My skin crawled and darkness crept into my mind. I clamped down the shield, blocking the memories. Now wasn't the time to break down.

I continued, "He accused me of not wanting to uphold my end of the negotiation, but there were no signs they were thinking of leaving. Not a single inclination. Where could they even go?"

King Noll shrugged. "Wherever they've gone before when we haven't been able to locate them. Not that we often tried hard enough to find them."

"You mentioned Viridessa to them?" Cian asked me.

King Steafan groaned, rolling his head. "Not this again."

I ignored him, as did the rest of the council. "I did. I thought it was the right thing to do. If we're able to see the opposition coming, they should too."

"Stop with this nonsense," King Steafan said. "The soul of that Mabuz is not going to terrorize our realm. We simply need to find a way to fix the balance."

"We're all ears for a useful suggestion," Queen Aisling said, leaning forward to look at him.

"The elves must go."

"And if that's not the answer?"

"Then Lia must go."

"Lia isn't going anywhere." I steeled my voice. "She'll deal with the consequences, but death is not it."

Calliope said, "Queen Elena is certain Viridessa exists. How can the rest of you be so skeptical?"

King Steafan's eyebrow arched, condescending. "Oh, and you spoke to Queen Elena yourself?"

Oh, no. Both Calliope and I looked to Cian. Were we not supposed to mention that? We knew parts of our conversation were private, but I hadn't realized we weren't supposed to say anything about visiting Elfland.

Thankfully, Cian gave a subtle nod to proceed.

"We did," Calliope said. "She allowed us into Elfland to discuss it. Her answers were more than convincing."

The others gaped, shooting looks at Cian, who remained impassive, not acknowledging their stares. Had none of them been admitted into Elfland?

"If it weren't that dire, do you truly believe she'd open her wards to us? If she didn't know for certain what we are dealing with?"

Even King Steafan didn't have anything to say in response to Calliope.

"I don't know about you, but our dead lands are bleeding into one another, creeping closer and closer to our main villages," I said. "By the next moon cycle, my fae will starve to death. They don't have enough food as it is, even with the elves missing. Before long, it'll be nothing but ash. If you don't believe it's Viridessa then please, offer another suggestion. Another solution to keep our realm from complete destruction. One that doesn't involve execution."

"What did Queen Elena say about Viridessa?" Queen Aisling asked. There wasn't a hint of suspicion or apprehension,

279

only openness.

Again, we looked to Cian. The last thing we wanted was to betray Elena in any way after she'd been so kind and helpful. She was Cameron's family after all.

Again, Cian nodded.

Calliope answered, "Last time Viridessa was woken up, it was for someone in Elena's family. A human who was kidnapped and injected with our blood for experimentation. Viridessa then appeared in Brigantia, a Weaver."

"We've heard the stories," King Steafan said dryly.

"Then you know what happened. It's not a tale. His family was butchered as punishment, and only then would Viridessa return Faylinn to its former thriving self."

"Then what of the fae who turned him?" King Noll asked. "What cost did they bear?"

We hadn't thought to ask Elena. There were so many things to grasp. At the time, we were most concerned about getting Lia the help she needed.

Cian spoke then, his voice bleak and somber, "Their ears and wings were cut off."

The council gasped. Calliope and I went rigid. We'd allowed Cameron's transformation. We might not have plunged the stellvial into his heart, but we gave our blessing to use the blood. Would Viridessa take our wings? Our ears? Cold terror surged through my veins.

Our eyes met, and the same dreaded thoughts swirled in Calliope's eyes.

"So, what do you want us to do?" King Steafan asked. "If the tale is true, there is nothing we can do to stop her. We could fight, but we would lose."

"We want to find her before all our lands have dried up and

there is no more food. We want to find her before she finds Lia," Calliope said, careful to leave out Cameron. Though there would come a time when he wouldn't be able to remain a secret, but today was not the day to bring him into the discussion.

"Queen Elena said the soul of Viridessa would awaken in a faery who recognizes life, death, and transformations. The only faery in Faylinn who can do that is Oliviana. She sings for our Fallen ceremony. I'm told most of you have someone similar in your kingdoms."

Every Royal nodded but Cian. What did they do for their Fallen ceremonies?

"Cian," King Noll said, "why don't you?"

"We haven't had a need for one as of yet."

"What do you mean?" Calliope asked.

"There's been no deaths in Elfland since our creation."

King Steafan said, "That's impossible."

Not with Elena as their queen. Not only were they protected with the solid force of her wards and armies, but with her healing abilities, if she utilized them on everyone... She mentioned another sister who probably did as well.

"If you understood how Elfland ran, then you might not believe it to be impossible." King Cian wasn't smug, merely confident, proud of his queen, his wife.

Calliope and I didn't say a word.

"Then tell us your ways, old friend." King Steafan eyed him, dubious. "Tell us how to lead such a thriving kingdom. You were spared from Adair's poison, after all. There must be more to it than Elena's wards."

King Cian only smiled. "Ah, but then Elfland would not be as secure as it is if our knowledge wasn't protected."

King Steafan scowled but said no more.

"We are not spared from Viridessa," Cian said. "Just as much of our land is dying as every other kingdom. No matter how strong Elfland is, we cannot escape Viridessa. It'd behoove the rest of you to accept that."

"So, you're saying she's awoken in one of our Songbirds," Queen Isolda said.

"If those are the only fae who can detect life and death, then yes," Cian said. "One of them will be the key to finding Viridessa."

"We already tried talking to Oliviana," Calliope said, "but she seemed just as concerned about Viridessa awakening as we are. I don't think Viridessa is in her."

"So, you'd like us to question our Songbirds," King Noll said.

"It's worth a try."

AFTER returning from the Royal council, I asked Kayne for a moment alone to gather my thoughts. They'd dispersed, promising to inquire with their Songbirds as Isolda called them, but nothing felt like we were any closer to identifying Viridessa.

Was it possible she wasn't real after all?

Entering beneath the archway into the study, my hand clapped my chest and a scream built in my lungs. My brain registered the tall figure looming in the middle of the tower before the scream escaped. "Marcus."

His broad, muscular frame faced me. "I'm sorry if I startled you. I thought Brae would've told you I was in here."

I let out controlled breaths to steady my racing heart. "There must have been a Keeper change because he wasn't out there."

He nodded. "Well, I'm sorry. I hope it's all right that I'm here."

"Yes, fine. It's great," I stumbled over my words, forcing a smile. "What's going on?"

Marcus's eyes roamed my face, reading me. I wish he'd stop. I'd already broken down once in front of him this week, and that was one too many. He made me too vulnerable. And he could never know about Tomas, what he'd done to me, threatened me with.

"Are you feeling better?"

Better since Kayne had to ask him to leave while I dry-heaved and sobbed in the corridor? Sure, grand.

"Much." With how much I was lying, I hoped I was growing better at it.

All Marcus did was nod. Maybe I passed. Or maybe he'd ignored my lie. "I heard the elves have gone missing."

Moving around my desk to put distance between us, I sat down. "Not even a barren trail."

"They're out there. You'll find them. Don't worry yourself too much about it. We have Oraelian Keepers searching as well."

I busied my hands with the maps and books on my desk, arranging and rearranging, keeping my eyes downcast. "Not that it would matter if we found them anyway. If we survive Viridessa, after telling Rymidon why the elves were here, a war is inevitable. Whether against me, or them, I haven't figured out yet."

Marcus stepped up and clasped a hand over mine, stopping my pointless shuffling. When our eyes met, I wasn't sure what he saw. Despair? Defeat?

His eyes searched, expression sympathetic. "What I think

you need is to get away."

"And go where exactly?" I chuckled with a curved brow. How could I possibly go anywhere during a time like this?

"Ondine."

The waterfall. *When she is feeling generous, she shares memories.* Marcus's words came back to me. Would she show me my family?

"Step away for a bit. It might help. Take some time for yourself, forget about everything going on. Take some time away with me."

The thought of spending time alone with him didn't fill me with dread or panic. Not that it should, but I expected it to. Instead, I nodded.

A comforting curve of his lips lit his warm eyes. "C'mon. I'll show you." Marcus slipped his hand in mine and led me from behind the desk. Maybe I should've stopped him. Chasing waterfalls wasn't the most productive way to spend my time today, but it felt like the most right decision I'd made in a long time.

After informing Kayne I didn't need him or any of my other personal Keepers, I let Marcus pull me through the corridors of the castle, his eyes lit with excitement. "You won't regret this, I promise."

As we soared through the woodlands of Oraelia, leaping side-by-side from limb-to-limb, Marcus smiled at me. It wasn't a smoldering smile or one of sympathy as I'd seen on his face so many times as of late. It was a smile of pure bliss and it transformed his entire face, dizzying me.

And while the threat of the elves still hung over us, and Viridessa was most likely days away from obliterating us all, this was the first time Marcus and I had ever done anything fun together, something that didn't involve forming a plan to catch an enemy. We'd spent dinners together and holed up in my tower for hours on end, but never once had we taken a break to breathe.

Thankfully, I'd thought more like Calliope today and wore a light-weight blue dress, making it easier to travel through the trees. It wasn't long before Marcus slowed and dropped to the forest floor, my feet lightly thumping the soil next to his.

He knocked his chin forward, motioning to a shrouded canopy of greens. The cove was protected by a drapery of trees and vines, and just beyond, the peaceful rush of Ondine spilled into the lake.

Marcus pushed aside a curtain of vegetation, holding it open for me. Lifting the hem of my dress, I squeezed through. What lay beyond exceeded my imagination. The rippling water was the deepest sparkling shade of turquoise. And Ondine, she was glorious. She poured over the ledge of a massive boulder carpeted in emerald moss. It curved with the edges of the small lake, surrounding the other side like a veil.

"Gorgeous," I said. "I see why you chose this place. I'd spend more time here than anywhere else if I could."

I was half-tempted to tear off the bottom of my dress, but settled for tying it at my knees and dipped my toes into the water skating over the lichen-covered rocks.

"It's hard to stay away from her." Marcus tugged off his black coat and tunic, followed by his ash-gray trousers, leaving him in a small pair of thin cream shorts—his underwear.

Oh.

He dove into Lake Lore in a perfect arc. When Marcus surfaced, he wiped the water from his eyes and the widest smile graced his face. A breath-thieving, heart-stumbling smile. If those were the smiles he was going to give me from now on, I'd happily wake up to him every morning. What a way to start the day.

"It's the perfect temperature." He beckoned with his hand. "Come on in."

"In my undergarments?"

"Have you never done that before?"

I shook my head, my cheeks heating.

"But I assume you don't swim in your dresses, either."

I hesitated. "I haven't gone swimming since I was a girl."

His gaze softened. "Well, now you really have to come swim." He chuckled. "Stay in your dress or not. It doesn't matter to me. If you take it off, I'll look the other way if it makes you more comfortable, until you're fully submerged."

Maybe it would make me more comfortable, but there was also a part of me that wanted Marcus to look. Possibly reckless, but I wanted to test my reaction to him. I couldn't shun him forever.

And I didn't want to.

There was no force behind his words, only tenderness and patience. He'd accept whatever I gave him, wouldn't make me uneasy or fear what he might do without my permission. In fact, I'd invite any touch from him.

When Marcus began turning away, I murmured, "It's all right."

He paused, his eyes verifying I meant what I said.

Starting with the lacing on my bodice, I took my time, undressing on my terms. Loosening the neckline, I slipped the dress down one shoulder and then the other before easing it over my hips. It fell in a soft heap, leaving me in a cream bralette and panties, my wings waving, languid.

I'd kept my eyes off Marcus until my toes touched the water, and then they trailed across the rich bluish-green lake before finding him treading water. He didn't blink or smile. He didn't make a sound. But he kept his distance and watched, with raw intensity, a slight part of his full lips.

I swallowed, the lump of saliva bobbing down my throat. Like a rabbit, my heartbeats leaped. The rocks dropped off when the water reached my knees, so I stepped off and sank below the surface. I swam a little way before I reemerged a few feet from Marcus.

He hadn't moved, meeting my eyes as soon as I swiped the water from them. His chest heaved with heavy breaths, but I was sure it wasn't from exertion.

"You're right. It's the perfect temperature."

Marcus's jaw tightened as he swallowed. *"Perfect."*

My cheeks warmed. He hardly blinked, like one blink was too long to keep his eyes off me. But he stayed put, treading water as he kept a proper gap between our bodies.

I hated to kill the moment, but I had to know. "Did you ever bring Nerida here?"

His brow furrowed, severing the heated tension. "No. Why would you ask that?"

"I don't know." I peered down at the water, my fingers dancing across the silky top. "When you described this place before, you made it sound so private. A perfect place for a clandestine meeting. I just thought, assumed, maybe you two…"

Marcus swam closer to me and I looked up. When I didn't swim away from his advance, he floated nearer. And then his hand molded to my hip. I didn't flinch. "This is my sanctuary. I've never brought anyone here but you."

I nodded because I couldn't speak, not with that kind of

confession. This was his haven and he shared it with me. Knowing how heavy my heart and mind had been, he brought me here to ease them. Because he… Cormac's disclosure of Marcus's feelings from the night of the Royal gala knocked me in the chest. Did he?

Marcus drew me in, our legs brushing beneath the surface as we kept our heads above the water. "Ask her," he whispered in my ear. "Not aloud, but with your heart. Ask Ondine."

Swimming to my side, he kept an arm around my waist, holding me close. We looked at Ondine together. I concentrated on her cascade, so vivid and pure.

Sakari. I just want to see Sakari. Please.

Within moments, a rainbow rippled across, and there we were, like a blown-up reenactment. Sakari looking just as he was when he died, and I, not much younger.

There was no sound, but as I watched us on the waterfall, our conversation played in my mind.

"That's better." Sakari rested his hands on my shoulders. "Relax your body a little more. You're overthrowing the knife."

I replanted my right foot forward and rolled my shoulders back. Aiming. Throw. The knife hit the inner circle of the target.

"That's it. That's it. You've got this."

Smiling, I said, "I'm feeling more comfortable with it."

"Good. I'm not surprised. You should." He moved to the target on the wall and pulled the knives out. "I better watch out. Soon you'll be a better knife thrower than me."

I laughed. "Doubtful, but thank you for the confidence boost."

"I mean it, Sarai." He spun to me. "You're more powerful than you know. You're kept safe in the castle for a reason. Believe in yourself more."

With his last word, the memory vanished, replaced with the rushing water as if it'd never been there.

"Did you see that?" I gasped.

Marcus shook his head. "The memories are only for you. What did she show you?"

"Sakari." With a shaky smile, I blinked away my tears. "He said exactly what I needed to hear."

Arm still around my waist, Marcus curled me into his chest, our bodies flush. "She's fairly intuitive."

One of my hands pressed against his hard pecs—the downbeat of his heart thumping against my palm—and the other looped around his neck. With ease, he kept us afloat, legs stroking with each motion. Water clung to the short strands of his hair, tousled and glistening under the warm sun peeking through the branches above.

"It's a relief to see you smile, for real," he said. "I've longed for the smiles you used to give me."

My smiles had changed. For him. For the world. They'd become more reserved, a shield of protection to keep me from fully feeling so much.

"It's been quite a while since I had a real reason to smile. Thank you for bringing me here. It..." I cleared the emotion from my voice. "It meant a lot seeing Sakari. More than any words could express."

"I thought you knew by now." He used the tips of his fingers to brush wet, stray strands from my forehead. "I'd do anything for you, Sarai. Just say the words."

I swallowed. The ardent sincerity of his eyes quivered my insides, heat swelling in my core.

Marcus's tongue tasted his bottom lip with a light teeth graze, his stare dipping to my lips. "I really want to kiss you."

Yes. Yes, I wanted that, too. I wanted to erase the last man who dared to touch me without my permission. To replace the tainted firsts. But could I handle it? Would Marcus's touch obliterate the unwanted memories? Or give them life?

Though it terrified me, there was only one way to find out. I had to know I wasn't forever broken.

"I won't stop you."

Eyes lifting from my waiting mouth, he searched mine, gauging their truthfulness. "If I do, there's no going back, Sarai. Once I kiss you, you're mine. Every inch of your skin. Every breath from your lips. Every beat of your heart. *Mine.*" His large hand trailed up my slim waist and brushed the bare skin of my ribcage. I didn't flinch.

I didn't flinch.

"But if you need more time, I'll wait. I can't imagine a more worthy reason to master patience." Mouths an inch apart. "...than for you." The water was warm, the air around us balmy, but I shivered. Goosebumps spread the entirety of my body. "So, I need you to be sure. I need to know..."

His. Marcus's. Deep in my bones, it became so clear. Without a doubt. There were much worse things.

I inched closer, the tip of my nose skimming his. "Then I'm yours."

Crash.

Our mouths crashed.

The most devastatingly beautiful crash.

It was a dance between urgent and savoring, like we had no time yet all the time in the world. His tongue wrote stories on my lips of his fierce desire and yearning. And I was a blank novel waiting for his resonant words to fill the pages.

He breathed. Hard. Fast. Like it was the last breath he'd

take before fate stole him from this world. Fingers fisted the hair at the base of my skull and clutched the sensitive place between my wings.

Lips devoured my neck, behind my ear, the slope of my shoulder, the outline of my collarbone. And every area his lips fed, his tongue followed. Sucking. Licking. Tasting. Marcus was everywhere and air no longer existed in my lungs.

My hands roamed the contour of his muscular back, his arms, his chest, and I realized I've never known this kind of hunger before. My body didn't lack nourishment, but it lacked the passion and devotion of Marcus and his magic hands and mouth. This was the kind of kiss with the power to strip away grief and fear and worry. None of that existed when we were braided limbs and tangled souls.

"Sarai," Marcus whispered into my ear. "I think my heart was missing you before it knew of your existence." His nose trailed up and down, our cheeks kissing. "I love..." He swallowed. "I love you."

One skip, two. My heartbeats found their steady rhythm once again and I squeezed my eyes shut, but a tear escaped anyway.

Nestling under his jawline, my lips pressed into the scruff, just a touch. "I love you, too."

He shuddered, and when I drew back, I thought I saw his eyes glisten with tears, but then he closed them as both of his hands cradled my face, kissing me again. I brushed a hand through his wet, silken hair and hooked my legs around his waist.

Marcus deepened the kiss, our tongues meeting and stroking, a tantalizing clash of passion. This was how it was supposed to be, this was how it was supposed to *feel*. Mutual desire and affection. A respect that ran so deep, you could free your mind and hand yourself over without pause, without restraint. He'd never hurt me again.

My wings curled around us in approval, forming to the corded muscle of his back. In the most vulnerable state, they accepted Marcus, sensed his worthiness. No matter what anyone else thought, no matter who might disapprove, we were unbreakable.

Marcus's fierce love had the ability to make me forget everything.

Everything.

THIRTY-SIX

MARCUS

SHE loved me.

THIRTY-SEVEN

LIA

AFTER we traversed around the darkened landscape of Novalora last night with a lantern of fireflies and no luck, we slept for a few hours under a massive blue flower. As soon as the sun dawned, Cameron and I trekked every mile left. There was no sign of the elves.

Pixies were gossips, so I knew they'd have told us if they'd seen them if we asked, but I didn't want to take their word for it. We needed to see with our own eyes and our hours were met with failure.

"This is what I expected when Calliope said she was a

faery." He pointed to a miniature lady in a yellow tulip dress and bare feet. The span of her pink wings dwarfed her tiny body.

"A pixie?" I chuckled as we passed a giant red mushroom with white flecks.

"The books and movies I've seen always depicted them that way most of the time."

"Bet Calliope blew your mind."

He chuckled. "You have no idea." Cameron walked a few steps before he said, "What if we left the faery realm and lived in the human world? What if leaving resets the balance?"

I hopped over a fallen oversized dandelion stem. "There's a reason faeries don't live in the real world, Cam. Remember that thing called metal? That's in basically every human necessity. Houses, transportation, technology. We'd never survive."

"I don't know." He shrugged. "We'd still have our abilities, right?"

I nodded.

"So, we could buy a few acres of land in the middle of nowhere, and you could help us grow crops. We could buy livestock and live off the land. Maybe build a house entirely out of wood and glass, plastic, anything non-metal, a quaint log cabin."

My eyebrow arched. "And what about pipes and plumbing?"

"You don't think I could rig something with PVC pipes and fittings? I'm a mechanic's son. MacGyverering is kind of our thing. And maybe we could find property by a lake. I could build a well and an outhouse. Bury our...bodily functions."

"Lovely. That'd be your job." I chuckled.

He smirked. "Well, I'd have to pull my weight somehow."

"And what about our ears and my wings? Might frighten a

human or two if we were seen."

"We can stay invisible, right?" He shrugged. "And if they did see us, they'd forget after long enough, right? Callie hid her wings and ears for quite some time. There are ways. Hats and hairstyles, leotards or ace bandages to wind up your wings around your torso. That's what Callie did, I think."

He'd really thought this through. "How about transportation? Are we going to walk everywhere? Or are you going to build us a wooden carriage and buy some horses to pull us?"

"It's not like we could go anywhere but the outdoors anyway. We'd just create our own Faylinn, hidden from the world where no one could find us."

I smiled at his hopeful imagination. "It's a beautiful thought, Cam, really, but we don't have any money. We'd have to get jobs, which would be next to impossible. While I'd love to afford lakefront property, we simply couldn't. And what about children? We'd have *fae* children. How is that fair to them? To force them to hide their true selves? Explaining to them how dangerous it would be to show their features."

"You want to make a baby with me, Ginge?" Cameron grew a lop-sided grin.

"Oh, shut up." I knocked him in the chest and he grabbed my hand before I could take it back.

He kissed my palm. Once, and again. "I want to make lots of babies with you. Or, just trying lots...and lots...and lots of times, then we have like two or three. That seems doable."

My teeth sunk into my lower lip, heat flushing my cheeks. "How about we focus on finding the elves first. Then move onto the whole resetting the balance issue before we get into the whole offspring talk. We haven't even bonded yet."

"You brought it up." He chuckled. "But while we're on the topic. Marrying you is my first order of business when the dust settles."

If we were still alive when all was said and done, I'd say yes in a heartbeat.

AFTER scouring Novalora with no luck, we headed back to the castle to check in with Calliope.

"They aren't in Faylinn, Rymidon, or Oraelia, either," she said. "Where in the world could they be?"

"What if we were to check their old land? Do you know what it was called?"

"Stefean mentioned it. It was...umm...Engalawood, I think?"

"Engalawood," I said aloud to remember. "Got it. Should we go there or Fortenberry first?"

Calliope pursed her lips to the side. "What if the Oak can't even take you there and you wind up trapped somewhere?"

"I'm pretty sure no matter where it takes us, we could get back to Faylinn or Rymidon."

"Pretty sure?" Cameron's eyebrow crooked.

"We've taken more hazardous risks than this. I think we can handle a little limbo if it comes to it," I said. "What about the other Songbirds? Are we just waiting to hear back from the other Royals?"

"Rymidon, Mirrion and Oraelia already contacted us. They don't believe their Songbirds are the ones. Apparently, all three were much like Oliviana, almost guileless. Now, I'm just waiting for Aurorali and Callastonia to contact me."

"Maybe that's their shtick. The more innocent you appear, the less people will suspect you." Like a second skin, my human Lia persona took over. I clapped my hands together, forcing enthusiasm. "Because, Calliebug, if they think their mission is important enough, they'll do anything to protect themselves!"

I hated reminding us where our friendship began and my deception, but the point was a crucial one to make.

She flinched but recovered, rubbing her bottom lip. "Yeah, but it's not like we can force Oliviana to tell us even if that were true."

"But you can," Kai said.

Calliope sighed, slicing her gaze in his direction in the window seat. "You know I hate using my Supremacy."

Kai's eyebrow quirked. "And you don't think if there's ever a time to use it, this is it?"

"Even if I did, I guarantee Viridessa is immune to it. There's no way she'd be able to be controlled by me or any of the other Royals. If she was, we'd have nothing to worry about when she showed herself, but a god would never be controlled by its creations."

As disheartening as it was, she had a point.

"Did the other Royals use it?" Cameron asked.

"I know Sarai doesn't. She hasn't touched her Supremacy since she became queen. She refuses, and after what Adair did, I don't blame her. But I'm not sure about the other kingdoms. Though, something tells me Steafan has no qualms with using his Supremacy."

"Well, we're not getting any closer to finding the elves here." Cameron took my hand. "Should we get going?"

I nodded. "We'll check in after we search Engalawood."

"If we don't wind up in a black hole," he snarked and I

rolled my eyes.

"Maybe I should send Dugal or Brokk or Declan with you."

"We'll be fine," I said. "You need them here with you more than we do."

"If you don't make it back in a few hours, we're coming for you."

"Thanks, Mom." Cameron waved as we walked out of the atrium.

I'D never tried to go somewhere I'd never been before, but I assumed it was much the same as anywhere else. When I pressed my palm to the trunk of the Waking Oak, I asked for safe passage to Engalawood. The wood groaned, underwinding a passageway. We couldn't see through to the other side; not that we ever could, but I hoped we'd at least see sunlight or some form of life, something so we knew it was safe. I didn't actually believe we'd end up in a black hole, but anything was possible.

Stepping through, holding Cameron's hand tightly in mine, my foot planted on land. Except rather than a cushy patch of grass or gnarly roots, my foot met solid dirt. My eyes lifted to a barren landscape. Not a single sprout of green. Though there were hills and valleys in the distance with no trees to block the view, all that was left was brown. Bare twigs and leafless fallen trunks on dry soil.

"How could the elves do this?" I took a step and something crunched under my foot. A bone from some sort of small animal. Radik or gorgan, maybe? Upon a closer look, mingling with the bald terrain were talons and bones and teeth. The remnants of whatever creatures roamed this land. "How hard is it to respect and nurture the world around you? The only land you have? Plant a seed, water a bush, feed your life sources. It's not that hard."

"They don't deserve Calliope's Arcshire. If this is what they'd make of it." Cameron sighed. "If Sarai sent the elves back here, they'd die in days, but maybe they'd deserve it. Do you think they'd even come back here to hide out or whatever? There's nothing here."

"I don't see why they would, but we need to search anyway. Let's make this quick. If we were in any other land or kingdom, we could scrounge up some water or food, but there are no signs of life here."

"And we know how hangry you get without food."

I rolled my eyes. "Without any forest or vine obstructions, it shouldn't take us long. I think I'll survive."

THIRTY-EIGHT

SARAI

OUR harvest isn't as depleted as yours, but it's nearing dangerously low levels. If we could offer Rymidon another round of barrels, I would, but Oraelians have to eat, too."

"I know." I waved Marcus off. "You don't have to justify why Oraelia can't continue with our trade agreement. I understand. We're all suffering. Ensuring your kingdom is taken care of is your parents' priority. I think all kingdoms have halted trade agreements at this point. As of now, we're making sure children are fed, while the rest of us eat enough to survive and hope we'll have another meal tomorrow."

"Most grown fae are getting one meal a day," Kayne said. "Some are rationing into two and three meals, while others are eating it as one, but they're getting enough to sustain themselves for the time being. Though, if our projections are correct from Arleen, in three days' time, the rations will be cut in half."

Marcus's hand ran down his face. "Oraelia probably has a few more days than that, but we aren't far behind."

Galdinon tapped on the open doorway. "Your…family is here, Your Highness."

My heart swelled when Calliope and Kai entered the tower with Lia and Cameron in tow. *My family*. Marcus moved aside, letting them file into the room.

"Your faces are a bright spot in my day." I hugged Calliope and a firm round bump nudged my stomach. My eyes shot up. She pressed a discreet finger to her lips with a light in her eyes that could only mean one thing before stepping away. I couldn't stop my smile but kept my thoughts to myself.

"We wanted to come check in with you and tell you where we're at," she said.

Lia crossed her arms over her chest. "Cameron and I wanted to make ourselves useful so we searched Novalora, Fortenberry, and Engalawood. There were no signs of the elves anywhere. No tracks, no fire remnants, nothing."

"It's like they vanished into thin air." I braced my hands on my hips. "I don't understand."

"What was Engalawood like?" Marcus asked.

"Lifeless and brown," Cameron said.

"Even after all these years, it didn't regenerate with new growth? Not a single lake or tree?" I asked.

"Nothing." Lia shook her head. "Engalawood was like a desert, just not as hot. No animals, no vegetation, but most importantly no elves."

"We also came because I heard from Callastonia and Aurorali while Cameron and Lia were in Fortenberry," Calliope said. "There was no luck with their Songbirds. Not one was suspected of being Viridessa. I don't know what else to do. Our harvest won't sustain us for much longer. The fowl and game in Faylinn are nearly extinct. We've left the fish alone for the sprites, but even those are declining. And the dead lands are less than a mile from creeping through our villages."

I heaved a sigh. "We're no better off. If my fae had more strength, they'd be rioting at the castle gates. They calmed when they learned the elves were gone, but it was short-lived." I turned to Kayne. "Where are *we* on tracking the elves?"

He straightened. "Last we heard, Callastonia found the remnants of a few fires on their northern lands yesterday, but there haven't been any other signs of them."

"How did they get through the Waking Oak without being seen by Callastonia Keepers?" Kai asked.

"Either they're incredibly stealthy, or they have outside help. The Keepers at the Oak denied seeing them. Something doesn't line up."

The musk of myrrh filled my nostrils as a flash of Tomas's dark blue eyes seared through the memories and the armor I'd donned. With the mention of Callastonia, I found myself trapped in that dining hall, against that wooden pillar. My stomach rolled and I clutched it.

"Sarai, are you all right?"

My head whipped to Calliope. "Hmm?"

"I asked if you were all right. You've got a strange look in your eyes."

"Oh." I swallowed, cleared my throat. "I'm fine. Just

thinking about everything."

"It was probably the mention of Callastonia."

"Kayne," I snapped, but he wasn't apologetic as he stared back at me.

"Why? Is there a problem with Callastonia?" she asked.

"No, no. Everything's fine." My eyes sliced to Kayne to keep his mouth shut. I was seconds away from tapping into my dormant Supremacy.

A swirl of remorse and determination rose in his eyes. "If you don't tell them, I will."

"No. *Stop.*"

His voice softened as he stepped closer to me. "It's hard. I understand. I can't fathom, but if it were me you were protecting, My Queen, I'd want to know. I'd loathe the darkness of ignorance."

"What's Kayne talking about, Sarai?" Marcus asked, farthest from me now.

Kayne's eyes narrowed like a big brother, just the way Sakari used to when I was in trouble, encouraging me to tell the truth.

I couldn't meet any of them in the eye, so I faced the window of the tower, overlooking my favorite mountaintops. *Peace, bring me peace.*

"After the Royal gala, Prince Tomas…" Nausea churned my stomach saying his name. "He invited me to Callastonia for dinner, so we could get to know one another better. The day we went to Elfland, his adviser asked if I was available that evening. I'm not sure why I went. My heart wasn't in it, but I needed a distraction. And I thought I owed it to Rymidon to try, to see if my heart would change.

"It started out fine enough, but it didn't take long before I realized the charm the night of the Royal gala had been an act, a very impressive act. When I told Tomas I didn't think we were a good match, he forced himself on me."

One of my hands latched onto the stone ledge as that night seized my brain. I clenched my eyes shut, trying to squash the memory of his aggressive hands and his mouth on my bare skin, my heart racing.

My words must've taken a moment to sink in because no one made a sound.

I took a heavy breath, releasing it slow. "He didn't get far, as he was interrupted by one of his Sowers—"

"He got far enough," Kayne said, gritting his teeth. "When I found her, her dress was torn and she was trying to fashion a shawl out of the table cloth to cover herself."

"Why weren't you with her?" Kai asked.

"I dismissed him and Galdinon," I said, cutting off the accusation. "It never occurred to me I couldn't trust being alone with Tomas, another Royal." Kayne would not be punished for something I asked him to do.

"Sarai," Calliope said on a breathless rasp. "Why didn't you say something?"

I exhaled through my nose, clutching the neckline of my dress. "He threatened to reveal Marcus's dealings with the elves, the knowledge about the scroll, the deceit I've been spewing to Rymidon, Cameron and Lia's transformation. Not just to the other Royals, but to every fae of every kingdom. I couldn't let any of you suffer more than you already are."

And then slender arms were holding me from behind, Calliope's cheek against the side of my head. "Oh, how I wish I'd known. I'll kill him. I will."

After a moment, I wasn't able to control my tears, my head

falling forward.

"Are you kidding me? That piece of scum dirtbag rotting sack of—" Cameron cut himself off. "You shouldn't have protected us, Sarai. Marcus and I would've marched up to the Royals ourselves and told them what we did. Hell, I'll announce it to every damn kingdom right now so that he pays for what he did to you."

When Calliope let go, I turned. My eyes were drawn to Marcus first. He stared at me across the tower, the most devastating anguish staining his eyes. He hadn't said a word yet. It was as if a death wrecked his world. He took one step, and then another until he was close enough to touch me.

"You protected me? Even after he tried—" His voice broke, a heartbroken crack. "Sarai." And once the fissure was finished with him, it lurched and spread, carving through my heart. "This is why you were so distant, acting so strange those days before, when you got *sick* and flinched at my touch."

I nodded, turning my face away. "Tomas didn't get to assault me and destroy those I love."

Marcus hooked his finger under my chin, so I met his eyes. "I— I don't— I can't—"

His hand covered his mouth as he looked to the ceiling, like the polished stone would give him answers. His hand shook, his breathing erratic.

"No," his voice broke, too fragile. Barely even a word. A fist gripped the roots of his hair. "No." And then he spun around, storming from the tower.

"Marcus. Marcus!"

"Maybe he just needs a minute." Calliope stopped me from following him with a hand on my arm. "Let him calm down in private for a moment."

"Tomas won't get away with this," Kai said.

Calliope nodded. "I don't care what he threatens. I'll send him to Arcshire if he tries. He can have fun with the elves, once we find them, that is. Or better yet, let's seal him off in Engalawood."

I nodded, blinking away tears.

"How are we going to handle this?" Kai asked Kayne, direct, no-nonsense.

"That depends. Are we going through the appropriate channels? Do I need to set up a meeting with King Eadric and Queen Isolda?" When Kai didn't respond right away, Kayne added, "Or do we want to handle this ourselves?"

Kai looked the way Marcus left for a brief second before focusing back on Kayne. "How discreet do you think we can be?"

"If we can get Marcus under control, as discreet as necessary. I've been envisioning what I'd do since I found her after it happened."

"Count me in," Cameron said, stepping up. "I don't care what it is. I'm there."

Kai glanced at the archway again. "We need to get Marcus. He'll want a say."

"What are you going to do?" I asked.

"It's better if you're not a part of this," Kai said. "No knowledge, no repercussions. This is on us."

"But—"

Calliope touched my shoulder. "Just let them do what they need to, Sarai. You aren't alone. You have all of us. Let them defend you for once."

With a resigned sigh, I nodded. "I'll try to find Marcus."

When I entered the corridor, Galdinon looked at me and

307

pointed. Marcus hadn't gone far. I reached the end and found him in an alcove with his head bent, hands planted on the stone wall.

"I should've been more insistent the night of the gala, made you understand," he said, sensing me there. "There's been rumors of his treatment of women, his affinity for using women to satisfy certain needs, but I didn't know he'd go that far. I didn't think he was a monster, that he'd try to take advantage. If I'd done a better job warning you away from Tomas, you'd never have gone to Callastonia."

I curled my hand around his thick shoulder. "We're not going to lay any blame right now. None of this is your fault. It happened; we're moving past it."

Marcus whipped around. "Tomas preyed on you because he thought he could, that our secrets would be more valuable than his." He gripped the sides of my face, gently. So gently, but ardent, bending to meet me in the eyes. "They're not. I'd suffer a fate worse than death to have kept him from harming you, Sarai."

I bowed my head, tears leaking without my permission. *Why don't they ever listen to me?* "I'll survive."

"You don't have to be so stoic or merciful." Frustration laced his words as he stroked my cheeks. "It's like you think because of what your father did, you have to do the exact opposite and let everyone take advantage of your good nature, that you owe them. You're allowed to be angry, to want retribution. To punish those who deserve punishment. Not everyone is deserving of compassion."

I raised my head, the intensity of my emotions burning through my eyes. "You don't think I'm mad? Of course I'm mad, Marcus. I'm *furious*. Tomas tried to steal something that should only ever be mine to give. I'm downright raging inside, but I have to keep it buried. I need to move forward and forget it."

"Why? What will that help? Other than feeding a festering wound that will never heal."

"Because I'm *terrified* that if I give in, if I follow through with all the cruel things I want Tomas to experience, I'll like the taste of it too much."

Marcus's head shook as his tongue swiped his bottom lip. His teeth sunk into the flesh, closing his eyes. "Oh, my sweet Sarai." Opening them again, he traced my jaw with the pad of his thumb. "You're not capable of the things your father did. It's just not in you. Are you kidding me? You not only spared the lives of the elves after they slayed twenty of your fae, but you also built them a damn village, provided food and protection. You're not only good, you're a damn saint."

My chin quivered. "And I regret ever negotiating that deal."

"Because you couldn't contain them soon enough to protect the fae, not because you want them dead."

"I want Tomas to suffer. I wouldn't hold a single hint of sorrow if he died."

Murderous. Marcus's gaze grew thunderingly murderous. "That makes two of us. Let him underestimate you, believe you won't fight back. You're a tempest clothed in flesh. He just doesn't know it yet."

Our eyes locked, unblinking. I nodded. I meant what I said. With every fiber, I wanted Tomas to suffer.

"Kai, Kayne, and Cameron want to talk to you back in the tower. I think they're forming a plan to confront Tomas."

Without hesitation, Marcus took my hand and walked us back to the study. The three men were huddled near my desk, speaking in low, assertive voices.

"When do we leave?" Marcus asked, breaking them up.

Kai turned around. "Are you levelheaded enough to not take matters into your own hands?"

"That depends on what you have in mind."

"Something that will keep us from murdering a Royal, but also bring suffering he'll never forget."

"I think we should leave them alone." Calliope slipped her arm through the crook of my elbow. "Come on, Sarai."

Lia closely followed.

"But—" I squeezed Marcus's hand.

"Go," he said. "We'll make this right."

I wanted that. I did, but it also worried me.

"Just be careful."

With a nod and light kiss on the cheek, Marcus let go of my hand and joined the other men.

THIRTY-NINE

CAMERON

We can't go storming the castle." Kayne's eyes met each of ours, ingraining his words. "They have two Keepers at the Waking Oak, so they'll know as soon as we arrive. And I assume you don't want King Eadric and Queen Isolda involved in this."

Marcus snorted. "At least then they'd know what a loathsome, rotten faery their son is, but no. I want this done quietly."

Kai nodded. "We'll need some sort of diversion."

"I'm good at those," I volunteered.

Kai eyed me, the corner of his mouth turning up in a smirk.

"That's actually not a bad idea. They don't know Cameron. If you can draw the Keepers' attention away so we can slip through before it closes, we'll have a chance to go unnoticed."

"Done."

"What do we know about Tomas's personal Keepers?" Marcus asked.

Kayne leaned his head into the circle. "They're skilled, especially Conor, but they don't guard him unless he leaves the castle."

"So, the only way to get to him is in the castle?" I asked. That didn't sound like a very discreet mission.

"No, we'll have to draw him out somehow," Marcus said. "We need him to be secluded."

"You can't kill him, Marcus," Kai said. "No matter how much Tomas deserves it. He's a Royal. You kill a Royal and Oraelia will have a war with Callastonia just like that." He snapped his fingers.

"I'm not going to kill him, just make it clear that he's never to touch another woman without her permission again. And make it a little *more* clear that he never should've *breathed* in Sarai's direction."

"I'm good with that." I shrugged. This piece of crap was going down. "So, how do we draw him out?"

"While they ate dinner…" Kayne's teeth grit, his nostrils flaring.

He must've carried a load of guilt for leaving Sarai alone with Tomas. It probably hadn't occurred to him that another Royal would have the balls to attack a queen.

"I chatted with his Keepers about what it's like guarding Sarai. They were jealous I had a young, single queen." He shook his head with a disgusted laugh. "But they mentioned or rather complained about how every night Tomas takes a walk around the village, strumming his balalaika."

"What's a balalaka?"

"Balalaika," Kayne said. "It's a stringed instrument they play in Callastonia."

"Why were they annoyed by that?" I asked.

"They were hinting at more, but I didn't quite grasp it until later. They said he doesn't talk to any of the Callastonians. He doesn't look at any of them, he just sings about blue flowers and how many he'd like to collect. And then he's ready to go back."

"Huh." Kai crossed his arms over his chest, wheels turning in his head.

"I'm guessing it's not just to get some fresh air," I said.

"I thought it was at first. A strange nightly stroll to show off his musical skills to his fae, but after he hurt Sarai, I couldn't stop thinking about it. She can't be the first woman he's forced himself on. He's always singing about blue flowers. Why?" Kayne's eyes pinched. "What if it means something to his Keepers, or a single Keeper? One who carries out Tomas's dirty work on the side. Maybe he's choosing his next conquest."

Marcus's jaw clenched, his fists curling at his sides. "We need to get there in time for his little walk."

"It's almost sundown," Kai said. "Let's head out."

WE clothed ourselves in hooded cloaks, like all the Rymidonian Keepers wear. I kept my hood off to look less suspicious when I entered the trunk first.

As I stepped through and caught sight of the Callastonian Keepers, I said, "Well, this isn't Mirrion." I leaped along the

313

roots, away from the Oak, hands on my hips, pretending to take in the landscape.

The two Keepers walked over, backs to the opening of the trunk. "Who are you?"

It started closing, but the other three hadn't come through yet. *Come on, guys.* "I'm just a little lost, I guess. Where am I?"

"Are you inebriated? This is Callastonia."

When there was only a crevice for them to slip through, all three darted out at the speed of light, rounding the back of the trunk. *Finally, fellas.*

"Oh, that's right." I slapped my thigh. "That's what I meant. It looks different at night. I'm supposed to meet my girlfriend in the woods for a little rendezvous, if you know what I'm sayin'," I stage-whispered around the back of my hand, nudging one in the arm.

He rolled his eyes and threw his arm to the side. "Get out of here."

"No problemo, capitan." I saluted, and rounded the trunk, meeting the others. With a nod from Kai, I flipped up my hood and we sped into the trees. Spreading out, so we were less likely to be seen, we darted through the forest. The foliage was thick, adding a little challenge to our course, but it didn't slow us down. In no time, the main village and castle peeked through the branches. As we approached, the ancient castle showcased more clearly under the moonlight.

A long, gray brick road curved its way through meadow up to the castle gates. Gold and light blue flame-shaped domes topped each of the five towers. It wasn't quite as large as the Rymidonian castle, but it rivaled it.

"Let's separate, surround the village so we're less likely to be noticed," Kai said, stopping my appraisal of the kingdom.

"I'm sure we'll hear Tomas when he comes through. Once we can gauge his route, follow his path and we'll meet at the perimeter and solidify a plan when we see how many Keepers are with him."

We nodded and fanned out. I found a pine tree closer to the castle that overlooked a good portion of the village and gave me eyes on the entrance. I'd see as soon as Tomas left the castle.

The village was quiet, most of the cottages dark or little light shining through the windows. Did they enjoy his serenading or were they sleeping and woken up nightly? If it didn't get me killed, I'd probably have thrown a shoe at him or maybe something harder.

We hadn't come a moment too soon. Just as I was settling against the trunk, the iron gates opened and a mellow melody drifted through the night. It was soft, but loud enough for fae ears. Two Callastonian Keepers alongside a blond with broad shoulders and a cocky gait ambled down the drive, approaching the village and picking a pathway on the north side. That must've been Prince Douche himself. I dropped to the forest floor.

As I darted from cover to cover, hiding behind trunks and bushes and buildings, I caught sight of Marcus. He was closer to Tomas, but remained in the shadows, watching. I couldn't see his eyes, but I imagined they were lethal. Had Lia been the one Tomas hurt, I might not have had the sense to make a plan before barging into the castle. Every witness be damned. It would have been worth it, too.

Once I was close enough to Marcus, his head turned in my direction, spotting me. He knocked his head to the side to follow him and we crept behind the village, keeping eyes on Tomas between each dwelling. When light allowed, gleaming from firefly lanterns, blue flower wreaths hung from a couple cottage windows. *Blue flowers.* The further we went, I counted. There weren't very many. Four, maybe? But they were all the same tiny blue flowers, and only in windows, one window of the houses.

A simple decoration or a secret message? Were they offering themselves up to him? What kind of sick and twisted fool was he?

The song was coming to an end when Kai and Kayne came into view, meeting us near the end of the pathway Tomas was on.

"You two get the Keepers," Marcus said under his breath. "Cameron and I will get Tomas. I'll give the signal."

They nodded and we plastered ourselves to the backs of the trees on either side of the darkened pebble path.

The strumming stopped and gravel crunched as footsteps grew closer and away from the village. "Lots of blue flowers out tonight." Tomas's low voice traveled into the trees. "Beautiful sight they are, gleaming in the dark."

"How many?" One Keeper asked.

Tomas paused. "All of them. They're only enticing as one when they refuse to bloom."

What kind of code was that? He was only satisfied if she refused him?

"Don't worry," he murmured. "I'll share my bouquet when I'm finished. As promised."

I kept my eyes on Marcus for the signal. One nod and we converged on the three Callastonians. Both Kai and Kayne grabbed the Keepers in chokeholds, dragging their bodies further into the forest.

Tomas's head whipped around, but with one punch, Marcus knocked him to the ground, the bala-whatever clattering down. He didn't get back up.

"Grab the stupid string thing and his feet," he murmured.

He didn't have to ask me twice. In less than a minute, we had the two Keepers tied up with sacks over their heads and Tomas laying at our feet on the dirt.

Kai smacked him, rousing Tomas, and he tensed when he took in our faces, hoods pulled back. He scrambled away on his hands and feet like a scared little mouse, but didn't make it far when Marcus took him by the throat and lifted him off the ground. With his feet dangling, he clawed at Marcus's hand, eyes bulging, face growing red.

"So, you enjoy preying on women? That's an interesting fact, Tomas. One I think the entire Royal council would like to hear."

"Preying is such a relative term."

Marcus's hold on his throat squeezed. "Not so relative when a woman tells you no. Maybe more than the Royal council should be made aware."

"You can't," Tomas choked out, a self-righteous gleam in his eyes. "I'll...tell...everyone..." As if he didn't have breath for more, he gasped out. "Elves."

"Go ahead and spill our secrets. I don't care. I'll happily accept the consequences, but just know, the moment you do, there won't be a soul in our world who won't know what you did to Queen Sarai. She has a heart of gold and you've tarnished it." Marcus's grip tightened, and I waffled with intervening, but Tomas remained conscious enough. "Everyone will know what a worthless piece of filth you are. And if you consider harming another woman, we will rain down an assault so brutal, you'll wish we'd finished the job here tonight."

Marcus finally loosened his fist, dropping Tomas to his feet, but he wasn't finished. With one hard, swift knee to the balls,

Tomas dropped to the soil, clutching his crotch. Kai and Kayne moved in and stripped him naked, handing his clothes off to me. He writhed in pain, unable to protest the loss of his clothes. I stuffed them in the crook of my arm.

Landing a savage kick to Tomas's stomach, Kayne bent down. "Let the wind chill your bones and the dirt and rocks embed your skin, so that you can experience a fraction of the humiliation and helplessness Sarai felt when I found her clutching the scraps of her dress to her chest." The visual shot visceral fury to my chest. "Breathe a word of this and every kingdom will know about your nightly strolls through the village and what you're really doing."

Tomas lugged himself to his knees, covering his junk, and found his hoarse voice. "This is treason, mutiny!"

"This is payback." I punched him in the face and he fell to the ground.

⨍ORTY

LIA

I paced the tower, the wool rug muffling the clop of my boots on the stone. "They've been gone for a while. Do you think they got caught?"

Calliope looked at me with her hands gripping the roots of her curls. "Gosh, I hope not."

"I shouldn't have let them go," Sarai said. "It's my battle to fight. I should've been the one to confront Tomas, not them."

"Are you ready to confront him?" Calliope's voice was gentle, her eyebrow cocked.

Sarai paused before shaking her head and stared out the

window once more. I couldn't imagine how I'd feel in her situation. Would the mere thought of his face fill me with crippling anxiety or would I try to chop off his manhood? It's not as if he deserved to keep it.

The door to the tower creaked open and one by one our men entered. First Marcus, followed by Kai, Kayne, and then Cameron. I released a heavy breath.

"What happened? What took you so long?"

"We got through and took care of Tomas undetected, but we had a slight problem leaving." Kai unhooked his cloak and tossed it onto the nearby chair.

"Took care of him?" Please tell me they didn't murder the Prince of Callastonia. Whether he deserved it or not, we didn't need that sort of complication on top of everything else.

"We just roughed him up a little," Cameron said, slipping an arm around my waist and planting a reassuring kiss on my cheek.

"What kind of slight problem?" Calliope asked, glaring at Kai.

"Cameron's second diversion backfired."

"I must've played innocent a little too well the first time around because nothing I did drew them from the trunk, so Kayne could slip in and open the passageway," he said. "I tried everything, short of pulling one in for a fat sloppy kiss."

"So, what did you do?" Sarai's eyes bulged with alarm from one to the next.

Kai sat down on the chair with his cloak. "Well, there were four of us and only two of them, so we kept ourselves shielded by our hoods and started throwing rocks at them from the forest."

"Rocks," Calliope said, unimpressed. "Chucking rocks was

your big plan?"

Kai shrugged. "It distracted them enough to draw them away from the Oak and search for us. Marcus and I darted around, circling and weaving, trying to throw them off while Kayne opened the passageway. We were able to dive in at the last second, the trunk closing before they reached us."

"You lucky sons of birches." I laughed.

"It was kind of fun. Let's do it again," Cameron said.

"No," the other men said in unison.

"So, Prince Tomas..." Sarai swallowed, her teal eyes a mixture of worry and doubt.

Marcus was the embodiment of intimidation and brooding. "Won't be bothering you ever again."

If I were Tomas, I'd find a nice big rock to hide under so Marcus could never find me again.

"But what about you and Cameron?" she asked.

Kai offered a crooked grin. "Something tells me he'll think twice before sharing anything from your situation or anything about tonight."

"What did you guys do?" My interest was piqued.

"Nothing you ladies need to worry about," Kayne said. "If it's all right with you, Your Grace, I'm going to retire for the evening. Brae and Eitri are on guard tonight."

Sarai nodded and he left.

"I'll tell you later," Cameron whispered in my ear, amusement dancing across his tone.

NAKED? You guys left him naked?"

"And screaming like a little girl." Cameron laughed as we

left the washroom after getting ready for bed. "It was amazing."

"Oh, I wish I could've seen that. Not his…you know, just the situation as a whole. I bet it was so satisfying."

"I don't know if it was as satisfying for Marcus; I'm pretty sure if it were up to him we'd have left Tomas without a heartbeat, but I won't say it didn't feel good to punch him. Especially after we heard that pig tell his Keepers to gather all the women with those blue flowers in their windows. We're still not sure what they mean, but we have a good idea."

"I know what it means."

"How do *you* know what it means?"

"Not because of that." I shook my head with a shrug. "Girls talk, which is all I thought it was before, rumors blown out of proportion." I drew back the comforter on the bed. "Before I came to Walhalla, I had friends in Callastonia, none who participated—at least they said they didn't—but there were those desperate enough to catch Tomas's attention. They'd wear blue flower wreaths in their hair. If one of his Keepers gave them a blue flower to add to their floral crown, then they were to place the wreaths in their windows at night to let Tomas know they were…willing. It started with one girl, but I guess word caught on. Of course they'd keep it hush-hush. No girl wants her parents knowing she's offering herself. And to a Royal no less, someone they could never have."

Cameron scowled, fluffing his pillow. "Well, he won't be *serenading* the village anymore. At least he better not."

"Men like that always find a way, Cam."

FORTY-ONE

SARAI

IN the gathering hall, Kayne stood at the base of the platform to my throne. "Our fae are growing more and more concerned about the lack of food. They'd assumed the elves were responsible, but without the elves in Rymidon and the increase in dead lands, suspicions are rising. They're questioning everything. Some have been communicating with other kingdoms, and finding out we aren't alone in our rationing. They may need to hear from you."

It was bound to come to this. "How can I tell them about the imbalance without revealing Cameron and Lia, the power of our blood and the elves? It doesn't help that Viridessa still has not revealed herself." I stood and stepped down to Kayne's level. "*I'm* beginning to question if she's even responsible."

Kayne nodded. "But we have to offer them something. We're days away from living off of one viga each. Some are volunteering to receive less of the harvest and game so it can be given to children and pregnant women. Fathers giving up rations to feed their families."

"They shouldn't have to live this way!" I shouted to the ceiling. Maybe my frustration would ricochet off the castle walls and reach the Mabuz. "If Viridessa exists, why isn't she showing herself yet? Deliver the consequences and leave our kingdoms be. The delay is cruel enough. Does she even care if we go much longer, Rymidonians are going to die? Faylinnians, Oraelians, every kingdom will have casualties. And for what? Because two beings fell in love and made a mistake."

Kayne kept his voice low. "Don't you think maybe that's the point? Strike us when we're at our weakest, when we simply cannot take another hardship. Let us suffer for disobeying."

"It's spiteful and falls in line with what we know about her, but why penalize the other kingdoms? Why penalize everyone? They know nothing of the transformations, of the imbalance."

"If what Queen Elena said is correct, then Viridessa hasn't woken since every kingdom was one. Everyone lived in Faylinn, so they all would have been affected no matter who was involved. Maybe she wants this to be a lesson to all, not just to the guilty."

I nodded. "She came sooner before. Faylinn didn't starve before the offenders were punished."

"But it was their first offense. As you said, she's cruel. This is most likely punishment for making the same mistake again. If our previous generations had been more forthcoming, trusted in our realm, maybe this could've been avoided again. We'd all be aware of the consequences of an imbalance rather than believing it to be folklore."

I sighed. "Kayne, what if we're wrong? What if this has nothing to do with her? What if we've been looking in the wrong place this whole time and we all starve to death because we didn't look for the right answer? That we relied on one woman's account of what it could be. Maybe we should be looking for a way to transform the elves, and Cameron and Lia back."

Kayne chewed on his lips, an uncertain curve to his shoulders. "I *have* been trying, Your Grace. I know you didn't ask me to, but through discreet avenues, I've been seeking solutions that have nothing to do with Viridessa. There has been no mention of the scrolls. I've kept the names out of it, and the involvement of the elves. I swear, but, My Queen, there are none. It simply is not possible to repair the dead lands or transform fae into humans without counterparts. If it is not Viridessa, then we are lost."

So lost.

I hadn't spoken with Marcus since the night he *visited* Tomas. It had been two days. Was he avoiding me? Needing space after I kept the degrading encounter from him? It was unlike Marcus, but I gave him time. As much time as my heart would allow. Our realm was suffering and I needed my match beside me. Because that's what he was. Marcus was my match. We hadn't said it aloud yet, but he felt the same. I know he did. Which is why I didn't understand why he avoided me.

When my Keepers and I stepped through the Waking Oak into Oraelia, it was a very different kingdom from the last time we came. Trees were barren, bushes nothing but naked twigs, not a flower in sight. Only patches of life dotted the land, fighting to survive. It looked much the same as Rymidon, and my heart plummeted. This beautiful, exotic kingdom lacked all the color and vibrancy it once knew.

"Queen Sarai. How lovely to see you, even under the less than ideal circumstances. How is your kingdom?" Queen Aisling greeted me as soon as Joran escorted us inside the castle, King Ronan by her side in their grand foyer. "I hope Marcus isn't overstaying his welcome."

"His welcome?"

"Yes." Her head tilted, smile dimming. "Since he's been staying in Rymidon for the last couple of days. I assumed he was assisting with the dead lands and dwindling harvest issues. Unfortunately, ours have worsened over the last several days. And we've had no success pursuing Viridessa. Nor any other solution."

"Oh." *That's odd.* "I was coming here to see Prince Marcus, actually. I haven't seen him in a couple of days and had a few things I needed to discuss with him," I bluffed. What I wanted was my other half, my true support. He'd never abandoned me before, even when I thought I wanted him to.

"Are you sure, my dear?" Her brow ruffled, her hand reaching out for King Ronan. "He isn't visiting someone else in Rymidon, maybe?"

"If there was another Royal in my kingdom, I would be the first to hear about it, especially Marcus."

"Maybe we misheard him," King Ronan said in a way that attempted to comfort Aisling, patting her hand over his. "Maybe he went to Aurorali to visit Cormac."

"No, I'm certain I heard Sarai's name because I was pleasantly surprised. A mother takes note of these sorts of things." She smiled once again, though it cracked. "He'd been more broody than usual since losing Nerida, but something changed when he began going to Rymidon all those moon cycles ago. He started smiling again. The radiant light he once carried in his eyes rekindled."

Her words should've warmed my heart, but they sunk like a stone in my stomach. Something was wrong. "Are you sure he hasn't come home at all in the last couple of days?"

"Positive, my dear."

Did he go back to Callastonia? Did he try to confront Tomas again? Was he tracking the elves? Hunting for food? Did Guthron find *him*?

"I'm so sorry. I need to go." I whirled around to leave but turned back. "If you hear from him, will you have him come to Rymidon or send me a message?"

"Of course," she said, her eyes falling more concerned. "Should we be worried?"

"I don't know yet." Aisling knew nothing of the elves and Marcus's involvement. This wasn't the time to tell them. "Maybe send a small unit out to search for him, though. It wouldn't hurt." I tried to keep my tone light, so as not to cause distress, but it was brewing like a hurricane in my veins.

Queen Aisling nodded, a mother's worry in her eyes.

Once Kayne and I were a few steps out of earshot, I said, "I have a bad feeling about this."

"Do you think it's Guthron?"

"Marcus betrayed him, tipped us off and we were able to retrieve all the blood they'd stolen along with the scroll. If

Marcus is in fact in danger, I guarantee, it has to do with the elves."

Once we'd returned, I sent out several units of Keepers to search Rymidon. I had little faith Marcus was there. There was a constant watch on the Waking Oak and he hadn't returned after he'd left two days ago, but I needed the confirmation before we expanded our search.

By nightfall, each troop reported back empty-handed. No Marcus and no elves. That settled it.

"I'm going out." I slipped from the study for my bedchamber.

Kayne rushed to follow. "It's late, Your Highness. I'll contact each kingdom and have them begin a search on their patrols this evening. He's a Royal. It's not possible to miss him. He'll be found."

It wasn't a question of finding him, but would he be found alive?

"Then I'll help them search myself." Entering my chambers, I headed straight for my armoire, trading my ornate dress for black pants, a long-sleeved tunic, and my fighting leathers.

"My Queen, I really think you should stay here. Let us handle it. We don't know what we'll find. It'll be safer if you remain in the castle. I'll go in your place, leave Galdinon and Brae with you."

I whirled around, clothes in hand. "Marcus is out there, Kayne. He could be in trouble or pain or—" No. I wouldn't go there. I couldn't go there. "And if Guthron does have him, I'm going to be the one to kill him."

Kayne stared at me, dumbfounded. I'd had enough.

Experienced too much loss. I wasn't about to lose Marcus, too. Guthron pushed his limits one too many times.

"Marcus is my match. There is no one else. I'm going, and you can't stop me."

He released an exasperated sigh and a delayed nod as I slipped behind the dressing screen to change. Removing my crown, I pulled my hair atop my head, securing it in place.

After retrieving all my knives from the weaponry den, Kayne, Brae, Eitri, and Galdinon followed me out of the castle and to the Waking Oak.

Every kingdom we entered Keepers declared there'd been no signs of Marcus or the elves. How was that possible? Would they lie? Lie to a queen?

"What about Fortenberry?" I asked. "Or Novalora? Engalawood?"

"The trolls haven't seen anything, either," Eitri said. "And Novalora is in Faylinn. Queen Calliope's Keepers wouldn't lie. Unless he somehow entered undetected, he isn't there. As for Engalawood, since Lia and Cameron traveled, I've had a unit check periodically. The elves aren't there, nothing would sustain them if they were. Not for this long."

"Aren't the trolls cowards?" I asked. "Anyone who threatens them will have the trolls lying to save themselves."

"It's a possibility, but Cameron and Lia search Fortenberry only days ago."

"And anything could've happened since then. We're going to Fortenberry."

Reentering the Waking Oak, Kayne stepped through first. I'd never been to Fortenberry before. We were well into the night, but there wasn't a soul in sight. Only the rush of waterfalls surrounded us in the rainforest, the humidity sticking my clothes to my skin. Though I'm sure the land was once flourishing, it was half dead, deteriorating just as the realm.

A stone bridge arched over the foot of the pitiful waterfall to the east. "That way." I pointed. "We'll begin there." I forged on, my Keepers trailing close behind.

We searched for miles, but never once came across a living creature.

"I know they aren't social creatures, but isn't it strange we haven't seen a single troll?"

"A bit," Kayne said. "Though we're nearing the dead of night, they might all be asleep."

"But there aren't even any homes or villages. Where do they live?"

As we climbed the rocks of a ridge, Eitri said, "They make their homes in hillsides and under bridges. They don't need much, just a warm place to sleep."

At the top of the cliff, I surveyed the land below. There were gullies and thickets. Some thrived, while others were desolate and dreary. In the distance, a grassy marsh was lit by the moonlight. In the center, a dark form hunched. It was difficult to tell, inanimate or live being.

"There," I said. "What is that?"

Kayne leaned forward, ever so slightly, squinting. "It's too dark. I can't be sure."

I leaped off the other side, and they followed. One after another, we sprinted to the wetlands.

Level with the foliage, I couldn't see above the tall grass. Water seeped into my shoes and up my pant legs as I waded through. The closer I grew, the dark figure peeked between the greens. Approaching with caution, I glanced over my shoulder at Kayne. He straightened as if he'd figured out what it was and pressed on in front of me with Galdinon, blocking my view, Brae and Eitri flanking behind me.

Grabbing Galdinon's shoulder, I peered around. When Kayne broke through the grass, he rushed forward, splashing through the swamp. The slumped body came into view, his head hung low with his arms stretched wide, each tied to a wooden post.

Marcus. *Marcus!*

I shoved past Galdinon and hurried my pace. "Marcus! Marcus!" I pushed Kayne aside.

"Wait, Sarai!" Kayne tried, but couldn't stop me.

Placing my hand beneath his chin, I lifted his face. "Marcus," I said, breathless, tapping his cheeks. Come on, wake up. Wake up! "Open your eyes. *Please* open your eyes."

Nothing.

I checked his breathing, but it was shallow. His head sunk back down when I removed my hand from his chin. I reached for one of his wrists to untie him, but the rope singed my fingers. I flinched back with a hiss, shaking out my hand. A thin cut stretched across my fingertips.

"Teadra," Galdinon murmured.

Teadra. Enchanted ropes. I didn't know much about them except no one could get out of them on their own. Marcus's wrists weren't just red from rubbing against the thin rope but burned and lacerated, bleeding.

"What can we do?" I asked.

"Your knives," Kayne said. "Try your knife."

Galdinon said, "It won't work." But even still, I tried.

I slipped one from my thigh and held Marcus's hand, careful to slip the knife inside without nicking his wrist. As soon as I slid the tip under, the cord tightened, digging the knife into his skin. I was quick to remove it, but I cut him just the same.

Soggy sludge!

"The enchantment tightens every time he moves or tries to free himself," Brae said. "I've seen it once before."

"How do we get him out of them?"

None of my Keepers had answers, standing with regretful gapes.

I spun back to Marcus. Bruises tarnished his face and torso, like patchwork, like he'd been beat over and over and he wasn't able to heal himself. How long had he been tied to these posts? Who did this to him?

"Marcus." I cupped his face, his beautiful, marred face. "Come on. Wake up, wake up. It's me, Sarai. I'm here. I came for you. Wake up for me." Tears clogged my throat, strangling my air. "*Please.*"

His eyelids fluttered.

"Marcus?"

His neck rolled a fraction, his head still hanging.

Oh, thank the Fallen Fae. I coughed a laugh. "Marcus?"

"Sarai?" Blinking, he pried open his forest eyes. "No," he rasped. "No."

"Yes, it's me. It's going to be okay. I'm here. We're going to get you out of these."

"No." He coughed, his voice raw. "Trap. It's a trap."

"What?"

"You have...you have to go." His head flopped down once more.

I spun. So concerned with Marcus, I hadn't noticed my Keepers stopped talking to me. There, in the marsh and thick grass, was a sneering Guthron among a horde of elves. And my Keepers gagged with their arms bound behind their backs. Ten hulking elves stood behind, trapping them against their chests. Their ears weren't as sharply pointed, their eyes not dark and deep set but rich in color. Transformed elves. More than there were before we reclaimed the blood. Too many more.

My spine straightened as I blocked Marcus. "Guthron, let them go."

"Or what?" He scoffed, stalking forward, the murky water sloshing. "You will banish me to the Waking Oak?"

I sucked in a breath. How did he know about that?

"We've negotiated once before. We can do it again." But they'd still wind up banished in that branch. I didn't care what it took.

"We are far past negotiations, little queen."

"Did you kill more fae?" I gestured to his henchmen.

The sinister curl of his lips twisted my insides. "I did not have to. Did you really think I would keep all the fae blood in one place? That I would have surrendered so easily? Allow you to take everything we worked so hard to achieve?" Guthron sneered, his towering figure advancing. "So naive. So foolish. *So* Sarai."

No. No. He couldn't. "But it needed to be fresh."

"There are ways of preserving it, darling. It is as if you think me to be unintelligent. How simple-minded do you think I am? Clearly, more dense than you."

There was power in my veins and vengeance in my heart, but I still suppressed a quiver, Guthron creeping closer and closer.

"If you don't want to negotiate, and you refuse the branch, you know what this means." I splayed my fingers at my sides, ready to unleash my element on every single elf here. After hurting Marcus, my mercy came to an end.

But then my arms were yanked behind my back, my wrists stinging as they were restrained.

I struggled against the hold, but the rope tightened, slicing through my skin. *Ouch!* When I whipped around, I was face-to-face with the Mabuz himself, Tomas. "You're looking beautiful as ever, Sarai."

My spine tensed, my shoulders pinched against the teadra. How had I ever found him handsome? Wickedness pooled in his blue eyes and swam on his smirking thin lips.

"Surprised to see me?" he taunted. "Don't be. This was inevitable. Especially after you sent your lackeys to do your dirty work."

"I didn't send anyone; they went on their own accord."

"After you leaked our little secret, of course. I thought we had an arrangement." He clicked his tongue. "Shameful. Did you forget I know your secrets? Which are much more damning than mine. What will your kingdom say when they find out about the bargain you made with the elves? And their future king's part in it. My, my what a betrayal. Not even *I* would consider placing my kingdom in such a predicament."

Realization dawned. "You were the one who told Guthron about the branch."

His smile that once fluttered fireflies in my stomach, drowned them and churned the tumultuous seas. "You don't think my mother shares Royal information with her son?" His golden eyebrow arched as he tipped his head with a nod. "Well, you'd be correct in that it wasn't this son, but the favorite one, Tadhg. It was just my luck when I overheard Calliope was creating a branch for the elves. Of course, I'd have kept that information to myself, but having the elves on my side seemed much more useful. I figured it would come in handy at some point. And look, here it is."

"You've been giving them a place to hide," I accused.

"In Callastonia, of course. I have some very loyal Keepers, as you know, who tend to turn a blind eye when asked, as long as I compensate them handsomely. Though, I couldn't have you searching Callastonia after we collected Marcus. What would Mother say? I'm surprised it took you so long to find us here. I half-expected Marcus to starve before I had the pleasure of killing him myself."

My spine went rigid. "And what exactly was your plan with the elves? Do you even know what they've done?"

Tomas shrugged. "I assumed I'd utilize the elves to *compel* you to bond with me, but after Marcus and his gang of buffoons ambushed me, I wasn't about to let him get away with it. You don't get to humiliate me and walk away without consequences." His eyes sliced to a drained Marcus whose heavy lids rose just enough to glare at Tomas.

"You *assaulted* me," I screamed, wriggling against the teadra without thought. The rope seared my wrists, but I held back my wince. "You're lucky he didn't kill you!"

"Oh, my pet." His voice gentled as his cringe-inducing lips skimmed the shell of my ear, pressing his chest to my back. "Is that what you thought that was?" His knuckles stroked down my cheek, down my jaw and my neck, sliding to the neckline of my top. "That was merely a preview of what you had to look forward to, what was in your future; that was until your puppets came for me."

I whirled around, catching him off guard, and spat in his face.

Tomas took a steady breath, that wasn't really steady at all, but restrained rage as he swiped my saliva from his cheek. Then he backhanded me.

"No!" Marcus roared, fighting against the teadra. "Touch her again, Tomas." His breathing was ragged. "I dare you."

"I'd love to see you try and stop me." Tomas yanked me back into his arms. Nuzzling his cheek against mine, the scratch of his scruff grating my skin. He pressed his lips there and ran his wet tongue from my chin to my ear. My eyes squeezed shut, jaw clenched, refraining from struggling with the teadra. Everything he did was to pull a reaction from me, to hurt me. I wouldn't let him see.

Marcus seethed, thrashing against the restraints. Blood dripped from his wrists as the teadra dug deeper.

"No, Marcus. *Stop.*" If he didn't, the cord would eventually slice his hands clear off.

Exhausted, he hunched over. His shoulders shook as short bouts of breath left him. Crying. Marcus was crying. Somehow that wrecked my heart more.

"So, what's your plan, Tomas?" I asked. "Are you going to kill Marcus, me, and my Keepers? Because that is the only way you'll get away with this."

"Why not?" He let me go with a shrug. Circling me, he twirled a knife in his hand. "The elves have a vendetta against you. They're the perfect patsy. No one would think to look my way."

I focused on Guthron. "And what do you get out of it if the entire fae world is after you for killing two of their Royals?"

"They are already after us. I warned you, Sarai. You broke our agreement. Your blood is now ours. And once they find us, it will not matter. Every one of us will have changed. We will be strong enough to fight back...and win."

"That's seven kingdoms against one. You really think the

odds are in your favor?"

"Do not worry about us, child." Guthron sneered. "We are more resourceful than you give us credit."

"And you," I whipped back to Tomas, "you're okay with this? With allowing them to slaughter our fae? Innocent fae, for our blood. To fight against us."

"They aren't killing me." Tomas tipped his head to the side with pursed lips, emotionless. "We made a deal. All I wanted was your two heads on a platter. They can do what they please from here on out."

"Psychopath," Marcus murmured.

"What was that?" Tomas cupped his ear, leaning into Marcus.

He raised his head with what little energy Marcus had. "I *said* you're a psychopath."

Tomas wound his hand back and smacked Marcus, sending his head flying to the side. The sound echoed around the isolated land.

With my hands tied behind my back, I couldn't aim well enough at the earth to call upon water. If I did, I might blast myself, or risk losing my hands in the process by the force of the element. Though, if Marcus hadn't used his element to burn the posts he was tied to, mine was probably dampened just the same.

"Get on with it then, Tomas," I said, a taunt. "What are you waiting for?"

"Sarai," Marcus wheezed. "What are you doing?"

He might be a monster, but I didn't think Tomas really had it in him to kill us.

"Well, before we move onto the main event, I think I deserve a parting gift, to finish what we started." Tomas gripped my chin, leaning in close to me, our mouths a breath apart. I'd sink my teeth into his bottom lip hard enough to draw blood if he tried to kiss me. "You're so conveniently shackled, it would be such a waste not to partake."

"Stay away from her!" Marcus growled, his wrists barely visible beneath the crimson ichor.

"Stop fighting the teadra, Marcus!" I cried.

"I'd rather lose my hands than have him touch you again."

The infuriatingly smug look on Tomas's face should be slapped away. "Good luck defending her handless."

I swallowed my tears. "He's not wrong. Please. Please, Marcus. Save your hands. Stop fighting."

"I'll never stop fighting." His eyes vowed. "I won't let him hurt you again. Ever."

I broke, tears pouring down my face. "You don't have a choice."

FORTY-TWO

CAMERON

DO you think Sarai has found Marcus yet?" I asked.

Calliope fell back in her chair behind the table in the atrium. "I was promised we'd know as soon as he was found, but it's been hours. If Sarai loses Marcus on top of everything else, she might very well die of a broken heart."

Lia scooted to the edge of the loveseat next to me. "Should we go help her search?"

"You two should get some rest." She massaged her temples. "I have my Keepers scouring Faylinn again, though I doubt he's here."

"But, if it is the elves, do you think they'd be foolish enough to keep him in one of the kingdoms?" I rested my forearms on my knees.

"Where else would they be?"

"Engalawood? Fortenberry?" I shrugged. "We checked days ago for the elves. They could've moved there at any point."

She nodded. "I'll have Brokk check with each of the kingdom's Keepers first to be sure. Once I know Sarai or her Keepers aren't in any of the other kingdoms, we'll go."

"What if it's Viridessa?" Lia asked. "The elves go missing first, now Marcus? She could be coming for me and Cameron next."

"For now, you're safe within these walls. Let's keep it that way."

My legs tingled, a creepy-crawling sensation spreading through my nerves. I shook out my limbs.

"I need to move. Walk the corridor with me?" I stood, holding my hand out to Lia. She interlocked her fingers with mine.

Calliope nodded. "I'll come find you as soon as Brokk returns with the report."

Lia didn't say a word as we strode the halls hand-in-hand, my head spinning out of control. A black cloud hung, unease twisting my bones with the impending fear and my heart pounded beneath my ribcage like it knew.

Our time to pay was coming, if it wasn't already here.

AN eternity later, Calliope found us on the opposite of the side of the castle from the atrium, Kai and her Keepers at her heel.

She called out, "Sarai isn't in any of the kingdoms, so she might've had the same idea as us."

"So, where do we go first?" I asked.

"We split up." Calliope turned to her Keepers. "Declan, I want you to take Dugal and Brokk and scour Engalawood. There's more ground to cover in Fortenberry, so the rest of us will head there."

With a swift nod, the three Keepers turned and marched down the corridor.

"The rest of us should suit up. Weapons, armor, the whole enchilada."

"I'm going to assume that means we go fully prepared," Kai said.

"Yeah, something like that." She grabbed his hand, but he stopped her. Bending his head close, he murmured low enough I couldn't make out much, but it was clear Kai wasn't comfortable with us going after Marcus. Maybe he felt the weight of Viridessa as I did.

"I'll be fine. Don't worry about me," she whispered, touching his cheek. "I need to do this for Sarai."

Kai didn't argue, but he wasn't happy as we followed them to their weaponry den.

I wasn't skilled with half of them, but I strapped a dagger to my waist and one to my ankle. I unhooked a weapon that resembled a machete and strapped it to my back. When I turned to Lia, she was equipped with a bow and arrows, her sapierces holstered to either side of her hips.

Calliope held out two pieces of armor that looked to be made of some sort of faery chainmail. "Just in case."

Lia and I slipped them over our heads. It was nothing more than the weight of another tunic.

When we passed through to Fortenberry, Calliope said, "It might be quicker to separate and search, but I don't feel comfortable with that."

"I agree," I said. "We stay close and we stay together."

We soared through the rainforest, or what used to be a rainforest, weaving through healthy and dry foliage. Steep cliffs that probably once had gushing waterfalls, had trickling water that was more like a leaky faucet. The stark difference between the dead lands and the living was more obvious than the other kingdoms with Fortenberry's abnormally colored trees and vines. One purple, another orange. And the next barren and colorless. A chaotic landscape.

We passed through skyscraper-sized cliffsides caked with shriveled moss and over rocky hillsides, though glens and over fallen trunks, only the stars and moon to guide our path.

Calliope came to an abrupt stop, holding out her hands. "Wait."

We silenced, listening for what she was. Her head tilted, ear directed to the north. She didn't say a word before she darted off again, and we trailed after her. When we came to the edge of a cliff, Calliope and Kai dropped to their hands and knees and crawled to the end.

Lia and I did the same and crouched beside them in a row overlooking a swamp. We were close enough that we could make out figures nestled in the tall grass, but it was too dark for details. Who they were, what they were doing.

Calliope lifted a pair of binoculars, or the faery version of them anyway. They weren't as big and didn't have lenses as long. "They're tied up," she whispered. "All of them. Sarai, her Keepers. Oh, Marcus. He's stretched out, strapped to wooden posts. There are about ten elves with Guthron. And that faery pig Tomas is there."

Kai took the binocular things from Calliope.

"Teadra," he muttered. "That's not good."

"What's that?" I asked.

"They're enchanted ropes. Both Sarai and Marcus are bound by them. Most likely her Keepers, too, but I can't see their backs."

"How can you tell?" Calliope asked.

"There's a subtle dark glow about teadra. I think I only saw it through the halaveinters because of the reflection off the lenses in the moonlight."

"So, what does that mean?" Calliope's eyes drew back to the silhouetted figures.

"The only way out of the rope is if the one who set the enchantment removes it or dies."

Dammit. "Well, that's bad luck. Do you think Tomas set the enchantment?"

Kai nodded. "Probably."

"So, there's nothing we can do?" Calliope's feet scraped the dirt as she shifted her weight.

"Not without knowing for certain who set the enchantment."

"And if it's Tomas?" I asked.

"He's not going to unlock the magic because we ask him to."

"But if we kill him?" Calliope asked, without a hint of hesitation or remorse.

Kai met her stare. "That might be the only way."

A scream tore through the gorge. Sarai. While I couldn't make out the details in the dark this far away, I could see a dainty figure flailing while another dragged her away.

"Tomas has her," Kai said, staring through the halav-whatevers.

Calliope bolted up. "The hell he does." And off the cliff she leaped.

"Calliope!" Kai hissed, darting after her.

Lia and I didn't wait, jumping down, too. We weren't close to the swamp, but that didn't stop Calliope.

"Get your filthy hands off my sister!" she roared, her hand jut out as she tore through the thick grass, parting it. Water sprayed from the murky pond hard enough to knock Tomas off his feet and release Sarai. She tumbled into the water beside him with a distressed cry.

Before any of us could reach her, Tomas was on his feet and had Sarai in his arms again, a dagger at her throat.

"Try that again, mutt queen, and you're next."

Calliope stopped at the water's edge. "You're awfully cocky for a man who has to force women to sleep with him."

"Didn't your husband tell you? I have women lining up for me every day."

"Oh, right. The desperate ones, but not the women you actually want because they can see past your true repulsive nature."

He glared but lifted a feral smile all the same. "Denying me was your loss, mutt queen."

"Right." Her fingers wiggled at her sides, readying to unleash another element. "What a tragic loss. How will I ever carry on?"

"I'd have made a much stronger king than your weak match who bows to your every whim."

The earth rumbled beneath our feet, Calliope's fingers pointed at the soil. She was about to bust the ground wide open, but surely that couldn't be her plan. Tomas still had Sarai.

A root sprang from the earth and whipped him across the face, loosening his hold enough for Sarai to get away. She stumbled to Marcus's side, barely catching herself before she fell into the water.

Calliope wrapped the thick root around Tomas's neck. "Unlock the enchantment on the teadra."

"Never." He continued to smile, vicious.

The root tightened, coloring leaving his face. "Let's try this again. Unlock the enchantments or die. Your choice."

And then, an icy wind blew through the wetlands. I looked to Calliope, assuming it was her, but the earth stopped quaking and she peered around, waiting. Searching.

Through the low-lying mist, on the opposite side of the marsh, behind Marcus, a group of women sauntered between the tall grass. Not just women—the Songbirds.

Though each had different hair color, skin color, and wings, their eyes were all the same vibrant light yellow, like starlight.

The one I saw in the atrium, Oliviana, stepped forward, walking on top of the swamp water like it was glass. "Is this what my world has come to? Elves torturing faeries? Royals torturing Royals? That just will not do." She swiped her hand to the right and the transformed elves restraining the Rymidonian Keepers dropped to the ground.

FORTY-THREE

LIA

I scoured the chests of the elves for a sign of life, but there was none. No steady rhythm of the lungs.

Dead.

Not knocked out. Dead.

"Viridessa?" Calliope's hold on the root around Tomas's neck let up and he tore out of it.

"In the flesh, my dear." She smiled; and though her face was so angelic, the curve of her mouth was sinister.

Calliope blinked, baffled as the rest of us were. "But when we talked to you in the atrium before, you seemed so unaware."

"And indeed, Oliviana was." The icy blonde sashayed around the marsh, weaving in between us. "You see, you do not get to summon me. I do not come when you call. It is not how this works. And that day I was with Marvina."

A brunette clothed in a beige dress accented with talons and turquoise wings, stepped from the line of the others. Her fingers traced down the tethered arm of the Prince of her kingdom as she rounded the right side of him. "And even if I had been present that day, I wouldn't have shown myself to you," she said, in the same tone Oliviana did.

We were surrounded by her. Viridessa was in all of them.

Cameron and I shared a look, speaking with our eyes. He realized it, too. Our hands clasped together.

"Ladies, ladies." Tomas raised his hands, trying to lay on the charm as he fixed his ruffled hair, wiping mud from his face. "Can we help you? I'm afraid you're interrupting a very serious Royal matter."

"Shut up, vermin," Marvina said.

His head cocked, intrigued. "Oh, what you may not know about me is that I like them feisty. Maybe we can work something out for later, when I'm done here." Tomas took one swaggering step and then another. "I also love to share. Myself, of course. There's plenty to go around." His arms swept out to his sides, offering himself to the Songbirds as he spun in a circle. The moron had no clue who he was dealing with.

His smirk was wiped clear off his face when Oliviana snatched his throat and lifted him off the ground as if he weighed as much as a feather. The man's neck couldn't catch a break. His legs flailed, his hands gripping her fingers, trying to pry them off and failed.

"How dare you speak to us this way? Had you kept your

mouth shut, vermin, I would have let you live. This matter did not concern you, but alas, your arrogance has deemed you unworthy of this world." She crushed Tomas's windpipe as if it was nothing but leaves and threw him to the ground, flopping like a rag doll, a bug to squash and nothing more.

Though none of us would miss him, the ruthless action choked my heart. With little to no effort, Tomas was wiped from this realm. It was a statement. The elves, now Tomas. Viridessa held the control here. And suddenly, the most powerful creatures in the world became helpless ants before her.

"Now," Marvina said in Viridessa's malevolent voice. She tapped her chin with a long, pointed fingernail. "Where were we? Oh, right."

Movement caught my eye, a lanky figure drifting backward, trying to remain unseen. Guthron.

"Not so fast, Elvenking," Marvina said. "You, the mastermind. Are you proud of yourself? Proud of the ruin you have caused in my world with your thirst for blood?"

Guthron stopped, but for a moment it seemed he'd try to run anyway. Then he gained futile courage. "Why should the fae be granted such abilities, such influence over the land? While we grovel at their feet." He sneered, puffing out his chest. *Smart, Guthron. Anger the Mabuz more.*

"Ah. Guthron, I see you have not changed, nor has your tribe. Did you truly think slaughter for sacred blood was the answer? If your pride had not controlled you, your kind might have realized Elfland was meant for you."

Guthron's eyes slimmed to disbelieving slits. "What?"

Oliviana smiled, roguish as she stepped closer to him. "Interesting, is it not? Do you think Elena named the kingdom all on her own? I whispered the name in her ear. It has been there all this time. All it required was someone worthy to find it. Elena did and transformed it into a beautiful sanctuary. And for that, I granted each who sought a world with a united cause the opportunity to create something for themselves. Your predecessors did not understand, but I had hoped you would be shrewd enough."

"But you stopped," Calliope said, butting into Oliviana's tirade. "After Farrah created Aurorali, no one else could break away."

She faced Calliope with an irritated glint in her eyes, flinging her bright blonde hair over her shoulder. "Well, it needed to end somewhere, half-breed. Not everyone was designed to rule."

"And yet, you allowed me. A *half-breed*."

Oliviana sighed, losing patience. "Well, Favner was not exactly tending to Faylinn as he should have. And while you are tainted with human blood, you were the last of my precious True. I needed you back."

I glared at Calliope to keep her mouth shut. She didn't pay me any attention, but stopped talking anyway.

"You…" Oliviana glided toward Guthron, sweeping aside the elves guarding him like they were the tall grass surrounding them. "You could have had a kingdom all of your own volition, but rather than cultivate your strengths, rather than gain insight into this realm, you chose to forsake the land you were given. You took and took and took from Engalawood until it was nothing but desolation, but what did you give in return? What have you provided this realm? Do you contribute anything?"

It was unusual to see the frightening being so unnerved for once. Finally, an adversary that could swipe the superior sneer from Guthron's ghastly face.

"You've learned nothing but greed and narcissism."

Oliviana stopped in front of him. Guthron was taller, broader, but it was very apparent which one was more intimidating. "Your selfishness may be the end of your kind if the next ruler does not make a change."

With widened eyes, he begged, "No, please." He couldn't say more before doubling over. My view was blocked from seeing what happened, but Olviaiana didn't lay a hand on him as he tumbled to the ground, lifeless.

If that was the fate of both Tomas and Guthron, what was going to happen to the rest of us? The same fate? Worse?

"As for the rest of you." With a flick of both wrists, Marvina stripped us of our weapons and armor.

I patted my sides and my chest, but there was nothing. Every piece scattered around us.

"Not that they would have been useful to you anyway, but their threatening presence is unnecessary." She weaved between us, holding our stares as she passed. "My, my, the trouble you have gotten yourselves into."

"What to do, what to do?" Oliviana tapped her chin. "Should I burn the whole realm to the ground and force you to rebuild your kingdom? Maybe I'll kill you all and start fresh. Hmm…" She raised her index finger in the air. "Or would the five of you like to atone for the choices you've made to save the rest of your fae?"

My eyes traveled around to my friends, my tribe. While there was fear, there was acceptance. We were prepared to take on what we had to in order to save everyone else, our world.

"Atone, is it?" Marvina weaved around Oliviana. "I thought so. It's too tragic that you did not heed my warnings. I assumed your ancestors learned from the last time I was rudely roused from my deep slumber. So, I gave you time, dampening your fae's abilities little by little, day by day. In every kingdom, I slowly took away your lands and crops, your livestock. But rather than rectifying the problem, you continued to let the miscreants live." She shrugged. "And now sacrifices must be made."

Miscreants? With the elves dead, was she referring to Cameron and me?

Marvina focused on me, and with one look, she sliced through any confidence I had left. My chest tightened as Cameron squeezed my hand. "You thought you could come crawling back to your fae form after forsaking her so many times?" Her head shook. "Foolish, foolish girl."

Oliviana sashayed to us and hooked her thumb in Cameron's direction. "And this human thought he could use the blood of fae and enter this world without permission? Without a counterpart?" Her head knocked back as she laughed, her long locks whipping with the wind.

A third approached Calliope with a blue floral wreath atop her head, her caramel hair braided over one slender shoulder rested along a cream cloak. "You handed over the blood, like it meant nothing."

"That's not true." Calliope shook her head. "I had reservations. I know how sacred the blood of our kind is—"

"And yet, you allowed it to happen anyway, half-breed," she said, her voice just as lethal as the other two.

Calliope clamped her lips shut, a mixture of fear and fury swirling in her eyes. Kai pulled her closer to his side.

Marvina smirked. "Oh, Rhona, we should at least call her Queen Half-breed. Don't you think? She deserves some respect." She turned to Marcus, "And you. You helped the elves. Knowing they intended to hunt down your own kind, you let them. You *encouraged* them as they stole precious, precious blood."

351

His head hung, lacking the strength to even lift it to her. If not for the subtle rise and fall of his chest, I'd assume he'd passed on. "I wish I could take it back," he said, his voice fragile as a pixie.

A fourth with dark skin, one dressed in leaves and flowers——an Auroralite Songbird—glided across the water, untouched by a single drop, stopping next to Oliviana. "Why do you faeries think that you can meddle in my world? I gave you life, remarkable abilities, healing powers, and you trample the rare gifts like they mean nothing." Her raspberry wings sharpened with her tone. "Flipping, flopping, forsaking your rare, sacred blood."

No one said a word, remaining stalk-still, as if a lone breath would draw her wrathful attention. Not even the rest of the elves cowering by dared after seeing their fellow king and tribe members' demise with the sweep of Viridessa's arm.

"This is so much worse than last time, Kianna." Oliviana toyed with the black curls of her kin. "I should obliterate this entire realm and start from scratch. Maybe the next era would show more gratitude." Her luminous eyes moved between us, from one to the next. "But today, you're lucky. I'm feeling generous."

Generous? She executed a dozen of us without batting an eyelash.

"Let us begin, shall we?" Another dressed in a fur vest and boots—Elfland—moved to the center of us. She spun in a circle until her starlit eyes landed on Cameron and me. "You two."

As Cameron and my grip tightened on each other's hands, my lungs constricted.

"I should kill you both for what you have done, but that would be too easy. Where is the suffering? The punishment?"

Her fingers cradled her delicate jaw as if in thought. "A sacrifice would be more fitting. A sacrifice to restore the balance you ruined." She spun her finger in the air, producing a low-floating cloud in the sky. A scene of Cameron and me I didn't recognize played across it.

"Oh, Evalina. I like the way you think." Marvina cackled, as if they weren't all the same.

On the cloud, I sat against an oak tree in a meadow, cradling a white blanket. No, not just a blanket. Closer and closer I became, as if zooming in, until there was something inside the white gossamer material. A baby. I held him close to my face, combing my fingers over his soft head as he lay sleeping. My lips pressed to his plump cheek and the scent of warm summer skin and sweetened milk filled my nostrils. A son. I had a son. Tears glistened in my eyes, a glow filling my chest.

The scene panned away from me to the glade and Cameron sitting in a circle with two little girls, weaving floral crowns. All three of them. The older of the two with fiery red hair and soft blue eyes smiled as Cameron fumbled with the yellow flowers in his masculine hands. She shuffled on her knees in an earth-toned dress to his side, showing him how to finish the floral crown with her delicate fingers. He kissed her cheek in thanks.

The younger girl with hair as golden as the sun stood on tiny legs, shorter than Cameron in his sitting position, and walked a step before she placed the crown of pink flowers she'd made on top of his head and patted his cheeks before placing a kiss there. Cameron smiled his big lovable grin at her, relishing her sweet affection.

When I blinked, it was gone. *Wait!* I wanted it back. More than *anything* I wanted it back, to see more. Was there more?

"The future you could have had, and will never be." Evalina

flicked her wrist in my direction.

A sharp pain tore through my belly and I cried out, doubling over. Cameron curled around me, bending to look me in the eyes. "Lia, what is it?" He brushed the hair curtaining my face.

Gasps poured out around us.

It was unlike anything I'd ever felt, an empty jagged ache, buried deep and untouchable. Tears flowed like rushing rivers from my eyes. When I caught my breath, I looked up, a coat of moisture blurring my vision. But through my blinking, Evalina held a bleeding organ in her hand, her head cocked. "Your womb will forever be barren."

"No," I cried, reaching for it to no avail.

She clenched her fist around it until it was nothing but mangled flesh and blood; and dropped it into the dirty marsh.

"NO!" Frantic sobs wracked my body. "*No.*" I gasped. "*Please.*"

With another flick of her wrists, Cameron went down beside me with a strangling groan. "And you," she said, "forever fruitless."

"No." I buried my face in my hands, leaning into him. That was our son, our daughters. We had children.

How was something being stripped away that I'd never even known I wanted fiercely, more devastating than losing my own life?

"Now you, dear half-breed queen," Oliviana said, slicing through my sorrow.

I looked up through my tears as Kai stepped in front of Calliope.

"Ah, Gallant King Kai." Oliviana clapped her hands. "Yes, I would not expect anything less from you than protecting your match, but this is a matter she cannot be saved from. Not even with her True Royal abilities."

"Please," he said. "Please, I beg of you." There was a desperation in Kai I'd never seen before. Snarky, brooding, and cocky were his go-to emotions, but never desperate.

"Begging will get you nowhere." Oliviana took another step toward Calliope.

"She's with child, please. Please spare the mother of my child." Kai dropped to his knees, his hands clasped in front of him. "Calliope warned Cameron and Lia, she warned them about the imbalance and the risk. It wasn't her decision for him to transform. He made it on his own accord."

Oliviana paused, as if sensing the pregnancy.

"Please," Kai rasped. Calliope gripped his shoulder, standing behind him, cradling her belly, which now as I paid closer attention, protruded beneath her gown, hidden under the layers of flowing fabric.

Another sob broke from my lungs.

"While consequences need to be dispensed, I am not without mercy. I have no desire to harm your innocent offspring, definitely not one of my dear True." Oliviana pursed her light pink lips. "However, Calliope cannot go free. Her offense may be milder than the rest, but she is still guilty of perpetuating the imbalance. In a place of power no less. I gave you Supremacy for a reason, half-breed. Use it."

We waited, on bated breath, no one daring to fight back.

She flicked her wrist, but nothing happened. Calliope and Kai shared a look, asking with their eyes if the other was physically harmed. What did it mean? What did she do?

A serenely wicked smile curved one side of her mouth. "Your beautiful baby girl. Oh yes, she will be beautiful. "

"A girl?" Calliope's tear-filled eyes shifted from Oliviana to Kai and back as she clutched his hand. They didn't know yet.

"Yes, my dear." Oliviana's head tilted, never blinking. "On her seventeenth birthday, she will become my next Songbird, to recognize the mortality of the realm. And I will bestow upon her a special gift no one else possesses. She will be a daughter of winter. While snow and ice will thrive within her, the sun will melt her skin." Calliope looked to Kai, distress furrowing her features. "Oh, yes. She will love winter, will live and breathe winter. Though that may make Faylinn a difficult land to live in."

Kai bolted forward, grabbing a knife from the ground and charged Oliviana. "You said you wouldn't harm her!"

With one swipe of her hand, Oliviana sliced Kai's cheek with his own blade. "Do not be foolish, young man. She will live and for that, you are lucky, but my mercy will only go so far. Push my limits and you will end up like Guthron and your fellow Royal." She pointed to Tomas's limp body, facedown in the marsh.

Calliope dashed to Kai's side, her hand replacing his, trying to heal the wound, but nothing happened as red oozed between her fingers.

Oliviana rolled her eyes. "My punishments cannot be rapidly healed by the abilities I have bestowed upon you, so do not bother trying. I control them, not you."

Calliope stood, her hands splaying out at her sides. *No. Don't try it, Callie. Don't.*

Kianna stepped forward, lining up with Marvina, Rhona, Evalina, and Oliviana. "Use your elements, half-breed, see what happens. Then you will see how truly useless you are against me."

Calliope's hands fisted and Kai pulled her into his arms,

away from Kianna and her clothing of foliage.

"Onto my favorite couple," Oliviana said.

"Oh, let me." Iona, who I recognized as Rymidon's Songbird, sauntered around Marcus. "It would be my pleasure."

FORTY-FOUR

SARAI

IONA smiled at me, the pure smile I'd grown familiar with since getting to know my kingdom, but her shining eyes held depravity, a thirst for retribution. She faced Marcus and grazed a slender finger down his battered cheek. A protective spark ignited in my veins, urging me forward, but I stayed where I was. He didn't so much as blink, his frame devoid of strength.

"Handsome, handsome Marcus of Oraelia." Iona plastered her hand over his chest tracing his tan pectorals. "You fell for the queen of the kingdom you swore to tear apart. What a conundrum. How will Rymidon ever forgive you if you become their king?"

Her wandering hand skimmed over his shoulder, down his corded bicep and forearm until she reached his marred wrist. The rope loosened and Marcus slumped to the ground with a splash, his other wrist still attached to the second wooden post. Though the enchantment was broken when Tomas died, Marcus must not have been strong enough to break free on his own.

"While you did not take any lives yourself, the blood of those innocent fae still sully your hands. Blood that was used to create such abominations." Iona pointed at the transformed elves laying lifeless in the mud. She flicked her other wrist and Marcus roared, a faint splash drowned by his agony. Cradling his now free arm against his chest on his knees, blood drenched his torso, pouring from his wrist, staining the water red.

"His hand," I gasped. "You cut off his hand!"

I took two rushed steps before I was stopped, Iona moving in between us. My hands were free, the enchantment lifted after Tomas. Though bloody thin gashes circled each wrist, I could have helped him.

"Eh, eh, eh." She wagged her finger. "This is not a wound you can heal. This is his penance, and I should not have been so lenient, which begs a question." She tilted her head to the side. "He ordered the slaughter of the fae you rule, the fae you love; and yet you *love* him, *hurt* for him as if his pain was your pain."

Iona circled me, one long finger following the line of my shoulders, from one to the other. I stiffened, preparing myself for my punishment, which surely would be the worst of them all. "You have suffered the greatest in your short life. Lost your mother as a child. Held prisoner by your own father for most of your life. And then you lost the rest of your family in that senseless, senseless war. My goodness, your heart should be nothing but stone."

"It isn't without effort, but I am not my losses. They shaped me; they do not define me."

"Indeed, indeed. You showed the elves mercy. You showed compassion to your enemy even after they murdered your subjects. And now, even knowing the truth, you want to bond with the man responsible. That either makes you foolish or forgiving; and forgiveness is not a trait I often see in this world." Her forehead creased, her eyes squinting. "I am not quite sure which it is."

"Forgiving," Calliope whispered, afraid to draw attention to herself once more or still too stricken with sorrow. "Sarai has a heart of gold. She's the most forgiving being in this world."

Iona blinked at Calliope before shifting her focus back to me. "I think you are right." She studied me. I nearly opened my mouth to beg her to get on with it. Deliver my suffering, so we could be done.

"For you, a gift." Though her features softened, her eyes remained orbs of ruin as she twirled a finger in the air.

"What is it you want, child?" Iona asked. "Anything. I can give you anything. Just say the word."

What? Anything. *Anything?*

"But, why? Aren't I more deserving of retribution? I forsook my fae by letting the elves in. I fell in love with the man who sought to ruin us. I gave the blood to Calliope for Cameron's transformation, harbored Lia and Cameron in Rymidon. I hid it all from my kingdom. I still hide it from them. Why should I not receive the same penance as the rest?"

"For precisely this reason." Another Songbird stepped forward, robed in gobs of gaudy fabric. "I see your heart. You feel deserving of punishment, asking to feel as your fellow fae do, but why? Will that make you feel better? More worthy of your kingdom? No, you will never tell them. This, Sarai. Living with the guilt *is* your punishment. So, a gift, what shall it be?"

My heart cracked. I looked to Marcus clutching his severed wrist; to Cameron and Lia huddled on the ground crying in each other's arms; to Calliope being held by Kai, stoic and yet aching.

As if reading my mind, Oliviana said, "Anything except taking away the punishments of your companions. I am afraid living with their consequences is the only way to reset the balance. This gift must be for you. So, what will it be, Raven?"

My head whipped up.

"Oh, wicked, Catriona, bringing in her cherished nickname." Oliviana cackled.

"Yes, my dear," Catriona said, drawing her jewelry-clad knuckles down my tear-stained cheek. "I'm aware of what your mother used to call you. Would you like me to bring her back? Or your brother, perhaps. Maybe more power is what you desire. I could make you as strong as the half-breed, if not more."

I blinked, clearing the moisture coating my eyes. There were so many things I wanted. Of course, I wanted my mother back, and Sakari. I wanted Calliope to have her father back. I wanted my friends, my family to not suffer. I wanted the realm to be replenished and safe. I wanted all of the fae to stop starving. I wanted a fair chance at building a thriving kingdom, one that wasn't hated or misjudged for actions that were not our own. I—

"I just want this to be over. I want peace." I cried, a continual stream of tears as I stared at Catriona. "Peace in Rymidon. Peace between the kingdoms. Peace between the elves and the fae. I just want *peace.*"

Catriona shrugged, unimpressed with my wish. "Then peace you shall have." All seven Songbirds' eyes lit up, brighter than the stars above us. "For now."

The glow spread to their faces, along the porcelain skin of their whole bodies until they were nothing but blinding light.

I shielded my face with my arm, closing my eyes against the brightness. It enveloped us, like a blanket of luminance so radiant, it couldn't be fully blocked. And then it went dark.

When I opened my eyes and dropped my arm, the Songbirds were gone. Cameron and Lia were still huddled on the ground. Kai and Calliope holding each other, their faces buried in each other's necks. And Marcus, he hunched over on his knees, curled forward in the swamp.

I dashed toward him, falling to my knees. "Marcus." Water and mud soaked through my pants.

It took effort, but he lifted his head. With his unharmed hand, Marcus reached up and caressed my face, tears streaking through the dirt and grim on his cheeks. "Are you okay?"

"I'm fine, I'm fine." I didn't care about me. I didn't suffer nearly enough. Right now, we had to stop the bleeding of Marcus's wrist. I stripped off my cloak and took his injured arm in my hand, tying the thick material around his wrist. "We need to get you back to Oraelia. Someone will know what to do to stop the bleeding."

"It needs to be cauterized," Cameron's ragged voice came from behind me.

"I don't have the strength to call upon my element." Marcus drooped forward in the murky water. I shifted under his arm, taking on his weight.

"Fire. Fire!" Calliope darted forward, stirring from her heartache. "I can do it. Take off the cloak." She helped me remove it, tossing the cloth aside.

She paused her hand over Marcus's severed wrist, eyes

lifting to him. "This is going to hurt."

He nodded once. "It can't be much worse than losing it."

Focusing on the narrow circumference, Calliope conjured a small flame. The flesh sizzled and sealed, but Marcus didn't make a sound.

I pressed my lips to his cheek, tasting the salty mixture of tears. "I'm so grateful you're okay," I whispered.

"I'm more worried about you." His cheek leaned into me. "Did Tomas hurt you? Are your wrists okay?"

"Don't." I shook my head, guilt near debilitating. "I'm fine. Let's get you out of here."

Kayne and Galdinon came forward, helping Marcus to his feet and guiding him out of the marsh. As day broke on the horizon, I followed with the other two couples, our heads hanging low.

"At least we made it out alive," Cameron said, but it lacked his usual humor.

"Is that what this is called?" Calliope met his stare.

No one smiled.

FORTY-FIVE

CAMERON

LETTING the back of a chair in the Rymidonian tower take my weight, I asked, "How's Marcus?"

Sarai moved around from behind her desk. "He's being taken care of in Oraelia. Knowing to cauterize it saved his arm. Thank you, Cameron."

"Just doing my part."

"Didn't think your boy scout skills would come in handy in the fae realm, now did you?" Calliope lifted a half-smile.

A small chuckle left me. It felt wrong. We fell into a silence, our minds and hearts still recovering from Fortenberry, only two days ago. Though the weight of Viridessa's threat lifted, we'd forever carry the fallout.

My stare fell on Calliope, holding her baby bump, Kai looping his arms around her shoulders to draw her to his chest. He'd hardly taken his hands off her since that day.

I didn't know much about pregnancy, and even less about faery pregnancies, but her stomach had almost doubled in size within the last couple of days. Wouldn't surprise me if she had less than nine months to prepare.

I wanted to ask more, to understand how quickly fae pregnancies worked and their differences, but with Viridessa's curse, it didn't feel right to bring it up. And it only fed the festering hurt, knowing I'd never get to see Lia that way.

A gentle hand settled on my back, and I lifted my eyes to Lia. She offered a slight smile, as if sensing my thoughts. Her hand drifted down my arm and interlaced our fingers. Together. No matter what happened, we were in this complicated, heartbreaking, extraordinary life together.

Sarai fell in a heap on the couch in the study. "I didn't want to leave Marcus, but he's stable enough for now and encouraged me to tend to Rymidon. Now, I just want to sleep for days."

"And how is everything here?" Lia asked. "Relatively back to normal?"

She nodded. "Viridessa made good on her promise for peace. With the return of our harvest and the absence of the elves, everyone seems to be content. At least no one has been coming with their torches to raid the castle, anyway."

I snorted.

"What about everyone else?" Lia looked to Calliope.

"I held a council with the Royals this morning. All the kingdoms have been restored to their previous thriving selves," she said. "And the remaining elves have been securely banished to Arcshire. Elena helped me with the wards."

"Do they have any idea how to…survive?" A quiet chuckle left Lia.

Calliope shrugged. "They can figure it out on their own. It seems Viridessa erased the knowledge of the fae blood from their minds, so they can't harm us anymore."

"At this point, as long as we're free from their harm, I don't care what they do." Sarai paused. "How was Isolda doing with Tomas's death?"

"She wasn't there. King Eadric came in her place, said she was in mourning, but he made no excuses for Tomas. He wanted me to relay their apologies to you, Sarai. Though they know it's no consolation."

Sarai nodded, but waved her off. "It wasn't their fault. And it's complicated, you know? Discovering the true nature of your son, but also loving and mourning him. Not just mourning his death, but mourning who they thought he was."

It took me a moment to realize, she spoke from experience. Maybe not a son, but a brother, a father. Complicated, indeed.

"And Viridessa's curse on…?" Lia's voice was gentle enough, but it still straightened my spine.

Calliope took a deep breath. "Well, we have seventeen years to figure it out, I guess. We've overcome harsher obstacles before, we can handle this. Together." She peered over her shoulder at Kai and he kissed her forehead, her eyes closing.

"We're stronger now than we were before, and tomorrow we'll be stronger still." He pulled her tight, lowering a hand to her belly, staring at the petite bump.

I glanced around the room, from Sarai to Calliope and Kai, squeezing Lia's hand in mine. "So, what now for us?"

"Well, we're going to leave it up to you two," Calliope said. "We're going to divulge the knowledge on the scroll about the blood to our fae. It won't remain Royal knowledge anymore. It's risky, but with the knowledge comes understanding and diligence. We all need to do our part to keep our realm safe."

"And Viridessa?" Lia asked. "Will everyone take her more seriously now? Treat her as more than folklore?"

"With the aftermath, it'll be hard not to. So, if you two want to remain in Faylinn or Rymidon, and questions are asked, you'll have to tell the truth. But they will know Viridessa punished us for it. I'm going to share my part and hope Faylinn accepts my faults and lack of malicious intent. They will know Kai and I paid the price." She choked on the last word and cleared her throat. Blinking rapidly, Calliope scratched her neck. As if all those things would hide the emotion drowning her.

Kai kissed her head. "We're keeping Sarai out of it, though."

"What? Why?" She scooted to the edge of the couch. "Do not shield me from this. I need to atone for my wrongdoings, too."

He shook his head. "Rymidon doesn't need to know. Viridessa was wrong about a lot of things, but not that. The elves are gone. You get your fresh start. Build up your fae. They don't need to question you when your intentions have always been pure. You wanted peace." His voice gentled. "Take it."

Lia and I nodded.

Sarai remained silent, tears slipping down her cheeks, but she nodded, too.

"But, Cam and Lia," Calliope said, hesitating, "You two have another option."

I met her eyes and knew. "Elfland."

367

She nodded. "It's up to you. Elena and Cian are happy to welcome you into their kingdom if you'd like, with a lot fewer questions. And…"

"My mom is there."

"It's not a bad option. You could reconnect with her, better understand her choice. You two missed so many years." Calliope raised her hands. "But I'm happy with whatever you choose. Just giving you your options."

Lia squeezed my hand twice. "I don't care what we do. Wherever we are, we'll figure it out." But in her eyes, I saw past her selflessness, she didn't want to stay in Faylinn or Rymidon, but she would, if I didn't want to go to Elfland.

After the last couple of weeks, I couldn't say I still held any resentment toward my mom. When death stared you in the face, perspective came. I didn't want to waste any more time without her in my life.

"Elfland, here we come."

"Are you sure?" Lia's hopeful tone solidified it.

"It's not like we can't visit Faylinn or Rymidon. Our lives aren't endangered anymore, but I think a fresh start is what's best for both of us."

She slipped her arms around my waist, hugging me to her.

"And what about your parents?" I asked.

Lia went rigid, pulling back. "What about them?"

"I might have something to add." Sarai raised a finger, her delicate voice cutting through the tension. "I was going to tell you, Lia, but then your black mark appeared, and everything with Tomas and Viridessa, there just wasn't a time."

Lia didn't say a word as she stared, her fiery wings stiffening.

"Your parents came to see me last moon cycle after you left

for Faylinn. They'd heard rumors about you being seen around Rymidon and they wanted to know if it was true."

"What did you say?"

"That you weren't there, which you weren't at the time. You were at Kai's safe house. I didn't tell them anything about your transformation, but they seemed heartbroken when they believed the rumors were false."

When Lia said nothing, Sarai continued, "I know you didn't tell me much when they turned their backs on you, but for what it's worth," she said, "I do believe they have had a change of heart. Of course, if you don't want them to know of your transformation, we can try to keep that quiet. But who knows, your parents might surprise you."

I brushed the edge of her wing, relaxing it. "If nothing else, it might give you closure."

Her eyes slid to mine. "I just don't know if I can," she whispered.

"And you don't have to see them. Not if you don't want to. Do you want to?"

It was in her eyes, though scared, before she answered, hesitant confirmation was there.

FORTY-SIX

LIA

WE garnered looks all the way from the castle, but thankfully no one stopped us. I couldn't wait to be in Elfland where we'd have anonymity, my reputation far behind us.

The familiar vine-covered cottage I grew up in peeked through the foliage atop a grassy knoll. My feet stopped, refusing to take me forward. A plume of smoke wafted from the pebbled chimney. Was my mom cooking? Warming her feet as she crocheted? Even when the weather was warm, her feet were always cold.

"We don't have to do this now." Cameron cinched his grip

on my hand, a reminder I wasn't alone. "You can wait, think things over. We'll head to Elfland and can come back another time."

I shook my head. "We need a *real* fresh start in Elfland. I can't do that without doing this."

A pause. "Okay." He didn't say anything more, letting me take my time.

Then, somehow my feet drove me forward and I knocked on the yellow front door.

Shuffling feet across the wood floors was the only warning before the door swung open. In place of the wood slab stood my dad, hair peppered in gray, blinking at me.

"Moira," he said over his shoulder, voice raised.

"Who is it?" My mom's silvery voice sailed through the air before she was next to him. Her hand slapped over her mouth, stifling a cry. "Magnolia?"

I'm not sure what my face held, but she approached me with caution, like any fast movement would scare me off.

"It's true." Her thin arms slipped around my neck, drawing me in with a gradual pull, unsure if I'd let her hug me. "You're here. You're yourself."

I didn't know what to say. This wasn't the greeting I was expecting, even with what Sarai said about their interaction. I'd kept a shield around my heart to keep it from hoping.

My dad had never been an affectionate man, so I was surprised when my mom let me go he didn't hesitate to take me in a firm hug.

I blinked when my vision grew blurry. Tears? They streamed down my cheeks. When he pulled away, I wiped my face.

"Well, c'mon now," my mom said. "Come inside and bring

your handsome friend."

Cameron chuckled quietly. My eyes whipped to him and he clamped his mouth shut. Laughing wasn't allowed. Not yet, not before I figured out what was going on.

Everything was much the same. Same antique furniture and maroon tapestries. Same artwork of the woodlands and portraits— *Portraits?* I stopped at the corner of the couch when I got stuck on one of me and Clover when I wasn't much older than five. Just before she was gone. My sister had me on her hip, grinning from ear-to-ear. Heartache punched me in the chest.

They kept us out on display, even after all this time.

"I love that painting of you two." My mom's voice carried across the kitchen as she opened and shut cabinets. "I had to hand over my favorite broach for Benen to paint that for me. Though, I still believe I got the better end of the deal."

She set a kettle on the stove, lighting it to brew up some letty tea. It was the only kind she drank.

"Go ahead, you two. Have a seat."

Cameron tugged me into the kitchen where we sat at the kitchen table, side-by-side.

"How is this possible?" My dad sat in his usual spot at the head of the table.

"How is it possible that I'm fae again?"

As my mom took a seat beside him, they nodded, and I took a deep breath. Their hospitality was going to be short-lived.

When I finished telling them everything—living with Cameron in the human world, the elves, the mark, Viridessa—all they did was stare with gaping mouths.

"She stole your womb?" My mother's voice rasped.

I nodded. "I'll never be able to have children."

I waited for their judgmental remarks, for scolding and

372

demands of leaving their home this instant.

My dad spoke first. "What a blessing from the Fates that we didn't lose you, too."

Record screech.

"You've been through so much." Tears glossed my mom's eyes. "Oh, my sweet Magnolia."

"Lia. My name is Lia."

She blinked, bewildered, but nodded. "The horrors. Everything you've endured, Lia. I can't imagine."

Glancing at Cameron who gave me an encouraging nod, then back to my parents, I said, "I don't understand what's happening."

They shared a knowing look, as if they'd been preparing for this. As they should have. The last thing my mother said to me before I went to the human world was, "Leave this house and never return."

Hand to her chest, my mom said, "We made a mistake when you agreed to work for Adair, and we've regretted it ever since that day."

"We tried to come to you after you returned when we were in Faylinn, but they refused to let us in the castle," my dad said. "And then with the battle, and your return to the human world, we thought we'd never get the chance again. There are so many things we did wrong; we were just scared of losing another daughter. We let our fear and pride obscure our judgment so much that we lost you anyway."

My mom reached across the table as if my hand was there for her to hold. I kept it clasped in my lap, Cameron's hand on top. "We understand if it takes time for you to forgive us. We're willing to do whatever you need. We just love you so much and are so grateful we get a second chance, with you here in

Rymidon."

"We're not staying here."

Her head reared back. "What?"

"Cameron and I are going to Elfland. By invitation of Queen Elena and King Cian."

"Why?" The single word from my mom's lips was drenched in desperation.

"After what we did, it's the smartest choice for us. We want to begin again. And Cameron's mom lives there."

"But I thought you were a human." My dad's forehead wrinkled.

"I was," Cameron said. "It's kind of a long story. Maybe for another time."

"Clover is in Elfland." My mom's voice was so quiet, I almost didn't understand her, but I thought she said...

"What?"

She swallowed, licking her lips. "You were too young to understand, and we were trying to protect Clover from Adair. He'd tried recruiting her to his forces, to be a spy in the human world, to the very same arrangement you'd agreed to, though she had no desire to bond with Skye."

"I don't understand." I blinked. "Clover is alive?"

They nodded, tears clogging my dad's voice when he said, "Safe in Elfland."

"Why would you keep that from me? You let me believe this whole time that my sister was dead?"

My mom's eyes plead for forgiveness. "You were *so* young at the time, we didn't want you to accidentally slip the truth to someone. We haven't seen Clover since the day we hid her in Elfland. We had every intention of telling you the truth, but then you grew close with Skye without our knowledge and there was nothing we could do. After you told us what bargain you'd struck with Adair, we spoke in anger, in a moment of weakness. We've regretted it every day since."

"I don't care about that anymore." A sheen of tears coated my eyes as I cut them off. "You're telling me I'll get to see my sister again?"

The softest of smiles stretched across their face as they nodded.

WELL, that turned out better than expected, right?"

We hadn't said a word since leaving my parent's cottage. I nodded as I placed my palm on the wide, knotted trunk of the Waking Oak.

I wasn't sure what I was feeling. I was angry with them, but I wasn't. How could I blame them? If I'd been able, I'd have killed Viridessa over the children in the vision she gave us and took away. And that was for children I didn't even know, children that would never be mine now. My parents protected Clover for all these years for good reason, and for that I was grateful. All wasn't forgiven, but knowing I would see my sister again somehow lessened my bitterness.

"Do you think Elena knows my sister? Could lead me to her?"

"Maybe." Cameron shrugged, but his voice was hopeful. "If she was someone Elena harbored, it's possible she'd remember her."

I hoped.

My mind replayed the conversation with my parents as we made our way into Elfland, through the wards, and were escorted through the forest. It kept getting stuck on the same deal Adair tried to make with Clover for Skye. Had Adair approached other girls? Altered his plan when asking hadn't worked?

My brain circled back to how Skye and I connected in the beginning. Him approaching me in the village and oblivious me being awestruck by the handsome ice prince who singled me out. Skye had picked *me* out of all the women in the kingdom, screwed with my head and my heart. Was it all an act? A part of a plan? Maybe feelings had grown for him in time, but I was probably nothing but a means to an end.

Skye never truly loved me.

Cameron squeezed my hand and I looked to him. He wasn't looking at me but at Elfland around us as we rose in the basket up the side of the fortress. It was just a gentle squeeze letting me know he was there, that my hand in his wasn't a simple gesture but a gesture of love and support, solidarity and comfort.

And suddenly, nothing about Skye and Adair mattered. Because I knew what real love was now.

QUEEN Elena herself showed Cameron and me to our new home. As we passed a stone cottage on the way to ours, a woman with golden hair spun on top of her head stood at the gate of her garden, watching us with a warm smile.

Cameron broke away from me and in a few strides had her in his arms. "Mom."

She buried her face in his shoulder and cried. A tear escaped my eye that I quickly swept away.

While they embraced, I turned to Elena. "My sister came to

you years ago. Clover Byrne. Do you remember her?"

"Of course, my dear. I remember all who seek my solace."

Promise bloomed in my heart. "Did you know she was my sister when we were last here?"

She nodded, but there was no apology in her eyes.

"And you said nothing?"

"It wasn't my place," she said. "You know this is a sanctuary, Lia. It only works because I give my kingdom my full protection and trust. I wouldn't betray it for anyone."

"Do you know where I can find her?"

"I do. Once we get you two settled, I'll escort you to her."

Nerves zinged through my veins, anticipation crackling.

"And my parents." I cleared my throat. "I don't know how all of this works, but if they wanted, could they move here, too? Or at least visit us."

Elena's gracious smile widened. "Of course."

AFTER we dropped off our bags in the cottage, Elena escorted us down the gravel road. She pointed, but didn't follow, needing to return to the castle. It was then I realized she didn't keep an entourage of Keepers with her. She sauntered away, head high, nodding and smiling at the fae who greeted her. The lack of necessity for the Keepers settled something profound in my chest. This was the perfect place for Cameron and me.

Two small children, a girl and a boy, jumped rope on the dirt pathway in front of a dwelling built into a hillside, the roof grass-covered, the door tall and oval.

As we approached, the light blue door opened and a young woman called, "Yanick. Mila. Time to come in for dinner."

Her hair was long and caramel, braided over one of her shoulders, the end swishing against her waist. When I took a step, my sister's jade eyes swiveled to me, her affectionate smile still in place. It shifted a fraction, but it didn't fall.

I took another step and she followed suit, a tilt of her head, eyes taking me in. "Magnolia?"

I nodded, unable to control my emotions. Tears poured down my cheeks, the taste of salt hitting my tongue when I smiled.

Rushing forward, we met halfway, tugging each other in. "Oh my Fallen Fae, you're here."

"And you're a mother."

She laughed and pulled back, holding my face as she combed my features. "You're so grown up."

All I could do was shrug and she understood. So much time had passed since we'd last seen each other.

"Mama, Mama!" Both of her legs were wrapped in her children's plump arms and legs.

She looked down at them with a watery smile. "Mila, Yanick, this is your Aunt Magnolia."

"Lia," I said with a chuckle, "I go by Lia."

There wasn't a hint of hesitation. "Okay." She nodded. "This is your Aunt Lia."

I bent down, meeting their shy grins. "I'm going to spoil you rotten."

They giggled, burying their pudgy, rosy faces into my sister's thighs, and a love I'd never known blossomed inside me. I was an aunt, and I would love these two as if they were my own.

When I stood, Clover was observing Cameron over my shoulder. "And who's this?"

I reached my hand back and he took hold, coming to my side. "This is my...match. Cameron."

He held out his wrist and she wrapped it in a Root. "It's nice to meet you."

"You, too." She looked at me the way I'd always imagined a sister would when they wanted all the juicy details, approval in her stare. "What have you been up to for the last hundred years?"

Taking a deep breath, I said, "Oh, sister, you're in for a tale."

FORTY-SEVEN

SARAI

IT had only been a week, but Rymidon was a new kingdom. Fear and starvation were a forgotten memory. Promise in the air. Without any heavy, pressing issues, I had a moment to walk the castle grounds, to appreciate the flourishing gardens and breathe.

Kayne met my lazy pace, catching me up on births and bondings. All the good news floating around the villages. I gobbled it up, reveling in the goodness.

"Your Grace."

I turned at the sound of Galdinon and my breath caught.

Marcus stood beside him and no one said more. There were

no introductions. Marcus didn't need it. Without asking, Kayne left after Galdinon, leaving us alone.

Standing on the stone path, Marcus's arms behind his back, there was a new lightness in his eyes, an easy tranquility.

I approached him, taking slow steps. "You seem better. Are you well?"

"Almost as good as new." Marcus held up the arm Viridessa injured. His unnaturally stiff hand was covered in a black leather glove. "It's not my dominant hand, so there's the silver lining." He smirked at the prosthetic. "One of our Craftsmen carved a wooden hand for me. Because it was a request he'd never received before, he's trying to design one that will be usable, but he carved this replacement for now."

A weighted breath left my lungs. "I wish we could have saved your hand. I should've at least tried."

He shook his head, dismissing my regret, though not callously. "I can live without it, not without difficulty, but there are worse sacrifices. I'll learn how to manage with time." Marcus closed the gap between our bodies, the sun glistening off his dark hair. "The worst part is not being able to touch you with both." His good hand cradled my face. His other came up, not warm flesh but solid wood under the leather. "How my hands love you."

I nestled into the crafted hand, closing my eyes. "I love this hand just the same."

There was a hitch in Marcus's breathing. "When Viridessa approached you, I was ready to cut out my own heart if she'd given you the same fate as Guthron and Tomas. I couldn't imagine living in a world where you don't exist. It would've been the most torturous punishment imaginable. Nothing would've been able to convince me to stay."

I licked my lips and swallowed, bringing my hand to his jaw, my nails caressing the short scruff. "When we found you strapped to those posts in the marsh, I thought you were dead. Marcus, never have I been so terrified, so devastated, the thought of losing one more I love, I almost died myself."

His forehead met mine.

Alive. We were alive. And our kingdoms were well, prospering. But nothing brought me more happiness and peace of mind than Marcus. Here. With me. The way it was supposed to be.

"Will you stand by my side?" I asked. "Will you be King of Rymidon?"

Marcus laughed. I've never heard him laugh—really laugh—before and the desire to hear the pleasant gruffness again intensified.

"Are you asking me to bond with you?" He pulled back just enough to look me in the eye.

"Yes." I smiled, a light laugh escaping. "Is that okay?"

"Okay?" His nose traced the length of my jawline until his lips met my temple. "Is that okay?" Marcus laughed again. Blissful. Elated. Euphoric. Every good feeling at once.

"I'm going to make you so happy, Sarai. I promise you. Your happiness will be my life's work, the most important thing I ever do."

His arms wrapped around my waist, lifting me in the air, and spinning. My hair whipped around us as I buried my face in his neck, placing kiss after kiss.

Setting me down, he captured my lips in a searing kiss. "Let's fill this castle with children and laughter and love. Let's make Rymidon our own utopia."

ACKNOWLEDGEMENTS

Coming back to Faylinn after four years was like a little homecoming. I love this world so much. The first world I ever created. And it's because of so many people that I keep coming back, even when I think I'm done.

To my Faylinn fanatics, you guys are the best.

Thank you to my cover designer, Regina Wamba, who created another gorgeous cover for the books.

Samantha Eaton-Roberts, thank you for cleaning of all my editorial messes and being so easy to work with.

To my beta Jo Pettibone, you always give me the best feedback. Thank you for being someone I can always turn to.

Michele G. Miller, doesn't it go without saying at this point? I love you and whatever.

To my favorite people, Ryan and Zoey Sue, thank you for being my own little cheering squad. I'm grateful for your patience and love when there were days when I was lost in Faylinn. I love you most.

BOOKS BY MINDY HAYES

<u>Faylinn Novels</u>
Kaleidoscope
Ember
Luminary
Glimmer
Daybreak

<u>Willowhaven Series</u>
Me After You
Me Without You
Me To You

<u>Standalones</u>
Stain: A Romantic Psychological Suspense
The Day That Saved Us

CO-WRITTEN WITH MICHELE G. MILLER
AS MINDY MICHELE

<u>Paper Planes Series</u>
Paper Planes and Other Things We Lost
Subway Stops and the Places We Meet
Chasing Cars and the Lessons We Learned

<u>Backroads Duet</u>
Love in C Minor
Loss in A Major

<u>Standalones</u>
Nothing Compares 2 U (novella)

ABOUT THE AUTHOR

MINDY HAYES is the youngest of six children and grew up in San Diego, California. After graduating from Brigham Young University-Idaho, she discovered her passion for reading and writing. Mindy lives in Summerville, South Carolina with her husband and beautiful baby girl.

. She is the author of Stain, the Faylinn Novels, the Willowhaven series, and The Day That Saved Us. Mindy is also the co-author of the Paper Planes series and the Backroads Duet, which was co-written with Michele G. Miller as Mindy Michele.

FIND MINDY ONLINE
Website: mindyhayes.com
Instagram: @haymind
Facebook: facebook.com/hayes.mindy
Twitter: @haymindywrites
Find me in my reader group on Facebook: Mindy's Gangsters

Made in the USA
Middletown, DE
06 September 2022